THE
VANISHING
OF
OWEN TAYLOR

<u>BOOKS BY KYLE MICHEL SULLIVAN</u>

<u>General Novels:</u>

The Alice '65
The Vanishing of Owen Taylor
David Martin
The Lyons' Den
Bobby Carapisi

<u>Adult Novels:</u>

Hunter
The Beast in the Nothing Room
Underground Guy
Rape in Holding Cell 6
Porno Manifesto
How to Rape a Straight Guy

<u>Out of Print:</u>
NYPD Blood

THE
VANISHING
OF
OWEN TAYLOR

Kyle Michel Sullivan

KMSCB
Buffalo, NY

Published 2016 by KMSCB

Cover design by JamTheCat
Photograph courtesy Shutterstock

Second Edition
Published 2021
Printed in the United States

— Acknowledgements —

Thanks to Vicki for helping keeping me on track, and to Brad, Scott, Andreas, and Michael for their backup. Additional thanks to The Depraved Minds Club on GoodReads.com for giving me so much support.

Table of Contents

Author Bio

Sample of
*Rape in Holding
Cell 6*

PART I

"Jake, why do you stick with Tone?"

It was my stepmother, Mira, asking. though what she really said was, "Iacob, what is your loyalty with this man, Antony?" English being her third language, after Farsi and French, and me being the only one allowed to call my guy Tone.

We were at a sleek Persian restaurant in Paris, not far from De Gaulle. I was en route to Copenhagen for my job and was already worried about my connection being delayed thanks to a winter storm blowing in, so I was not in the mood for my father's second wife to diss my guy. I loaded some duck fesenjan into my mouth to give me time to work up a polite answer.

"Do you remain beside him because others say you should not?" she continued. "Are you to be stubborn, in the way of your father?"

"Mira," I snarled, still half-chewing, "I love Tone."

"It is not love to remain with someone when it is to your own detriment; it is self-loathing."

Oh ... typical psychologist; Here's your box, little man, and aren't you ashamed for being in it? I wouldn't be surprised if she analyzed my half-brothers-and-sisters in the same way.

I swallowed, sipped my beer, took a breath and snarled, "Psycho-lady ... q'est-çe que c'est?" Tried to make it jokey; didn't work. Her expression turned quizzical, like she was thinking, *This lab rat used to be smart, so why's he screwing up the maze leading to the cheese?* "Has Antony told you all that he has done?"

She knew damn well he had. And yet ... while I knew more about him than anybody, even I didn't know it all.

I pushed my plate aside, leaned against the table, folded my hands, looked her straight in the eyes and asked, "This is why you had me change my travel plans? So you could diss my guy to my face?"

She hesitated then took a sip of her wine. Pinot noir with a lamb salad ... there's something wrong about that.

"I apologize," she said. "I am too used to being ... to being circumspect with my patients."

"Circumspect?" Said in my Texas twangiest with my grin my goofiest. "An' here I thought you was bein' blunt."

She looked straight at me. "Do you know that your mother has contacted your father?"

And I got blunted right between the eyes. I kept my voice steady as I said, "So?"

"So ... she has done this twice. That I know of."

"Okay ... again — so?"

"One telephone call refers to your uncle, Owen Taylor. As I understand what has happened, he is vanished, and she wishes to find him. She asks Faraz to use his influence to bring forth an investigation."

My appetite dropped to zero, because this ... was ... bullshit. Uncle Owen was mom's half-brother, and she did not give a single solitary damn about him. Why? Simple — he was gay, and she blamed him for me choosing to go that way and *be of the devil*, which she had actually screamed at me as she kicked me out of the house. Besides, my uncle wasn't the kind to just disappear; my mother was. I can't tell you the number of times I'd get dumped at my grandmother's so she could run off to some hunting trip or seminar or church retreat, while we always knew where Uncle Owen was, even if he wasn't in constant contact. But now she's calling her hated ex-husband about her hated half-brother because she can't find him? No way in hell.

"Mira, Uncle Owen's in Palm Springs; my father's based here. What kind of influence can he have?"

She gave me that maze-rat-screwed-up look, again. "He has investments in California. Some in partnership with your uncle."

Which I did not know. "Which means he has his contact info. So what'd he find out?"

She hesitated. "He has yet to locate him."

Wait ... my father, with all his resources, couldn't track down my uncle? "So ... so what's this got to do with me?"

"Her most recent telephone call was to ask for your contact details. I find it interesting she did not already have them."

"Why? She told me years ago, I'm not her son."

"Words spoken only in shock ... and anger ... "

"You really gonna excuse someone you never met?"

She sighed, nodded and sipped more wine.

I downed some beer, trying to sort my thoughts, then asked, "How'd you find out she called?" I asked.

That made her blink. "You do not think Faraz has told me?"

"I know my father and his secrets as well as you do."

She had to smile at that. "Yes. Well ... his assistant keeps nothing from his wife, and may Faraz never learn of this."

More bullshit; dad had used his assistant to feed Mira this crap. What was he up to? And was she really dumb enough to fall for it? I doubted that.

"When did she call?"

"The last was two months ago, is my understanding."

"I got no idea what to say," I said, making myself finish my meal. "She hasn't called me. All I've gotten from her and dad is ten years of Catholic and Islamic hate."

"Iacob, if Faraz truly despised you, like this, he would not have allowed you back into his family."

"That was Tone's doin', not his. And you're the one who kept me in. And you will never know how grateful I am ... "

Her face grew tender. "I would have it no other way."

I gave her a soft smile back. "So what does Tone have to do with all this? Aside from the fact that both my parents hate his guts ... and that, you cannot deny."

Mira sighed, in response. "I merely wish to ... understand why you remain in America when your future is in Europe."

"Texas and her crappy brand of justice."

"That is Antony's legal situation. Yours is finalized."

"What hits him, hits me."

She all but rolled her eyes, then poked at her salad, as if to see if it's alive. "Did you know he has ... demanded his therapist share his notes with me?"

No ... but my only response was an American shrug.

No fooling her. She almost smiled. "When you speak of those who love secrets, Iacob, perhaps you should look to him. Now let me clarify my initial question. Even if you do love Antony, is it wise to remain with him? Is it not true he faces still the possibility of a prison sentence?"

"Who told you that?"

"That is unimportant. What is of importance is your future. And to remain with a man who may be jailed — "

"He won't. It's just this new Attorney General tryin' to renege on the deal we worked out. Like he's got any say in it."

"Nor have you any influence over this."

"The hell I don't. What's goin' on here, Mira? Why you goin' down this road?"

Another hesitation. Another sip of wine. "I ... I have been talking with Ari."

I barked a laugh. "Nobody talks with Uncle Ari; you listen, because he chatters enough for the world."

She smiled back. "True. But he compliments your graphic abilities to me. He tells me his clients now ask for you. He wishes for you to partner with him, but he worries you may refuse because of Antony's legal situation. It is an excellent opportunity, Iacob, and as you are now a citizen of Denmark you may do this. But you cannot maintain this long-distance manner of employment; you must return to Copenhagen to live. Once Antony has his legal obligations met, he could then join you."

Jesus ... more crap? Ari may be dad's brother, but guess who couldn't keep a secret to save his life? And he hadn't said word one about anything more than me meeting a new client and tossing out ideas for an ad campaign, on this trip. That actually hurt.

"Mira ... I thought you had some respect for me."

That made her blink. "Of course I do."

"Then why're you handin' me this nonsense? My mother's worried about my uncle and ... and Ari's got ... he's got plans for me and I ... I'm screwing up my life and ... and what the hell is goin' on? What's it got to do with my uncle goin' off the grid? What're you really trying to tell me? Is there somethin' in Tone's notes I ought to know?"

She looked at me for a moment then pushed her plate away. "It was wrong of me to inform you of those."

" ... Jesus ... that bad?"

She finished her wine. "This ... this you must discuss with Antony. It may have been a violation of ethics to even mention him sharing them. I will say no more."

Perfect. She's shut down, and trying to get Tone to talk about something he did not want to talk about was like an ant trying to tear a hole in a brick wall — in concept, possible; in reality, never gonna happen.

I downed the last of my beer, shaken. Part of me wanted to push and find out what the hell Mira was really trying to tell me, but I needed to get back for my flight, and I did not want to leave my one ally in France on a bad note. So I sighed and shrugged. "Okay, I get the message ... but my grandmother taught me you don't abandon someone you love when they're in trouble. I'm surprised you even begin to think I could do that."

Again with the rat-screwing-up-the-maze look. "No matter what the cost?" I just smiled. "Nor would I ever have thought of you as one with a martyr-complex."

"Okay, first off," I snapped, "back off. I'm not one of your patients. An' you know what Tone's done for me — "

"So you remain from gratitude?"

"Don't categorize me, Mira! I told you — I love him."

"Does he love you?"

"He was almost killed, helpin' me. What do you think?"

Mira sighed, her eyes a bit sad. "I think ... now ... to be with him harms you. And I hope you at least will consider what I have suggested. You are a young man still ... "

"I'm twenty-seven."

"An American twenty-seven. You have much to learn of the world, as yet. It is ... it would be so much better for you to do this somewhere other than where you are, at this time."

That hammered the message home. My so-called parents were up to something, and it centered around me and Tone, and maybe my Uncle Owen ... and she wanted me to be someplace safer than Texas, once it went down. Near family who cared about me. What that something was, she either didn't know. Or wouldn't tell me, if she did know. I'd have to work that out for myself.

She dropped me at De Gaulle, and while waiting to board I did some research into my folks via my phone. Nothing unusual came up. With mom, it was newsletter crap about the company she worked for, all years old and boring, along with her running a blog for some

Catholic Church fundraisers. The only thing that dug at me was her connection to an anti-gay group called PSALMS, who were fighting the expansion of the gay agenda. Yeah, by forcing the right-wing agenda of glorious intolerance down everybody's throat. Good ol' mom, still with the hate.

As for my father, it was all *Forbes 400* and *Business Week* and *Financial Times* crap about which group he bought in the EU and what he sold in South America and investments he suggested in Asia, and on and on. Mira was the brilliant lady-psychologist he'd married, who had borne him five children — the implication being: like a good woman is supposed to do. It was nice to know misogyny wasn't just an American trait. How she wound up with him made no sense to me ... unless she was fronting a study on sociopathic businessmen.

Ten million references to Owen Taylors came up, and none of the first pages held anything about my uncle. I sent texts to Tone and our buddy, Matt, to let them know I was here and ask if they would find out what they could about him. I said nothing about my conversation with Mira; that could wait till I got home, where Tone and I could have a serious talk ... in private.

Then in Copenhagen I got another jolt. I kept my apartment there because it kept me as a legitimate resident ... and because I loved the place. Vaulted ceilings above open rooms; a balcony that overlooked Koge Bay; furnishings by Ikea; eight months of peace and happiness when Tone and I lived there. I could not wait to get this hell in Texas done with so we could come back.

Our landlady stacked our mail by the door, so I grabbed everything and sat on the balcony to glance over it, ignoring the sharp cold breeze. In it, I found a letter from a publisher about a graphic novel I'd submitted; they agreed to publish it when I was done with it. That was a nice boost that set me to drifting and remembering this one winter's day where I'd sat right here, trying to figure out why I was having so much trouble with it. Got cold to the bone. Finally gave up to come inside ... and Tone had made hot cocoa. With a dark chocolate bar mixed in it. Topped with little marshmallows. I had to be careful sipping it; he loved to boil that stuff, and the foam stuck to my moustache. He wiped it off with his fingers and licked them, smiling like a joyful puppy. Such a simple thing, but it gave me the hint that I was overcomplicating the story and now? It was going to be published. Life was exactly what I wanted, then.

The rest of the mail was crap or magazines we liked or bills telling me my bills had been billed to my bank account, but at the bottom were a couple of envelopes.

From Uncle Owen.

One was postmarked the day I returned to Texas, on my last trip here. In it was a house key and a printed note that read, *You'll need this when you come. O. #4870*.* The other was a pre-stamped blank postcard sent a couple days earlier that said, *Dear Jacob, I need to see you, ASAP. O,* in block letters.

Dear Jacob? He never addressed me like that. And he knew my cell phone number; why not just call me? Text me? E-mail me?

I tried to call him but got voice mail, and it was too full to accept more messages. An e-mail bounced back, so I contacted the service and found out his in-box was at capacity. Not at all usual for him. But to send these messages here? And now even mom was looking for him? That did not sound good.

I'd planned to stay in Copenhagen, a couple days, to visit with my cousins ... but now? I needed to find out what was going on with my California uncle. Meaning I'd have to have a talk with my mother. Something I hadn't done in ten years.

Jesus, I'd rather be back in prison.

— II —

I guess it would help to tell you, my name is Jacob Michael Blaine, born and raised in Texas. Initially, I was Iacob Merhzad Darya-Bendari but that got all Americanized after mom divorced dad and took back her maiden name. She's Irish-Catholic, never wrong, and didn't want anyone to know she'd been involved with a Persian who wasn't a feline. My father is a conniving asshole who was in Texas for the family oil business. My grandmother, Nana, once told me I look like both of them, thanks to mom's cheekbones, dad's hawkish profile and their thick dark hair. I also got her big eyes, his trim build, and enough brains from Nana to see there's more to the world than a self-important state that has gone bat-shit crazy.

But neither one of them was noted for their sense of time, which I also got from them, so as I came in from the balcony I noticed my meeting was in less than an hour. I scrambled to shower, shave, and pull on a suit — the only occasion where I'll wear one — and make it to the restaurant before they arrived.

I beat them by two minutes, then Uncle Ari, the client, and I had a nice, leisurely five-course meal with two bottles of wine and too many after-dinner drinks. I showed off my portfolio, using my laptop, and discussed my upcoming graphic novel ... and the deal was sealed. By then, it was after one am, so I changed out of that suit and headed to the airport to catch an early flight back to the States.

Now I've done jackrabbit trips like this, before, and had next to no trouble with jet lag. I used to do it twice a month, which is why I go business class — so I can grab a nap. And it was my intention to talk with Tone as he drove us home. This time? My brain got lost in trying to figure out what the hell was going on with Mira, mom, dad, and Uncle Owen, and how Mira knew Texas' new Attorney General had suddenly begun talking about sending Tone to jail. So a little more background is in order.

Five years ago, I was arrested by a deputy sheriff on bogus drug charges. Why? Because I made a cousin of his pay for damage to a city car she had borrowed. With the help of a conniving Assistant District Attorney, I was convicted and sentenced to four years in a Texas prison. I made parole after twenty months. Then less than a year later, I was exonerated and my record vacated ... thanks to one Antony Patric St. Lazarre — AKA: Tone. He proved my arrest was a set-up, so I got a nice settlement that helped us move to Denmark so I could work with my Uncle Ari.

The reason Tone got involved in my case was because of a man named Collie ... Collier Winston-Royce. He got busted by the same deputy sheriff, as me, for just as stupid a reason — he gave a relative of that deputy's a bad grade in a college class. The bastard's only intention was to mess with him, but Collie wound up beaten to death in a jail cell and Tone careened into a near psychotic need for revenge. By the time it was over, he'd brought down that deputy sheriff, the ADA, a crooked Texas Ranger who'd helped them, and a state judge ... and nearly gotten himself stabbed to death in that same jail. It was a rough time.

Problem is, Tone committed a few felonies to do it, which is why we were still there. His plea to lesser charges in exchange for probation was handled by the Department of Justice, not the Texas Attorney General, at the time; there were too many questions about how dirty that bastard was. Then the new AG decided the deal did not apply to Tone's involvement in the kidnapping and questioning of another crooked Texas Ranger, and he was threatening a nasty trial and even nastier publicity.

Our lawyer was pretty good — Rene Castillo. He snapped and snarled right back at the AG over every detail, and sometimes it was fun to just sit and watch their pissing contest. But Tone had a hearing coming up to determine if he could gain an early release from probation ... meaning if the AG would stop trying to prove he had a big dick, we could go home.

Instead, the bastard was growling that he would drag Tone into a trial for attempted murder. All to keep up his self-professed image as a *law-and-order* man. It was bullshit, but he didn't care about anything else.

The whole thing was depressing Tone and pissing me off, but we'd kept it quiet. Mainly because Castillo was sure once the AG got down to serious negotiation behind closed doors, he'd see this was a no-win situation for him and stop the posturing. And secrecy was the best way for that to happen. Yet somehow Mira had found out. It made me wonder if that was in the notes Tone's therapist shared with her. Which made me wonder if she now knew everything I'd deliberately not told her. Which made me wonder if this would mess things up with my half-brothers-and-sisters.

Which meant I didn't sleep a wink on the flight.

So I arrived totally zoned out. I didn't return to life till a mug of coffee was right next to my nose. I sat up, saw I was in our bed, took the mug and did some cooling action. Tone boils the stuff, so I'm always careful with the first sip. But damn, even scalding it tastes like heaven.

"Okay," I murmured, "I'm starting to feel human, again."

"Is'ums sure?" he said, and the mommy-to-baby-jokiness in his voice made me smile. "'Oo was weally out of it."

"Lemme shower first," I said. "What time is it?"

"Almost ten. I'd offer you brunch, but ... "

It was light outside. "Whoa, what happened to the rest of Wednesday?"

"Sleepies."

"Whoa," I chuckled. "So why no brunch?"

"That doesn't start till Friday."

"Says who?"

"Says the rules."

"Since when do you follow those?"

"Since I became a convicted felon. I now cross the street at the corner, go one mile per hour under the speed limit, come to a complete stop at stop signs, and bake a potato to go with my steak, as is the law in Texas."

I yawned as I said, "Tell the judge that an' he'll laugh you out of court. We still got a hearing on Tuesday, right?"

He nodded. "How 'bout a grilled cheese with tomato soup?"

"Oh ... woof."

"It'll be ready when you are."

I looked him over. A bit shorter than me. A bit trimmer. Brown mop flopping in his face. Eyes that warned you not to get too close. He had on a black t-shirt with a green skeleton's hand on the front, and it was snug on him. That and his almost-loose jeans, coupled with his clean face ... it amazed me how sexy he could appear without a thought.

I realized I was naked under the sheet and blanket, so put my hands behind my head and took a deep breath. "Don't ya wanna watch me bathe?" Then I stretched.

He squiggled a finger from my nose down through the hair on my chest as he said, "Maybe tonight."

"Carefuuuul," I sighed. "You'll get somethin' starrrrted."

"Yes. The soup. Don't take too long; Matt has news." Then he patted my belly and was gone. No kiss? My breath must be really crappy, which wouldn't surprise me, considering the crappy airline food.

I flipped the covers off and jumped to my feet to stretch some more. Man, it felt good to be in a place where you don't have to give a shit. We'd stayed with his folks the first couple months of dealing with the state ... till I realized we'd be here for at least two years so rented the left side of a two-story duplex. It wasn't new but was built solid, with hardwood floors and two baths. Furniture was courtesy of his parents' storage space.

Matt moved into the extra bedroom, from Florida. Matt Zehavi. He's a computer geek about my age, who builds online games and designs websites; he built a beauty for Uncle Ari and still does occasional graphics videos for him. He got mixed up Tone's shit, too, yet managed to get out of it cleaner than either of us ... the little shit.

Tone was pretty limited as to what he could do and where he could go, thanks to a monitor on his ankle, but he was still making his own way, teaching English as a second language and preparing people for the Citizenship test. The work gave him something to focus on besides the state's nonsense, and making your own money matters.

I looked out the French doors at the back garden. It was drizzly and gray, the perfect day for soup and a nice long run. Winter was coming early here, too. I didn't mind; I liked the cold and snow of Denmark. I'd hinted to Matt about joining us, there, and he sort of seemed interested ... but not massively.

I showered, thought for two seconds about letting my heavy whiskers grow into a full beard, then sliced off everything except my goatee, decided to get my thick mop cut down to an easy length, brushed my teeth, and wrapped myself in a long, clean robe; clothes were for later. I also decided not to see mom till tomorrow. There was still no response from Uncle Owen, and I wanted time to contact some of his friends.

When I got to the dining area, Matt was seated at the table, grinning and munching on a sweet pickle as he tried to sneak bites of the grilled cheesers, like he was a kid. Hell, he looked like a kid — short, trim, big-eyes and smile, always in a t-shirt and jeans ... and thinking about it, that was his shirt Tone was wearing; no wonder it was snug.

I plopped on a stool beside him and let him pop a gherkin in my mouth as Tone ladled out the soup and sat with us, then I plowed into my sandwich. Man, I love grilled cheese. Marry that up to some tomato soup, I could even handle watching *Cabaret* or *The Rocky Horror Picture Show* for the hundredth time.

When I finally came up for air, I looked at Matt and said, "You look happy."

"New client," he grinned. "In Ireland. We're working up a game based on Celtic legends, sort of an anti-*Game of Thrones*. I'll show you some, later. First comes what you asked me to look into. When was the last time you talked to him? Your uncle."

"On the phone?" It took me a moment to remember. "Just after the Fourth of July. And a text, the end of that month."

"Nothing else since those two notes?"

I shook my head. "The only time Uncle Owen was big on e-mails and letters and crap was when I was in jail. I'd get a package from him, every other week, and he'd drop in every other month. But after I was out, when he did send an e-mail it was huge. That's why those messages're so weird. What's up?"

"Did you know your uncle was arrested for solicitation of prostitution?" Matt asked.

I nodded.

Tone blinked and frowned. "And you didn't tell me?"

"He didn't wanna share with anybody, Tone."

He nodded. "Of course ... understandable," he said, his voice shifting into even and calm, which always makes me wary. It means he's got something else going on in his brain. "You had no more contact with him, at all?"

"None, but it was only a misdemeanor; he was handlin' it."

Matt munched another gherkin as he said, "Well, on August 2nd, a felony complaint was filed against Owen Taylor for having sexual relations with a male not of the age of consent."

"Bullshit!"

"No shit. And apparently he skipped bail the day after charges were filed, to avoid prosecution."

"No," I snapped. "No, he wouldn't do a runner. That's the mark of a coward, and my uncle was anything but."

"That's what we've learned, Jake," said Tone.

"I found out who his lawyer is," said Matt. "We thought you

might want to call him, see what you can find out."

"I know his name," I said. "It's in the e-mail he sent me after he got busted."

"What'd he say?" Tone asked.

I thought about it, for a second, then said, "Better if you read for yourselves."

So I fired up my laptop and let them.

— III —

Jake, you will not believe what happened to me. I drove down to Page's convenience store for some milk, butter, eggs and bread, and was arrested. By a police officer in plain clothes. Who claims I asked him to have sex with me. For money. Right there! In the parking lot!!

Talk about ridiculous. The man looks like one of those puffy body-builders who give off the air of greasiness and psychosis. I seriously believe if he had taken in too deep of a breath he would have exploded, that is how tight his skin was over his face and body. Probably on triple doses of steroids, and I would swear he had bitch-tits under his tee-shirt.

He followed me all over the store and was doing everything he could to make me notice him and think he was available for some fun. It did not matter where I went, the moment I stopped, he would appear next to me to "look at something for himself." Then he would cast me a glance and all but lick his lips to send out that age-old signal of "blow-job." It made me nervous, so when I went to the cashier and he appeared behind me, before she could begin ringing me up I said, "I forgot something," and scurried to the back of the store to check in the coolers for ... whatever. I just wanted him to leave.

When he finally did, I took my time paying for my things. But he was waiting outside as I exited. He approached me and asked me if I wanted to have some fun. He said that he was really horny.

I told him, "That's not where my head is, right now, thanks."

He frowned and said, "C'mon, I know you're gay."

"What does that have to do with it?" I asked, more than a bit

peeved. Because I'm queer I will jump on anything with a dick, whether in the mood or not? What a stupid thing to say.

He followed me to my car, saying, "C'mon, man, I really need to fuck with somebody, tonight. I'm so fuckin' horny."

I grew even more nervous. His insistence was beginning to seem pathological. A number of gay men have been beaten and robbed, over the last year. One is still in the hospital. So I put my groceries in the car and said, "Damn, I left my cell phone on the sales counter. Tell you what — let me get it, first, then we can talk some more."

"Get some beer, too. Something to eat. I'm kinda hungry."

That made me think he might be panhandling, in his own awkward way, so I said, "Why don't I give you some money?"

I started back to the store, but he grabbed me and said, "No need, faggot. You're under arrest."

"For what?" I asked.

"Solicitation of prostitution." The words leapt from his mouth as if they were just waiting for release.

I pulled away from him, angry, telling him, "You're no police officer!"

That is when he held up his badge, saying, "And that's resisting arrest and assault."

He slammed me against the side of the store, handcuffed me from behind and pushed me over to a new black Camaro, handing me the Miranda saying the whole way, even as I protested. I was taken to the county jail down in Indio, booked, fingerprinted, dressed in prison attire, glanced over by a nurse, and put in a cell. Thank God no one else was around.

I've never been arrested before so I cannot say for certain all jail cells are like this one — but it was vile. A toilet in a corner of the room with nothing in the way of privacy. A sink was beside it but the water came out in a trickle. A pair of bunk beds jutted from a wall. A heavy Lucite door. A vague aroma of urine. Hardly "Architectural Digest." If this is what you dealt with when you were in stir, you're a better man than I am, Gunga Din. Thank God I was alone in there.

I was given nothing to eat or drink until seven am the next morning, and it was nearly forty-eight hours before I was taken to a judge for a bail hearing. The Assistant District Attorney handling the arraignment was a Ms. Ginty, this huffy little blond thing who looked like she would blow away if the breeze was too strong. The moment the bailiff finished reading the complaint, which included indecent exposure charges, she said, "People ask for one-hundred thousand dollars bail, your honor."

"What?!" shot out of me.

"The defendant accosted a decorated police office, exposed himself and attempted to entice the officer into following his lead by offering him money. When he learned he was talking to a policeman, he became irate, attacked the officer and tried to escape. Indications are he would be a flight risk."

"That's nonsense your honor!" I snapped. "The officer approached me and asked me for sex, and when I said no he — "

"This is preposterous on the face of it, your honor. The arresting officer actually told the defendant to leave him alone in hopes he could just drive away."

"You want to talk preposterous?" I cried. "That I'd risk being beaten, robbed, or killed for someone who looks like him, let alone try to buy him!"

The judge told us to be quiet and asked me, "Do you have an attorney, Mr. Taylor?"

"I do."

"Where is he?"

"He's out of town, your honor, so I called another lawyer I know, but all I got was voicemail. Your honor, I own property in this town. I have no criminal history. No arrest record. I don't even have an unpaid parking ticket."

"Is this true, Ms. Ginty?" the judge asked.

"We haven't fully vetted his background, sir."

I nearly spat at her. "Why not? I've been here two days."

"Is that a yes or no, Ms. Ginty?"

"So far as we can tell — "

"That's the same as a yes." He turned to me and asked, "Do you wish to make a plea now?"

"Not guilty," I shot back.

"Bail is set at five-thousand dollars, cash or bond." Then he slammed his gavel down.

I posted bail and, after I was released, who should I meet but this priest I've had some unpleasant dealings with. His name is Father Paul, but I say more like Father Puke. He's been going out of his way to tell me I will go to hell if I do not change my ways, and I would not be surprised if he had something to do with my arrest. We've had a nice little back-and-forth for the last year, or so. On this lovely occasion, he followed me, telling me he wanted to help me get right with God and enter ex-gay therapy and on and on ... until I threatened to sue him for harassment and making terrorist threats. And I think I still will, just to make a point.

I took a cab back to Page's to get my car. Of course, most of the food was ruined and the interior stank. It took two detailings for it to even begin to smell right, again. As soon as I arrived home, I bathed and fed myself something decent. What they foist upon the inmates appears to be more like microwaveable dinners than real food. I despise pre-prepared meals, and do not even begin to trust anything that is gray-brown but claims to be edible.

I called Preston, again — Niemczyk, that trial attorney I know — but he was still in New York. I wanted to stop this in its tracks, so I spoke with Lorinda — Waller-Burke. She's my real estate attorney. She had contacted Baskin, Baskin and Reed to come help me; small wonder they never showed up. I once had dealings with the elder Baskin and was not impressed. But I sucked it up and met with Scott Baskin; he is the one Lorinda suggested. I believe she has a crush on him, and while he is adorable, he is not the brightest bulb there is, and he did not believe me when I told him I had done nothing wrong or illegal. His mantra was, "I can get a deal for public nuisance or disturbing the peace." Apparently, the fact that I am innocent made no difference. Well, I prefer to have someone who believes me defending me, not some pretty fool going through the motions, so I waited until Preston returned to fire back.

He and I met with a deputy district attorney about my case, today. His name is Warren Philby, and he is the epitome of an aging metrosexual. Ms. Ginty is his assistant. The two of them tried to force me into a deal.

"It's an excellent one," he said with all the sincerity of a used car salesman. "Disturbing the peace. Six months probation, some

community service, and if you meet all conditions, the conviction will be expunged. This is the best I can offer."

I told him, "I've done nothing wrong or illegal, so I see no reason to say I did just to make your job easier."

"Oh, stop it," said Ms. Ginty in this really snotty voice. "We have a witness who backs up the officer's version of the arrest."

Which was nonsense. There was no one around but me and that officer. I told them this, and Philby shrugged. "That's not a workable defense, telling the judge everyone's lying about you."

Preston responded. "Aw, cool, we'll have a trial by jury."

"The jury won't believe you," Philby said, giving off this heavy-hearted vibe. "I've had convictions with less evidence."

"Then you should be ashamed," I snapped.

"Who's this other witness?" Preston asked them.

"Officer Roy Harper," said Ms. Ginty.

Preston laughed. "Another cop? Aw, this is easy-peasy. C'mon, Owen." We rose and headed for the door.

"If you leave there will be no deal," she snapped.

In answer, I slammed the door, behind us. Well, tried to; it was on one of those auto-close pump-action set-ups, whatever they are called, so it only bounced back and then slowly settled shut on its own steam. So much for my Bette Davis exit.

Of course Preston already had a copy of the arrest report. Not a word of there being a witness on it. Hardly a surprise. So I immediately went back to Page's and got a copy of the security surveillance video. It is all indoors so doesn't show any of our interaction, but it backs me up in so many other ways, this trial will be quite the experience.

A friend is facing similar charges and Preston is his attorney, as well. Our trials are scheduled for the same day, so this will be doubly interesting.

The only problem now is Father Puke. He arrived in Palm Springs a couple of years ago, and he set up this homophobic group called PSALMS Forever, who protest anything pro-gay. The conniving little bitch actually appeared up on my doorstep, today. With protesters! He demanded I stop living my life of evil and come back to the lord. Our local version of the Westboro scum. I slammed the door in their faces, so the assholes began warning one and all that I was a danger and would rape their sons. This is private property, so I called my security service on them, but by the time they sent someone over, the vermin had left. No one here was paying them any attention — the only two neighbors who would were at work, thank heaven — so they went in search of a better audience. Typical.

  Palm Springs has changed. Be glad you're not out here.
  Owen

Then I told them about the phone conversation we'd had, after the e-mail.

"The video's our backup, Jake," Uncle Owen told me. "We can use it to cast doubt on his version of events."

"But if it don't show anything ... " I'd said.

"It shows he's alone. And he followed me all over the store; I did not follow him as he claimed in his report."

"You haven't given it to Philby, yet, have you?"

"Are you insane? Officer Chet already changed his story with this witness; I'm not giving him cause to change it more."

"Chet? Seriously?"

"Yes. Officer Chet Morrow. Doesn't it just drip of porn? I'm close to deciding we ought to depose him. Get his version locked in before the trial."

"When is it?"

"The Thirtieth. Doesn't help the DA's proven himself to be as much of a dick as his predecessors."

"They're all dicks, Uncle Owen."

"And as in life, some are bigger than others ... but his dickishness would gag a horse."

"Shit, what'd he do?"

"Didn't I tell you about the previous asshole who was DA? No, wait, that would've been about the time you were dealing with probation and the psycho in your life. Speaking of which, how is Anthony doing?"

"An-TONY," I'd laughed. "You ever call him anything besides that, you'll find out what a dick really is."

He'd laughed. "Okay, actually it started with the previous-previous DA. The Palm Springs Police Department set up a sting against gay men, one night. One of those entrapment set-ups, where a cop begs you to expose yourself then arrests you for public indecency. A number of the gay community got together and fought the charges. After all, they don't have female cops do the same thing to straight frat boys, and when heterosexual couples are caught going too far in public, they're warned off whereas gay men are arrested. He ignored us, so we pumped our money into his opponent during the next election and kicked him out. It helped that the Palm Springs Chief of Police was caught on tape saying some very not-nice things about gay men during that sting; he wound up resigning.

"So ... we put a new DA into office and what happens? He repays our help by still pushing through with the criminal cases against the men who were arrested. I told the son-of-a-bitch in the next election we'd fight to have him kicked out, too. His response was, *The law is the law; if you don't like it, change it.* Instead, he was changed. Now we have a new one who at least is willing to talk. But Philby was hired under the first DA, and no one will put a leash on the SOB. Plus the police still pull their stings. I'm trying to make it an issue with the press and such, but getting no traction. It's demoralizing. Most of the arrestees have just taken deals. I think they thought I could be forced to, as well."

"You think the arrest was aimed at you 'cause you opposed the two previous DAs?"

"I doubt it. Her Majesty Chet seemed more upset at the fact that I didn't find his ass attractive than anything."

"Not a muscle queen, huh?"

"Oh, stop. I'm no more interested in fake men than straight men are in breast implants."

"What do you know about straight guys?"

"The lad who tended the grounds was straight. Tiago," he sighed. "He and I discussed it."

"Tiago? A name like that and he's a breeder?"

"Yes. And beautiful. And knows it. Works shirtless. Shows off his buff chest and broad back and slim hips ... and those legs in those holey cargo shorts ... " Another sigh. "But nothing's going to happen. He got a girl pregnant and split so he wouldn't have to marry her. Even left his little brother behind."

I'd chuckled. "Why don't I hop over durin' the trial? Moral support and all that? Maybe spit in Father Puke's face."

"Thank you, but I have several friends to back me up. If we present my case correctly, I doubt it'll go to verdict."

"Juries can be worked over."

"True. And a couple of the accused probably did do what they were arrested for. Erect. But that hardly makes the arrests right, and taking a deal does not work for everybody. This one man who was caught is from Upland. His career would be harmed by a record, so he brought in a couple of big guns from LA. God knows how much it's costing him, but Philby's hinted at backing down, in his case."

"Bullshit."

"No shit. They went after the arresting officers' records and gave interviews to the local press on the DA's homophobic policies. Preston's copycatting, especially with Don's case."

"Don?"

"Rice. You met him when you came out, that time."

"I did?"

"Six-six. Blond. VERY much a Viking. Dressed up as Blanche, Our Lady of the Golden Girls for Pride?"

"That's Dion, Uncle Owen. And you introduced him as Rose."

"You're right; I'd forgotten. His real name's Donald, but don't tell him I told you."

I'd laughed. "I don't think I'll ever see him, again."

"You never know. Anyway, Preston started making noises to the local paper, too. We even used a couple of his comments in flyers we mailed out against Philby, so I think he realizes it's better to get the LA boys out of here before the rest of us fags catch on how best to fight back against his bullshit."

"They never fought back, before?"

"We do, but I cannot tell you how many queens I know just give in because they think this is the way of the world."

"Maybe it is ... "

"So why didn't you take a deal when you faced prison?"

"Some nights ... some nights I wish I had."

"Stop it!" His voice cracked like a whip. "If you hadn't

fought, you might still have wound up in jail, and you would not have had the moral authority to make them acknowledge what they did to you was wrong. You did the right thing, Jake. I know it's hard to believe but — "

"You don't know what I had to do to survive in that place."

"I have an idea. And it only makes me prouder of you. Your grandmother felt the same way. We knew you were innocent, and you making it through that hell without being destroyed by it proved to us the kind of man you are. Someone who can stand on his own two feet. So no self-denigrating allowed, you little mutt; not in my long-distance presence."

I'd nodded then said, "Yes, sir."

"Now I am going to end this call before I get weepy."

"Lemme know how things go, okay? And I mean it — if you need me out there ... "

"I've been standing in my own opera pumps for a long time, dear. Do not think that I cannot handle this shit. Your job is to take care of Antony. See, I do know his name."

Then he'd ended the call. Our last contact was a text the end of the month saying, *I was half-right*. I'd texted him back, asking what he meant, but he never responded.

— IV —

They read the message and Matt did some cross-referencing on his diamond-sharp laptop as I spoke, popping in with, "Okay, got that here," and, "It fits." He also found a chart showing Warren Philby had a ninety-five percent conviction rate and was talking about running for Riverside District Attorney in the next election. As a Republican with a Tea Party bent.

Already I hated the prick.

That's when I noticed Tone looking at me with his quiet, wary expression, so I snarled, "You don't believe my uncle'd molest a kid, do you?"

"No." He frowned like he was insulted I'd even asked him

that question.

"So what ... is ... it?"

"I dunno. It just doesn't line up with ... well, your father called your mother, asking about your uncle's condos and — "

"Condos? He had more'n one?"

"Four. One he lived in; three he rented out. He also owns some other property."

"Whoa, whoa, whoa, how d'you know my father called mom?"

"She ... she told me."

I nearly fell off the chair. "My mother called you?"

Tone blinked and looked away. "Uh ... looking for you. I ... I told her you were ... you were out of the country."

"When?"

"Day before yesterday."

Man, I should've gone to see her the second I got back.

"What'd she say to you, Tone?"

He sighed. "She knows why you're here. And she ... she said stuff like, *That's just like you, to let people drag you down.* Then she gave me her number and address — "

"I know that shit," I said. "I'm goin' straight over."

"She's moved, Jake," said Matt.

"She sold her townhouse? She loved that place."

"Just telling you what she told me," Tone said. He gave me a slip of paper with a phone number and address.

"This is south side," I muttered.

Tone shrugged. He wouldn't know, but my mother was one of those types who only want to live around *acceptable* people. In her eyes, Southside was ... borderline ... at best.

"Matt, we'll be right back." I went around the counter, took Tone by the arm and guided him up into the bedroom, then closed the door, sat him on the bed and kneeled before him, looking hard into his eyes.

"Y'know, I had lunch with Mira. Is there anything you want to tell me?"

He hesitated then looked straight back at me, his eyes sharp as cut diamonds. "That therapist I'm seeing ... that the state's making me see. I ... I asked him to talk with her. Told him she's a psychologist and has a clinic in Paris and ... and I wanted her to know everything that happened was on me. Not you."

"She already knew that."

" ... Maybe. This verified it."

"And you talk about me not tellin' you things?"

"I ... uh ... I didn't think she'd let you know."

"Great defense. So what's in those notes?"

He looked away. "You already know everything in them."

I took a deep breath. "Tone ... what. The fuck. Is goin' on, here?" He just stared at the wall. No expression. I took his face in my hands and made him look at me. "Okay, whatever it was that my mother said to you — keep in mind ... that bitch kicked me out of her home when I was seventeen. I haven't seen her since, so what she knows about me and who I am is zero. Zip. Nada. Anything she says is just her messin' with us."

He shrugged me off and said, "But she's right. You wouldn't be here except for me."

"You're right, you little shit — I wouldn't. I'd be fresh out of jail. Or still livin' in Nana's house. Barely existing. I'd never have met my brothers and sisters in Paris, or gotten to work with my Uncle Ari, or become a Danish citizen. I'd be an ex-con. But I'm here, alive, because of you. So what. Did. My mother. Say. To you?"

"Just ... just what I told you."

"Bullshit!" No response. I sighed and sat cross-legged on the floor. "You don't wanna talk, don't. But this is a woman who told her only child that she hates him bein' queer."

"Maybe ... maybe you shouldn't go see her ... "

"I got to. Somethin' is goin' on with my uncle and the only way to get the truth of what she knows is a face-to-face."

He ran his hand through my hair. God, I loved it when he did that. Then he whispered, "Should I stock up on alcohol?"

I sighed from the emotion in his voice and nodded. "Twelve-pack. No, fuck it — Tequila."

"I'll get some mixers and we'll make a nice queeny night of it. A Christian, a Muslim, and a Jew had a party ... " He snorted. "Sounds like the setup for a joke."

I made him look at me. "Hey, I'm half Catholic."

His hand whispered over my cheek and his eyes grew hurt, again. "My all-American mutt."

All I could think to say was, "Don't let mom mess with us, Tone." He ruffled my hair then got up and left the room.

I leaned against the bed. He'd lied to me. My mother's crap comments weren't bad enough to rip him up. There was definitely something else going on in his head, and he'd used them as a wall to hide behind.

Well ... sitting on the floor wasn't getting anything done. I got up, got dressed, and headed over to the insurance company where she worked. I wanted a professional environment around us, in case things got nasty, because she was damn well going to explain to me what the hell she was pulling.

Only it turned out she hadn't worked there in nearly three years.

Man ... I had a lot of catching up to do, with her.

— V —

My mother didn't answer her phone, so I headed for her new address in an older, carefully planned area of the Southside. A golf course of sun-burned grass just beginning to grow, again. Ponds filled by a creek that finally had water flowing down it instead of trickling. Pecan trees and nuts littering the ground.

Man, I love pecans. Nana'd had a couple trees in her back yard, and I'd pick up two and crack them together and eat them straight out of the shell. Tasted a hundred times better than the ones you get in packages. The drizzle had stopped, so I pulled over to gather some up. But one was rotten and the other barely had any meat in it; it was too soon after the drought. I dropped them on the ground and headed on.

A mile later, I found a complex that was a good forty years old — meaning big rooms, wide windows, tall ceilings and cracks in the walls thanks to the foundation settling. The doors and windows had been painted over a dozen times without first being stripped, so it reeked of low-rent. Tone must have written the address down wrong.

But then I saw mom's silver Lexus with its red and green pinstripes parked behind her unit. She bought it new, a month before she kicked me to the curb; now it had faded paint, nearly bald tires, dings and dents in the fenders and bumpers ... and a tear in the driver's seat that had been duct taped.

Duct taped? To my mother, that was the first sign of being white-trash, so she wouldn't let it in the house. Me? I use it, nonstop.

I instantly figured out which was her apartment, thanks to this freaky wire peacock she owned. It had blue and green metal feathers, and its head was on a coil that bounced if you touched it ... and was on backwards, so it looked over its body instead of looking ahead. She'd bought it my last year of high school, and when I asked her why, she'd told me, "It makes people wonder."

I heard organ music from inside and almost backed away, thinking I had the wrong unit. Instead, I knocked ... no, pounded on her door and the music stopped. A moment later this little, bird-like woman with black hair showing silver roots opened it ... and I had to swallow hard to keep from gasping.

The big cold eyes were my mother's, as were the cheekbones and long nose, but she'd shrunk by half and looked twice as old as I remembered, and her hands trembled as she glared at me.

"Jacob," she said, like she was stating a fact.

"Mom," I whispered, my voice not very steady.

"You've grown." I nodded. "The extra weight is right for you. You never did eat enough to keep a man alive."

"You moved," I finally croaked out.

"You noticed. Come in. No sense letting the warm air out."

Warm air, hell; it was a friggin' sauna inside. I took my jacket off and followed her through the kitchen into a living room that was almost empty. Just a couch, coffee table, floor lamp, TV, and a Hammond organ in one corner with a bench. Mom'd had this gorgeous set of matching French Provincial everything, with dozens of lush plants and off-beat knick-knacks tucked into the open spaces. She and Uncle Owen would fill their homes with that crap, to the point of it being too much, so sparse was not what I expected.

She noticed my expression and said, "Sold it. All of it."

"And your townhouse?"

"Repossessed by the bank."

"How? My father paid cash for that as part of —"

"I thought you understood how mortgages work, Jacob. You borrow money, use your home as collateral —"

"Okay, okay, okay, I get it. Jesus, mom, what happened?"

"It's what's known as a merger. Two insurance companies become one and consolidate their operations in one place or another. My department moved to South Dakota; others went to India. Five hundred people were kept; fifteen hundred were not. Which group do you think I was with?"

"But you must've had savin's and a 401-K to raid ... just to tide you over till you found a new job ... "

"I'm sixty-one years old — either too expensive for an employer, or they think I have no concept of how to use Quickbooks or an XL Spreadsheet."

Then I noticed a basket of prescriptions on a table. All different-size bottles. She noticed I noticed and nearly spit.

"Another issue hindering my job search. The remains of my cancer treatment. I'd be dead if it hadn't been for the ACA subsidies and unemployment ... and now disability. But while my doctor says I'm cancer free, employers still see me as a risk. And my 401K is gone."

"Why didn't you tell me?"

"You cut off contact."

"You knew how to get hold of me if you wanted to."

"When mother was alive. Sit. I'll bring you some sweet tea, with lemon."

"This is bullshit, mom. What's really goin' on, here?"

For a moment, her eyes shot daggers at me and she almost flashed back to the imperious bitch she could be. But then she took in a deep breath and said, "I've made changes in my life, Jacob. While you sit in that chair watching the poison they use drip into your body, hoping it kills the cancer before it kills you ... you do a great deal of thinking. Now I'll get the tea."

I followed her into the kitchen.

She kept on with, "I heard you had left the country, so I

contacted your father for your information. He always knows how to reach you. Why, is beyond me."

"I thought dad called you." She cast me a frown. "You told Antony he called you about Uncle Owen's condos."

"Antony?"

"Cut it out; you know who I mean."

Her eyes glittered with anger as she spat out, "Yes, that thing you live with. He'll drag you to hell, with him."

"Is that what you told him?"

"He knows that perfectly well, the little demon. He has one in him, you know. Your father filled me in on what he's done."

"Faraz told you — ?"

"Jacob, listen to me — that person is dangerous and ... and the things that — that he did — "

"Cut it! Now did you call dad, or did he call you?"

"What difference does it make?"

"He called you." Things were starting to make sense. Dad was up to something and had fed Mira a line to distract her.

"All right, he did. He had spoken with Donald Rice and wondered if I had a way to contact your uncle, and — "

"Uncle Owen?"

"Jacob, stop interrupting! You know perfectly well Owen is the only one who would be a part of this sort of conversation. I told him my contact information was no longer valid, then we began to discuss that thing you live with. He's concerned about his children by his second wife."

I had to snarl. "They've never met Tone."

"They will eventually, so he has every right to be worried. Look at Owen. I never wanted him near you, but my mother ignored my wishes and let you visit him, while I was gone. And when I learned he had influenced you to be homosexual — "

"Don't go down that road, mom!"

" — I called him and asked why he'd brought you into that lifestyle. It did not end on a good note. It's been ten years since we've spoken. Even at mother's funeral we said nothing and ... and brother and sister should never be out of communication for so long, ever." She looked at me, her eyes hard but filled with pain. "It's also true between mother and son. By throwing you into the street — I — I did wrong."

My anger bolted into this weird light-headedness, and I asked, "Are you really cancer free?"

She sighed. "They say I am ... but the treatment so weakened my heart, it could stop at any time. I don't ... I don't want to die with you hating me."

I leaned back against the counter. "Why do you care?"

She hesitated then opened the fridge. All it had were jugs of water, a pitcher of tea, and slices of processed cheese. I almost laughed at how obvious it was.

She gripped the pitcher. "I now drink it the way you used to. It's the only way I can taste it. Do you want ice?"

She could barely hold it, so I took it from her and set it on the counter. "How broke are you?"

She began to shake so grabbed the sink to keep it from taking over. Her voice quivered. "I can't even pay for my burial. I tried to ask Owen — "

"What about Uncle Norbert?" He's mom's younger, full-blood brother and lives in Dallas.

"He has two children in college."

"Short answer, he said, *No*." I looked at her. "What about Catholic Services?" She said nothing. "Did you even tell them?"

" ... Yes."

"Your own church won't help you?" More silence. I had to laugh at that. "So you're beggin' me and Uncle Owen?"

"You're family. Blood. You think I'd ask either of you for anything if I didn't have to?"

"Great salesmanship, mom," growled from me. "It'll be hard to get Uncle Owen to do anything, right now. He's vanished."

She almost laughed. "Don't be ridiculous. He would work out an itinerary for his trip to hell, and I would not be surprised if he worked out yours, as well."

"Gotta believe in it, first." I put the pitcher back in the fridge. "How're you gettin' groceries?"

"I still drive. My car is in fine mechanical order." I just looked at her. She sighed. "SNAP. And disability. My apartment is section eight. If I had been able to refinance my mortgage until I sold my home, I could have done all right, but the bank would not work with me. And they're having difficulty selling it. Market's soft."

"They know you're sick?"

"Of course."

I got my jacket. "Give me their number and contact name."

"What good can you do?"

I looked at her. "You want help from your blood, or not?"

She wrote the information down along with her checking account number, and I left. I had Tone wire a thousand bucks into it then asked Matt to research the bank as I checked out mom's old townhouse. It was on the river, a prime location, and every other unit was occupied. What was even better? It had no For Sale sign. Having difficulty selling it, my ass; they weren't even trying.

Matt found out the bank had been absorbed by C&B Trust Company, out of North Carolina. One of those states where anything a corporation wants, it gets, and screw the people. I asked him to check into the laws about mortgages in Texas, then called the guy handling mom's account. I wanted to talk to him, face-to-face, but the only address the office had was a P-O box. It took three tries to get hold of him and tell him I'd pay the mortgage off.

"I see it's already in foreclosure," he said, "so — "

"She owes a little more'n fifteen thousand. I can wire transfer the funds — "

He cut me off with, "We can't do anything about it."

"Oh, you wanna play?" I growled, "Who's your supervisor?"

"Mr. Blaine, I can assure you — "

"Who. Is. Your. Supervisor?"

He took a breath before he said, "Just a moment."

A woman came on the line and she tried to be even snottier than him, so I shot back by referencing Texas homesteading laws — thank you, Tone. And I quoted, "In Texas, every family and every single adult person is entitled to a homestead exempt from seizure for claims of creditors, except for encumbrances properly fixed on homestead property." Of course, Matt had found out mom hadn't set her place up as being on a homestead, so that could get tricky if they checked.

Matt also found out C&B was quick to take taxpayer support and nasty about reworking the mortgages of people who were a day behind and an inch underwater. They'd even foreclosed on people who were current with their payments, then made a deal with the Justice Department to keep it quiet. So I told the bitch I was going to sue them and be very vocal about it and parade my very sick mother before the media and point out how they'd kicked her out of her home so they could resell it at a profit. I'd also demand they be audited, and see to it all past mortgage foreclosures were investigated, in detail, killing the deal with Justice. Then I told her I'd pay twelve thousand for mom's mortgage.

"It's more than fifteen thousand and you said — "

"Now it's ten-thousand. You fight me more, I bring in my lawyers. You want it or not?"

They put me off for a day, but I think once their attorneys heard of the situation, they told the bank's officers to stop being idiots and take the offer. It'd take a lot of cash to defend the case ... and I'm pretty sure they feared I was right about the investigations, audits and deal going bad. Better to cut it loose. The bitch supervisor tried to put off finalizing the deal till next week, when the monetary transfer would clear, but I'd learned they'd left the community fees, utilities and taxes in mom's name. That was not at all legal if the joint is in foreclosure. She backed down and the title was physically turned over to me ... at 5:59 pm, that Friday.

Now that I owned mom's home, she couldn't get into the same mess, again. I also set up a transfer of a thousand a month into her account, so she could eat and live, and I arranged for everything else to be billed to me. Plus she finally agreed to get CareLink, but in *Fuck The Poor* Texas that wasn't guaranteed.

Just to be clear, the only reason I put this dent in my settlement money was for Tone's sake. After his encounter with her, if I'd let her just sink into her own filth, he'd have blamed himself. Now he could see everything was fine with her and me and could keep his focus on his own crap. Maybe that'd calm him down, some.

I did make one condition to my mother — she was never to call Tone or Matt, again. If she did, I'd toss her in the street like she had me. She didn't mind; she hated Tone's guts ... but she is who she is; you have to expect this kind of crap.

I hired some cleaners to come in on Saturday, and movers to take everything over, Monday morning. By that evening, she was reinstalled in her home. Helped that there wasn't a lot to move or set up or clean since the place had only been vacant about a year. Mom must have left it in pristine condition.

Throughout this, we kept digging into my uncle's vanishing act. Tone found out that he headed up a group called GALAIATH — Gays And Lesbians Against Injustice And Targeting of Homosexuals — and they were doing battle against PALMS demonstrations and the police stings.

Matt noted that he'd developed a townhouse community called Playa Royale — Queen's Beach — where he lived. Of course. He also had an apartment complex and seemed to live off the rents from that. There were some other projects in the works, now that the economy was back on track, but those were pretty blurry.

I finally got hold of Preston Niemczyk on Monday to learn more about the criminal charges.

"Totally bogus," said Preston in what sounded to me like a New York accent. "We had a response, to it. He had no reason to do skip bail."

"He didn't," said. "There's somethin' else goin' on."

"I do not disagree, but until we know for sure ... "

"The police are treating him as a fugitive?"

"You got it. So you coming out here?"

"Yeah, Wednesday."

"I'm in court all day; gimme a call Thursday and we'll work out a meet-up. Okay?"

I agreed then ordered in Chinese for dinner, which I'm not wild about but mom loves. That made her happy, so she told me why dad was looking for my Uncle.

"There is some property Faraz wants to buy," she said, "but he's unable to locate Owen. Apparently your uncle is partners with some other people in it, and he's the one in control. Faraz wondered if I knew where he went."

"Bullshit," I snapped. "He's got a thousand ways to find Uncle Owen, an' he knows you two haven't spoken in years."

"Your father's tried his own resources. He wants to buy the land as soon as possible."

"What's it for? This land, what's he want with it?"

"I have no idea."

"Who're these other owners?"

"He didn't say."

"Have you talked to Uncle 'Bert?"

"He's heard nothing from Owen, either. My fear is, he's lying dead in his home."

"That's been checked on."

"Are you sure? Homosexuals are so self-involved — "

"Hey, this self-involved faggot just put you back in your townhouse, at considerable expense."

She glared at me. "So that's how it's going to be."

"You spit shit like that 'round me — damn straight."

Then I stormed out, leaving half my meal behind, and drove straight home. But Tone was off at his therapy session and Matt was out, so I just had the four walls to rant and rave at ... till I noticed Matt had left a note on the counter — *Fugitive warrant issued for Owen Taylor; indications are he went to Mexico; nothing else since 3 months ago.*

Shit. Shit. Shit. Shit. Shit. Shit.

The next day was that hearing with the judge overseeing Tone's case. I was hoping we'd clear everything up and then Tone and I could drive to Palm Springs, together. Instead, Castillo and the bastard AG agreed on a continuance to the following Tuesday. Perfect.

Castillo told me not to worry; this gave him more time to fight and finagle with the guy and he thought they were close to an understanding, but he was paid by the hour so no wonder he's happy. Me, I was thinking this was geared towards draining me of every penny I got in settlement from this fucked up state.

So I booked a flight and packed a bag, and the next morning headed for Palm Springs. That gave me five-six days to find out what the hell was going on with my uncle. Should be plenty of time. Right?

When did I become such an optimist?

— VI —

The second I told Tone I was going to Palm Springs, he shifted into being way too careful in his words and kept bouncing back and forth between holding on to me and not letting me near him, like a cat that wants to be petted then left alone then petted ... and on and on. Initially, I thought he was worried the AG and Castillo would come to an agreement while I was gone, but then I started wondering if he was about to vanish, again. Like my uncle did. Like my mother would. Like he had, twice before. Which segued into me wondering if Mira's question was really about me being around people who had no problem putting me second when it suited them.

Of course, I was low on the ladder of meaning in prison, but that was a survival mechanism. Beta dogs last longer than Alphas because all they had to do was bark and growl and join a fight, not face one down.

So I flew out on the cattle car line and arrived at LAX just before ten, in the middle of one of SoCal's rare cold snaps. My thought was, so what if it was over a hundred miles to Palm Springs? There was a better selection of flights, and cheaper. What I didn't count on is, it takes three solid hours to get there, thanks to LA's non-stop stop-and-go traffic ... not to mention drivers who refuse to watch the road or care about the other people on the freeway. By the time I reached the 111 exit, I'd damn near been sideswiped twice, almost rear-ended once, cut off forty-seven times, and was ready to rip somebody's heart out. The long quiet stretch between the 10 and the city was heaven, in comparison.

I used GPS to find Uncle Owen's new place. It was on a road off the 111, up a glorified alleyway stacked with low-slung houses up to a private gate. Beyond that was a drive that curled back and forth up a steep hill to some 2-story stucco townhouses perched on top, looking like a Moorish fortress standing guard over its domain.

Turned out the number my uncle sent me was the code to that security gate — his birthdate. It swung open so I drove in, twisting and turning till I reached a short drive that ended in a cul-de-sac. There were eighteen units, all two-story stucco with clay tile roofs. The ones to the left were even with the drive, each with its own small front yard and driveway to a built-in garage. In back, a sloping yard and deck looked out over the city.

To the right, the hill rose higher so the front yards and driveways were slanted. The back yards nestled up to a high stucco privacy wall surrounding the complex that was made less severe by non-stop succulents draping from it and cacti planted along its base. The units curled around a cul-de-sac at the end and the landscaping was desert casual. Overall, very nice ... if you like the desert, which my uncle did.

"It's pure," is what he told me when I asked why. "If you look close, you see the beginnings of life."

"Yeah," I sighed in response. "All the ants and scorpions and snakes, oh my. But no cool breeze, tall trees, winter snows, or happy streams."

He'd just patted my cheek, smiling.

His unit looked straight down the cul-de-sac, so he could see whoever was coming in. I pulled into his driveway and got out to look around, and you want to talk about having the high ground? Even from the unit's side fence, you could see across miles of city, desert, mountains, and wind farms. The unit to the left of Uncle Owen's had broken windows, an open front door, and cracked stucco. Two other units sported For Sale signs; another was Sold. But all of the grounds were perfect.

I tried the key he'd sent me on the front door, but no-go. So what was it for? No one answered the doorbell, and the blinds were drawn, so I peeked through a small window in the door and saw massive stacks of envelopes and fliers, and hints of the furniture inside. The fortress was watched over by a security company with no number on its signs. I rang a couple of other doorbells but no one answered, so I finally called Matt.

"What's that management company you mentioned?" I asked. "The one Donald Rice called from?"

"Palmetto Properties," he said, then gave me the address.

I GPS'd it, saw he was just up Palm Canyon, so headed over. I could've called, I guess, but I was here ... and thinking about Dion ... remembering him ... my heart felt lighter.

I'd just graduated and was headed for college in the fall. Mom was off on one of her trips, so Nana paid for me to visit Uncle Owen. I flew straight into Palm Springs during what must have been the hottest Pride Week ever ... and talk about culture-shock. Texas' gay communities are vanilla compared to the six-thousand flavors I found there. Men and women of every shape, size and interest playing grab-ass and tit-pinch with each other and hugging and kissing in screaming voices ... I was sure I'd get laid the second I stepped out Uncle Owen's door.

Instead, I got this weird vibe off guys I was introduced to, like I was beneath them. Granted, I wasn't as built as I am now, but neither was I skinny or shapeless. Later, I overheard this one circuit-boi dismiss me by saying I was just a Tex-Mex, while another guy said I didn't look Mexican; I looked Cuban. But neither culture was interesting to them. It wasn't till I met Dion that things changed.

We were at a pool party behind this sharp-angled mansion of white paint, black glass and over-watered lawn under a blazing sun, surrounded by pumped up muscle queens of all colors in the wildest assortment of Speedos and thongs and Spandex that had been made tighter. Everybody was scream-chatting and diving into the Olympic-sized pool and never-ending supply of rainbow-colored drinks and nothing nibbles as they showed their pumped up chests and kick-ass legs and implanted butts. I saw at least a dozen hook-ups, and was getting pissed because it looked like mine would just be my right hand.

Dion wasn't the only one dressed in a costume but he stood out because he was this six-foot-six combination of *The Flying Nun, the Creature From The Black Lagoon,* and *Joan Crawford.* To about his hips. From there down was just a nice ass, crotch and pair of perfect legs under sexy net stockings and rhinestone-studded flats. My golden giant ... and seriously, I had to look up to see his baby-blue eyes, pug nose, and kick-ass smile.

Uncle Owen introduced us then wandered off to grab another glass of neon something or other and sit near his buddies — Cliff, a sort-of-buff African-American with cafe-au-lait skin and sloe eyes, and Ian, who was from Ireland, had a past-fifty-pudginess and was en route to a nasty sunburn. They looked like a Greek Chorus in their t-shirts, cargo shorts, and flip-flops.

Dion was the first guy under forty who paid attention to me instead of the preconceptions of others, and let it be known by saying, "People call me Rose of the Golden Girls, but you may call me Dion. Are you from Egypt? You've got this really amazing Omar Sharif vibe going."

Which was bullshit. I'd seen *Funny Girl* and *Lawrence of Arabia*; the only similarities between us were the dark hair and olive skin. But I knew what he was getting at and told him, "Mix of Iranian, Irish, and a touch of Italian. Makes me all I's."

"A real live *Persian Boy*. Have you read the book?" I had no idea what he was talking about. He smiled and caressed my chin and said, "By Mary Renault. A book about Alexander the Great and his Persian slave boy."

"Is it porn?" I asked, grinning.

He laughed and patted my face and said, "Only of the heart." Then he had taken off his winged hat and removed his top to show he wore a dark, electric blue classic-cut Speedo that accented his abs and chest. Another difference between him and the other muscle queens was, he still had glowing blond hair on his body ... and in all the right places. The boys took notice, believe me. He moved to dump the costume on a wall and stretched his way back to me, saying, "It's too hot for this shit."

I noticed a space in the pool by us and cried, "Let's cool off," then grabbed him around the waist and pulled him in ... and we had a great day, together ... great night ... great two weeks ...

Dion lived in a sleek apartment complex off South Palm Canyon, two buildings over from Uncle Owen. Most of the parties happened in high-walled homes you could walk to ... so long as you went early in the morning and didn't come back till the sun was down; otherwise you got roasted. Uncle Owen always wore a safari hat and carried a cup full of ice. He'd dip a bandana in the cup's cold water then either drape the wet cotton around his collar or over his head and down his neck, using the hat to keep it in place.

"Old Texas trick," he told me. "Natural AC."

Dion used a huge green and black umbrella he had bought in Ireland, for shade, so I shared that with him. He always smelled of coconut oil and loved to rub it on me almost as much as I enjoyed slathering it on him. He even talked me into wearing a red Speedo, once, which got my ass grabbed way more than I thought possible. But not once did I think of being with anyone but Dion. Leaving him at the end of my two-week stay was hard; I came so close to telling my uncle I wanted to stay.

And sometimes it hurt to think of how things would have been if I had.

— VII —

I parked outside this 1980s-style mixed office and retail building — all weird-shaped concrete in desert hues mixed in ways that really shouldn't be, with silvery-black windows, tall palm trees, and more cacti and succulents than a nursery. The parking lot's asphalt had been sun-bleached into such a soft gray, the white lines designating the spaces almost blended with it. Several stores were vacant, and few cars were in the lot.

I went inside and upstairs and down a hallway then cut left instead of right to find Palmetto Properties. Nothing grand or glorious, just a sign spelled out in sticky letters on the cheap panel door, with the *E* in the first word and the first *E* in the second word showing only the ghost of their adhesives.

Inside were four cubicles behind one of those metal desks faked up to look like wood. It had stacks of paperwork and a couple of In/Out trays on it along with a flat calendar and a multi-line phone. Obviously the receptionist's, but no one was sitting at it.

Then this bright blond head popped up over a cubicle to say, "Be right with you — " and stopped and his big blue eyes got bigger. "Jake?"

It was Rose of the Golden Girls.

"Hey, Dion," I grinned back. "How's trickin'?"

He burst around the cubicle to grab me around the waist and haul me into the air. "Oh, my God, you've gotten all butch and buff and oh, my God! You're gorgeous. I can't believe it. I haven't seen you in what? Nine-ten years? Oh, my God."

"Shit, Dion, did you grow?" I grunted as he crushed me.

He laughed. Still had a boyish face and eyes with little crinkles that danced for joy when he was happy and stormed like thunder when he wasn't and a smile that made me think of heaven. Maybe not as buff as he used to be, and in business casual, not Speedo sexy, but no mistaking him for anybody but Dion.

"I go by Donald, now," he chuckled. "And I grew another inch a year after you left. And ... there's these."

He set me down and showed me he was wearing purple leather cowboy boots with three-inch Vaquero heels.

"Jeez," I said, "What does that make you now? Seven-ten?"

"Drop it by a foot and you'd be right. Intimidation factor. I haven't taken 'em off in six months. How the hell are you!?"

"Doin' great. I live in Denmark."

"That's what Owen said. He kept me up on everything about you. Don't know why." And he winked at me.

"Really. He told me nothin' about you."

"I got slapped around by love and married a chef. Can't you tell?" He patted his belly, which was nowhere near fat.

"Still fishin' for compliments, bitch?"

"It's the Blanche in me. C'mon back to my office."

He led me into his cubicle, with its mountains of paperwork and erasure-boards covered in notes and schedules. Under it all were hints of a desk and an ornate rolling chair. I think I heard a phone ringing, but it could be coming from next door. He took a stack of folders off a plastic patio chair and plopped into his.

"Oh, my God, it's so good to see you. Y'know, those weeks we were together ... it's a fallback memory for when things get too intense."

"What d'you mean?"

"Oh, the last couple years've just been crazy. Doesn't help that I've got kids, now."

"Wait, is this chef female?"

"Honey, please! They're from his first marriage. His wife dumped them on him so she could follow her bliss. To Eureka. Certain family members were not happy, but she signed the papers giving him full custody and the courts agreed they were valid, especially since

Kent and I are legally married. So now I'm co-care-giver to twin six-year-old girls who will soon be seven, a ten year-old boy, two dogs, a cat, and a yard in the suburbs."

"I can't imagine you a dad."

"I'm not; I'm a papa. Kent is dad. So, you out here for Owen? You know where he's gone? I hear Mexico, but ... "

"Dion, I ain't heard from him since he was arrested."

"Oh. Didn't he tell you about Philby's fresh charges?"

"Found out on my own. I called but I can't get hold of him. I was hopin' you knew where he was, or maybe had a key to let me into his place."

He leaned back, sighing. "Of course I do. I even went over there to make sure he wasn't lying dead in his bed and being feasted on by desert rats."

"Was he sick?"

"No, but the night before he vanished he called me, upset."

"I thought he won his case."

"Not exactly. Philby got a continuance. He didn't tell you anything about it?"

I shook my head. "Just that it was happenin'."

"Oh my God, the way Owen doles out information. Well, I got busted, too, and my trial was just before his, so I stuck around to offer moral support. Several of us were there."

"Yeah?"

"Oh my God, we made it a party. You remember Ian and Cliff, right?" I nodded. "We sat right behind Owen, casting evil glares at Philby and Ginty as that bitch cop told his story. Then Preston started questioning him, and let him know he had video backup, and Philby bolted up and asked to meet in chambers. Like it was an episode of *Law and Order* or something. They came out fifteen minutes later, Philby huffing in anger."

"Owen tell you what happened?"

"Only that the judge gave the persecution a couple of days to verify the video. We saw it, that night. It proved that bitch cop was lying and there was no witness anywhere."

"He told me the video was inside the store."

"It was. But the cop said Owen came out right behind him,

and the video showed it was more than two minutes later. Plus, the cop went to the right when he got outside while Owen went to the left. But here's the killer part." He leaned in close, like this was choice gossip. "You actually saw the cop's shadow cross the main door to follow Owen, proving he did the chasing, not the other way around. What made it fun was, this other cop, some long, lean, butch little bitch named Roy Harper, of all things, swore in his report that his buddy was stopped as he rounded the corner of the store to get in his car. Where Roy was sitting, waiting. Parked on the street. Flat out lied. Both got perjury complaints filed against them."

"And Philby fought that?"

"He used the continuance to work up charges of underage sex against Owen. Little Sir Roy even came over to threaten him with it. Connie says they would've punched each other out if she hadn't stopped them."

"Connie?"

"She bought my place when I moved in with Kent. Owen didn't tell you about her?"

"Wait — you lived in Playa Royale, too?"

He smirked. "Honey, you need up your research game."

"I ... I got ways to find out stuff."

"Uh-huh," and the look he gave me would have wilted a cactus. "Well ... I had the first unit on the left. Moved in the second it was finished. I was rolling in cash, at the time. Anyway, Connie's on the city council and had just got home when she saw them arguing and got between them. Philby'd filed the rape charges, that morning, and confiscated his computer and files. He really didn't tell you any of this, himself?"

"No. Shit, I'd have come straight out, whether he wanted me to or not." Which might be why he didn't tell me.

"That's not what I wanted to hear. I've got tons of stuff to go over with him."

"Like what?"

"I handle the townhouses and his apartment complex. You do know about those, right?" I flipped him off. He grinned. "There've been repairs and one of his apartment tenants moved out, last week, so their deposit has to be worked up. Taxes are coming due and the bank is claiming he's behind in his mortgage payments, so they're adding on penalties and fees — which he isn't and they shouldn't, but I can't find out what's going on because my Power of Attorney ran out two months ago."

"Shit. How long's this been going on?"

"Since just after he left. And what a coincidence."

"Who're you talking to at the bank?"

He reached behind him to dig into a pile of papers and pulled out a partially crumbled business card for one Grace Nieri, then handed it to me. "This cunt. Oh shit, sorry."

"For what?"

He blinked and his grin went lopsided. "I've been trying not to cuss so much; the kids, y'know."

I laughed. "Shit, bitch, you *are* Rose of the Golden Girls!"

"I was all Blanche, till I met you."

"Yeah, right."

"No, seriously. Remember that day? When Owen brought you in, I thought you were his trick."

"Bullshit."

"Oh, my God, I was so happy he'd finally become human and spent the money for a little fun, and I was hoping he'd give me your number so I could show you what fun was all about. That's why I strolled my little ass over — "

"Little? I couldn't get my hands around it."

"And it's served me well. But then I saw you up close, and you had this lovely, lost look about you, and I learned you were the nephew he raved about."

"Don't oversell it, *Donald*."

"No, seriously — of all his nephews and nieces, you were the only one he thought was worth a damn. That's why when he started to tell you my name I said Rose instead of Blanche. Don't you remember how he frowned at me?"

"Not really ... "

He shrugged, a wistful glaze in his eyes. "It's funny. I went over hoping to give you a blow job, but then we talked, and you pulled me into the pool, and something changed inside me."

"Me, too. I got wood the second I touched you."

"You're sweet to say that."

"I mean it," I said, my voice growing soft. "Truth is, those memories were a fallback for me, too."

He gave me a tender smile that almost ached. "When I heard you got disowned, I told Owen he should let you stay with him. Or I could put you up; I had room in my bed, then."

"He never even suggested it."

"Well, that was about the time he started building Playa Royale. He said he'd think about it. I guess he got sidetracked. Then I met Kent ... and things turned serious between us. What's funny is, I don't think they would have if I hadn't had such a lovely time with you. It showed me I had the potential for a relationship, and now I have the proof. Over nine years, me and Kent. Longer than both my sister's marriages, put together."

"Wait, together nine years but twin six year-olds?"

"Yeah ... his ex invited him over to talk about school for Joel, and one glass of wine led to another ... and we almost broke up. I'm so glad we didn't. Wouldn't even think of it, now."

It took me a moment to focus on that last comment. "Dion, is everything okay with you?"

He sighed, the grin dashing back to his lips but not his eyes, and said, "It's just Don, Jake. Dion's dead. And it's fine, basically. Kids're great. Kent works so hard. It's just — I've lost half my clients in the last year. They sell their place or don't renew their contract and go to other management services." He waved about the room with his arms. "I used to have five employees; now it's just me. Noticed how quiet the phone is? Two years ago, I couldn't have held any kind of a conversation with you. Now Owen's properties are my main source of income, and they're taking Playa Royale away from me, too."

"Who is?"

"The community committee. When Owen vanished, this tool named Lionel Tinley took over. He bought the unit across from Connie about six months ago. She's fighting him, but another guy ... uh, George Simmons, he goes along with Tinley."

"Why they doin' it?"

He shrugged. "The economy's still weak, out here. Couple of people lost their jobs. Two of the units are in foreclosure and three others are behind in their fees. And Owen's not around to back Connie up."

"Sorry to hear it."

He gave me his lop-sided grin, again, and said, "Oh, dump that stuff. How long you in town for?"

"I need to be back in Texas by Monday for my guy; no longer than that."

"Oh?"

"It's just legal crap; you know the justice system ... "

"Shit, do I ever — oh, sorry."

"I dunno, Dion," I smirked. "I think my virgin ears have just been violated."

He chuckled then eyed me in a way that made my heart race, just like he had all those years ago. "Tell me ... was I the first one to violate you?"

"Naw, there were a couple of jocks in school ... who'd never admit to it, now. But you were my first man. Tell me — you mind if I ask you why you got busted?"

"Oh, my God, I brag on it. Kent and I were at a bar — our first night out in over a year — and I'd had a few too many. While he was getting the car — we never do valet, anymore; can't afford it — I was waiting outside when this guy comes up. Tight jeans and t-shirt. Nice body. Starts talking to me and not really believing I'm a real blond, and then he said, I'll show you mine if you show me yours. Which he did. Not all of it; just a hint of the shaft and his pubic hair. I showed him my pubes. He was a cop, and he busted me for public indecency. Said I'd shown him my erect penis."

"Did you?"

"Honey, I wasn't that drunk and he wasn't that hot. Next thing I know, I'm in a cop car being hauled down to Indio for booking. Kent had no idea where I was till they let me call him. Since we knew Preston through GALAIATH, my man got hold of him and I got bailed, that night."

"So what happened?"

"Honey, weren't you listening? The stupid little punk said I showed him my dick. Erect." He leaned forward, his expression stupidly seductive. "Do you remember my penis, my Persian Boy?"

I nodded. It was long and sloped and had three rings around it, thanks to skin discoloration — red near the tip, pale cream in the center, and a brown base. "Raccoon Dick," I said.

He chuckled and nodded. "Preston set the little bastard up, so beautifully. Got him to swear he'd seen my cock, with plenty of light and no obstructions and on and on and on ... then asked him to describe it. The cop tried to weasel out of it but Preston just kept harping on it till Philby dropped the charges. It was lovely." He chuckled.

"You took a chance."

He shrugged. "I had to. I'd been in jail, before, so if I'd taken any kind of a deal, the county could've used that to show I was a serial criminal, or something. Drive me and Kent apart. Take the kids away. Instead, the liar is under investigation for perjury, too; Preston made sure of it and Owen made sure the press knew that was three cops connected with two cases facing perjury charges. Of course, the investigation'll probably go on just as long as it takes for people forget about it."

"Yeah. So much for justice, right?"

"Honey, it's okay to lie, cheat and kill if you're a cop."

"No shit — oh ... sorry." And I smirked.

He laughed and slapped my leg. "Here's an extra set of keys to Owen's," he said, digging them out of an overstuffed drawer and tossing them to me. "Security code's his first name. Same for the gate."

"I thought it's his birth date. It worked when I input it."

"Really? Wonder when he changed it?"

"Don't you need it to get in?"

He shook his head. "I have my old one. I ... I hope you can figure out what's really going on. Philby claims he skipped bail to avoid trial for the molestation charge."

"What do you think?"

He grew very still. "I don't want to think what I think," he said. "But like I said, I ... I talked to him just before he vanished. He was really upset about something. Almost crying. I told him to come over, but he never did. And he didn't answer his phone when I called back. And now ... " His voice trailed off.

"You remember when that was?" I asked, softly.

"August 2nd. Samantha lost a baby tooth. Y'know, I tried to

file a missing persons, but the cops' attitude is, they're already looking for him as a fugitive."

I made myself smile. "You should've brought donuts."

"I wonder ... " he muttered. Then he hopped up and said, "Oh my God, once you're settled in, come by the house for dinner. I'll introduce you to Kent, and I know he'd love to cook for somebody besides me, for a change. All the kids want is Mac & Cheese, 'burgers or peanut butter and jelly sandwiches."

"It's a date. Dion."

He put his hand on my neck, his eyes filled with memories, then leaned down to kiss my cheek. "Dion's dead," he whispered.

"Not to me," I whispered back.

He grew misty, so turned away and wrote his home address on the back of a business card and we set it up for six ... then I wandered back to the car, my brain scrambled.

Dion had suggested I come back out here. Even offered to put me up so Uncle Owen could keep his space, but the offer was never passed along. Of course, I'd never asked, but if he'd suggested it just after I got kicked to the curb? I would have. Or maybe not. Nana let me live with her. I'd been accepted to a damn good school in town. Had a good job. Then I was in jail. And prison. And had a record so couldn't have left if I'd wanted to, not without a shitload of trouble. Then I was facing East, not West. But it felt weird, considering how supportive he'd been. I couldn't believe he'd do that without some better reason than he got busy building condos.

I drove back to the fortress to let myself in. The mail was nothing but postcards from all over and charities begging for money and insurance scam offerings and your-best-new-credit-card applications and fliers for parties and bars and political rallies and causes and politicians who promised they really are there for you mingled in with brightly colored ones for Sunday services and seminars at a church called San Sebastian — the patron saint of athletes ... and a holy death ... at the hands of archers. Talk about phallic symbolism.

The electric and gas were still on. Dion told me Owen had gone paperless with his bills, so everything was charged to his credit card. He'd always been anal about that, just like mom. And me.

The townhouse was filled with that French Provincial crap, like mom's once was, everything in its place. Patio door by the kitchen. Stairs to the left leading up to a pair of bedrooms. It was so much like his apartment had been ... except there were no pictures on the walls, just hints of discoloration and dust where they'd once hung. Nor were there any plants, anywhere; my uncle had filled his home with them. And dust covered every square inch of surface, including the TV screen. He was too much of a neat freak for that to be allowed.

I checked the fridge; just wine, water, and canned mixers in it. Nothing perishable. No dry or canned goods in the pantry. No alcohol in the bar. No dishes or glasses or silverware in the sink or dishwasher, just in the cupboards and drawers. It was like this was a model home no one really lived in.

I checked his bedroom; everything was in perfect order except the clothes in his closet had dust on them. Neat stacks of underwear and socks sat folded in drawers. I found his luggage in a storage space in the bathroom, which was spotless. The other bedroom was his office, and it had nothing out of place — except there was no computer on the desk, just the cables that connected it to the power and printer. On top of that, I couldn't find a backup file anywhere, and I knew how anal he was about that, too. I checked his filing cabinets; all empty. Looked like the cops had taken everything they could.

Shit. I got this weird, sinking feeling at seeing just how perfectly placed every object was, as if his home was waiting for him to return from a trip he knew he'd never come back from.

Like he'd gone off into his beloved desert and ... and ended it.

I headed back downstairs, telling myself there was no way that could've happened. He'd never have given in to that sort of despair, no question in my mind. Well, I was definitely family, so I'd be filing that missing persons report, in the morning, and flat out dare those fucking bastards to blow me off and —

"Open up! Police!" jolted me, followed by pounding at the door. "Open up!"

I scrambled over to the foyer to yank the door open before they had a chance to break through it — and there stood a pair of mean-freak automatons in black uniforms and flak jackets, microphones on their shoulders ... both with their pistols out and at the ready. If I wasn't careful, I'd be tomorrow's headline — *Burglar Killed By Palm Springs Cops!*

And no one would even try to question it.

— VIII —

A two-inch difference in height was the only thing that kept these two uniforms from being twins. Everything else, from sunglasses to jackboots to hip-holsters to gloves to haircuts, was straight off the butcher-than-thou cop assembly line and meant to intimidate. All it did was irritate me.

"What the hell is wrong with you?" I snapped. "You damn near gave me a heart attack!"

"Do you live here?" the taller one snapped back.

"No, I'm visiting," I snarled back. "I'm the owner's nephew. That a problem?"

"Hey, watch your attitude!" His pup-partner snarled, trying to show me who's boss. It was obvious he thought the gun in his hand meant his dick was bigger than porn-size.

His alpha-buddy said, "Can you prove it?"

I handed him my Danish passport and Dion's business card. "These people manage the property. They'll verify who I am, and let you know they gave me the key to get in, *and* the security code. The fact that the alarm did not go off should have told you everything's okay."

"This passport real?" He seemed genuinely confused.

I rolled my eyes. "Denmark has a consulate in Los Angeles. Call them."

Then a woman's voice called out, "Wait — are you Jake?" Counterpointed by some mutt's yapping.

I looked past the cop to see a voluptuous Hispanic woman heading up the drive. Stylish, black hair nicely cut, very business-like. An elderly woman was approaching on the sidewalk, with an orange Pomeranian on a leash.

"Name's Jacob Blaine," said the prick before I could speak.

"Says he's Danish."

"Don't look Danish," snapped his partner, still trying hard to be belligerent. "They're blond."

"Then you've never been there," I growled.

"Guys, I'm sorry," she said. "I thought it was a break-in."

The elderly lady called, "Connie, is everything all right?"

"It's fine," she called back, offering me a well-manicured hand in a perfect politician's move. "I'm Consuelo Test, part of neighborhood watch. So you're Jake."

"Is he okay here, Ms. Test?" the puppy asked, wary. He showed her Dion's business card.

"Yes," she responded, her eyes glancing over the card then settling on me. "I'm friends with the owner and he's talked about Jake so much, I feel like I've known him forever."

The little prick must've been really pissed he didn't have an excuse to splatter me to hell and back, because he walked away without another word. His buddy flipped the card and passport back at me and followed him, with a shrug, brushing by the old lady as she headed over.

"Well-mannered," I said loud enough for him to hear. They both cast me a glare as they got in their cruiser.

Connie touched my arm and said, "Sorry about this, Jake — may I call you that?"

"Sure, Ms. Test," I said, smirking after the cops as they drove away.

"It's Connie. Please. This is Meredith Dolmer."

The elderly lady held out her hand, gently. She had one of those faces that remind you of quiet strength and bemusement — or maybe amusement; it was hard to read — with short white hair swept back and light. She wore casual slacks topped by a warm sweater and must've been close to ninety, considering how gently she moved and the way she focused on you when she spoke.

"And here is Geordi," she said, referring to the happy, yappy mutt, her voice hinting an accent. "So you are The Jake."

"I recognize you now, from the picture," said Connie.

"Picture?" I asked.

"On Owen's desk. I thought you were a model."

All careful lighting and Photoshopped. I'd got it done just before I was nearly destroyed. But it wasn't anywhere in the place. That could be a good sign ... or another bad one. Shit.

So I smiled and said, "I'm not male model material."

"Owen would disagree," said Meredith. "I believe he is very proud of his nephew."

"Very," said Connie, and the look in her eyes carried way more meaning than Meredith's words. Then she leaned in close and softly asked, "Do you know where he went?"

"Don't you?" I asked.

"No. His voice mail's full and he's not answering e-mails."

"Did he come to stay with you, in Denmark?" asked Meredith.

"Did he tell you he was?" I asked.

"No," she sighed, "it was more of a hope."

"I hear he skipped into Mexico." So she thought he was skipping the rape charge, too. Some friend.

"Let's return to my home and have some coffee," Meredith said. "Owen has been gone so long, I'm sure the food in his refrigerator is spoiled." She turned to Connie. "Also, I have some of your chili left."

"Coffee's great," I said, "but I gotta pass on the food."

"Jake ... it's an award-winning recipe," Connie fake-whined.

"Careful. I was raised in Texas; I know from chili."

She leaned closer and whispered, "You only think you do. I got to the national cook-off." Then she let two fingers caress my right hand. Man, she was anything but subtle.

"Sounds temptin'," I said, "but I got a dinner date."

"Already?" Connie smirked. "You work fast."

I made myself smile at her. "You got no idea."

"Wanna bet?" And the certainty in her voice convinced me there's no way in hell I would.

Meredith's home was the second unit down from my uncle's, and was filled with comfortable furniture and rugs and colorful afghans she'd probably crocheted herself. Pictures of her and a lovely blond woman covered the top of a baby grand piano and a couple of end tables. Her plants were thick and healthy and made the place feel like a country conservatory. Few works of art were on her walls. Sliding glass doors opened onto a back yard lush with succulents, with a light cabana top to keep the sun from being too much. It felt just right the moment I walked in.

And man, she makes coffee that's as good as Tone's ... but no scalding here, baby; it was perfect. Connie joined us and, as Meredith fed Geordi little strips of turkey bologna, we had a nice chat about nothing ... that told me way more than you'd have expected.

For example, when my Uncle Owen developed Playa Royale you had to be recommended by someone he knew, and that was just to be allowed to see the blueprints. Buying in was a whole 'nother game. Despite the housing crash, he'd sold out before the first shovel was turned, except for the units he kept as rentals. Meredith was in one, Cliff and his boyfriend, Ned, shared the one between hers and my uncle's, and four circuit boys were on the other side of her.

"You know about Circuit boys?" I asked Meredith.

"I'm Meredith's dictionary," Connie laughed. "Hell, I've partied with those boys, myself."

"Now you scare me," I chuckled, only half-joking.

She laughed even harder and slapped a hand on my shoulder. "Don't worry; my handcuffs will stay locked away when you're around."

"Connie, please." Meredith was not amused.

"Uh ... Don says you bought his townhouse, Connie."

"Down by the gate. He wanted to move in with his husband. I took over the mortgage and was underwater from the beginning. Who knew the value could drop so much? But I'm on top now."

"You're on the Playa Royale committee, too, right?"

"Wow," Connie said, "Donnie filled you in good."

I wondered if she's ever had the nerve to call him Donnie to his face ... and figured, probably.

"Lionel Tinley decided it would be better for himself to manage the property," said Meredith. "In exchange for free dues for himself. He lives in the unit across from Connie and thinks Donald is too expensive. I like how well everything is kept, so I am against it."

"But she's not an owner, so she doesn't have much pull," said Connie. "A couple of people don't want to change, but Lionel's convinced the rest they can lower their dues and get the same service for seventy-five dollars less a month, each. Doesn't sound like much, but a few owners are having serious financial troubles and the bank's being their usual self."

I found the card Dion gave me. "Palm Valley West Bank?"

Connie nodded. "Owen set up the mortgages there. He knew a president or VP or something, and got some excellent rates."

"They were taken over by another bank a year ago," said Meredith, "and they have made the fees and rules impossible to deal with. I had to move my account."

"They're all like that, now," said Connie. "Me, me, me, and to hell with you."

"Unless you're rich," I said.

"Or have connections," purred Connie. "Owen knew people who didn't know they knew people."

"Where does it stand with Don taking care of the place?"

"His contract's up the end of the year," said Connie. "If Owen doesn't get back here, Lionel and George won't renew it."

"Idiots," Meredith whispered.

We kept chatting till it was close to six, but I didn't learn anything more. They walked me back to the townhouse, where Connie gave me her card.

"If you do find out what's going on with Owen, please tell us," she said. "Him running off like this ... it's not the right thing to do. He should at least let us know he's okay."

"If I can figure it out," I replied. "He always kept his life private from me."

"I don't think any of us truly know him," said Meredith.

"Jake ... didn't you two share details of your conquests?"

"Neither of us kisses or tells," I said.

"Too bad." But I got the impression she didn't believe me. "Tell you what, let's have a get-together of GALAIATH and see if they can help. Say, my place, Friday night?"

"Sounds great," I said. "That way I can let you know if your chili's any good." I winked at her.

"Game on," she shot back, all but licking her lips.

She moseyed on down to her corral and I got the hell over to Dion's before she could lasso me. Jeez. She was no fag hag; she was a budding serial rapist.

No way in hell was I ever going to be alone with her.

— IX —

Mr. Rice lived in a pale yellow bungalow in a pleasant part of town. Yard of green gravel. Date trees hugging the corners of the house. Azaleas mixed in with lots of succulents. Way more suburban than I expected.

I heard barking then Dion popped open the door before I could hit the buzzer. He was in the same clothes and boots and lifted me up in a hug, again, as he called, "Oh, my God, Kent, he's here! And he looks hungry as a wolf!" Then he focused on a golden retriever and an Australian sheepdog, whispering, "Zoë, Zebra, calm down. He's a guest."

Two seconds of sniffing my hand and they were ready to do some lickin' an' get some pettin', as Nana would've said.

"Not the best guard dogs," said Dion.

"Here," I said, handing over a six-pack of Shiner Bock, one of the few good things about Texas. As Nana'd taught me, you never go to a home empty-handed, and it shocked the hell out of me to find that beer in a local grocery store. Goes great with anything, even whatever was behind the way too promising aroma that hit me. "Damn, Dion, what's on the grill?"

"Steaks with Kent's own marinate. You better be starving."

"The steaks aren't that large," said a smiling voice, and then I saw a dark, slim man with bright, gentle eyes and an outstretched hand approaching, half of him hidden by a cook's apron, the top of his head level with Dion's chin. "I'm Kent Mixta."

"Jacob Blaine. Thanks for havin' me."

"Please. D, pull the kids away from their game."

"They're eating with us, Jake. Be prepared."

Dion led me through a wide open home that was a chaos of toys and clothes and cozy furniture on top of the two happy dogs and one curious cat — all with the usual shedding. Before I'd gone five feet, my jeans' legs were covered in it. "How do you keep their hair off you?" I asked.

"Packing tape," he replied. "I use a roll a week. And they only ride in Kent's car, not mine."

"What does Kent do?"

"Sous Chef on Indian Canyon. He changes clothes at work. I get the kids to school so he can sleep in, he picks them up, then at four scoots to the restaurant. I'm on mobile from then and handle anything that way. He's off Sundays and Wednesdays, and I don't do weekends, if I can help it, so we get one full day together where we all just ... enjoy."

"Sounds rough."

"Worth it. Don't you want children?"

"Ain't ready for middle-age yet."

"Bitch," Dion gasped in a whisper, then he led me into a game room that was as chaotic as the rest of the place. Seated before a huge TV screen were a boy and two girls straight out of Hollywood's version of what children should look like, playing Super Mario on a Wii. "Yo, clan, here's your victim!"

The girls bolted over with squeaks as the boy put the game on hold before he even thought about joining us.

"Okay, Jake, this one's Samantha, this one's Sarah, and Mr. Cool here is Joel. Be gentle with him, kiddles."

First thing I did was note that Sarah had a gold clip in her brunette hair while Samantha's was red; I'd need that to tell them apart. Joel casually smiled and shook my hand with a surprising maturity. Then it was five minutes of questions from the girls as Joel watched. "Where you from?" "Denmark." "Where's that?" "Europe." "Europe? You sound like papa." "Jenny Gross's mom's from Europe and she talks funny." "You don't." "I was born in Texas." "Did you have a horse?" "Nope." "What about a ranch?" "Too much trouble." "No they're not." "Horses are great." "Papa takes us riding, sometimes." "They like to stop and eat the grass." "It gets papa fussy."

I tried to picture Dion on a horse. Cowboy gear. Legs all the way to the ground like he's on a tiny pony. Not pretty.

Thank God Kent called us to dinner before I said anything too dumb, because lemme tell you ... the CIA could learn some interrogation techniques from six year-old girls ... and calm intimidation from a ten-year-old's steady gaze.

What made up for it is the best damn steak of my life. With baked potatoes (as is the law in California, too, it seemed). Green bean salad. Cornbread. In portions that don't overwhelm. Bock for us boys, sparkling juice for the kids. Heaven. By the time dinner was over, I'd told the little monsters everything I was willing to share in my life, and they'd decided to visit me in Denmark.

Once the plates were cleared, the kids scurried back to their game. "Homework's done when they get home," said Kent, "so they'll be in bed by eight-thirty."

"Give us some time to be adults," said Dion.

"Y'know, I met Connie," I said.

"Did she pull her Sexy Sadie crap on you?" asked Dion as he sipped a beer. I shrugged. He chuckled. "Offer to take her up on it. Watch how fast the excuses fly."

"So she's messin' with me? Weird. Normally I can tell."

"Oh, my God, Jake," Dion laughed, "if she really was that way, we wouldn't have helped on her campaign."

"Connie's runnin' for office?" I asked.

"Already on the city council," said Dion. "I told you."

"Right, I got it confused with Playa Royale's committee. I met Meredith, too."

"She's sweet. Like a little doll. She doesn't like the committee much."

"Don't blame her."

"Connie's good," said Kent, "and she's been good for us, on the council."

"A couple of born-agains got elected," said Dion, "and want to run anyone gay or with an Hispanic last name out of town. Oh my God, this one asshole — sorry, jerk — Kent, was it Fletcher?" Kent nodded. "He called Connie a wetback, in a council meeting."

Kent shook his head. "What he actually said was, he didn't need advice on wetbacks from someone like her."

"Patriot scum. Next meeting, she brought in birth certificates showing she was born in Fresno, her parents in El Centro, and her grandparents in Blythe!"

"Fletcher moved here from Kansas, four years ago."

"I thought he was from Utah."

"Wrong side of Colorado."

"Wrong side of life. Anyway, she made him apologize. She's a real ally, Jake. That's why I sold her my place."

"Well, it was also time to get rid of it. Imagine if we had to deal with the bank over that, on top of everything else."

"Oh my God, half the people we knew at the bank are gone, and these new idiots ... you wonder how they made it through high school, let alone college. I had one put my deposit into our money-market instead of the company checking and couldn't figure out how to correct it. Plus there was a two-day hold on the checks, so I couldn't even go online to shift the money to the correct account. I wound up with two-hundred in fees, and that's with them waiving half of it; they wouldn't waive everything despite it being their damn mistake. Said I shouldn't have waited till the last minute."

"That's why we shifted our business to B of A," said Kent. "The restaurant's willing to do direct deposit of my check to them. They wouldn't with Palm Valley."

"Wasn't Ian having problems with them, too?"

"No, it was Ned. Ian's with a credit union."

"Wish there was one for people like me."

"Why don't you start one?" I asked. "Gay and Lesbian Federal Union of Credit, Karmic Universe."

Dion got it, straight off, and laughed. "Oh my God, you are still a bad boy!"

"What?" asked Kent.

Dion whispered to him, "First letter of every word."

"G-L-F-U-C-K-U — ?" he muttered, then his face lit up at realizing. Dion chuckled and caressed his cheek ... and I thought of all the times I'd done that same thing with Tone ... and him with me. Just a touch to let you know you're in the same zone. It hadn't happened in so long, I felt a sudden ache behind my heart ... and a sigh drifted out of me.

It was time for the girls to bathe and hit their beds, so I finished their game with Joel. Well, tried to, because I sucked. Princess Whatever would have vanished forever if he hadn't been piloting Mario.

He finally looked at me and said, "We don't have to play this.

I do it 'cause the girls like it."

"Is there one you'd like to play?"

"It's too late. Did you know papa before he was with dad?"

Whoa, talk about left field. "Uh, yeah."

"Did he leave you for dad?"

Holy shit, should I even be talking about this with him? "No, I was visiting my Uncle Owen. You know him, right?" Joel nodded. "I met your papa while I was here, then went home. That was before he even met your father."

He nodded. "Uncle Owen's cool. He watches us, sometimes."

"Yeah, he is cool."

"He's been gone a while."

"Yeah, he has."

"This kid said he ran off so he wouldn't go to jail."

"That's not true."

"You sure?"

"Yes." What the hell am I supposed to be saying here?

"Then where is he?"

"I ... I don't know. I've come to find out."

"Okay. Do you think I'll grow up like papa and dad?"

Jesus. "I ... I don't know. Why you askin'?"

"This kid at school says if you got two dads, you wind up like your dads. You gotta have a mom to wind up normal."

"Not true. I had a mother and a father and I didn't wind up like them. Why does it even matter?"

"Just wanna know."

"Well, whether you have two dads or two moms or a mom and a dad or just a mom, you grow up like you're supposed to. Anybody who says anything else is stupid."

He just looked at me, and for a second I saw a forty year-old man in his eyes, then he stood up. "I gotta get ready for bed." And he left.

I felt like I'd said the exact wrong thing.

Later, as Dion was seeing me to the door, he asked, "Did you get EIT'd by our little J Edgar?"

"EIT'd?"

"Enhanced Interrogation Techniques. Apparently, he's been

asking people very blunt questions about me and Kent, thanks to idiots at school filling his head with stupidity."

"You know what it was about?"

"What he's gonna be when he grows up. Looks like he's trying to build a consensus. Kent and I've left it alone. Hope he comes to us with it."

"He will, and you'll do fine when the time comes."

"Thanks." Then he hugged me and kissed me on the cheek. "Don't be a stranger, anymore. Please?"

I nodded, got in my car and headed back to the fortress. I had to drive through a section of town where there were next to no streetlights, making it seem even darker than it already was. There was little traffic, and the whole feeling was one of wariness and fear. I didn't like the edginess it gave me, so I cranked up the stereo to blast it away.

Man, Palm Springs had changed since I visited. Granted, I'd only been here a little while, but what I saw then was a city that was open and carefree and willing to accept anyone and anything. Now? It felt suspicious and wary.

A lot of it might be due to Southern California's real estate crash. When you tear apart somebody's bankbook, they start looking for people or groups to blame for the lack of certainty, and politicians prey on that. Feed it as long as they can. I had a feeling that's why gays and undocumented workers were being targeted; people thought the former had all the money and freedom they wanted, and the latter were taking away their jobs. It was nonsense, but since when does reality matter to a mob?

There was also the dismissal of Prop H8 by the Supreme Court. The anti-gay crowd had put a lot into keeping exclusive rights to marriage and had lost. Completely. So now we had push back from the anti-fag crowd still fighting for their cause, as lost as it was.

It was obvious my uncle saw the cancer of intolerance slowly destroying his version of Utopia. He'd tried to fight it, but the other had side fought dirty, so maybe he had grown to feel it was hopeless and had, as Dion feared, taken himself out of the equation. I still couldn't see it, but that reminded me of how little I knew about him. I didn't know if he had a lover. I didn't know what kind of food he liked or what his goals were or anything. I hadn't even known how he made a living till I found out he was a developer and landlord. His problems with the DA were shrugged off with a text message, even though it threatened a hell of a lot more than a fine and community service. It made me feel like I couldn't be trusted.

But then, why would he send me a key that didn't fit any of his locks? And his security code? And a message that didn't ask me to do anything but expected me to do something? It was weird.

"Shit, he and Tone're built from the same DNA," I muttered. "I should call him to find out how Uncle — "

Flashing lights rolled up behind me and I was beckoned over. But why? I wasn't speeding, hadn't had any beer in a couple hours so wasn't weaving over the road, and I hadn't even passed a traffic light, yet. Plus, this was a rental car; I could be pretty sure all its lights worked. Of course, cops can use a traffic stop as an excuse to get at you, if they feel like it, but why would they be doing that with me? I hadn't been in town twelve hours. Had they been following me? Why? Only Dion really knew me here, and I hadn't messed with anybody ...

Except those two cops at Uncle Owen's. Oh, man, were those two mutts gonna get some back, from me? Prove who's the alpha and who's his pup?

I glanced around. No street lights burned. Huge empty lots sat on both sides of the road. The main drag was another three blocks away. I was alone in a place I didn't know, and I didn't have a safe-recording app on my cell phone to prove what was about to happen. I flashed back to the night I got busted on a bullshit charge, chucked in jail and my life damn near ruined. Shit, I couldn't handle that, again. No way in hell.

Okay, when I got fucked over the first time, I was too dumb to understand what was what. Now? If this was anything but a traffic stop, I'd play nine kinds of hell with these assholes. I speed-dialed Tone's number, hoping to God he wouldn't answer. He did.

"Jake, do you know what time it — ?"

I cut him off with, "Tone, hang up. I'm callin' back. Let it go to voicemail."

I heard him whisper, "Shit," then say, "Okay."

I redialed and set the phone on the console as I pulled to a stop. The cop stayed behind me, lights still flashing, high beams blasting straight into my mirrors. He got out, slow and easy, and sauntered my way. All I could make out was a half-silhouette of something that looked male.

Then another cop exited the passenger side. And stayed there. As a witness.

Shit, shit, shit. Yes, my calmer side was insisting, *It's just a misunderstanding; it'll be cool, keep calm,* while my paranoid side damn near screamed, *Your uncle vanished, now you're going to, too, dumbass.*

Like hell, motherfuckers; bring it on.

— X —

I kept my hands on the steering wheel and said, loud enough for the phone to hear, "It's almost eleven, Wednesday night, California time, and I'm being stopped by two police officers just inside the Palm Springs city limits. Without cause."

The first cop wandered up, his hand twitching to go for whatever torture toy he liked. I didn't move. He stopped by the back door.

"Driver's license and proof of insurance," he snapped.

"It's a rental," I said. He must've already known that. What game was he playing?

"Rental agreement."

I nodded and offered him my Texas driver's license; I'd yanked that from my wallet the second I put the car in park. I hadn't had a chance to shift to a Danish license, yet. "The agreement's in the glove box," I said. "Is it okay if I get it?"

"No," was the snarly reply. "Unlock the doors then keep your hands on the steering wheel. Hey, Roy, come get the rental agreement from this guy's glove compartment."

In case he has a gun in there? What kind of bullshit was this, and why would a cop be so stupid as to — whoa, whoa, whoa, whoa ... *Roy?* One of the cops connected to my uncle's arrest was named Roy.

No ... no, it couldn't be. How would they even know I was here?

I used the rearview mirrors to watch Roy stroll up to the door, a long, lean block of serenity like he knew it was a game.

I kept facing forward as I said, "I don't understand; what's the problem?"

"You ran a stop sign, back there."

There weren't any stop signs on this road. Period. I didn't argue; just take the ticket and fight it in court.

"Shit, Roy, this fag's from Texas."

"Yeah? Nothin' but steers an' queers there."

Okay ... the only way they would have the nerve to make a crack like that was if their body-mikes and the camera in the patrol car were off. Why do cops always think they're flashing a really big dick when all they're proving is their little head is smarter than the one on their shoulders?

"Jacob Blaine?" said the guy by me. "This your license?"

"Yeah."

"You look Mexican, to me. Got proof you're an American?"

"What d'you mean?" I snapped. "I'm black Irish." And half-Persian, but no need to mention that. Assholes like this love to use anything unusual to hang you with.

"Rented the car at L-A-X-ative," said Roy, his voice hard and chuckling, as if he'd made a funny.

"What's a cocksucker like you doin' in California?" said the guy with my license.

"I'm here — I came to see my uncle!" I almost said, *I'm here for Owen Taylor, asshole* ... but something kept me from it. It couldn't be more obvious that these guys were trying to force an incident, but I wanted to know why before I started howling.

"No shit? Your uncle. How much is he payin' you?"

"Cheap bastard didn't even spring for a decent ride," Roy sneered.

"Hope you got your money up front."

Okay ... that did it. Time to put the pups in their place. So I gasped in an oh-so-surprised voice, "Wait a minute — Roy? Roy?! Could you be that hot cop he's told me so much about?"

"What the fuck you talking about, fag?" Roy was not happy.

"Hey, dude," I said, still not moving, "You can supplement your income any way you want, and from what I hear, you got plenty to supplement it with so — "

The cop behind me yanked the door open and screeched, "Out on the ground, faggot, face down! Now! NOW!"

I started to do it but he grabbed my jacket to sling me to the asphalt ... so I hooked a finger in his holster and he came down with me. Slammed his face against the edge of the door. By the time Roy had scrambled around from the other side of the car, his taser out, I was lying flat, hands and legs stretched out, not moving an inch and fighting to keep from smiling.

"What the fuck, Chet!?!" was all he could think to say.

Chet? CHET?!

Holy fuckin' shit, it was both of the cops Uncle Owen told me about. Paranoid me took over. No way this was a coincidence.

"The son-of-a-bitch grabbed me," Chet snarled.

"What you talkin' 'bout?" I yelled, letting fear tint my voice. "I was gettin' out of the car when you yanked at me, and slipped. It's my fault you can't stand up straight?"

"Motherfucking cocksuckin' faggot son-of-a-bitch!" Chet bolted to his feet and kicked me in the side.

It hurt, but I really played it up with a scream and howl and cry of, "Why're you doin'?! What'd I do?!"

"I'm gonna cut your fuckin' balls off, motherfucker! Fuckin' faggots!"

He kicked me, again. I coughed and choked, and didn't need to play that one up; I think he broke a rib. He got ready to kick me again, thinking he was going to make me fight back, but I took worse beatings in prison, so I got ready.

Then Roy shoved Chet back and barked, "Hey, hey, HEY!" His voice gained an octave on each word.

"What the fuck is — ?!" His voice cut off. I heard some rustling behind me then my phone was shoved in front of my face by fat, bloody fingers, Chet snarling, "You were on the phone?"

I looked at him and spit, "To my boyfriend, asshole. I got his voicemail. This is gonna be some fuckin' message he finds."

Chet's mouth dropped open, working like it wanted to close

but couldn't figure out how. Blood trailed down his face from a gash in his forehead. He rose. A second later, Roy straddled my butt. Ground me against the asphalt like he was trying to fuck my ass and pulled my hands behind me to whip a strap-cuff around my wrists. I cried out from the pain, especially when he forced me to my feet by yanking my hands up. And the whole time he whispered, "You're under arrest for assault on a police officer. You have the right to remain silent. Anything you say can and will be used against you in a court of law."

"Good," I croaked. "Puttin' a collar on you'll be fun."

Chet howled and grabbed me and slammed me on the cruiser's hood, face up, and punched me in the gut, twice.

"Fuckin' coward," I muttered, trying not to hurl.

He was aiming to smash me, again, when Roy got between us. "Don't."

That is when I finally got a good look at Chet, and he was so damn typical — well into his thirties, with the puffy jowls, bad skin, and thin hair that goes with the juicer-culture of bodybuilders. What's more, his torso barely fit into his extra-extra large uniform shirt while his legs all but vanished inside his trousers. No wonder he toppled so easy.

Roy was Laurel to his Hardy, and looked more like a cop ought to look, right down to the white t-shirt under his uniform and the oh-so-earnest expression countering the five o'clock shadow on his long face. His hair was thick and dark, like his eyebrows, and he probably had zero percent body fat. The one imperfection on him was the nails of his long lean fingers were bitten to the nubs. I noticed because his hand held Chet back. He knew they were in deep shit.

"C'mon," he said, his voice wavering a little, "it's gonna be hard enough to explain this, as it is."

"Who's gonna take the word of a fag against two cops?"

"Your words, asshole," I choked. "Not mine."

"Illegally recorded," said Roy, without conviction.

"We'll see," I growled back.

They worked me into the rear of the cruiser. Two minutes later, a tow truck arrived, and when I saw the character driving it, I was glad I had extra insurance on the car. The keys got handed over and I was driven to jail to be booked for assault on a cop and resisting arrest.

Silence all the way.

We stopped at the back door of a blank, low-slung building, construction finishing up around its sides. An expansion. Of course. Plenty of money for prisons and none for education.

I got printed, mug shot, personal effects taken, and slapped into an orange jumpsuit within ten minutes of Chet and Roy dragging me in. During the whole process, I croaked, over and over, "I need to see a doctor. Please. I need to see a doctor." I never heard a word in response, so I figured it was going to be a long nasty night.

Finally, I was taken into a small holding cell that had nothing but a bench attached to the wall. There was no non-painful way to sit or lie on it, so I lay on the floor ... and the hell with how nasty it was.

Until that point, I'd been on top of what had happened. But it didn't take long for the adrenalin rush to pass and memories of my previous dance with the law to come crashing in.

Back then, I was nowhere near as built as I am now, and I was scared shitless. A non-violent guy accused of having drugs locked in a jail cell with murderers, rapists, armed robbers, you name it. Alphas like to prove straight-off who their bitch is in there, so a couple shoving matches came close to me having to fight somebody. One stopped when a guard passed by; the other when a trans prostitute was tossed in with us and the other guys forced her to give them all blow-jobs.

I was offered a go, but I told them a cop busted me for fucking his seventeen year-old daughter, so I was spent for the night. Not a word about drugs being planted on me. Not a word about me being gay. I had a feeling lies about screwing a girl were safer than the truth, though one guy did insist I describe my night in detail as he used the prostitute's mouth. I used the sex scene in *Titanic* to spin a beautiful pile of crap, and nearly got sick doing it.

Then five mean-as-shit-looking black guys were put in. All solid muscle and cold-eyes. All focused on me. The second the cell door was closed and the guard was gone, they told the guys I was a punk for the cops and a fag and started tearing at me. At my uniform. At every part of my body. I swore they were lying, but no one listened. Instead, the other guys in the cell screamed for them to get harder and nastier, like they were the audience at a gay porn shoot. I fought them, but when five guys want to fuck you, they will. And it went on and on and on, like forever — hands on me ... groping me ... grabbing where they wanted in this sick sort of intimacy ... with slaps and punches and pain that never let up ... and I was damn near sick just from the memory and ... and son-of-a-bitch, I'd kill anybody who tried that with me, this go-around.

Fuckin' kill 'em.

Wouldn't even hesitate.

— XI —

The slashing memories kept up until an old man in a white coat was let into my cell. He had long silver hair, weary eyes, more wrinkles than a Shar-Pei, and the first words out of his mouth were, "Get up on the bench."

I was shaking, thanks to my brain, so it took me moment to snarl, "I can't. It hurts too damn much."

He frowned and sat on the floor, and helped me off with the top of my jumpsuit then felt the bruising on my side, soft and easy as he muttered, "Don't feel like nothin' broke. Prob'ly just bruised. Gonna hurt for a while. Who did it?"

"Like it matters?" I asked.

He eyed me then tapped the tattoo covering my right bicep and shoulder. "Celtic?" I nodded; no need to point out some of the symbols were in Farsi. He nodded back, rose, pulled out a form and rapped on the door, calling, "This boy's for the ER."

A guard appeared on the other side of the door. "You so sure he's not just faking — ?"

"That wasn't no request!" the medic shot back, filling out the form.

The guard blinked then vanished.

Man, I liked this guy.

"Thank God I'm back on days, next week," he sighed, then shot me a glance of apology. "Ambulance'll be here, shortly. Don't move if you don't have to. No heavy liftin' for a good six weeks. And I sure hope that ain't the side you sleep on."

"I'll live, Dr ... ?"

He grinned and said, "Sandoval." Then he pounded on the door and the guard came to let him out.

As the guard shut the door, I said, "Don't I get a phone call?" The only answer was complete silence.

An hour later, I was taken to a nearby hospital under armed guard, like I was a terrorist or presidential assassin or something, and examined in every way from touchy-feely to x-ray to anal probe before I was admitted for overnight observation. One deputy whined about that, but the doctor just shrugged as she said, "Not your call."

I was set in a solitary room with my left ankle handcuffed to the bed and the door locked. I couldn't find a way to get comfortable enough to sleep, but it was a hell of a lot better than my first night in jail. And one positive aspect of being chained up was, whenever I started drifting back to that crap, all I had to do was yank on the cuff to send a sharp pain jolting into my brain to bring me back to the here and now. Made for a long night, but not a freaky one.

The next morning, a different doctor came in, checked my chart, checked my x-rays, poked and prodded my side, coughed like a guy who slammed through a pack a day, and finally said, "Cleared for release," without once looking me in the eye. The deputy on guard smirked.

"May I make a phone call?" I asked. Again, no response.

I was handed my jumpsuit and told to get dressed.

"I'm still due a phone call," I snapped. This time, I got a shrug.

I dropped the hospital gown and had just grabbed my briefs when the door slammed open and a Young Republican Female barged in — pinstripe dress-suit so sharp, you could cut paper with it; blond hair in a stylish bun; lips tighter than a hundred year-old nun's, made even tighter by the little gold cross around her neck; and if she ate more than a leaf of lettuce a day, it would have surprised me. She was flanked by two massive uniforms of the Deputy-Sheriff variety, one male, one female.

"Mr. Blaine, will you come with us?" she said, a bit breathless.

"I got a choice?" I snarled, glancing between the two cops.

"Please," she said. "My boss wants to see you in his office."

"And you are ... ?"

"Elizabeth Ginty, Deputy District Attorney Warren Philby's assistant."

Holy shit — *this* was the bitch Uncle Owen talked about? Paranoid me came scratching at my gut.

I croaked out a whisper of, "Ms. Ginty, I'm a citizen of Denmark. I ask to be granted access to representatives from my embassy or consulate."

"Mr. Blaine, please," she retorted. "You're an American with a criminal record who is in no position to demand anything more than the minimum required for any convicted felon."

Whoa, whoa, whoa — she had access to my Texas criminal record? That crap was supposed to be expunged as part of the settlement. Shit. That is when I let a real snarl come into my voice. "Look at my personal effects, currently in the jail's vault or whatever you call it. You'll find my Danish passport. I became a citizen eighteen months ago."

She looked perfectly shocked as she asked, "You did? Why?"

I played up the pain angle with some grimaces and catches in my voice. "I have family there. And a ... a job."

"That means you have dual citizenship. So the waters get pretty murky, here."

I quietly choked out, "Lady, do you even know what waters we're in?"

She gave off the barest of hesitations before she said, "Get dressed. We have to go."

Tone told me they'd pulled this same crap on him, once — popping up for a talk while he was bare-assed, to put him on the defensive. Well, this bitch could see whatever she damn well wanted, so I tossed the briefs and carefully forced myself into the jumpsuit, still playing up my achiness. "I need to pee, first."

"You can do it when we get there. It's not far."

Well ... at least I now knew Ms. Ginty, and I could see why Uncle Owen had despised her. She hit me as one of those people who goes to church every Sunday and prays to God and thinks of herself as the purest of the pure even as she tears apart other people's lives, all because those other people are *the others*. She probably had a husband who was her twin and maybe even two-point-five babies she was proud to bear in the face of the Femi-commies who wanted to abort all children and yap, yap, yap, like an excited Chihuahua. Yeah, she had no idea what waters she was swimming in now.

Problem was, neither did I.

— XII —

Not far meant driving a mile through the most backed-up traffic ever, past the jail and Larsen Justice Center to a newly constructed office building. We could have walked faster. By the time we arrived, I was close to pissing on the floorboard, but her pit-bulls were just daring me to try, so I held it in.

We strode in then headed straight up an elevator to a blank reception room policed by a receptionist whose attitude screamed *Don't mess with me*, then past a blank wall into an office that still reeked of fresh paint, old criminal files, and dusty books; no chance to take a piss.

Seated behind a desk that was perfectly positioned before a wall of framed photos and citations was a man who fit the TV ideal of a strong DA way too perfectly. His profile crisp and clean. His salt and pepper hair cut as perfectly his suit. His nails bright and polished. His smile so calm, cool and condescending, I could have sworn I saw him on some version of *Law & Order* — and may have; in So-Cal, everybody's an actor.

Seated in a plush chair in front of the desk was his near twin in polish and attitude, just with silvery-blond hair, a windbreaker over a Polo shirt, tan slacks, and deck shoes. He rose and offered a hand with light calluses on it.

"Mr. Blaine?" he asked in a voice that had been trained right. "My name is Gregory Mikkelsen, with the Royal Danish Consulate. I apologize for the manner of my dress; I received the call a short while ago, on the fourteenth hole, and came here, straightaway. Are you well?"

"As well as can be," I croaked.

He nodded. "Yes. Well, I am here to represent the interests of Her Majesty, whose interest is in making certain her citizens are cared for." He turned to the guy behind the desk, who hadn't moved. "This is Warren Philby, Deputy District Attorney."

The viciously polite tone in Mikkelsen's voice made Philby rise and offer a hand. "Mr. Blaine. Will you have a seat?"

Well, paranoid me was in total control. I'd been targeted, and having some heavy-hitting backup from another country may be the only thing that keeps me from disappearing like my uncle. I wondered if he'd been arrested and conveniently forgotten about in some jail somewhere. If that was the case, I'd make the bastards fry.

I carefully settled into the other chair before the desk. Mikkelsen sat after me, as did Philby.

"We were about to have some coffee?" Mikkelsen directed at Philby, who just barely tensed.

"Yes," he said, his voice under serious control. "Mr. Blaine, would you like something?"

I let my voice crack even more as I said, "Water, please." The need to hydrate had smacked around the need to pee.

"Of course," said Mikkelsen. "Coffee, please. Black."

Philby nodded and looked at Ms. Ginty. "Would you?"

I could hear her stiffen, behind me. "Warren ... "

The look he cast her would have killed an elephant from a thousand yards. I heard her breathe in and leave. He softened his glare and turned it on me.

"I want to apologize for the misunderstanding about your arrest, Mr. Blaine," he said. "Things went a bit far — "

"A *bit* far?" Mikkelsen asked, his voice silky but sharp as a knife, even under this charming smile. "I thought the British owned the power of understatement."

"We will, of course, investigate the situation completely," Philby continued, his voice so deliberately calm, it was like atonal music. "I promise you."

"Of course," I sneered.

He eyed me a second then said, in the same atonal voice, "Mr. Blaine, would you please tell me your side of the arrest?"

"Cut it out," I snapped, because as much as I wanted to take pleasure in the whole setup, I was nervous enough to where I didn't need to just pee, anymore. "You heard the tape, and it hurts to talk ... "

"So they did beat you?" asked Mikkelsen. I nodded. "Were you seen by a physician?"

"I was brought here from the hospital."

"Which also tended to the officer you injured," Philby snapped, "who received two dozen stitches — "

I sighed and gave Mikkelsen my most hurt expression as I said, "Do I have a lawyer, yet?"

Mikkelsen almost smiled. "I am an attorney licensed in the state of California, Mr. Blaine. I can assume control of the case on behalf of you as well as Her Majesty's government, if you so wish."

"I do."

He turned his near grin onto Philby. "Well, Warren, this formalizes the fact that you are now dealing with me. So let us dispense with the dueling versions of the arrest. Has Mr. Blaine been arraigned?"

"C'mon, Gregory, this is ridiculous — "

"No, I haven't," I croaked, and I wasn't playing it up. I was getting desperate for that water, and the Ginty bitch was taking her time. "Please, could I have something to drink?"

Mikkelsen looked at Philby. "Wasn't Ms. Ginty bringing us coffee?"

"She'll be back in a minute," Philby shot at him, his eyes never leaving me. "Now listen up, Blaine, a guy with your criminal history doesn't have a leg to — "

Mikkelsen cut him off by rising and whispering an icy, "Excuse me," then he walked over to the door and opened it to find Ms. Ginty talking to the receptionist, a bottle of water in hand. I could hear coffee brewing in the background. He held out his hand and she sheepishly gave him the water, then he politely closed the door and returned to the desk.

He twisted off the cap before handing it to me. I thanked him with a nod then guzzled some. As I drank, I listened to him turn his steely voice onto Philby.

"These games are for children, Warren. I expect better of you.

Has Mr. Blaine been arraigned?"

"No. And it might not be necessary if he's willing to hand over *both* his American and Danish passports to — "

"You have my personal assurance he will not be leaving."

"That may not be enough for a judge."

"Then let's go before one. Now. We can find out."

"He's not due for arraignment for another twenty-four hours and I don't think — "

"Warren, there are numerous judges in the Larsen Center who can handle an arraignment. Surely one is in chambers."

Philby roared to his feet. "Don't get pushy with me, Gregory, because I can — "

Mikkelsen just stepped back, pulled out his cell phone and hit a number as he shot out, "Excuse me." His call was answered immediately, and he spoke in Danish. I was nowhere near fluent in the language, yet, but I could figure out what he said.

"Erik, here is Gregory Mikkelsen. I need you to work up a writ of habeas corpus concerning one Jacob Blaine and take it to Judge Alexis Montoya for signing, then bring it to me at the office of Warren Philby. Angelika has the address. Then please contact the State Department and apprise them of the situation."

"Okay, okay, okay," Philby said, waving his hands. "There will be no charges filed."

Mikkelsen just glared at Philby as he said, in Danish, *"Take care of it at once, Erik."* Then closed his phone.

"Gregory, being reasonable would be a lot more — "

"Warren," Mikkelsen said in a voice so calm and cold, it stopped the man dead in his rant, "I will make decisions about this case based on my own judgment, since yours is so obviously impaired, and since I do not yet have the coffee you promised me. I will also file a complaint, on behalf of my client, against both police officers for brutality and hate crimes."

"You won't get far with that."

"No? We heard what is on that tape."

"Which was illegally recorded so — "

"Bullshit," I snapped out. "I was interrupted while leaving a message. It's not my fault those two cops were stupid enough to be caught, accidentally caught, on tape, spitting out some of the most homophobic crap I've ever heard. And on top of that, they deliberately disable the cameras on their cruiser and their bodies? Who're you kiddin'?"

"You don't know that they disabled — "

I cut Philby off with, "Wanna bet?"

Mikkelsen's near smile almost broke through his face. He turned to Philby and said, "Well, Warren, this does put an interesting twist on the situation."

"Listen," he said, "let's have that cup of coffee — "

"The time for that was five minutes ago," said Mikkelsen.

Philby glared at him, then sat down. "I'll send the necessary forms to the Booking Clerk," he said in a voice so calm and collected, you'd never know he was red in the face. "There will be no charges. Clothes and personal effects will be returned, at once."

"What about my car?"

"It was impounded, Mr. Blaine. You'll need to — "

"Warren," Gregory said in his sharpest, most diplomatic voice, yet, "I think it should be released and brought here."

"That's completely out of my hands," said Philby. "The best I can do is arrange for all penalties and fees to be waived. You'll have to go pick it up."

I growled, which was a mistake; the room began to swim so I leaned back in the chair.

Gregory looked at me. "Are you all right, Mr. Blaine?"

I made myself look at him and sigh, "No. My side is killing me, my head's about to fall off, I need to pee, and I haven't eaten since last night. If this goes on much longer ... "

Gregory glared at Philby and lowered his voice just enough to made it all but scream. "I suggest you arrange something about the car, Warren. We'll be out front in an hour."

Then we left.

— XIII —

An hour later, I had my clothes back on, four tacos, a DP, a double-dose of Advil in me ... and the relief of taking a ten-minute dump. Man, there is nothing like it, even when it hurts to even think about trying to hurry things along. I almost felt human, again. Mikkelsen and I were standing outside the new building, at a corner, trying to ignore the construction noise of the new jail. My phone was cracked and futzing in and out. I tried to call Tone to tell him I was okay, but the call wouldn't go through. Same for Matt. Not good.

This was a tacky area of town, where the 111 squeezes down to two lanes each direction; it's only a mile to the freeway and a bit farther to Coachella, and traffic was non-stop. Mikkelsen sipped at a cup of decaf he'd bought out of a vending machine; I had a bottle of water. He still looked like he'd just dressed after taking a shower while I'm sure I reeked.

"You should have another doctor check your injuries," he said, basking in the sun like a lazy kitty-cat. "It's best to have as much evidence of the abuse as possible."

I nodded. "I'll hit an ER soon as I can. Sounds like you've known Philby for a while."

"I met him only this morning," he smiled.

Damn. "I'm glad you're on my side."

"I've been many years in the diplomatic corps, Mr. Blaine."

"Jake."

"You may call me Gregory. I learned a long time ago when to be nice and when to be nasty. And when to be both."

"All with a smile."

"That's what makes it diplomacy," and his smile became a grin. "You, however, seem to know the art of when to keep silent and when to scream from the rooftops. That also can be useful."

"I don't get you," I said.

"Don't you? May I ask — it was my understanding you were in Texas; why are you in California?"

Boy does his research ... or has it done for him. "My uncle."

"Visiting?"

I shook my head. "Dead."

Gregory blinked. "Oh. My condolences."

I just nodded. I hadn't meant to say that, because I really did not know it, but voicing that word had sent a sharp jolt of truth through my body. I had been trying to ignore the growing fear that Uncle Owen's disappearance was not temporary. But knowing how anal he'd always been about his life, and all the crap over the last twenty-four hours ... no question in my mind — he was dead. And I would not be one bit surprised if the cops already knew it. Maybe he died in a cell. Maybe on the way to jail. Maybe he did it himself. Maybe it was done to him. I had no idea. I just knew he was gone.

And I felt my heart shred into nothing.

I gazed down the road at the flat country and distant mountains and blue open sky, cloudless and cold and ... and Jesus, how could this bright gleaming city be so full of shadows? Dark and bleak and meaningless. Vicious in their sharpness. Making me feel completely, totally and absolutely lost. It was all so damned wrong.

That's when my car was brought up via tow truck, filthy and scratched. The guy dumped it right on the street, and I signed off on everything. I was too depressed to make a scene over the damage; I just took pictures with my messed-up phone so the rental company could.

That is when Erik showed up with the writ. He was a younger sandy-haired version of Mikkelsen and twice as polite, if that was possible. Gregory slipped the writ into his pocket.

"Just in case," he smiled. I thanked him, and he gave me his card. "This won't be the end of it," he said, still smiling. "They've had their feelings hurt, and will want to take it out on someone. And keep in mind, the statute of limitations is six years. They can file the charges any time they choose. I would tread carefully until you leave town, were I you."

"Like they needed an excuse, last night?"

"Jake ... " He said it in a chiding way.

I knew what he meant. I was on their radar now. Any action I took, any statement I made, anyplace I drove, I would have to have some way of backing myself up when they finally decided to take revenge for not letting them fuck me over, and they can get away with it because the citizens they claim to protect stupidly believe their hype about how they seek justice for all.

So I thanked Gregory, got in the car and drove straight to an urgent-care facility. As I waited for them to see me, I focused on my phone. Its lens was shattered and the cover was scuffed. And all my phone numbers and messages had been erased.

Motherfucking babies, these people are.

I was still able to going online and check the Riverside morgue, see if they offered information on people who died around the time of my uncle's disappearance. The accidents and one suicide I found had names and the one John Doe was the wrong age range. So I dug into the online edition of the local paper to see what had been reported about his trial. There was nothing until four days afterwards — a nice page 3 headline about him running away from charges of molesting a child. Of course, the story was crap straight through, like Philby had written it.

The phone was blanking in and out, so I shut it down and tried to read some weeklies that were piled up in the dinky office ... but nothing took my brain away from this one reality — my uncle was dead. No way would he go this long without being in contact with me, not after asking me to come here. And his home, it was like he knew he would never be coming back and wanted nothing there to be remembered by. Or to be lying around that might embarrass him ... or me when things had to be addressed. Like what to do about his estate.

The belief that he actually had killed himself crusted around me like ice, because I could understand why he would want to. I'd considered it when I was sentenced, but no way in hell did I want to die in jail. Instead, soon as I was inside, I found out who the alpha dog was and aligned myself with him. It cost me; Jesus Christ, it cost me. The things I did. The things he had me do. To other guys. With other guys. I never asked why, not even when I was free. Morality was out of my price range.

I thought I got that backbone from Nana. My uncle. Maybe even from my mother. None of them put up with shit. But as much as I hated to admit it, Mira was right when she said I was a lot like my father. Especially the willingness to do what you had to do to make your way. Of course he had always had enough money to buy his morals, proving they were nothing but a petty exercise for an uncaring person's mind that had zero to do with their soul. I guess that was why they could be adjusted so easily to mean anything anybody wanted them to.

Uncle Owen had fought from a place of righteousness, but just as he was winning the opposition changed the game. And if he'd won that battle, they'd have come back with something else. Until it got to be too much — the fighting and the hate and the attitudes of scum who've got nothing better to do than crush the people they don't like. I could see where he'd get to where he no longer felt it was worth it.

But why not come to me? Call me? At least give me a hint he was in trouble? I'd have been here so fast to back him up. Done anything he needed. He was the only one besides Nana who stood behind me when I was busted. Without even asking if any of it was true. And he'd sent me money while I lived with her and tried to get my art going. He'd even visited me, in prison, and brought books and magazines and newspapers. Their support kept me sane enough to at least try and rejoin the world once I was free. To cage the animal I had become, in there. To give me pause enough to see Tone ... and to change my own spiral of self-destruction so I could pull him back from his.

Now my blood backup was gone. Yeah, I still had Tone and Matt, but they were in Texas and there was no one here to lean on but Dion, and I couldn't do that to him and Kent. Not with all they were going through, right now. And I had seen nothing in the way of a note in my uncle's perfect handwriting to let me know what he had done or wanted me to do for him or why he had even asked me to come here. I was just plain lost.

So I stood in the doorway and watched the traffic pass under a cloudless night. A billion stars overhead, but no matter where I looked all I saw was darkness.

They finally called me in and verified Sandoval's diagnosis and the ER doctor's ... and gave me a prescription for something that was a hell of a lot better than Advil. I got it filled, swigged one down with a Dr. Pepper, bought a pack of gum and had to fight to keep from pointing the car down the 10 and not stop till I was back in Tone's arms. Hoping to God he was in his granite mood instead of little bleak psycho.

Only I couldn't. Uncle Owen had stuck it out for me. He'd done right by me. No way could I abandon him, no matter what I found out ... and I did have to find out what happened. What it cost was no longer important. If he had ended it, I had to find out what drove him to that point. And if punishment was due, make sure it was paid.

I owed him that much, at the very least.

— XIV —

I still had no idea what to do when I finally got back to the fortress. I was stumbling tired, aching all over, desperate for a shower, and so many miles down the road to being depressed as I parked, I couldn't work up the will to even get out of the car. I looked around. Saw a few other vehicles parked in the cul-de-sac and on the driveways, blank shapes barely visible in the darkness. Many of the buildings had lights on, inside and out, so it wasn't quite a ghost town, yet ... but the deep black shadows still overwhelmed me.

Then it hit me — there was a light on in Uncle Owen's townhouse. I knew I hadn't left one burning. I bolted from the car and slammed up to the door, pissed as hell. If those cops had pulled some kind of shit without legal authority —

But an aroma whispered up to me, killing my flames and fury. Reminding me of peace. Of home. I entered. Saw a pair of ratty loafers on the floor in front of the sofa and a jacket dropped on top the coffee table. My laptop was open, papers scattered around it. Words drifted from its speakers — *"I know what you're thinkiiiing, you wonder why I chose herrrr, out of allll the ladies in the worrrrrrld"* ... Joel Gray singing about being in love with a Jewish gorilla, from *Cabaret*. I let my sense of smell lead me back to the kitchen and, oh dear God, there was Tone, looking at me as he poured steaming hot cocoa into a soup mug. He plopped marshmallows in. Gazed at me with gleaming eyes.

My shoulders grew straight. My heart was close to bursting. I couldn't take my eyes off him as I leaned against the counter separating the kitchen from the dining room. He offered me the cup. I took it, and it was hot. Jesus Christ, he loved to boil this shit, but how safe and strong and perfect it was. I sipped at it, careful, not wanting to ruin the taste by burning my lips or tongue. The marshmallows had already melted, building sticky white foam over the top. And he had mixed in a Hershey's dark chocolate bar, giving the flavor a little bite. I let the aroma fill my soul. He reached over, wiped the cocoa and marshmallow from my moustache, and licked it off his fingers, smiling.

He was granite. He was granite.

The last twenty-odd hours must have shown in my face, because his eyes flicked over me with concern and he came around the counter and wrapped his arms around me and I winced from pain and set the cup down and held him close.

Oh my God, the feel of him. The warmth of him. The rise and fall of his breath as his arms pulled me tight to him. I lay my face onto side of his neck and God, himself, could not have made me move, right then.

This was all I wanted. All I ever wanted.

I don't know how long we stood like that before I gave his neck a gentle kiss to let him know it was all okay, again. So he brushed his cheek against mine and tipped his nose to mine and his voice trembled as he said, "Your cocoa's cold."

No, it was just warm enough, now. So I sipped more of it.

"I checked the fridge," he said, his voice still soft, "and made a trip to that rip-off of a place called Page's. We're having Tilapia with saffron rice, steamed carrots, a green salad with oil and vinegar, and a nice cold Chardonnay. I know you don't really drink wine, but you're having some. Okay?"

I just smiled. Not a good idea to mix barbiturates and alcohol, but I could tell him that, later, when I had words.

"Matt's flying straight into Palm Springs and should land about nine, so we'll save the fruit and cheese till he gets here, then he and I can finish the bottle off. We'll see how he feels about sleeping on the couch, tonight, and we can rent a bed for the rest of the week."

I frowned. Tone tensed.

"He's already on his way, Jake. The only reason he didn't come with me is, we needed someone at home to be in contact with the embassy, in case things didn't go well."

"How'd you know?" I half-choked out.

"Your voice. I've never heard you so scared."

"I wasn't, really. I ... I ... "

He just looked at me, one eyebrow cocked.

I sighed and nodded. He was right. I could admit it and he wouldn't think less of me for it. He'd been there.

He put a hand to my cheek and stroked his thumb under my eye. "Is your uncle coming back?" I gave a slight shake of my head. "Oh, baby." He slipped that hand around my neck and brought me into the softest, tenderest kiss he'd ever given me and whispered, "Now you're definitely having a glass of wine."

I nodded. I'd do anything he said, right then. "How'd you get the AG to let you come?"

"We'll talk about that after dinner."

Then he slipped back into the kitchen and pulled the fish from the fridge. I looked at his ankle; the monitor was there, its light glowing green. I followed him.

"Tone, how'd you get on the plane with that monitor?"

"I drove."

"You did get the judge's okay to do that?"

"Kind of hard to do when you're leaving at one in the morning."

"You broke probation?!" I spun around, fighting the belief everything was about to crash and burn. "That monitor's probably screamin' all over the goddamn state — "

"Oh, that. Matt reworked its coordinates so no matter where I am, that's where it thinks I should be."

"Until they do a readout! Shit! We were so close to gettin' you released and goin' back to our lives and away from that fuckin' state and — " And then it hit me. "Wait, you DROVE?! When did you leave?"

"Soon as your message was done. I called the embassy, gave them my PIN so they could hear it, and they said they'd take it from there."

"But it's twelve-hundred miles!"

"And it's nineteen hours since you called. Let's just say, I didn't take a nap till I got here."

"Shit. How'd you get in?"

"Rose of the Golden Girls. I filled him in, then he called Preston Niemczyk — what kind of name is that? Czech? Anyway, he found out you'd been released, so Rose led me here, where I've been waiting for you. Just between you and me, I really think he's more like six-eight."

" ... He wears boots. Intimidation factor."

"It works. He's beautiful. But tell me something."

"What?" I moaned.

"Is all of him in ... well, in proportion?"

"What?" Then it hit me what he was asking. "Oh ... since when're you a size-queen?"

"I'm not. I like you, don't I?"

"Hey!" I shoved him, and winced. That was the wrong move to make. I tried to smile as I murmured, "He's normal, not proportionate."

His eyes got their sharp focus. He came over, slapped my hands aside and lifted my shirt to see I was seven shades of black and blue. His voice had a razor in it when he asked, "What'd they do to you?"

"Usual shit. I ... saw a doctor ... "

"That where you were?" I nodded. "I tried your phone — "

"It's screwed up. The ... the doctor gave me some stuff."

I showed him the prescription. He took in a tight breath. I indicated I didn't want to talk about it, anymore; things were too mixed up, so he shifted into gentle mode and said, "Lay down and get some rest. You ... you need it. Soon as Matt's settled in and I've got you in order ... and had a good night's sleep, I ... I can ... I'll head back."

"What'd you bring him into this for? I don't need — "

"Matt hacks, and you need someone to cover your ass — "

"I got people here, already."

"Then why didn't you call them instead of me?"

I shut up. I had input both Dion's and Connie's numbers into my phone, so I could have dialed either one of them and got a faster resolution. But now that I felt like Uncle Owen was dead, I trusted nobody but my pack. Plus the idea of having my own tech-meister to bounce ideas off of made too much sense.

"Maybe I should get a shower, first," I said.

"You could use one," he said. "But first, the wine."

He pulled out a bottle from the fridge and half-tossed it to me, and I barely caught it, my side hurt so. I halfway think he did it deliberately, the little shit.

"Opener's on the table, by the couch," he said, eyeing me.

"I can't drink any — "

"I can, so pour me some," he said as he put the fish back in the fridge. "And don't worry. I'll be home by Sunday night. And I'll tell my probation officer the monitor's acting weird."

"Tone, if they find out you came here — "

"I'll handle it," he said, his voice thick with emotion. "I'll have to."

Oh, shit, he was up to something. But I couldn't wrangle an answer out of him now, not when my mind was nowhere to be found.

It hurt my side to even try opening the bottle, so he pushed me to the couch and guided me face down on it. Then he started his tender, magical, caressing massage thing, and the heartbreaking sensation of his fingers whispering along my skin and up my arms and over my shoulders and down my back and around my hips and up, again, replaced all the pain and hurt and anger with memories of how perfect our life had been, for a while, standing on our balcony and watching a storm whip up Koge Bay, barely wrapped up against the cold, hot cocoa in hand, side by side, his head on my shoulder, the world at our feet ... and the next thing I knew, he and Matt were back from the airport.

Dinner wound up being Taco Bell and a dozen beers ... and me knocked on my ass from mixing up the hops and chemicals, despite Tone telling me not to. But I felt alive, again. Strong. My pack was with me, so God help anybody who messed with us. We could fight back.

And would definitely ... most definitely ... fight dirty.

PART 2

The next morning I woke up achy but relaxed. Tone was already down in the kitchen fixing breakfast, so I took a nice hot shower then called Connie and told her I'd buy whatever she needed for that night. She gave me a list as long as my arm, including a case of Negra Modelo, saying, "My chili tastes best with that." I liked the beer, so no argument.

I didn't mention Tone and Matt being there; I didn't want anybody to know about them, yet.

Matt found a powerhouse WiFi relay under the kitchen sink so cracked in to use it for his research, starting with Palm Valley West Bank. They were declared insolvent fifteen months ago then a couple of holding companies tried to take them over, but the Feds gave it to C&B Trust.

"Isn't that your mother's bank?" Tone asked.

"Not anymore," I said. "I made her change."

What interested me was Grace Nieri, the bank president; she was the one giving Dion so much trouble. The picture Matt found online was of a woman Nana would have called handsome. About fifty. Careful make-up. Her expression so devoid of expression, she looked like wax. Divorced. A son. Nothing more. She was brought in a year ago to handle the merger, and was doing everything she could to make the bank profitable, again.

Which meant screwing people left and right. For example, they used to do automatic payment withdrawals at five pm on the day the payment was due. It got shifted to nine am, and deposits were posted to the account afterwards. Even direct deposits to a checking account now had a forty-eight hour hold on them. With new fees attached.

It looked like Uncle Owen stayed one step ahead of the changes by setting up to have money transferred from his savings to cover the mortgages. So the bank began waiting till after his payment bounced to do it, adding on extra fees. On top of that, Nieri canceled the grace period and instantly listed his mortgages as delinquent, none of which started until after he vanished; prior to that, he always had enough in his account to cover it all. Something else, he didn't get hit by this crap till after Dion's Power of Attorney had run out ... which stank.

I called Dion to ask about the POA.

"They had a copy," he said. "They insisted on it when the bank changed hands."

"Do you have copies of the mortgages?" I asked.

"Yeah, I think so."

"Can I swing by and pick 'em up?"

"Baby, for you — anything. But you gotta pay me."

"Pay you?"

"Details on why you did your own little vanishing act, the other night. Deal?"

"Nosy bitch. But deal."

Then Matt found out something that wasn't posted on Palm Valley's website bio. "Grace Nieri handled another merger for C&B Trust."

Tone sighed. "Where your mother banked."

"Bitch gets around," I said.

"C&B's been in the news a lot," said Matt, pulling up a couple of news articles. "Here — Lamar Davis Lawton's the new CEO ... no, that's from a couple years ago. Here. Story about them expanding by taking over failed banks in the southwest."

"Who's Lawton?"

"Used to be a Congressman. Indicted for campaign fraud. Resigned."

"And probably on a first-name basis with the FDIC guys," I sneered. "No wonder they got Palm Valley West. Can you pull together a list? See who else they got and who they're owned by? Who else bid on taking the dead banks over?"

"Jeez, Jake, do you really it's possible to do something so very, very hard?" His disdain was punctuated with a snotty look.

I flicked the back of his head. He snickered then shifted into gamer-junkie mode as his fingers flicked over the keyboard.

Meanwhile, Tone made an inventory of everything left in the apartment and burned photos of them on a thumb drive via my laptop. He also made notes about what was obviously missing, like the computer and files and pictures off the walls, where the hooks sat and waited. Books were gone from the shelves, too, and the layer of dust on their empty spots was lighter than that where the computer monitor had been.

"By a month, at least," he said, "like someone took them after the computer. And why take the monitor? A PC tower hooks up to just about anything. And they also grab his backup files?"

"Is it normal for the cops to take that much?" asked Matt during a break in his fix.

"Depends on the search warrant," I said.

"I found a storage box of owner's manuals," said Tone, "There're some for a laptop and couple of digital video cameras, but none of those're here."

"The cops may've taken them with his desktop," I said. "And there's no receipt to show what they do and don't have."

"Wouldn't they have left one?"

"Not really," said Matt. "According to this one site, all they have to do is leave a copy of the warrant, and give the judge who signed it an inventory list."

"But there's no copy of the warrant here. Can you find out who issued it?"

Matt bopped his head in a yes. I left them to work and went to get my phone replaced. That only took two hours. Then I hit the police department to file a missing person report.

Of course, the cop at the desk refused to do it because my uncle was considered a fugitive and had a warrant out for his arrest and yap, yap, yap. I asked to see what had been done and was told I was neither his lawyer nor was I a known relative. I showed him letters from Uncle Owen that mentioned I was his nephew; Tone made me take some, from Texas. Still no go. Not till after a half hour of arguing; then he took the report just to make me leave. I made him give me the file number; I knew they wouldn't do anything, but at least it was in the system.

Then I went to the bank and asked to see Grace Nieri. I was ushered up some stairs into an office that was all chrome and glass to be met by a woman who was even colder, thinner, and less human in person than in her picture. She now had silver hair styled smooth and was closing in on sixty. Plus, her whole manner of dress and attitude were so severe, it's like she was either a bad drag queen or Hollywood's version of a transsexual. The only human thing I found on this long, lean block of ice were perfect French nails manicured to within a millimeter of being scary.

She sat behind a brutally neat desk and said, in a voice that reminded me of HAL in *2001*, "You have no legal right to know any of his business with our bank." Then t-t-t-tap, she drummed that set of French nails atop her desk.

"My uncle is missing, Ms. Nieri — "

"A man who runs away to avoid facing trail is not missing, Mr. Blaine; he's a fugitive." T-t-t-tap, t-t-t-tap. "And until such time as he returns to answer for his crimes, and then hands you or Mr. Rice legal authority over his accounts, the point is moot." T-t-t-tap. And the more I heard the damn things, the more certain I was they were fake, the sound they gave off was so plastic. Then she very calmly rose and whispered, "So we are done." And she nodded to the door.

I didn't argue. There'd be time for that when I was locked and loaded.

And would we have fun, then.

— II —

I hopped over to Dion's and told him everything that'd happened. He let a rare frown cross his face.

"But why target you? How'd they know you were here? And oh my God, why be so stupid about it? Owen hit them with perjury charges, and you're his nephew and — it's dumb."

"I don't know any cops who can think beyond their nose," I sighed. "And it's not like IAD's gonna really do anything about it. Not till my uncle's situation is settled."

"Palm Springs has changed," he sighed. "You wanna hear the latest about Joel? One of the teachers at his school — this bitch who wasn't crazy about me and Kent being his parents — she overheard him ask a janitor if he's going to turn out gay. She must've done a hundred yard dash to a phone to let me know, and her voice dripped with *I told you so*. I'm sure she spread it all over the school, by now, the gossipy cunt. Sorry."

"How can she get away with that?"

"Some parents back her up. When the kids began living with me and Kent ... oh my God, they were not kind. A couple even pointed out the twins were born after Kent and I were married."

"Like it's any of their business."

Dion's eyes were close to thunder. "No question they're his. We ran DNA, because the way things were with Yvette, we wanted proof. Oh my God, was that a fun conversation."

"I bet."

"At least Joel got a good teacher, his first year here. She shot people down, all over. And he made friends with other kids. That's what's so sad about this. The little shit who's filling him with this crap — he and Joel were real buddies till this year. Now it's non-stop bullying. Kent and I decided to talk him into going to a different school. One that's ... oh, let's just say ... it's better for science and math. He loves those subjects. One of the positive things about owning land. Even if it's a hillside, you legally can say that's your residence."

"You buildin' another house?"

"Oh, my God, Jake, your research is crap. It's the side of the hill the townhouses are on. All Owen bought, to start with, is the top. I went in on it with him and Ian — you'll see him, tonight. Did it when I was flush, and it was a good tax write-off. But now it's more of a drain. At least I can still use the old address and have the mail forwarded here."

"You always were a sneaky little fuck."

"Who you callin' little, bitch?" he chuckled, but his eyes stayed somber. "Truth is, I'd rather sell it; I could use the money."

"Oh, shit ... you need Owen for that, don't you?"

Dion shrugged. "Lorinda's checking it out. We only did it because Owen got word someone else wanted to buy the hillside, and that'd give them control of our drive. I can't imagine why anyone would want it; it's really too steep to put a house on. Except this is California; they love steep, no matter how many earthquakes there are. Now? I don't live there. And Ian's about to retire. He wants to move back to Ireland. Go from extreme heat to extreme wet."

"I understand. I like Copenhagen."

"That'd almost make you neighbors."

I laughed, grabbed copies of the mortgages and POA to my uncle's properties, and left. I was a couple miles down the road before I realized I had forgotten to get Lorinda's info, so I called him and asked him to bring it to the meeting.

I swung by Page's to buy Connie's ingredients. It was a nice store with plenty of parking around the Pueblo-style building. Inside were long narrow aisles packed with everything you could think of and lots of loud tourists.

Once my basket was full, I spoke with the day manager, a sweet thirty-ish woman who wore natural everything and carried the vague scent of recent reefer. She remembered Owen's arrest. It happened just before closing, but they knew nothing about it till they found his car in the parking lot the next morning. They were about to have it towed when someone noticed the passenger door was unlocked and the bag of groceries was in the front seat. So they called the police, who shrugged it off. The next day, my uncle appeared, very upset.

"He had to buy fresh food," she said, "and air his car out. Never told us what happened; he just left."

"But he came back for a copy of the surveillance video."

She nodded. "Almost two weeks later. We burned him a DVD. Normally we won't, but he's a regular ... "

After some more chit-chat, a bit of flirting ... and twenty bucks worth of her own blend of aroma therapy ... I got my own copy of that video, though I had to make a quick trip to Staples to grab a thumb drive to dump it on.

I dropped Connie's stuff off just as she got home. Outside, her place may look like everyone else's, but inside it was clean, simple and spacious, all in glass and brass except for dozens of green plants situated everywhere. It reminded me more of an office than a home.

She had already heard about my arrest was fascinated. "Was it really the same officer who arrested Owen?"

"Maybe," I said, keeping it cagey. "I haven't seen the report, yet."

"I'll get that, for you," she said as she dumped olive oil and peppers into a huge pot.

"I dunno; I've already spit in their faces."

"Don't want to stir up a hornet's nest, huh?" I nodded. She shook her head and stirred in fresh-diced tomatoes; no canned shit for this baby. "The police have been so stupid, lately."

"Nothing new about that," I chuckled, already impressed with the aroma of the pot that was currently simmering. "Tell me, what do you know about Roy Harper?"

"He joined the force a couple of years ago," she said. "Was in the Marines ... divorced ... I think."

"That fits."

"You a fan of jarheads or divorcés?" she oh-so-sweetly asked.

I grinned. "No comment."

"Oh ... you're such a tease. Now leave. It's time for secret ingredients and nobody sees those but boys in my bed." And she winked at me.

"I'll be back around five-thirty, to set up," I laughed.

"Damn," she said with an exaggerated sigh, "I'm losing my touch."

"It's not you, Connie; it's how I was borned."

"Go, before I do pull out those handcuffs and bring you back to reality."

I went. It was obvious she saw a gay man as a challenge, just like lesbians are to some guys. They get this mindset going that all it takes is the right one in bed, and their world will shift straight. As if sexual identity was that simple. I saw how contradictory and complex it was when I saw homophobes in prison pair up with guys who were willing ... or weren't ... once they got lonely enough. And when they got out, they'd go right back to the girlfriend or wife as if they had just gone for a walk.

Me ... since I didn't smoke and didn't do drugs, I'd swap those for condoms, because I did not want to get HIV, and because those straight butch boys would never get themselves tested. They stupidly figured since they were pitching instead of catching, they were immune. So I never went without one. Even on the occasions I was leased out. I could make it part of the whole process — slip the condom on with my lips, prime the guy up before he entered, and made damn sure he felt like he was raw inside me. Which is probably the only reason I'm still negative.

That was another positive of having a protector ... until I was built up enough to take care of myself, if the guy gave me a hard time I could call the boss over and the bullshit would be shoved aside with a simple, "Shut the fuck up and get done. You ain't got him all night." And I'd act like I was really happy about the whole thing.

Shit ... just thinking about it makes my stomach flip.

But it kept me safe. In fact, the only time a situation even began to get close to me being taken over by a group, he stopped 'em cold by grabbing this short, wiry Latino gangsta who was talking to some buddies. Then he'd snarled, "Don't touch my cunt," and shoved the gangsta at them. "This one's a virgin."

The guy didn't figure out what was happening until he was in the toilets fighting to keep his virginity intact. But like I said, if five guys ... or seven, in his case ... want to fuck you, they are going to. And you think the guards give a shit? But that's the way it is; animals always attack the weak, and all we were behind those bars was animals. And my thought about it? Better him than me.

Back at the townhouse, Tone had finished his inventory and Matt had a stack of info, mainly on Lamar Davis Lawton. After he left office, he got all born-again ... along with his fourth wife. He was installed as CEO of C&B three years ago, with a kick-ass salary, benefits, and stock options, and was the driving force behind the company's regeneration and expansion. Not because he did any work; it was his former position on a number of Congressional committees that left him with plenty of contacts in DC that made the difference. He also had speaking engagements and was invited to the Sunday morning talk shows and right-wing radio broadcasts to discuss the week's events, and he always plugged C&B. The fresh, new motto he brought them? *We're here for the real America.*

"As opposed to the surreal?" Matt asked.

"Small wonder they don't have a bank in San Francisco,"

Tone smirked.

"Or Orlando," grinned Matt. Both of us looked at him, so he shrugged and said, "Trust me, Disney World makes Salvadore Dali look boring." Then Matt showed us a press release; Lawton was also big on holding seminars that told people how they could make themselves a Christian millionaire.

"So easy," snarled Tone. "Start a church and tell people cash donations will pay off their sins."

"Catholics've been doin' that for centuries," I said.

We watched Page's security video on my laptop, and it was just like my uncle said — Officer Chet followed him all over the store, exited 2:18 minutes ahead of him, going to the right, then my uncle exited going left, and you could see the cop's shadow flash past the door as it closed. It was obvious he followed my uncle, not the other way around. So why would Philby have been surprised by this? He wasn't stupid. Arrogant?

"By the way, here's this," said Tone as he handed me a folded sheet of paper. Uncle Owen's Will. Written in his own neat hand and notarized and filed with the county a couple years ago. "It was in the middle of the laptop owner's manual. You're executor and he left everything to you."

His Will was hidden in an owner's manual? Like he knew the cops were going to pull some kind of crap and he didn't want it found after he vanished? That ripped into me. Few people pay attention to pamphlets for electronics and such, but I always read those things when I buy something new, so I'd have gone through them, eventually.

"The crazy thing is," Tone continued, "the Will doesn't match what Matt found through the bank."

I was barely listening. "What d'you mean?" I asked.

"It only lists these four units and the apartment complex as properties owned."

I made myself focus on Tone. "So?"

"Antony found a pad of unused checks," Matt said.

"In the kitchen," Tone said. "Under the microwave. They were pretty dirty. Probably pushed in by accident."

"Gave me access to his bank account," Matt continued. "It

only shows deposits from rents. Could be he's got checking in some other bank ... "

"What are you getting at?" I snapped as I popped some Advil. My side hurt and dealing with a bunch of queens, that night, was the last thing I wanted to do hopped up on barbiturates. So Tone and Matt drawing things out irritated the shit out of me.

"I found a reference in the bank's mortgage files, for your uncle, about a building on Conestoga Lane. Like it's delinquent and he owes taxes on it, but I can't find any income from it. No expenses. Nothing."

More weird crap. Shit. "Got an address?"

"Yeah. Looks like a car dealership. On a huge lot."

"Text it to me, will you?"

Tone chimed in with, "In those manuals was a PDF printout for a high-power server. Maybe he had an online business."

"His home's not wired for it," said Matt, "but a place like that might be. And he might have set up a business account at another bank."

"You can't find any other reference, in his checking?" I asked. "Tax liens? Anything?"

Matt shook his head. "Just the usual crap, and fees."

"Didn't he talk to you about his business?" asked Tone.

I shook my head. I was beginning to see Uncle Owen had kept his life in shadows, presenting only a careful façade to family and friends. Like he trusted no one. Yet he'd set it up so I would find his will and be executor and ... it made no sense.

My only hope of finding out what the hell was going on with him was tonight's meeting, and I wasn't feeling all that jacked about it. Who could've figured my feeling was both wrong ...

... And right?

— III —

By this time it was five-thirty, so my pack joined me at Connie's. Tone wore a pair of jeans that bunched around his ankles, to hide the monitor, so I figured there'd be no problem. But then he met Connie, and both of them bolted into this sharp wariness ... like a couple of pedigree poodles who weren't sure if they were friends or foes. It was all, "Lovely home you have." "Thanks, wish I could spend more time here." "Don't we all? Chili smells wonderful." "It's an old family recipe. I hope you approve." "If it tastes good, I'm happy." Murmured with an icy politeness that would've warmed Gregory Mikkelsen's near-smile.

With Matt, however, Connie was all momma hen. "You've got such beautiful eyes," she cooed. "You remind me of a boy I dated in college. Almost married him."

"Why didn't you?" Matt asked, loving the attention.

"He was Jewish, and I'm Catholic. We both wanted to raise our kids in our religion, and wouldn't give an inch. So we parted ways. He's now the father of six."

"And they said the Fifties were dead," Tone half-joked.

Connie didn't even look at him as she replied, "Nothing dies if it's good. Matt, what do you need to make this work?"

"Just a power outlet," he grinned. "I'm setting Killer up in the middle of the room and — "

"Killer? Sounds wicked." And I swear to God, she was all but cooing as she said it.

"You tell me." He showed her his black diamond of a laptop. She all but stroked it. I figured I'd better give Matt a heads-up about Connie and her handcuffs.

As for her chili — I snuck a couple chips full and nearly died from the beauty of it. No beans. Chunks of steak so tender they melted as they touched your tongue. Just enough jalapeno and habanera to snarl and kick as it went down. Shredded carrots to counter. The exact right blend of garlic, onions, spices, and I'd swear a hint of cinnamon. She did chili right, all right.

While Matt set up Killer, Tone and I put out everything you needed for a buffet dinner.

As we worked, I whispered, "You got a problem with Connie?"

He looked at me, confused. "You like her?"

"She's okay."

He hesitated then asked, "Have you ever been with one?"

I jolted to a halt. "What?"

"Been with a girl? Tasted the Sapphic pleasures?"

"Fuckin' shit, Tone, where's this comin' from?"

"Just wondered. She likes you. A lot."

I tried to make it snide and wicked and a touch queeny as I said, "Now don't be jealous."

"It's not that. She just ... makes me uncomfortable. The way she talks to you; the way she looks at you. And I mean you, not Matt. He's got nothing to worry about from her."

"You don't think she's gonna rape me?"

He shrugged. "Just ... don't be alone with her."

I almost laughed. "Already decided that. And just to let you know, I've been with girls, twice. It was okay but it wasn't right, for me. Or them. You been with one?"

"No." The word was short and sharp, and his voice was tight and closed off to me. "Drop it. I shouldn't have asked."

Aw, shit. More of his push-away crap. My first instinct was to make him tell me what was going on, but that'd mean a nasty fight; I could tell from how quiet he got. So I made myself put it aside till after the meeting. We could talk then.

The first one to show up was Ian, a nurse who still had his Irish lilt. I remembered him, even though he was pudgier, now. He floated in wearing paisley silk pants and a cashmere sweater under a light jacket. It was chilly out, but a couple shots of whisky'd taken care of that; you could smell it a yard away. He lived in the Fortress, so no worries about him in a car.

Next came a married pair of biker chicks, Billie and Beth, on a Harley. Both were round, wore identical jeans everything, had buzz cuts, were pierced and tattooed, and lived in one of the more upscale trailer parks. The only way I could tell them apart was, Billie was white and Beth was black.

Then Cliff showed up, and I got the feeling he'd had work done, his skin was so tight, and his clothes were twenty years too young for him. He was accompanied by a semi-buff, tattooed muscle-leather-boi in his thirties, Ned, who was more interested in posing in his outfit than anything else.

They all chatted like they hadn't seen each other in years, and they loved my guys and vise-versa, though Cliff called Tone Tony — which was politely corrected — and Ned tried to put the moves on Matt, to Cliff's displeasure ... but not Connie's; guess Tone was right about her.

Beth laughed about me having my own harem, to Billie's displeasure, while Ian fawned over me with the *My God, you're grown so butch and buff* kind of crap. But that wasn't the worst; he started sharing stories about me and Dion with Tone and Matt.

"Dear God, but the second Dion saw Jake, he was like a fox after a mouse, and the two of them were inseparable the full two weeks. I doubt Jake saw five minutes of his uncle while here. It was so fun to watch."

"Uncle Owen was with us a lot." I shot back.

"Your chaperone?" asked Beth.

I smirked. "Uh ... nope."

"He painted them, together, once," said Cliff. "Nude."

"Nothing serious showing, dammit," said Ian. "Dion was seated, his robe half off his shoulders and one gorgeous leg visible; Jake was standing, revealing his lovely posterior, and he was bent over, a little, kissing Dion. All very tender."

"It was beautiful," sighed Cliff.

"And life-sized," sighed Ned.

I turned so they couldn't see me roll my eyes at Tone.

"Sounds cool," Matt said. "What happened to it?"

"Donated it to a gay museum in San Francisco," said Cliff. "But he had a serigraph made. It hangs in the foyer."

"It's not there now," Tone said.

"It was, the last time I was at Owen's," said Ian.

"When was that?" I asked.

"The night of his trial. We came over to celebrate him kicking Philby in the balls. Watch that video."

"Discuss revenge," said Cliff.

"Especially on Officer Harper," sighed Ned.

"Sounds promising," laughed Connie.

That made Tone roll his eyes at me.

Ned nodded. "But I remember — that picture was there. I

talked with Owen about getting a copy of it."

"Maybe it's at a print shop," said Matt.

"Then I'd like one, as well," said Ian. "You lads made a lovely couple."

Tone's eyes grew sharp. He was not happy.

"Okay, guys, careful," I said. "Dion's comin', too."

"I'll bet he did, with you," smirked Ned.

Cliff and Beth laughed. Now Billie rolled her eyes.

Ian patted Tone's knee and said, "Of course, that was ten years ago. It was so much nicer here, then."

"God, the fun we'd have," said Cliff, almost sad. Then they got into a discussion over whether the White Party of 2005 was better than the Splash Party of 2009.

Oh, jeez, this was gonna be such fun.

— IV —

The first pot of chili was almost gone but Dion, Meredith, and Preston hadn't shown up, yet, and I was starving. I still waited until everyone else had served themselves up before I grabbed a bowl. There are a lot of things I don't like about my mother, but she instilled a definite sense of propriety in me. Especially as host. So I got the dregs of the pot ... but it did not matter. Sprinkle on some cheese, chopped onions and salsa, and I was ready for heaven and earth to fade away on my tongue. Only just as I was about to chow down, Meredith and her happy, yappy Geordi arrived, to everyone's happy, yappy joy.

"I apologize for my tardiness," she said. "Geordi insisted on marking every cactus on his walk. Do you mind?"

Connie laughed. "If you think we can hear over him."

"Oh, he'll settle once he's had something to eat." Then she pulled a package of turkey bologna from her purse. He stayed right by her, waiting for it ... which she gave him in little bits. Man, if that was how she fed the mutt, it's a wonder he wasn't too heavy to pick up.

"Second pot of chili's almost done," Connie said.

I held mine out. "But we saved you a bowl."

"Thank you," she replied, "but I never eat before eight."

"Perfect timing," Connie said as she stirred.

"God, Connie," said Cliff, "you're destroying my diet."

"Part of my evil plan," she grinned back at him.

Ian took a sip from a flask as he looked around the room, then asked, "Isn't that Owen's fern in the corner?"

I looked at this massive explosion of crinkled leaves feathering out from a hanging jade green pot.

"Yes," she said. "He gave it to me a few days before he vanished."

"I killed the last two plants Owen gave me." That was Billie talking.

"You didn't live with me, then," said Beth.

"Is he coming? I haven't seen him in months."

"That prick of a DA filed boy-rape charges against him and he split for the border," said Ned. He was sweating from the chili's bite ... and probably how hot his leather was.

"Shit," said Beth. "Should've said somethin'. I could of told him places to go, down Baja."

"That's why I asked you all here," I said. "I'm tryin' to put together what was goin' on after the trial. See if I can figure out what ... uh, where he went." And why nobody was worried about him just vanishing like he did.

"When was that?" asked Billie.

"Beginning of August," said Connie.

"That would be when I saw him last," said Meredith. "He was having that argument with that young man."

"Roy Harper," Connie said as she came over to take a chair, Negra Modelo in hand. "One of the jerks who arrested Jake."

"Arrested?!" The word burst out of just about everybody at the same time. Shit, I didn't want that as a distraction.

Connie nodded. "Chet Morrow was the other one. Idiots."

Now I had to hand over all sorts of details, including repeat how Harper straddled my ass to cuff me, thanks to Ned's tight, wicked interest. It took ten minutes to get the focus back on Roy and my uncle, and Tone did not look at me, once.

"What was goin' down between 'em when you arrived, Connie?" I asked.

"They were about to hit each other. Owen was livid."

"Excuse me," Ned cut in. "Are you absolutely certain it was Roy Harper, that night?"

"Yes," said Connie. "I know him."

"He's a busy bitch," said Ned, smoothing his hand over the leather on his thigh. Then he quickly added, "He tried to get me for PI but — "

"PI?" It was Meredith asking. Geordi was interested, too.

"Public intoxication, all because this cock ring I was wearing was too tight to let me walk straight."

"Oh," whispered out of Meredith as she focused on Geordi.

"You've never walked straight," Ian cooed at him.

"Except to bed," sniped Cliff.

Ned gave them a *but-of-course* shrug and said, "Then they threw in everything you can think of. Public indecency. Assault on a police officer. Resisting arrest."

"Assault!" Ian laughed. "You even touch a cop's ass, they charge you with that shite. Then it's your word against his."

"And the judge always take his side," added Ned.

"Little bastards. You can be Sir Perfect your whole life and he can have complaints out the tail," Cliff muttered, "but in the courtroom, he's truth incarnate and you're a thug."

"Ned," I said, "you had all your charges dropped to just disturbing the peace? Really?"

"Blood test came back showing I was under the legal limit. That snippy Ginty bitch still wanted to force a deal on me for everything else but I refused till they offered that." And he looked very proud of himself as he said it.

"You're luckier than me," said Ian. "I had to plead, but my lawyer said it's the best he could do, and it's good I did. By meeting the terms of probation, my record was vacated. If we'd gone to trial, I'd have been found guilty, and since Catholics Incorporated has taken over my hospital, they've been dismissing all who have a criminal record."

"Who represented you?" I asked.

"Scott Baskin," he sighed. "Lovely boy; waste in court."

"Not Preston?" asked Cliff.

"This was years ago, before he moved here."

"I got busted for DUI," said Billie. "On my bike."

"We were both drunk as skunks," laughed Beth. "I don't remember a lot about it, except I got the worst case of the giggles because that silly pig was being so dead serious about it all. Like we were aiming to plow through a field of babies. At two in the morning!"

"No, shit," said Billie. "It took everything I had not to hurl on his ass."

"You were wonderful." And they kissed.

That's when Dion showed up, looking frazzled. "Sorry," he said, "babysitter dumped me."

"Who could do that to you?" I asked, playful.

Dion sighed at me, "Try a sixteen year-old girl who just got asked out by a seventeen year-old jock she's had a crush on since, like, forever, and who is probably going to lose her virginity, tonight. Girls are such idiots when it comes to boys, and if you think I'm gonna let my two get like that ... "

I had to hide a smirk over Dion's huffiness. Nothing's dumber than a goofy boy in love with the varsity quarterback. And I speak from experience. They're little gods, in Texas, and usually look like something carved by a Greek sculptor. I almost sighed at the memory ... and at a few other memories he and I made, before he hit the big league, got married, and grew both straight and narrow.

Dion ended with, "All I can say is, thank God for Lemm."

"So he watches the children?" Meredith asked.

Dion nodded. "I got him just as he was leaving work. The twins have a crush on him. I'd say Joel does, too, but Lemm plays catch with him. Baseball; who knew? I'm raising a butch baby boy, guys."

"We'll love him no matter who he loves," Ian grinned.

"Lemm?" I asked. "Why didn't you mention him before?"

Dion cast me a WTF look. "Oh, my God, Jake, I know a thousand people. You want to meet all of them, tonight?"

Talk about taking what I said wrong. Then I caught Tone

giving me one of his sideways gazes, like he was trying to study me and Dion without us noticing. Made me uncomfortable.

Ned put a hand on my knee and said, "Don't worry, Jake, you can't help but meet him. He's staying with us."

"I thought it was just you two in there," Connie said.

Cliff cast an irritated glare at Ned, then growled, "He's only here for a few days."

Ned grimaced and muttered, "Till ... um ... well, till things get sorted out." Then he got up for another beer.

"I haven't seen him around," Connie said, then she joked, "Is he in hiding, too?"

"No, nothing like that, no," said Ned, sharp and quick.

"Please, guys," said Cliff, "don't tell anyone he's at our place. We don't want word to get out."

"If he's in trouble," said Connie, "he could come to me."

"It's that priest," Ned all but snarled. "He's built a hard-on of hate for the kid, and if he finds out he's staying with a couple of fags ... well ... you can just imagine what he'll start screaming. The bitch."

Connie smiled. "Lips're sealed." Everyone else agreed.

"Thanks," said Cliff, and the look he shot Ned was anything but happy.

Which was all so very interesting.

— V —

The last to arrive was Preston Niemczyk — short, swarthy, hairy, with happy, dancing eyes and a wide grin, and unable to sit still for a second. He also wore a thick wedding band and had the same vaguely frazzled look as Dion.

"Wife's gonna have a baby," he said, after we'd been introduced. "So Connie, if you have any chili left over, pity a poor broke lawyer with it? Maybe that'll make her happy."

"If there is," she laughed, handing him a beer and heading to the kitchen to do some stirring before rejoining the group. "When's she due?"

"Late June, early July. We just found out."

It took another ten minutes of congratulating Preston and asking to finally meet the wife — seems she worked in San Diego and was shy — before we got back to business.

First thing I learned was, my uncle was the quiet but driving force behind GALAIATH, with Dion his backup. And they'd been pushing Preston to run for District Attorney of Riverside County.

"That's why I'm getting so much gay business," he said. "I fight as dirty as the prosecution, and I'm cheap. Too cheap."

"So are you goin' after the DA's job?" I asked.

"Aw, I haven't decided, yet," Preston shrugged. "Election's years down the road."

"Doesn't hurt he's won so many cases," said Ian. "Even got some monetary settlements."

"What about my uncle's rape case?" I asked.

"Like I said, typical DA bullshit," said Preston. "Up the ante to try and bluff their way out of a clear case of perjury on the cops' parts. I filed complaints on Morrow and Harper, both, and gave IAD a copy of the video to back it up."

"Did you talk to the kid claiming Owen had sex with him?"

Preston tightened just a bit and said, "Yeah, and he says Philby forced him to say it. He also told Owen. We discussed it on the phone. Aw, guys, you ready for this? Gossip 'round the courthouse is, Philby has solid evidence Owen split for Mexico, back in August. Not good."

"What was this kid's name?" I asked.

"Not gonna share," said Preston. "He's already been through too much. If Owen wants to tell you, that's up to him. But when he comes back, I'm filing a complaint with the Bar Association against Philby, for this crap."

"Good luck with that," sneered Cliff.

"The cops took his computers and files, Preston," I said. "Can you get those back?"

"Depends. Check with me, Tuesday."

I turned to Dion. "Who was Owen's real estate lawyer?"

"Oh, shit, Lorinda — oh, sorry — uh, I told you I'd have

that for you and ... dag, I've got it at my office; remind me tomorrow and I'll get it to you."

"Thanks. So how's GALAIATH doin' now that Owen's gone?"

"It isn't," said Cliff.

"It's not as bad as all that," said Ian.

"He was the one always e-mailing us with updates and asking for help on things," said Billie.

"Doing phone calls and raising money," Beth chirped. "Drove PSALMS crazy with his push-back."

They kept on and on about my uncle's ideas — like holding an *In-Your-Face* street-party fundraiser in the fortress, with Ned and Dion wearing thongs or Speedos and getting dunked or doing dances or even stripping down for every hundred bucks donated while Meredith, Kent, and Connie served up food.

Meredith smiled. "Sondi showed me the secret to her funnel cakes."

Dion whispered to me, "Sondi and Meredith were together for nearly fifty years, till ... " and he indicated she died.

"I have an in at a beer distributor so we'd have got that at wholesale," Ian added.

"It would've been a great party," said Ned.

"No kidding," sighed Connie.

Tone cast me a near grimace. I had to hide a smile.

Owen also made sure every time Preston won a case against Philby, the papers and TV news were made aware. And he sent out e-mail blasts and fliers ripping the county for selective enforcement of the law. He'd mentioned this one of the times we spoke, but I hadn't connected it to an actual campaign.

"My favorite," said Ian, "was the *Straights* one."

"I still got that," laughed Preston, then he turned to me. "It points out that they don't put female cops outside of bars and tell frat boys they'll show their tits if they'll show their dicks, then bust them for public indecency."

"I think he filed a complaint with the Justice Department using that reasoning," said Cliff. "Or the ACLU. One of those."

"Aw, he tried," said Preston. "Blew him off."

"And not in a fun way, I'm sure," smiled Ned.

The more they talked, the more it sounded like my uncle was a one-man political movement for gay rights in Palm Springs. Which was crazy; even I knew the city was twenty-five percent gay and had dozens of gay organizations. There was the main center on South Palm Canyon for crying out loud. And I said so.

"People get complacent," said Ian, "and some are leaving."

"Driven off," said Billie. "The pussies."

"Don't agree," said Preston. "Couple of the guys beat up, lately, were activists pushing for the same things as Owen."

"Counter-attack over gay marriage," said Dion. "It's made the right wing louder and meaner and more focused."

"There's still plenty of people who don't go along with the hate," said Ned.

"Too bad they don't speak up," said Beth.

"We do," said Connie, sipping her beer.

"Aw, you and I are the exceptions that prove the rule, Connie," said Preston.

They did have local backing, but very little money. So how the hell was my uncle paying for all this? Which made me wonder, since none of that information on GALAIATH was in his townhouse, had the cops taken that, as well?

We were at the point where all they wanted to discuss was how supportive Owen was of everybody, and how he loved being with his friends ... like a wake. The only interesting detail after that point was when they spoke about a guy who did repair work for Owen on the townhouses he owned.

"What was his name?" Billie asked. "Tigger, right?"

"Tiago," groaned Ian.

Meredith touched my arm and whispered, "Lemm's brother."

"Wait, is he the guy who tended grounds here?" I asked, remembering Uncle Owen's reference to him. "He did repairs?"

"Lemm helped on his days off," sighed Ian. "Such beauties."

"No man who looks like that should be straight," said Ned.

"Thank God he is," said Connie as she got up to get herself

another beer.

Then everybody got busy comparing Tiago's perfect pecs, ass and arms with Lemm's and on and on, something even Connie and Beth were willing to discuss. It was beginning to feel porno, so I figured I'd got as much out of them as I could, that night.

It wasn't till everyone started leaving that I was able to get Cliff to himself and ask, "What's up with these guys, Lemm and Tiago?"

"Haven't seen Tiago in months. His girlfriend got preggers so he split. Left Lemm on his own. Now this priest is after him, saying stuff like, *You're a faggot and rape kids so shouldn't be allowed to live,* kind of crap."

"The same one who harassed my uncle?"

"Yeah, I think so. Father Paul. Father Prick. He banged on Lemm's door, last week, yelling that he sold another kid into sexual slavery. Freaked the whole complex out. Some residents attacked the kid. Accused him of being after their sons, too. The bastard tried to pull the same thing at Lemm's job, but the owner made a big show of being an open carry freak. With an assault rifle. So Father Prick scurried away and used that for his sermon or something. Wait, do Catholics have sermons?"

"Why do you think mass goes on for an hour and a half?"

Cliff grimaced. "Anyway, Lemm's staying with us till he figures out what to do. Sleeping on an air mattress in the office nook. Talking about quitting his job. Leaving the state. He has a green card so I was trying to get him a job at the TV station, but the station manager's a wuss. Soon as word got back to Father Prick and he showed up to complain, Lemm'd be gone."

"Why'd the bastard go all Topeka on him?"

"He's gay. Isn't that enough? I thought the prick was just a closet case, but no pings on the gaydar."

"What's he look like, this priest?"

"Google up a picture of that Marine fuck who had the big brown eyes and earnest expression, during Iran-Contra. Father Prick looks a lot like him, but with better teeth."

"Lemm have a car?"

"No, it's bus or beg a ride. I'm picking him up."

"Let me."

"You sure?"

"Yeah, I'd like to meet him." And see if I could get more info. I mean, a priest driving someone out of their home? That's more of a bible-thumper move than Catholic.

Cliff grinned. "Thanks, it's been a rough day, and ... well, you'll like Lemm; he's a sweet kid. Doesn't deserve this."

"That don't keep it from happenin'."

He gave me a shrug of agreement.

I told Tone what I was planning.

He tensed and asked, "Are you okay to drive?"

"Yeah," I said. "All I drank was Dr. Pepper."

"That's not what I mean. The cops have you on their radar. I ... I ... I'll come with you. Or Matt ... "

"No, it's better if this is one-on-one. I'll get more info that way. And if somethin' does happen and either of you're in the car?"

"But they've got the rental car's number, now. Take dad's Chrysler. It has Texas plates so they won't notice it."

"Tone, they will track that car back to you, and that means nine kinds of shit. I'll take Palm Canyon back, this time. It's out of the way, but there's lots of traffic on it. Especially on a Friday night. With two of us in the car ... is that okay?"

His eyes said it wasn't, but his words were, "If you're not back by eleven ... "

"I will be, or I'll call."

"Like the other night?" He touched my bruised side, then turned and stormed back to Uncle Owen's. I watched him all the way up to the door, where he cast me a quick look that was way more complicated than him just being pissed; there was hurt and fear in it. Something was going on in his crazy-assed brain, and it was about more than just the cops harassing me. Shit, it's all *I like you unless you like me, then I won't like you until you don't like me and then I'll like you. Maybe.* Like a fucking cat.

Of course, that's when Mira's question drifted back — *why do I stay with him?* How do I explain that I'm like a wolf and mate for life? Even now, when I get pissed off at him, it's more because I feel like I'm not as much a part of him as he is me, and I was starting to think maybe I never will be.

Jesus, he gets me so confused. But there's a corner of me that'll never give up on hoping he'll change. I wondered if I could ever explain that to Mira in a way that meant all I wanted it to mean ... and not have her think I'm an abused spouse?

Probably not, since I can't to myself.

— VI —

We got to Dion's about ten-fifteen, and crept in to find the twins asleep, then checked on Joel, who was also lost to slumber without a care in the world. Probably because he had the sweetest, gentlest guard dog sitting on the corner of his bed, a guy who couldn't have been more than nineteen, a tiny flashlight clutched in an elegant hand shining on a jigsaw puzzle depicting Niagara Falls. His Polo shirt and Dockers added to the flow of a male-model body. Not some skinny guy who lives on the thought of food, but lean and clean, with skin was so tan and smooth, he could've been Photoshopped.

He looked up to reveal the most perfectly proportioned face I'd ever seen in my life. Big brown eyes. Straight nose. Gentle smile. Good clean chin with a hint of stubble on it. Mother Nature could use him to show off how well she does symmetry.

He put a finger to his lips and carefully slipped off the bed to glide over to us. Dion closed the door as the guy whispered, "Joel wished to talk," his voice carrying a heavy Latin accent, "so I sit on the bed to listen. He tries to stay awake for you, but ... "

"What's the trouble?" asked Dion.

"He wishes to know if he should tell you of a problem he has at the school. More than that, I cannot say."

"He doesn't know he can tell us anything he — ?"

I put a hand on Dion's shoulder and cut in with, "What'd you tell him?"

Lemm turned his eyes on me, and they were so deep and open and passionate, my heart began to pound and my face tingled. "I tell him he must speak with his fathers."

Exactly what I should have said. I kicked myself for not thinking of it. "Dion, my bet is, you already know what he's gonna talk about."

Dion took a deep breath and said to Lemm, "Thanks, baby." Then he jolted and put his hand on my back. "Oh my God, Lemm, this is Jake. Old friend of mine. Nephew to Owen."

Lemm widened his smile and nodded to me.

"Hi," was all I was able to come up with.

"Does Cliff not come with you?" Lemm asked Dion, his voice nearly musical.

"That's why I'm here," I said, and it popped out of me a little too fast. "Give you a ride back."

"Thank you, but can we now leave? I am very tired."

"Sure," I said.

Dion slipped a couple of bills into Lemm's hand, saying, "Thanks for helping out, baby. You're a lifesaver."

Dion walked us out to my car, and I have to say ... Lemm's catlike stride was so cool and elegant, I damn near stopped breathing. I jolted myself back to now with, "Lemm, you ... uh, you're having trouble with a priest named Paul, right?"

He looked at me, his dark eyes narrowing. "Why you ask?"

Oh, smooth, Jake, grill him from the second you meet him. Great way to build trust. "It's just ... uh, my uncle was havin' a problem with someone like that." His wariness turned into a frown. "Owen Taylor."

Lemm grew even warier. "Owen told you of him?"

Dion popped in with, "Baby, you can trust Jake as much as you trust anybody. More, even."

The guy took in a deep breath and said, "The priest I have some trouble with is Father Paul, yes."

"Didn't he drive you from your apartment?" I asked.

It took Lemm a moment to respond. "No, he tells me only that I will go to hell. That I threaten children. The people who live beside me, they hear him. They make me go away."

"But why pick on you? There's lots of gay men in this town, probably in the same complex. And I understand you know this priest." Lemm gave me the hint of a nod, his eyes hurt. "So why did he turn on you? Did he tell you?"

Lemm barely shook his head.

"Could be he just found out," said Dion. "A guy at the restaurant was pals with Kent till he realized he's married to me; then it became all, *Stay away from me; I don't wanna go queer*. He's not there, anymore, thank God."

"I think he does not know before this. I do not tell of who I am ... but I do not hide. Gloria knows."

"She's the girl who had Tiago's baby," Dion whispered, as if Lemm couldn't hear him.

I nodded. "This priest bothered you at your job, right?"

Lemm shut down on me. "Who tells you these things?"

Dion jumped in with, "It just came up, Lemm. At the meeting."

He nearly spit. "Ned. There are no secrets with him."

"Sorry," I said. "I didn't mean to sound nosy."

Lemm looked at me cool and blank. "Father Paul does not know where I work. He thinks he knows, but he is wrong."

"So the guy with the gun's a story?"

"No, the story is true. I know him; he knows me; he does not like Father Paul. So he talks with Gloria to say I work for him. But I work in another store, to prepare the shelves."

"Market on Marimba at Nasun," Said Dion. "Oh my God, they have the best produce."

"I ... I'll check it out," I said.

"I am to work tomorrow; ask for me and I get you the best."

"Y'know, I think that priest got his celibate self loving Lemm and he's acting like a brat to get him to notice him."

"I can see why he would," slipped out of me faster than I could censor it.

Lemm half-smiled at me then turned to Dion. "Please allow Joel to come to you with his trouble. Then will he be more open."

"Your wish is my command." But Dion's eyes twinkled when he said it.

Lemm told Dion good-night and got in the car. I slipped behind the wheel, trying like hell to ignore Dion's smirk as he closed the door on me.

"Drive safe," he said, way too much meaning in his voice.

I shot him a look that said, *Go to hell*. His grin only widened as I pulled away.

I kept to the exact speed limit because I wanted time to build some trust with Lemm. I didn't dis-believe his story; I remembered Uncle Owen's comments on how Father Paul'd locked and loaded on him. But living in Texas you catch on pretty quick that after all the posturing is done, Catholics are just hypocrites; it's the bible-thumpers who're the bullies.

I drove in silence until Lemm asked, "You stay in Owen's home?"

I nodded. "Did you know him very well?"

"Yes." His expression hinted at pain. "He is always very kind to me. I wish he still was here."

"Lemm, this Father Paul — what else is goin' on with him?"

He looked at me. "I have told you what I know."

"Have you? You're hidin' from the guy, so there has to be somethin' more. Has he physically threatened you? Is he gonna try an' get your green card revoked?"

He tensed and glared at me. "Stop the car, please." I did, expecting him to get out and walk. We were on Palm Canyon so he could easily have caught a bus. Instead, he put a hand on my shoulder, his face tight and serious. "Look in my eyes."

I thought about refusing, because ... man, you could drown in those beauties. But I took a deep breath and did as he asked. Saw flecks of gold in them, with shadows and corners he'd never let anyone into. Wary like a creature that's been brutally hurt. Tone's eyes, only Lemm was in control of his shadows; aware of his corners. He could unlock any door...if I'd help him ...

His face relaxed. He leaned back, breaking the spell, then said, "Two weeks before today, a man pays me to be with him. Father Paul is angry for this. Perhaps you will keep driving?"

Okay ...

I put the car in gear and eased back into traffic. Lemm didn't say another word for a couple blocks, then he continued, "The place where I work before ... it had no need for me. So I am without money before I find this job. When you do not have all the payment for your rent, three-hundred dollars is very much."

"Wouldn't Dion have given you more time?"

"He tries. The bank refuses."

"Dion manages the property, not them."

"The building is owned by Owen."

"So it's his decision, not theirs."

He frowned at me, exasperated. "And he is not here. And the bank has the mortgage. And he is behind with his payment. If I do not pay when I must, Owen becomes more behind and they use that to hurt him."

"Who handed you that line of crap?"

"Crap?" He seemed taken aback. "A ... a man calls me to ask about the payment. I told him I work, again, and that I soon will have it, but he explains to me what will happen. That Owen will be hurt bad. I try to borrow the money but no one has it to lend to me, and because I am new to my store, they will not advance me money." Another silence, then, "So this man, he tells me all he wants is ... is ... to be with me. Then he will pay me. So I ... I go with him. and he brings me the beer. It is open. He thinks I am stupid. I refuse it, so he ... he becomes angry and drags me to the bed, and I ... I see rope and ... and horrible things and I ... I fight him and run away. He knows me at this new job so comes to my store. He wants his money — or to use me. But I do not trust him and I have already paid the rent. I say I will return the money to him, but he does not believe me. I think he has told Father Paul, and that is why he turns to disappointment and anger. He has helped me and Tiago and now he is betrayed. He tells people of me and they are afraid for their children."

"He didn't tell Father Paul where you worked?" Lemm just shrugged. "Are you plannin' to get away from Palm Springs?"

"Where do I go? I do not know where my brother now is, and only here are my friends." He was silent, again, before saying, "Dion tells me I can trust you, so please tell no one what I have done. Ned ... he says he is a friend, but when he hears I sell myself, to his eyes I will be someone to be used."

"I got it. And Lemm, I don't blame you. For any of it."

He looked at me. "This is an easy thing to say, but — "

I cut him off with, "My uncle tell you I was in prison?"

He blinked. "No."

"Well, while I was in there I did things that ... that ... even after I got out ... shit. When my grandmother died, I was totally broke. Uncle Owen was bringin' me some cash, but he wasn't due till the next day, and there wasn't any food in the house, so I hit over to a supermarket and stole a couple cans of Spaghetti-O's and a quart of milk. If I'd gotten caught, I'd of gone back inside, and nobody would've give a damn as to why. But when you're hungry, all that matters is bein' fed."

His expression softened. "You sound like Owen. To him, always there is more to every story."

"He backed me up." Lemm nodded, not looking at me. Sadness enveloped him. Then a thought hit me. "How long've you known my uncle?"

He shrugged. "Since six years. A little more."

Oh, shit. "Lemm, are you under eighteen?"

He tensed then said, "I am soon to have nineteen years."

"You know what happened to Owen? What Philby did to him? After the trial?"

Lemm put his hands together. His left thumb rubbed into the palm of his right hand. He seemed to want to say something but couldn't form the words or thoughts or whatever.

"You're the guy Philby used to charge him with rape."

He stopped breathing for a long moment, then his breath whispered from him. He gave a bare nod and the words tumbled from him. "Mr. Philby hears that I know Owen, so I am taken to him by two police, and he says I am used by him, since many years, and I tell him this is not true, but he tells me I lie, and the police tell me I will go to jail and they will tear up my green card and I must return to Chile, and they say it over and over and over and ... and ... " He couldn't continue.

"So you said he did."

He nodded, eyes filled with hurt.

So there it was. After getting reamed by both Dion and my uncle, Philby had used everything he could to force a scared kid into making a fake claim so he could get the upper hand over one of them. And a middle-aged man like Owen being nice to a pretty boy like

Lemm? Two and two would add up to forty-seven, in most people's minds, it fit the stereotype so neatly. Wouldn't matter if the story was so full of holes it made Swiss Cheese look solid. Wouldn't matter if the truth was known to half the city. The other half would still tar him with Pedophile. And the gay community by association.

I was building a nice hate for motherfucking Philby.

"Those officers," I said, "do you know their names?"

He shook his head. "But one is a woman, very angry. I am sure Father Paul has now told to them I offer myself for sale. This makes it more hard for Owen. Do you not blame me, still?"

"Lemm, I ... I told you, I ain't judgin' nobody."

"But I am why Owen must go away ... "

I had no answer to that.

We curled up the drive to the fortress. It was dark and ghostly. Below us, a million shimmering stars were caught in an elegant spider's web supported by shadows. It would have been magical if I wasn't so pissed off at Philby and his pit bulls, using Lemm to start their intimidation against my uncle with as much force as the Gestapo did against the Jews.

The Chrysler was in the driveway, so I stopped in front of the townhouse. Lemm didn't move to get out. I stayed put.

He finally said, "I wish Owen asked me to go with him. Since Tiago is gone ... I do not do so good. He is smart. Clever. He has eleven years more than me, and my parents are dead. I come to this country with him, since eight years. He does the painting for Owen and brings me to help. And I help with the garden. Owen is very kind to me. With my brother gone away, I come to him. I am afraid because people ... they tell me Tiago did not want be husband to Gloria or father to Cara. But Owen says maybe Tiago is caught by immigration and deported."

"Didn't he have a green card?"

"No, his father is American. A man who was with the Embassy in Santiago. Father Paul makes him to sponsor Tiago, so he is American, too. Then Tiago shows my mother and father are dead and he is my only relative, so ... "

"So that's what you meant when he said that he helped you? Father Pri ... uh, Paul got you both legal."

Lemm nodded. "Tiago likes the woman. Father Paul thinks the same of me ... until he learns I do not. Then he is angry. He knows already Owen keeps my rent low for my apartment. I work the gardens on days I do not have the job. Owen gives to me money for this. I swear he takes nothing in return. Mr. Philby thinks here is the proof. He does not understand, Owen is father and brother to me. Nothing happens between us."

"When was the last time you saw my uncle?"

"Two days from his trial. I tell him what I have done. I cried. He is angry but tells me to not worry. The next day, they take his computers and files and sketches he makes."

Oh, shit. "Sketches of you?" He nodded. "With dates on them?" He nodded. "Nude?"

He smiled. "No. My face, only. I do not pose without my clothes, not even for Ned."

"Ned?"

"He says this is *art photography*." He pulled a small card from his wallet. "Here is what he does."

I took the card, one of those business types with a good headshot of Lemm next to his name: Leonardo Díaz de Valdés, along with an e-mail address. "Ned did this?"

Lemm nodded, his eyes weary. "He thinks I should become the actor. Model."

"Move to LA? Get rich and famous?"

"It is not so easy a business. I do not know if I can act."

"You've got the look for it."

"Such things do not last forever. And my accent ... I am good only for Telenovelas or to model."

I leaned back in the seat and examined his face. In the sharp shadows and filtered light, it came across as even more perfect and clean. Fact is, everything about him was so smooth and right, I wanted to touch him to make sure he was real.

"Says here your name's Leonardo. How'd you wind up as Lemm?" I was whispering, my eyes locked on his profile.

He smiled and his eyes grew distant. "As a niño, I say my name Lemardo so much, Tiago christened me. Two Ms." Pain washed over his face as he said, "I am so sorry. Owen now is my only family and I betray him and — "

THWACK! Pellets of the car's rear window flew over both of us as some lunatic screamed, "Fuckin' faggots!"

A baseball bat cracked down on my side of the windshield. I slammed my door open against the bastard wielding it and bolted out. He stumbled back then took a swing at me. I ducked, gave him three punches in a kidney then yanked the bat away before he could even think and smacked him in the left knee with it. He dropped to the ground, screaming in agony. I think I broke his kneecap — no, I hope I did.

Someone else grabbed me from behind and my side shrieked in pain as another guy swung at me. I kicked him between the legs then dropped forward and rolled the guy holding me into the car's front tire, knocking him out. One thing prison teaches you is how to fight quick and dirty, even if you're a beta-doggie.

I was back on my feet by the time Lemm was out of the car. Cliff and Ned bolted from the townhouse as other people rushed outside and Tone and Matt appeared at the door.

"Somebody call the cops!" I yelled.

"They're on the way," said Ned. "What happened?"

That's when I looked down and saw the guys I'd just messed up were teenage jocks, in designer jeans and jackets.

The guy I'd kicked started to get up but I cracked the baseball bat on the pavement next to him and snarled, "Don't move." He stayed down, his hands holding his crotch.

The first guy whined, "You broke my leg, motherfucker."

"Shut the fuck up," I yelled, "or I'll break your fuckin' head, you fuckin' understand me!?"

The second guy moaned, "Shit, man, we thought you was faggots."

"I am a faggot, you fuck," I snarled back. "And I just beat your fuckin' ass." Then I yelled at the top of my lungs, "Did everybody hear that? This faggot just beat the shit out of three little assholes! Wanna send more my way?"

Tone grabbed me by one arm, saying, "Jake! They're under control." Then he murmured, "You'll hurt yourself, more."

He was right; the adrenalin was already beginning to fade

and my side was screaming about how unhappy it was. But then I saw the car had dings with the busted windows and I jumped back to roaring and raised the bat, snarling, "You're payin' for the damage, you little fuck! Every goddamn penny of it! I'll take it out of your hide if you don't!" Matt had to help Tone hold me back.

I finally heard police sirens approaching. The animal in me whispered a last growl and I dropped the baseball bat; there was enough of a crowd around that the little bastards couldn't get away even if they'd been able to walk.

Now came the fun part — dealing with the cops.

Again.

Not a habit I liked getting into.

— VII —

The police cruiser roared up the drive and squealed to a halt, then two cops popped out, one yelling, "Everybody back away. C'mon, let us through. What's going on here?"

The voice sounded familiar so I tried to turn and look at him. Big mistake; I nearly fell over from the sharp sudden pain. Tone made me sit against the car's trunk. I didn't fight him. It hurt to even breathe.

He nudged Matt. "Get his meds." Matt scurried off.

That's when everybody started talking at once, adding to the chaos of my mind. I was aware of the cops seeing the car's damage, seeing the bat, seeing the three little shits on the ground, and seeing me in all my pain and anger ... and the first cop still stupidly repeated, "Well, what's going on?"

I shook my head, in awe, and snarled, "They hit my car with a baseball bat and called me faggot. So I stopped 'em."

The second cop said, "You? All by yourself?"

His voice was too familiar, so I made myself stand up to look at them. The pain from my ribs ricocheted all over my body, but it was worth it ... because it was the same alpha and pup who'd tried to mess with me in Uncle Owen's home. They knew who I was, too;

I could see it in their eyes.

"Yeah," I snarled. "I know how to fight."

"You better hope these kids aren't bad hurt," said the pup. He knelt beside the unconscious one. "Call EMS. Kevin's bleeding all over the pavement."

"You know these little shits?" I asked.

"High school kids," snapped the first cop. "I don't think mom and dad're gonna like you much."

Oh, so that's the direction they wanted to go?

I snarled, "Mom and dad ain't gonna like the bill they get for damage to the car, either."

"Don't you have insurance?" asked the second cop.

"It's a rental. And I'm pressin' assault charges against the little angels. As a hate crime."

"Hate crime?"

"Somebody calls me a faggot as he's tryin' to bash the shit out of my brains? Hate crime. You got a problem with that?"

"You need to calm down, buddy."

"ME!?"

Tone stepped between us and said, "Jake, it's all right. You're all right. Okay?" Matt ran up with the pills and a bottle of water. Tone shoved one on me and said, "Here, c'mon."

"Oh, so he's on meds," said the first cop.

Tone shot at him, "OxyContin, thanks to two associates of yours." Then he did his magic massage on my shoulders.

The cops exchanged glances. Meaning they probably knew about Chet and Roy, and that these three brats had pulled this before, and they needed to do something to head things off, so I got ready for them to be even more asshole-ish.

Then Connie's voice bellowed, "What the hell is this?"

She was striding up from her townhouse, dressed in a heavy robe and moccasins, pissed as hell.

Well ... a city council person witnessing them pulling any kind of crap would not be ignored, even if they did know her. So they calmly took my statement and politely informed me as to who they were; alpha was Officer Stettlin, pup was Officer Janovich. No more names for my assailants; I'd have to get that from the police report.

Connie surveyed the damage and glared at the two conscious brats, shaking her head. "Stupid boys," she muttered. "It amazes me you'll graduate high school and go to college. Parents having money makes all the difference in the world, doesn't it?"

Neither of them had the balls to look her in the eyes.

Two more cop cars roared in and did absolutely nothing, then EMS finally showed up and took two of the brats to an ER; the third was handcuffed and taken to jail. All so nice and casual, I knew the little shits would be released to mommy and daddy within the hour. If Philby was anything like I thought he was, they'd plead to disturbing the peace ... if it went that far.

What the hell was going on? I'm in town just a little over forty-eight hours and already I'm in my third confrontation? One even gets me put in the hospital. And then these dipshits badges know the kids who tried to bash my head in? Were Philby and Ginty using the uniforms as their pit-bulls, and the pit-bulls using these brats as their snarl-pups? What the hell had I done to bring on this kind of push-back except meet with my uncle's friends? This made no sense.

Tone broke my train of thought by saying, "Jake, let's go back in. C'mon."

My side hurt but it was manageable, so I said, "No, I'm takin' pictures of this shit. And it needs cleanin' up."

"I can do that ... "

"Tone, I'm in control, okay?"

But I sure as hell wasn't up for talking to anybody, so I used inspecting and photographing the car as an excuse not to.

Fortunately, Lemm appeared and took the focus off me. He'd slipped into Cliff's townhouse to hide, and I didn't blame him. Hell, I'd have been surprised if he hadn't vanished. But now they were gone and Connie was back in her home, so it was safe.

I introduced him to my guys, and Tone was handed some cool indifference, but he was too focused on sweeping up glass to pay attention. However, Lemm and Matt got to talking about computers and his job and life. Not what I would have expected.

I had a dozen shots on my phone so pretended to be viewing those photos as I surreptitiously watched everybody else.

Cliff said good night and went into his place; Ned slowly

followed, his eyes not leaving Lemm till he closed the door. A couple of Connie's circuit boys — with the tall, clean, classy looks of serious party animals — returned to the unit on the other side of Meredith. I saw she had watched the whole thing from an upstairs window. And a young married couple headed into the unit next to Connie's.

The last two guys to go back inside were a short, balding man in a workout suit, well into middle-age, who never left the yard of the townhouse across from Connie's; and a tall, geeky kind of guy in baggy shorts and a button-down shirt along with his mousy wife, who slipped into the one next door to him. The other units stayed dark. So ... that was Lionel and George.

Why did they remind me of pinch-lipped old ladies?

— VIII —

A few minutes later, Ian drove up and got out, horrified. He was still wearing those paisley pants and sweater, had a brown bag in the passenger seat and even more whiskey was on his breath. It's good he'd waited till the cops were gone; he'd have been so busted for drunk-driving. I had a good mind to bawl him out for the stupidity of it, but his alarm cut my anger in half.

"Christ, Jake, what's this with your car?" His brogue was so thick, that he was understandable amazed me.

"Some brats took on more than they could handle."

He eyed the damage. "Three of them?"

"They been here before?"

He nodded to the torn up vacant unit. "It wasn't the wind broke those windows."

"You call the cops on 'em?"

"Of course. And you think they sent anyone?"

Tone joined us with a bag of shattered glass in one hand and the broom and dustpan in the other and said, "Ian, would you look at Jake's side, please?"

I all but howled. "Tone, I was checked at an ER!"

"Is that a fact?" asked Ian. "Which one?"

"On Marimba, in Indio."

"An urgent care facility?" Ian's look was so condescending I nearly laughed. "Inside, lad."

"Ian, I'm fine — "

"If you think I'm going to pass up the opportunity to put my hands on your hot little body, you're mad. Get inside."

"Please, Jake," said Tone. "Please." His voice was tight.

I went in and pulled off my jacket. It hurt like hell. Tone dumped the bag of glass in the kitchen and helped me, then undid my shirt.

"This is stupid, Tone," I muttered.

"Shut up." His voice was tighter, if that was possible.

I was close to firing back at him when Ian's ice-cold hand on my back jolted me. "Jesus, Ian, some warnin', next time?"

"Dear God, and a tattoo," he muttered, caressing it. Then he touched my bruises. "Is this what you're talkin' about?"

Tone looked down my side and nodded. I tried to look, but I heard Ian say, "Jake, are into pain, at all?"

Before I could say, *No* – BAM! Lightning slammed into my side and I screamed, "IAN, WHAT THE FUCK!?"

"Just smoothing over those lovely ribs of yours. One was a bit out of place."

"I noticed it," Tone muttered, his voice shaky. "Must've happened in the fight."

"Fight?" asked Ian. "You took on those three bastards?"

"They ... picked on the wrong fag." I made it sound jokey, but Ian noticed my hands were shaking. I hurt like hell.

"Sorry I missed it," said Ian. "You'd best sit down, lad. Not all the way." He guided me onto the arm of the couch. "I'll get something to wrap your lovely body with."

"What good'll that do ... for ribs?" I muttered.

"Hold you in place and remind you not to try something like this, again. So what was the outcome?"

"Two to the hospital, one to jail," said Tone.

"And lovely, here, wasn't arrested, as well? Amazing."

I looked at him. "You think the cops put the little fucks up to it?"

He put his ice-cold hands on my ribs, but this time it felt good. Almost soothing.

"Jake, I'm from Belfast. The Constables there worked with hoodlums, like these, all the time. It helped them maintain control of Catholics. The Brits used the same strategy. They even had a policy of shoot to kill, till they began killing innocent Catholic boys and it became too obvious to all. That's why I came here; to get away from that. For all the good it did. Back in a flash." Then he patted my back and drifted out.

Tone sat behind me. Draped his arms over me, careful and easy. He was shaking. "I'm not leaving till this is done."

I rolled my eyes. "Tone ... "

"I'm not leaving you," he snarled in his don't-fuck-with-me voice.

"We got a hearin' before the judge on Tuesday," I said. "What if it takes longer 'n that to sort this out?"

"It won't. Between you, me and Matt, we'll kick some ass by Monday. But I'll call Castillo and have him ask for a continuance. If Texas can do it, so can we."

He ran the tips of his fingernails over my two-day whiskers, trailing along my chin. Oh, dear God, how nice that felt. And hearing the steel in his voice. I leaned into him and whispered, "Love it when you're granite."

"Hmm?"

"Nothing. God, I'd love to soak in a tub."

"Pain pills kicking in?"

"Yeeeeesssssss ... finallyyyyy ... "

"C'mon, I'll help you upstairs, old man junky."

I chuckled at him. "Bitch."

He helped me undress, then I took a nice, long, hot shower. I was feeling human by the time I was done. When I came out of the bathroom, I noticed he was ending a phone call and was back to being Mr. In-Control. He patted me down with one of my uncle's big, thick, obscenely comfortable towels then wrapped me in it, like I was his child. It got me going, so I pulled him close and kissed him and did some ass-grabbing.

He pulled back and said, "Ian's waiting." Dammit.

He led me downstairs and there Ian stood with a body-wrap. He shot a quick photo of me with his phone then let out a long sigh of approval at how semi-dressed ... and semi-hard ... I was.

I smiled as I said, "If that goes on the web, I know whose ass to kick."

"Nothing like that till you're healed, luv, and this is for my pleasure only. Now stand still."

Tone watched him wrap my torso so he could do it, himself, and let out a good-natured growl when Ian's thumbs flicked my nips, making me giggle.

"My tip," the old fart said.

"Okay," Tone said. "But if you touch his ass ... "

"Understood." Then he looked at me. "Do I at least get a thank you kiss?" I gave him a nice, long, tender one. No tongue; the whiskey on his lips was close to going sour. His hands stayed on my waist till we parted, and he sighed, "Now I've something to dream about, tonight."

"Thanks, Ian," I said.

Tone led him to the front door, saying, "At the meeting, tonight, Preston mentioned there had been some attacks on gay men. What have the police done about that?"

"I understand they arrested some Latino lads. Said it was merely robberies happening. No hate crimes here; we're Palm Springs, not bloody Kansas." Said with a wink.

"Thanks." Then Tone gave him a peck on the cheek.

Ian got flustered. "Two lovely lads kissing me in one day? Haven't had that happen since I was Dublin, last. Which was far too long ago." Then he patted Tone on the butt and quickly said, "You didn't say I couldn't touch yours," before scurrying out.

Tone closed the door and looked at me. "I should've slapped him, but he was so cute about it ... "

I smiled and pulled Tone into an embrace and rested my chin on his shoulder. My side still ached but I didn't care.

"Why can't we stay like this forever?" I murmured.

He just sighed.

"So what do you think?" I asked. "Cops're usin' those little shits to beat up gay men? Set 'em on me?"

"You ... you sound like a detective from some Forties Noir movie. They beat me up to warn me off."

"Instead of beat me off to warm me up?"

His fingers curled in my hair, then let go. His voice was soft. "You're not being careful, Jake. When you were in prison, would anyone have been able to sneak up on you, like this?"

I looked at him, wary. "I'm not in prison."

"I know. It's just ... " His eyes hid behind bleak shadows.

My voice grew soft. "You do think I was targeted."

He tried to joke. "Jake, please, don't give my paranoia any ideas."

A laugh popped out of me; not a good thing to happen, thanks to my side. I grunted. "Now you know how I felt when you disappeared and nearly got yourself killed."

He held my head in his hands. Drew his thumbs across my cheeks. His eyes sharp and dangerous. "That is not funny."

"Okay. So ... so what do you want me to do? Stop? Give up on my uncle? Leave? I don't run from fights, Tone."

"I ... I just don't want to see you hurt."

"Okay ... so what do you think's goin' on?"

"I don't know. None of this makes sense, and what I thought it might be isn't and ... and I've got to check some things, but I can't do anything about it till ... till Matt gets back."

"Where is he?"

"Still talking to Lemm. On Cliff's front steps."

"Uh-oh ... "

Tone nodded. "I've already been there and back."

I put my nose to his. "What's your take on Lemm?"

He took a while to answer. "He's the first guy I've met who's darker than me."

"Bullshit, nobody's as dark as you."

"You only say that because you love me."

"Nice of you to notice," I fake-whined.

"That's one of the few things I can trust in." He took my hand. "C'mon, we'll give Matt that little talk in the morning."

I let him lead me upstairs and into the bedroom then pulled him close and kissed him.

"Y'know, I ain't that tired, yet," I whispered. "And Ian got me goin'. And them pills ... coolness. You up for somethin' quick and dirty?" Then I toyed with his nips through his shirt and nibbled at his neck.

He pulled back and said, "Not tonight. I ... I'm still kind of freaked out about what happened. Maybe tomorrow night, okay?"

Oh. Okay ...

He guided me onto the bed, still wrapped in the towel, and pulled a sheet and blanket over me. Then he lay beside me, fully clothed. And held me. And caressed my arms and neck and chin.

And all of a sudden I locked in on his comment.

My love was one of the few things he could trust in.

He only trusted that I loved him? He didn't know I did? And he didn't say he loved me. He hadn't once, not since he got here. Now he'd backed away. Put me to bed, like a kid. Why?

Was it because I didn't follow this one little scenario he liked? After he got arrested and was nearly killed in jail, he'd locked in on the whole process of watching me shower. Then he'd join me to kiss and fool around, then towel me off and bounce onto the bed to get down to business. Which wasn't easy, thanks to that stupid monitor.

I didn't mind it like that, but then one day I'd slipped up behind him in his folks' kitchen and put my arms around him and played with his nips through his t-shirt, and he'd started gasping and shaking. It took half an hour to calm him down.

The one good thing about Texas being assholy was, they forced him to get a mental evaluation. To my surprise, he liked the therapist who did it so much, he started seeing the guy every Monday. After his freak-out, the guy had taken me aside and explained why Tone lost it. When we'd lived in Copenhagen, those eight months before he got caught up in the mess in Texas, the last time we made love was like that scenario. Repeating it anchored him in a pleasant time, and deviations jolted him out of his comfort zone and into the reality of what happened. He said to take it easy and it would be okay, with time.

As we were headed home, Tone had looked at me and said, "I asked him to tell you. I should've told you myself — "

I'd cut him off by putting my right hand on his neck to massage it, and he'd leaned forward like a cat and let me stroke his hair. Then we'd gorged on Tex-Mex and Margaritas.

Sure enough, once we had our own apartment, he'd relaxed and sex had started to be fun, again. Until a few months ago. When he'd started pushing me away while pulling me close. Now I could see it meant he didn't trust me enough to tell me, himself.

He didn't know I loved him; he only trusted that I did. And he meant it, because he didn't say he loved me.

He didn't say it.

He didn't.

Shit.

I was a fucking idiot.

— IX —

It was still dark when I gave up on sleep and slipped out of bed. Tone shifted but didn't wake. Lying there, peaceful, in the shadows, he looked like Joel. Innocent. Pure. Beautiful. Heartbreaking. Just looking at him made me ache.

God, I was so confused. I thought OxyContin was supposed to make you feel euphoric. Maybe a run would give me a chance to sort my scrambled brain out, and screw my aching fucking ribs.

Except ... first I had to replace the car and fill out an accident report. So I wound up sitting on the doorstep of the rental agency's Palm Springs office until the morning clerk showed up. I didn't even fill the tank. All he had available was an SUV and, Jesus, how he whined and whimpered and tried to talk me into taking the damaged car back to LAX. But finally, he handed over the SUV's keys and I grabbed my crap and tossed in the back then headed off.

I asked the clerk about a park to run in, and he sent me to the saddest excuse I'd ever seen — two baseball diamonds side by side next to a long, slim field barely covered by greenery, with nothing but the occasional tree for daytime shade. Probably the best I'd find, so I parked in the lot next to the community house, did some light stretching, and took off down this path between the diamonds. It led me around to a paved walk so I ran on the grass to where it jumped through an opening in the cyclone fencing and ran along the golf links. Then it ran out and I wound up on a street that curled around to an area of what used to be million dollar bungalows but now were too old-fashioned and too close to the airport's flight path to be that valuable.

It was chilly, and all I had on was my sweats and hoodie, a t-shirt and pair of sneakers, but one good thing about Palm Springs is it's flat and monotonous. I could keep a nice pace, as the body-wrap kept my side's pains to a minimum; too bad I didn't have something like that for the turmoil in my brain.

Mira's voice kept ringing in my ears. "Why do you stay with Tone?" Suddenly I could see what she was aiming at. It wasn't me being weak or putting my career on hold or her distrust of the man I love; it was her seeing this was still too much of a one-way street, going from me to him.

I could've stayed in Copenhagen and let him come to me, if he wanted. That would've been the smart way to handle things. But like some dumb mutt whose loyalty for its master never stops, no matter how much it gets kicked, I'd gone trotting after a guy who didn't know I loved him; who just trusted that I did.

I kept telling myself, he'd given me my life back. Given me a future. But the more I looked at the reality of what he'd done, back then, the more I could see that ... hell, none of that was for me. It was for Collie, the guy I came after. A man named for a dog. He was the reason Tone ripped into the deputy sheriff and ADA and crooked-assed judge; they'd caused the death of his beloved, and he wanted revenge. I was just the replacement mongrel. Collateral justice.

Had I mistaken me being in the wrong place at the right time meant he wanted me? Needed me? Loved me? Because if all he does is trust that I love him, that's nothing but another wall. A backhanded form of control filled with expectation. Tolerance. Fondness, maybe. But not an ache in your soul when your partner hurts. Not anger when he or she is misused. Not joy when you see them for the first time that day. Not peace when they hold you. Not the certainty that they care for you as much as you care for them. It's barely a shadow of those ideas.

I felt all those things for Tone. But apparently he did not with me. He did not believe that he's my mate forever.

Shit!

SHIT!

I ran and ran down wide residential roads lined with long houses landscaped to the max while dawn slowly expanded. A few cars passed. Some trucks. Some people out on their own little runs. Early risers who were probably in bed by ten, even on a Saturday. I paid them no attention. In fact, my brain didn't even begin to stop swirling till I'd caught my second wind.

That is when I remembered that dealership Matt mentioned. He'd texted me its address, so I fired up my new phone to see where it was. Turned out to be about a mile from where I was, back the other side of the airport. There were also two messages from Tone and one from Matt. I shut it down, found a twenty-four hour drug store just ahead, stopped in for a water and doubled down on some Advil, then headed over to it.

Finally, I saw a flat-walled monstrosity with boarded up windows, peeling paint and crumbling pillars. It sat in the middle of an asphalt parking area, graffiti splashed all over. Wide, empty, weed-and-sand-filled lots surrounded it. A chain-link fence blocked off the section leading to what were once open-air service bays, and it was caught with debris. More trash cowered against its walls. Its gate was locked with a push-button contraption. Talk about deserted.

I took a while to catch my breath; my ribs were demanding attention, even with the Advil, so I gripped high on the fence to stretch them. Not the best idea, pain-wise, but it cut the chaos in my head ... and let me notice a neat door hidden from easy view, leading into what had once been the showroom and offices. No big deal, except it had a fairly new push-button lock on it.

I looked at the lock on the fence; it was newish, too. I punched in the number Uncle Owen sent me, and it popped open. I slipped through the gate and over to the door. That lock was electronic, like it was linked to an alarm, and there was a deadbolt lock above it. The key I'd been sent was in my wallet. I tried it ... and it fit. I wasn't surprised. I punched in the numbers, again, and the light shifted from red to green. I entered.

First came a short hallway, dark but clean and neat. A couple of doors along one wall were labeled men, women, and employees only. The first two were exactly what they claimed to be — restrooms with rolls of toilet paper and soap and towels in them. The last was a room of lockers and toilets and a couple of shower stalls with high-end liquid soaps, shampoos, and towels of all types and sizes. All with just a hint of dust on them. Half the tiles in the false ceiling were gone, and C-clamps were attached to some of the cross-beams.

I continued on into what was probably once a waiting room. It was brutally neat, with a desk, chairs, makeshift kitchenette of microwave, coffee maker, apartment fridge, toaster oven, mugs and condiments and such. A bottle of vodka was in the fridge's tiny freezer compartment; nothing else. The desk's drawers had note pads and pencils and packets of chewing gum and mints. And condoms. The carpet was old, but clean.

A wider hallway kept going past some offices to what was once the showroom. Now it was just an open, empty, cavernous space, with one column in the center of it all. Bleak darkness was cut by shafts of early-morning light that snuck between the plywood boards covering the windows. The floor was covered with dirt and debris.

To my immediate left were three topless cubicles. The one nearest to me was about fifteen by twenty-five foot and held a desk, couple of chairs, an old computer tower and monitor, a few plants, and crap like pencils, paper, paperclips and such. Mini-blinds gave the idea of a window along the back wall. The barest minimum needed to give an official feel to the place. Overhead, a movie light was positioned on bars that ran at an angle across the cubicle, its cable held by another clamp. The carpet had been cleaned; the desk was scuffed but neat.

The cubicle next to it was the same size and set up as a jail cell with cheesy bunk-beds, a fake toilet, and bars made from PVC pipes that had been sort-of spray-painted dark gray; the floor was painted. Movie lights hung from above it, too.

In the corner was a larger cubicle with a metal-frame bed

holding a queen-size mattress covered with plastic and flanked by two nightstands, books on top of them. Across from it was a recliner, also draped in plastic; next to that was a massive wardrobe cabinet. Then ... directly across from the wardrobe ... I saw the serigraph of the painting Owen did of me and Dion. A soft layer of dust over it. I picked up one of the books to look inside; there was a plate in it with my uncle's name done in his neat hand. I put it back. The few plants were not dry.

Another door was locked and labeled private ... and it took that key. Of course. This was the largest room and held more lighting equipment, ready for use. A desk in the corner. Two cameras. A server humming and blinking. A laptop connected to them, along with a second monitor. A rolling chair was parked against the desk ... and more framed sketches were stacked behind it ... all of them my uncle's; I knew his style.

Hanging from racks in another corner were leather and latex costumes of the kinky variety, for males and females, with dog masks. Cat masks. Gags. Rope. Chains. Collars. Hand cuffs. Leather cuffs. Storage file boxes were stacked in another corner. I looked in one to find adult toys. Lined along a wall were sawhorses and restraint chairs and stainless steel gurneys with leather hand and ankle straps on them, all neat and clean.

I turned back to the laptop and hit the space bar. All the screens came to life. A video-editing program was open with a project uploaded and partially edited. I clicked on the project, and one monitor filled with the video image of Cliff and Ned playing a leather-bondage sex game, by the showroom floor's column. Both wore black chaps, boots, and harnesses along with white jocks, with Ned tied to the column and a ball-gag in his mouth. The floor was well-swept. Cliff half-heartedly pitched as Ned catched in a series of shots that hinted at this being domination or rape, but Ned's impressive dick had worked out of the jock and was having way too much fun, and he was all but giggling from Cliff's tentative, fussy hands.

The laptop's screen had files with other angles and moments that had been shot of the same project, and in every one of them the place looked as dark and alone and deserted as possible. In the last one I looked at, they were at the end of their game, because after maybe ten seconds, Ned fired his load. From three different angles to make it seem like ten times more. He must've said "Oh, yeah," a hundred times.

I sighed and hit pause; no surprise there. A couple of other files were also on it, all recently edited and with very heterosexual couples playing the same games. Then I noticed a project was still in the queue to be edited. Titled O-T. I clicked on the file. Up jumped a man lying on that bed in the cubicle, seen from an above angle, face down. Tan, lightly hairy legs spread wide apart. Ass barely covered by a pair of tightie-whities. He was looking to his right, smiling, a little drunk, and saying in a heavy accent, "Wha' you doin'?"

He looked too much like Lemm to be anyone but Tiago. A back strong and well-shaped. A perfect butt under that white cotton. Taut thighs flowing from his hips. He'd be sex incarnate to anybody — gay, straight or kangaroo.

The camera zoomed in on his glorious rear as the long lean fingers of a right hand trailed up his left leg to grab at the white cloth and tear the material open making Tiago yelp and slur, "No — don' — " and the image froze ...

And my insides exploded like a 9.5 earthquake as memories of what happened to me in jail tore into my brain and my side was forgotten, my whole life, and this whirlpool of chaos swept over me and dragged me down, down, down, and Jesus Christ, I could still feel every second of that night. The fear. The pain. Locked into each man's way of having fun. Like the asshole who slammed my head against the wall, over and over and over as he ... as he rode me. And one who slapped me a half-dozen times then forced himself into my mouth, saying if I wasn't careful with the teeth, he'd kick 'em all out of my head. And another one with his ass and ... and ... Jesus, the taste ... that God-awful taste ... it took years to get past it ... and the smell and the gut-wrenching certainty I'd be torn to bits if I didn't do what they wanted and more ... more ...

I couldn't stop the pictures in my head ... the retching jolts in my gut that made me glad I hadn't eaten ... they kept on and on until somehow ... somehow I managed to stagger out of the office and slam back to that center column and drop down to a crouch. Dust billowed around me, adding to the chaos as I fought to regain control.

That night ... Jesus Christ, that night ...

That night is why, when I arrived in prison, I decided if all I had to offer was my hand or mouth or ass, it would be with someone I could live with. I didn't care if he was black, white, pink or purple; I did not want that night to happen, again.

My "angel" wound up being a hairless skinhead with tatts on his tatts. Slaughter. Bastardized from Sylvester. He proved the devil walks the earth, the son-of-a-bitch. Made me shave the hair on my body off, so I'd look more like a girl as he used me. Gave me to guys he owed favors to or needed a favor from. Had me pass off cigarettes laced with PCP to those he was pissed at, then let the guards know. And worse. And I did it. Gladly. Because there were too many other devils in that hell-hole to deal with, and his protection gave me time to build up and smarten up so I could protect myself.

I drifted into reliving how a guy dragged me into the laundry and tried to make me blow him. Slaughter was in solitary for one of his fights, so the fool though he could pull any kind of shit he felt like. But I fought hard. And I got hurt, but so did he before he gave up and left me to bleed on the floor.

When Slaughter found out, the asshole wound up as the asshole for a pack of thugs. He'd screamed about it, as if the guards would care, then noised-off that he was going to have his lawyer sue. And wound up a suicide ... according to the official report.

Unofficial report — never threaten guards or thugs.

But that's when Slaughter got the hint that I could be more of a threat than anybody. I knew his every weakness, and I let slip that if anything happened to me, the whole prison would, too. Which actually got me a bit of respect from him.

That tiny sliver of memory ... of me finally able to take care of myself ... is what helped me claw my way back to here and now. Leave the shadows behind, again. I'd beaten the devil, once; demons were nothing, in comparison.

So I stopped shaking, stood up, dusted off my sweats, locked up and left. I was cold — no, fucking freezing, but that meant less than nothing, at that moment. I'd been cold before.

And ... now I knew how my uncle financed GALAIATH.

I didn't care. Till I was attacked, I'd liked porn. And this building ... it made sense, coming here to shoot; those ratty walls were almost as picturesque as the desert. Plus, being in Palm Springs it's near the muscle boys and the randy Marines at Twenty-Nine Palms, who'd do anything for a buck, a beer and a blow job. It was isolated enough so they could play hard with no one to hear them scream or holler with delight. Hell, even with all the amateur crap being posted on X-tube and such, kink was still lucrative, so long as you did it in ways that kept 'em coming back. But it is not a smart move if you're in politics.

I doubted Preston knew about this place. He was sharp enough to understand that even with a dozen layers between it and him, Philby would've sniffed it out. The bastard probably *was* aware of it and just waiting for the right moment to reveal it. Like the primaries. Have ads screaming, *Preston's backers are accused pedophiles who made sex videos, and one jumped bail to escape justice,* until people freaked out and sent the son-of-a-bitch into office.

Man, politics makes ice hockey look like a knitting club.

— X —

I walked back to the SUV. It was closing in on nine, so I headed over to Dion's. He answered the door in a pair of shorts and a wife-beater that had grease stains on it, both dogs at his side. He looked beautifully flustered. I looked like shit, but he didn't let on.

"Jake? Oh, my God, you're up early."

"Sorry," I said, "you in the middle of somethin'?"

"We're just finishing breakfast. You want a bite?"

The idea of food slammed me into a nod. His eyes lingered on me, then he said, "C'mon in. It's French Toast. Kent's still asleep so keep it low. Coffee or juice?"

"I'd kill for some coffee," I said, following him inside. The dogs stayed by me, alternating between sniffing my butt and begging for some petting. I absently tickled each one's ears. "I just ... I dropped by to pick up Lenora's info."

"Lorinda. That's at the office — no, no, wait ... I may have her card on the fridge. Lemme see."

He led me into the kitchen, where Joel, Sarah and Samantha were seated at a small round table, finishing lightly battered bread topped with fruit and drizzled with maple syrup. Half-full glasses of orange juice by each of them. I smiled at them. Joel kept eating, but the twins eyed me with distaste.

"Ew, you're dirty," said Samantha. I think.

"I was runnin'" I said. "Workin' out."

"Before breakfast?" asked Sarah. I think.

"Yeah," I said. "That looks great. Mind if I join you?"

"Wash your haaaaands," said Samantha.

"Right."

Dion absently pointed to the sink, so I rolled up my sleeves and sloshed soap and water on my arms and face.

"Don't forget behind your eeeears!" Followed by giggles.

I didn't. The hot water felt fantastic. I even ran it over my hair. Then Dion tossed me a dishrag to dry off with and I got handed a steaming cup.

He pointed to a rolling table. "Milk and sugar."

I fixed my coffee as the twins set up a space between them for me to sit, and I sat where I was told to.

"Papa's taking us to the zoo," said Samantha ... I presume.

"They have one in Palm Springs?" I asked.

The girls giggled as Joel condescended to say, "L-A."

"Griffith Park," Dion chimed in as he looked on the scores of notes and drawings and cards on the door of the fridge.

"I don't want to keep you," I said.

"You won't," he smiled. "Oh, my God, I do have one."

He handed me a neat card for Lorinda Waller-Burke, with a nice bright photo of a pretty professional woman on it. She was both a lawyer and real estate agent, and your best chance at a real deal on a house or condo.

"You think she'd be workin' today?" I asked.

"It's Saturday; she'll be out in the field, but that's her cell phone. Call her. Buy her a coffee then just try to get her to shut up."

"Thanks."

Dion looked the table over as he slopped bread into the last of some whipped egg. "Do I see some empty plates that need to go in the dishwasher? And three little travelers who need to get dressed? Do I?"

"Papa, you're not wearing that!" said Samantha. Probably.

"I ... guess not. But I bet I get changed before you do."

The kids scrambled to put their dishes away then hurried down the hall to their rooms.

"Quietly," Dion softly called after them. He turned to me. "We're giving Kent a down day. Rough night."

"Oh?" I sipped the coffee, and even with milk and sugar, it damn near took the enamel off my teeth, it was so strong.

He nodded and flipped the French Toast. "Business is slow at the restaurant so they're cutting back to five nights a week. Got rid of two servers and a busboy. If Kent wants to stay on, he's got to do lunches, as well as dinner. Split shift."

"That messes with your set-up."

"A little. Where's your other half?"

"Tone? He's ... he's not a morning person."

"You two have a fight?"

I frowned at Dion. "Why'd you ask that?"

"Sorry. I'm being nosy little ol' Blanche, again."

"No, it's not that. It's just ... I felt like goin' out for a run and ... and ... Dion ... how well did you know my uncle?"

"Oh my God, Jake! I trust him with my kids. I don't do that with people I don't know."

"So you knew what's going on in that dealership he owns?"

He looked at me. "What dealership?"

"Just off the main drag. Big. Middle of nowhere."

"Okay ... " He flipped the toast onto a plate and set it before me then pulled a bowl of fruit from the fridge. "It was a Ford dealership that went under in the crash. What makes you think it belongs to Owen?"

Dion was genuinely confused. I held up the key. "This fits the lock to it. Could he own property you don't know about?"

"How? His capital's all tied up. We found that out when he

tried to buy the unit beside him before it went up for sale. Oh my God, Lorinda worked her butt off on it. He got turned down by three banks and two mortgage companies, and he has good credit."

WTF? "Dion, can you get into the county's tax records?"

"No, but I think Lorinda can. So what's in that building?"

"Nothin'," I said. "Just bullshit." Then I grinned and grimaced and added, "Sorry."

"Oh, stop."

His grin unleashed my appetite. I ate that French toast in four bites and even drank more of his coffee ... just not a lot.

Before he had a chance to question me further, the twins came running in. "We beat you! We beat you!"

"Quietly, kiddles. Daddy needs some sleep."

"Why isn't daddy coming with us to the zoo?" And I refuse to speculate whether it's Sarah or Samantha who asked.

"He's been working real hard, so we're going to let him rest," Dion chirped. Then he glanced at me. "But y'know what — I think we'll have a cookout, tomorrow. In the back yard. For your new Uncle Jake. Have some friends in. Play in the pool. Does that sound like fun?"

"It's cold," the girls said, in unison.

"I'll turn the crystals on. Warm the pool, too."

"Cool," said Joel as he entered the kitchen.

"So what do you say, Jake?" Dion asked. "Will Anthony be up by eleven?"

"Antony," I said, my mouth full of the last of the French toast. "Yeah, I ... I think he will."

"Then it's a date." And even though he was grinning, I could tell he knew something was up between me and Tone, and he was going to find out what it was. And he'd take my side; I already knew it. That was the beauty of him.

"God, I wish you'd asked me to stay," I said before I could stop myself.

His grin became a tender smile as he said, "We're hitting the road, soon as I change. Want to join us?"

Yes, I'd love to, but I got the harshest, meanest *Don't even think it, buddy* glare from all three of the kids. This was going to be their day with papa; no stinky strangers or best behavior crap.

"No," I said. "But thanks. This was great."

Dion changed into an I'm their Papa t-shirt and cargo pants, and I accompanied them out of the house to his car. Then they headed for LA and I headed back to the fortress. I needed to check something out, now, now, now, because if I was right it meant suicide or jumping bail were not the only explanations for the vanishing of Owen Taylor.

He might have been murdered.

My uncle. Might have been deliberately killed. By someone here in Palm Springs. That one thought slammed total clarity into my brain ... and churned my gut with anger. Because if that was the case ... if someone had actually done that ... to someone as decent as him ... oh my God, would I make that motherfucker pay.

No matter what.

PART THREE

I left Lorinda a message en route back to the fortress, which took nearly an hour, thanks to weekender traffic.

Tone met me at the door, in snarl mode. "Do you have any idea how — ?"

I cut him off with, "What? I went for a run and stopped by Dion's. He's havin' a cookout there, tomorrow. Eleven am. You're both invited and be on time; Dion hates it when you're late." Then I pushed by him and Matt and ran upstairs to dig Uncle Owen's note from my suitcase. I ran back downstairs, and dove under the desk to look at my uncle's printer — an old ink-jet.

I slammed the printed note down and muttered, "Shit. I'm stupid. Fuckin' stupid."

"What's going on?" Matt asked.

"This note's off a laser printer, not an ink jet."

"So?"

"So he didn't send it to me."

"Then who did?" Tone asked, his mood iced down.

I flipped the note over and wrote some names on the back. "I don't know, yet. Tone, I'm gonna grab a shower. Would you find out what organizations these people belong to? Anything that's been in the news since the beginnin' of last year. I don't care how dinky it seems." I shoved the paper in his hand and turned to Matt. "Can you find out the name on the title of that dealership? And when it was last sold?"

"Sure." His voice was wary.

"Thanks." Then I headed upstairs.

Tone followed. "Jake, what's going on?"

"I've been lookin' at this all wrong."

I entered the bedroom and stripped off my hoodie and tee-shirt. He stood in the doorway, watching me. Almost like he was afraid. "What ... what do you mean?"

"I gotta talk to some people, Monday. I'll know then. Did Matt do what you needed?"

"Oh, uh, no ... not yet," he said. "I was talking to Castillo about ... things ... "

"Oh?"

"He's not sure he can get another continuance."

He was watching me like a hawk. Waiting for me to react. All I did was pull off Ian's body wrap and sigh, "Okay, then you better head back. Be there for it."

He frowned. "Don't you want to know what it's all about?"

I shrugged. "If you want to tell me ... "

"Jake, you always insisted on information — "

I glared at him and kicked off my shoes. "Which you keep offerin' me in itsy-bitsy spoonfuls. And then you don't tell me everything, anyway, so why bother? Well ... I'm not gonna drag it out of you, anymore." I yanked off my socks, sweats and briefs. "I need to keep my head clear to figure out what's happened with my uncle, so if you want me to know somethin', tell me; if you don't, shut the fuck up about it!"

I stormed into the bathroom and slammed the door. Then I got the shower going and stood under the steaming hot water, kicking myself. I'd meant to keep it cool and ignore his crap, but two seconds of his hinting and I turn into the Tasmanian Devil. Real cool, Jake; doing your own research, now.

I was back to aching so soaped up and rinsed, nice and slow, and took my time drying off. The body wrap needed washing so I tore a towel into strips and tied those around me. Not perfect but better than nothing, and Ian was right — that little bit helped lower the pain, but I still popped an Oxy. Then I dressed and went downstairs.

Matt heard me but didn't look up from his laptop as he said, "Ready for this? That dealership's owned by an investment group. OT and Associates. Why didn't I check his initials?"

"There's a thousand OTs in So-Cal," I said.

"Know what else? It's got an office located at — "

"The dealership," I said. He nodded. "Anything else?"

"It changed hands just under a year ago. Before that, it was in foreclosure. A new mortgage was set up with Palm Valley West Bank. Package included a few plots of land ... two of them next to it, like they were planning to develop something."

"I want all those addresses, and who else they affiliated with. Partnered with. Any other company or organization. Tax ID number. Who the associates are. Anything, okay? And do they have any other mortgages? I want to know where their office really is."

"I told you; it's at that dealership."

I shook my head. "I was there. It's not."

Matt blinked then spun into his Zen thing; he'd let me know when he had everything he could get.

I noticed the front door was open so went to it. Tone was sitting on the front step, drinking wine from a juice tumbler.

"It's not even noon," I said.

He took a sip and held up the list I'd made. I took it. He'd gotten what I needed.

"Thanks," I said.

"Fuck you." He was pissed as shit.

I sat beside him, and it wasn't easy. The Oxy hadn't kicked in yet and my side was back to screaming from that run. I let myself settle in then asked, soft and quiet, "Tone, what did my mother say to you?"

"I fucking told you."

"No, you gave me some bullshit that's not enough to mess with you, like this. C'mon. Dump it."

"Dammit, Jake, you act like I don't trust you when you don't even begin to trust me and — !"

He was about to go into his usual Tone meltdown, so I smacked the wine out of his hand. It hurt, but I didn't care.

"You got no right to be mad!" I snarled. "All the shit that's goin' down between us is on you, not me. So you fuckin' tell me what she fuckin' said to you." Then I added, "And I don't mean the last time you talked; I mean the first."

That jolted him. "How ... how'd you know?"

"Just ... tell me. Shit." Because the truth is, I'd only guessed at her calling him, before. But it made sense.

He got this lost look about him. I'd seen it every time he thought he was being Little Sir Brilliant and suddenly realized he was anything but.

"You ... you're right," whispered from him, "you shouldn't trust me. You can't." He wrapped his arms around himself and started shaking. He finally sighed, "She said you'd leave me, some day. That I'd go too far in something and you'd have to back away ... to save yourself ... because I was driving you to it."

"You told me that, yourself, years ago."

"And you told me about that wolf your father had. As a pet. When he was still in Iran. That always loved to see him. No matter what he did to it. You never told me that ... that one day he teased it too much and it attacked him. And he killed it. She said someday that'll happen with us. I didn't believe her, so I ... I called Ari. He verified the story."

"Tone ... "

"No, look at how I treat you. I'm as much of an asshole as your father. Maybe more. I'm not a decent person, Jake. Seems the only way I know I did something wrong is when I hurt you, because that hurts me. But how much longer can you deal with that and keep any kind of respect for yourself? And one day have too much and go after me? And me lose control and ... and ... "

I sighed. "When did she call?"

"Couple months ago."

"Why didn't you tell me?"

"This ... this was between her and me."

"What my mother says about me is between her and you!?"

"That's what ... what we decided."

I took in a deep breath. "What else? C'mon."

"She just ... she kept talking about how much you've given up for me. Life and money and career. And how little I give back."

"Tone ... you gave me my life back."

He wouldn't look at me. "Now I'm taking it away. Dragging you under. I ... I think once you're done, here, maybe you should go back. Back home. Denmark."

"We've been through this before ... "

"I can handle things on my own!" he snapped, then softened, "Well, me and Castillo. I ... I think maybe ... maybe it's better I stand on my own, now. You've been holding me up for so long, I need to know if I ... if I can face this myself."

"That's what Uncle Owen always said."

"He's right. It's ... it's better that way, Jake."

It took me a moment to ask, "Don't you love me, no more?"

He took in a sharp breath and held it; that told me without question he still did. But what he said was, "How do you want me to answer that? I don't know, I don't know anything, nothing, you should go home." The words tumbled out of him. "Let me sink or swim on my own. Please. That's the only way I can keep from hurting you. From pushing you too far. It's better for both of us. You should go home. I'll handle this. Me and Castillo. And you can ... you can get back to your life."

"Now you sound like Mira."

And now I had an idea about the last few months. Tone had been trying to drive me off, like you throw rocks at a dog that's followed you home, hoping it'll go away. And my mother was pushing it. She'd snuck her poison into him, straight from her playbook of manipulation and hate, hell-bent on pushing him away from me. I was so fucking sorry I'd helped the bitch.

What could I do now but murmur, "Maybe you're right."

He swallowed then almost chuckled, like he'd geared himself up to pull more tricks to convince me and was shocked he didn't have to. "One of the few times in my life," he said. He pulled away and stood up. "I'm sorry. You deserve so much better than me." Then he picked up the tumbler and went inside.

I just sat there.

I could see where he was coming from. Didn't matter that he was my mate for life. It was always going to be up to him how it worked. And he's got some kind of scar in his brain that won't let him believe in anybody, not even himself. That's why I cut him so much slack. But he was right. In my heart ... my soul ... I need my mate to believe in me. Not just trust in me. Need it more than anything. And eventually that need would explode. And we'd lose what little control we had. And one of us would be killed or crippled. So how could this work out? How could we keep going like this? I just did not know.

It had grown bright and sunny but there was still a biting chill in the breeze. I had jeans and a light shirt on, deck shoes, no socks, so it cut into me. I should've gone inside and got a jacket, at least ... but I've been cold before.

I looked up at the mountains, soft in the morning haze. They lay under light caps of snow and were ringed with whispery clouds. I bet it was green and wonderful, up there. I wondered how far you could see on a day like today? Maybe once this was done, I'd go up and find out. Touch the snow, again, like I was back in Copenhagen.

Our one winter there had been so easy and alive. The wind off the Baltic could slice you to ribbons but it was honest and real. And watching the storms on the sea from our home ... our own little fortress ... it was like living art. Nobody messed with us. Tone believed in me, then, and in himself. Did all right, on his own terms. I only had to go into the city twice a week, to see Uncle Ari; I wouldn't have gone that often if I could've avoided it. I wanted to stay in those cozy, upstairs rooms, forever. I wondered if we could ever get that back, or if mom's poison was too deep-rooted.

My thoughts were broken by a car backing out of a garage. Lionel Tinley was behind the wheel of a three year-old Malibu, a sharp-featured woman in the seat beside him. He cast me a snotty glare as he backed onto the main drive. I just sighed.

Too bad Uncle Owen hadn't kept the whole damn fortress for rentals and surrounded himself with the protection of his own little family instead of a few like-minded people ... except he had tried to do that; he just couldn't maintain it.

Guess you can't keep anything for long, in this world.

No matter how hard you try.

— II —

I stood up and headed next door. I wanted to find out what was up with Cliff and Ned and that dealership, and now would be the best time, because I was in no mood for anybody's bullshit. But no one answered the door, so I found myself at Meredith's.

Outside, these units were landscaped like my uncle's, the desert flowers and plants meant for low water consumption. Like all the rest, the stucco walls and double-pane windows kept things quiet; I could barely hear Geordi yapping.

A moment later, Meredith swung the door open, wearing a lovely brocaded blouse and plain pants, and telling the mutt, "Hush, it's Jake, you little fool." Then she looked at me and smiled. "Maybe you should give him some bologna?"

"Don't wanna make him too fat to yap," I said, forcing a smile and crouching down to let him sniff my fingers. Then he yapped even more and spun in a happy circle. "But I bet he needs the fuel."

"Small dogs are the worst when it comes to nervousness. Come in. Come on." She shuffled on into the kitchen. I followed. "How about some tea? I have a fresh pot."

"That'd be great," I said, rubbing my arms and looking at the photos of Sondi on the piano. "How long were you together?"

She noticed my gaze and said, "Forty-eight years." Then she motioned for me to sit at the counter and watched me out of the corner of her eye as she brought down a couple of china cups and saucers. "You left early, this morning."

"Went out for a run. How'd you know?"

"I'm a very light sleeper, and Geordi is very nosy. That's why I'm in the front bedroom — so he can see what's going on at all times, and I can report it to Connie, if need be."

"Like when I first arrived?"

"No, I was in the back yard. I didn't notice what was happening until the police came. Should you be running?"

"Why not?"

"Ian told me what happened. I saw him when he was leaving for his shift, this morning."

I sighed. "It wasn't that bad."

Geordi was whimpering and skittering around the base of my stool, so Meredith handed me a slice of bologna and I absently pulled off bits of it to drop down to him as I continued with, "You saw the argument, that last night Owen was around."

She nodded. "With Officer Harper, but I told you that. I was about to go down, I was so concerned for Owen. But then Connie drove up and calmed them, both."

"So you watched it from your bedroom?"

"Yes, it was quite late."

"Did you hear what they were sayin'?"

"No, but I could tell Owen was very angry."

"Not Harper?"

"He seemed very impassive."

"Meredith ... did my uncle have many people over at his place?"

"How do you mean?"

"People you didn't know? Or recognize? Guys."

Geordi started yapping, so I fed him more bologna.

Meredith eyed me, for a moment. She knew what I was getting at. "Not that I know of, outside of the group you met. Cliff and Ian were probably his closest friends. Dion would bring the children over. Sometimes Owen babysat, and I'd drop Geordi off to play. Lemm was there, a few times. And Tiago, when he still worked for us. But thinking about it, I don't believe I ever saw Tiago go inside. Owen would bring out refreshments, and they'd sit on his steps to chat. Geordi liked to join them."

"You never did?"

"Once or twice. If Connie was around, she would." She leaned in to whisper, "I think she liked Tiago."

No, really? "Was there anything else that happened just before the argument with Harper?"

"Nothing I can think of. Until he started GALAIATH, Owen led a very sedate life. Usually with a Bloody Mary."

"I remember those," I said, grimacing. Tall, spicy, with a lemon peel wrapped around a stalk of celery to stir it. I hated the taste. "Uncle Owen had these rental units and an apartment complex for income, but did he do anything else for a livin'?"

"Don't you know?"

"I'm findin' out I didn't know that much about him."

She looked at me. "What should he have told you?"

I shrugged and sipped some tea. Irish breakfast. It tasted so good. Warm. Another reminder of winter nights in Copenhagen, sitting on the couch by Tone, with hot mugs as we watched an old movie. Or I sketched and he read. Like we had a home.

"Owen sketched," I said. "Nice work, too."

"The painting he did of you and Dion was lovely."

"He sent me a picture of it," I murmured. "He ever ... ever give you an idea of why he didn't want me to come out here?"

She gave me a long look. "I was unaware he didn't."

"He gave me all kinds of support, but he never offered. I get ... I get the feelin' he's glad I never asked, so he wouldn't have to say no. And I ... I don't understand."

"Owen's the only one to answer that."

"Would've been so nice ... so much better ... "

"Had you lived with Owen, you would never have met Antony and Matthew."

" ... Yeah ... "

She put a tender hand to my face. Caressed my cheek, like Nana used to do. And she said, "You were sitting on those steps a long time, Jake. So was Antony. And in that cold, cold wind."

"Sortin' things out," I smiled. "Tryin' to. Nana used to tell me, *Only a fool trusts everybody, just like a fool trusts no one.* I thought I worked out what that meant when I was in prison, but I'm still tryin' to figure who should and shouldn't be counted on. Puttin' my faith in the wrong people. Settin' myself up to get hurt."

"Because Owen didn't invite into his home?"

"Naw ... no ... it's more'n that."

Meredith sighed. "I would never expect self-pity from you."

I flashed back to Mira calling me a martyr, and I snapped, "That's not what this is! I'm tired. And I ache and I'm cranky."

She nodded. I studied her face. Every wrinkle outlined a life that had been through so much more than me, since she could've been put in jail just for loving someone.

"Sorry," I whispered, "I bet it was rough for you, when you were my age."

She poured more tea, a smile on her face. "Oh, it wasn't so

bad. The one issue I had was when a firm I worked for began to supply engine parts to Grumann. This was during the Republican Red Scare, so one day, I was called into the CEO's office and told since the parts we made were for Naval aircraft, I was a security risk. Being a lezzzz-bian." She smirked as she said the word. "I was informed I would have to be let go. I was sent back to my desk, under armed guard, to pack everything that was mine. Then I was escorted to my car and off the property. It was all very humiliating, and meant to be. Those silly men acting as if I had committed a betrayal of America by not wanting to be in their beds."

"Jerks has always been jerks."

She smiled and handed me a tiny sandwich with the crust cut off the bread. "Cucumber and cream cheese."

"Thanks." I politely bit into it. "Did you have trouble findin' another job?"

"In the defense industry? I was more likely to be committed by the state for the mental illness of homosexuality than find another position, now that word was out. But I had savings, and Sondi managed the sportswear department of a Macy's, and they didn't care. Also, I was in what is now called supply-chain, and I was very good at it. So good, in fact, they called me back in to demand that I explain my system of ordering to my big, buff married-with-children male replacement. I refused. Then they said they would have me arrested for treason."

"Bullshit," popped out faster than I could stop it.

"No, it's not," she said. "I was visited by a pair of rather menacing gorillas from the FBI, who informed me I was sabotaging a vital part of the nation's security and I could be put in jail."

"I don't get it," I said. "I did a version of supply for the city, when I worked there. It's not that hard."

"All it takes is the ability to think one step ahead of everyone you're dealing with. What helped my cause was, the man who replaced me was a lazy, condescending fool who could not lower himself to deal with those he considered beneath him." She leaned in close to whisper, "His father owned the company."

I nodded, with a smirk.

Meredith's eyes twinkled as she continued. "He waited for the heads of various departments to tell him what they needed, which put him about ten days behind the curve on ordering. The truth is, department supervisors are rarely of any use; I always went to the workers, themselves, to find out what they were running low on. They're more accurate. So I always kept them well stocked. They grew used to my way so didn't tell anyone they needed materials until they were very low. Everything ran out, and the production line had to be shut down. Which angered the union. And Grumann.

"Finally, my replacement's father came to me, begging me to show Junior how to make things work smoothly, again. It seems he had also alienated some of our suppliers because he blamed them for not getting the materials to him quickly enough. If there is anything you do not do, it's anger your supplier, not unless you have a backup.

"Well, I refused. I also mentioned I was being considered for a position at one of his competitors. The next day, I had security clearance, back pay, and my job, again. And, because I had a good relationship with our suppliers, I cleared everything up within four days, and made certain the production lines never shut down, again. I remained there thirty-three years."

"Why? They treated you like shit."

She gave me a look that would've stopped a charging bull. "And I rubbed Junior's nose in it, every day I was there."

I laughed. "Don't mess with the Meredith."

"Sondi was sure I'd be carted off when the FBI came, so stayed in the kitchen on the phone to an attorney. She always was more nervous than I. She worried that I would die before she, and she wouldn't know what to do. I think that is why she never made a will; she thought it might jinx us. Obviously, she passed away first. And I now live here instead of my home."

"You got thrown out of your house?"

"Sondi's brother was given control of her estate. By the state. He took everything that was in her name, which included our bungalow. I got my car. An insurance settlement. Stocks and bonds ... the ones I could prove I purchased with my own check. I took the furniture without giving him a chance to say anything."

"That sort of happened to Tone. Before he and I met. When a guy he was involved with got killed."

"It's pathetic, how common it was. That's another reason Owen started GALAIATH. He wanted gay men and women to not only stand on their own, without the permission of society, but look out for each other. He knew there would always be those who opposed us." Her eyes grew gentle. "He also saw how some of the national organizations would rather schmooze with politicians than tend to the needs of the gay community."

"And now GALAIATH's gonna fall apart."

She set more tea in front of me, with milk and sugar on the side. She'd noticed how I make it. "You think he's gone." I nodded. She sighed. "So do I."

This sense of futility began to overwhelm me. Uncle Owen had been strong. He'd fought back ... but even though he'd had lots of people around who cared about him and admired him and would stand shoulder to shoulder with him, that wasn't enough to keep him safe.

Jesus Christ, how could I even hope to know what to do to the bastards once I'd worked the whole thing out? How could I even face it? I'd already had a taste of how easy it is to crush somebody, but at least I'd also seen the sons-of-bitches who did it to me go down in flames. Thanks to Tone.

My Tone.

My big bad fucking Tone, who just loved to go bat-shit crazy and fuck with my brain ... like a fucking cat.

And who wanted me to go away.

"What'll I do without him?" I murmured.

"Live," Meredith said. "Keep making him proud. He was proud of you, Jake. Very. Considering some of the things he said, when he spoke of you, he was pleased you stood on your own, and relied on others only when you wanted to. You never cried for help but faced the world. As he did. As we all must do, I suppose."

I realized she thought I was talking about Uncle Owen, so I nodded and made myself ask, just to be sure, "Was ... was my uncle despondent after the fight with Harper?"

"I have no idea. He left immediately after the young man drove away. I spoke with Connie, but not even she knew what they'd argued about. All she noticed was they were about to come to blows. That was the last time I saw him. His car was still gone when I took Geordi out for his morning walk."

"What time was that?"

"Usually about six."

I fed Geordi another piece of bologna. "Did you see my uncle as they were cartin' off his paperwork?"

"No, I was out most of that day. They were finished by the time I returned home. I found him standing in the doorway, holding the warrant, shaking his head. I asked him what was wrong and he said, *Stupid bastards; if they want to know about me, they took the wrong computer*." Her eyes grew soft. "That was the last time I spoke with him."

I jolted. "Wrong computer?"

"Hmm? Oh ... yes, he said his laptop was in his car and they never asked for it."

"Oh, jeez ... " I knew where his laptop was, now.

I thanked her for the tea and sandwiches and hurried to get my keys and wallet. Matt was still at his computer.

"No other street address for OT and Associates," he growled. "Just a P-O Box. I can't find if they've done business with anybody or have a bank account — "

"No other mortgages?"

"Nothing."

I pulled on a jacket and handed him Gregory Mikkelsen's card. "Matt, if I'm not back by five, call Preston. Then call this guy. Here's the number."

"Jake ... what're you doing?"

"I'm gonna try an' stop bein' stupid."

I drove straight to the dealership, let myself in, went in to the editing room and woke up the laptop. Then I ticked on the little Apple icon, and sure enough, at the bottom of the droplet was my uncle's name. It belonged to him ... but he hadn't put here. He was being connected to porn production to damage him. Hurt his reputation. His credibility in the eyes of most people. The implications kicked me all over the room.

I started to shut down the editing program and disconnect the laptop when something in the frozen image of Cliff's and Ned's video hit me — the floor around them was swept. But dust had billowed up around me when I crouched down by that column, earlier today. I checked the date on the video; it was only a couple of weeks old. I ticked onto a couple of other videos and saw they ranged over the last few months, and the floor was clean in them, too. So was the carpet in the waiting room and cubicles.

I looked out at the showroom; the floor was consistently filthy, from one end to the other. I slipped out of the room and examined the ceiling and walls. Past the cubicles. Walking slow. Careful. Keeping watch for snakes, scorpions and spiders. The windows still held glass, and the boards were tight against them. No place for much dirt to get in.

I crossed to that column in the center and stopped, where Cliff had played his game with Ned. Its paint was scratched, some of it stripped away. The dust was shifted aside, where I had crouched down, revealing a dark stain in the concrete. I squatted and brushed away more dirt to find the stain billowed away from the column ... and every nerve in my body tingled.

So here it was. That spot was hidden by dirt because it used to be covered in blood. And it didn't get there by accident. If the whips and chains Ned and Cliff so loved had cut too deep, so what? That would be no reason to try and hide it. But someone had deliberately brought in dirt and trash to cover up evidence of ... of where my uncle had died? Was that it?

A sick feeling in my stomach told me, *Yes, and this is why you were sent that key.*

Somebody knew what had happened here, and wanted me to find out. Somebody who couldn't go to the cops, themself. So they'd sent me those cryptic notes, hoping I'd work it out. Somebody still here in Palm Springs. Watching. Waiting.

But who knew my Danish address in this town? The only ones who might were the cops who took all my uncle's files. My info would be in there ... but then, so would my Texas contact numbers. Those could be verified in a heartbeat.

What the hell was going on here? Was I supposed to find out one of my uncle's friends had killed him? Or was I being used to deflect blame for his death onto someone innocent? Whichever it was, I couldn't let him be associated with anything in this warehouse.

The possibilities were too destructive.

— III —

I didn't find any security cameras hidden in the dealership so I cleared those cubicles of my uncle's books, albums and sketches. No way did I want anything of his anywhere near this. I kept his laptop powered up so I could look at it later, then wiped down anything I'd touched in the place. I was glad I had the SUV; everything barely fit into it.

Of course, Lorinda called as I drove away. She was in Palm Desert and wanted to connect at a California Pizza Kitchen, near her. I was torn between finding out more about my uncle and taking everything back to the fortress, but it might be my only chance so I popped off with, "Then let's do lunch." She laughed, and we set to meet in an hour. I zipped over to a Lowes by the airport, bought a tarp and covered everything in the back.

The CPK was in a strip of faux shops facing away from the main drag — and you want to talk about totally California? It had a bar area walled off by glass panels, high tables with chairs, and servers that ask you every five seconds how it's going. And damn near everything on the menu has chicken in it, like they're really California Chicken Kitchen. I got a table and ordered a tea.

The second she burst in off the street, I knew her real name was Little Miss Sunshine. Her clothes were bright and business casual, her hair bleached and hair-sprayed just right, and even in heels she looked ready to drag you through a hundred homes that day ... if you could keep up. And Dion way-understated her ability to chatter.

Oh, and she just a-*dored* my uncle.

"He's like the uncle you always wish you'd had. Like cool and calm and sweet. My mom met him and she's like, *You know what a Dutch Uncle is? That's Owen.* But I didn't know what a Dutch uncle is, so I'm all, *Mom, what do you mean?* And she's like, *He's practical, direct, outspoken, stubborn, blunt, well-organized, and thinks he's always right.* And I'm like, wow, that's him. Who knew? And when I told him she'd said that, he laughed for like half an hour, he thought it was so cute."

She paused long enough to take a bite of her salad, so I hopped in with, "Did you handle all of his real estate deals?"

"Oh, no, I only took over two years ago from the guy who was doing it, because he and Owen didn't get along. But there hasn't been much for me to do except make sure he like keeps up on his taxes, though I did handle some legal stuff. Like when he wanted to buy that condo. We tried like crazy to work it out but the bank wouldn't say yes, and once word gets around everybody's like *No, I don't think so.* And you can't get them to change their minds, no matter what you do, so don't even try."

Another bite.

"When was this?" I asked.

"A year ago, maybe more, maybe less. Time gets away from you so fast. Like I thought today was Friday and I'd have a day to catch up but it's not, so I'm scrambling to make all my appointments and I'm like wondering why I set so many up, but some of them look good, so I can't say no. Can I?"

Another breath. Another bite of salad. Whooh.

"I know my uncle owned four of the townhouses and an apartment complex. Was there any other property?"

"I don't know. Like I think there was some property he bought, like some kind of partnership under Baskin and Baskin, with some other people and ... oh, they're not like the ice cream place, where you get all those flavors and cones. Like Baskin Robbins. No, these guys're like really serious lawyers, so they'd handle anything he'd partnered with people on, so you ought to talk to them. But you have to wait till Monday. They're big enough to get weekends off. I'm like scrambling to find time to do my nails, and they really do need a touchup."

"Can you check the county tax records?"

"Just to see if there's like tax liens against a property, and if the city's got like plans for that area or restrictions."

"Could you check under Owen's name?"

"Sure, but he's like current on everything, and he'd be the one to tell you about that. But check with me Monday — no, wait, uh — make it Tuesday ... except I've got to be in San Bernardino. Got a good prospect for a commercial building. Try Wednesday. Or better — call Baskin and Baskin."

"When my uncle got in trouble, they're the ones you referred him to, right?"

"Oh, yeah, Scott, oh, yeah. He said he'd deal with it and I guess he did because I like didn't hear anything more about it, after that, but then that's just like Owen to get things done and taken care of without telling you. And cheap about it, too. But he is cheap. Like back when we were planning to buy that townhouse, he had some illegals come in and paint it before the bank said okay because they were available, and when they said no, he was like really upset. The bank said no. Not the illegals."

"Illegals?"

"Couple of Mexican guys. Brothers, I think. They looked a lot alike, but one was like way too young for me, but the other one — makes you want to break the law."

Another bite. A moment of silence, broken by me before it was broken by her. "Break the law, how?"

She leaned close to whisper, "Oh, you can't sleep with an illegal guy. People might think you think it's okay he's here."

"But ... what if he's a citizen?"

"But he was like Mexican."

"There's lots of people of Mexican descent in California; it's like Texas; it used to be part of Mexico."

"Then why don't the cities have Mexican names?"

Okay, that so startled me, I went blank for a second. I covered it by asking, "What about this Scott guy? What do you know about him?"

"Baskin. The old man's grandson. He does rock climbing and he is like so much. Ooh. With him, nothing would be illegal. Not one thing. Nothing." She actually fanned herself. "But he and Owen didn't get along, so Owen went his own way. Just like a Dutch Uncle. I need to call him and find out what he's been up to. Owen, not Scott. Oh, wait, didn't he like run off, right, a couple months ago? Owen? Some legal thing, I think. And it's time to talk about property taxes. Like, so quick. Ugh. He better hurry back. Riverside doesn't like give you any leeway."

Two seconds later, she was on her own way to her next appointment, leaving behind a third of her salad and half her tea. I was left to catch my breath ... and pay the bill.

Since the apartment complex owned by my uncle was in La Quinta, I made that my next stop. It was flat-roofed two-story buildings on three sides of a swimming pool, all connected by a covered walkway, looking like a motel that had been made over into living spaces. What had probably once been the front desk/reception area was now a larger apartment with picture windows and vertical blinds that were crooked. Some older cars were parked along a stucco wall that blocked in the courtyard. Graffiti had been painted over a dozen times and re-graffiti'd, yet again. Felt on the cheap side, which is probably why the place was completely rented.

I stopped and peered through the security gate. It seemed like nobody was around, and Uncle Owen's birthday numbers and name didn't do anything with the lock. I noticed a couple of teenage girls watching a bunch of kids playing soccer in a vacant lot nearby. Most of them were Hispanic boys and girls in shorts, t-shirts and sneakers, despite the cold, and a couple of them were really good at the game. The two older girls were bundled in thick sweaters and jeans, and both gave me a wary eye as I smiled and wandered over.

"Hey," I said in my best Texas. "Maybe you can help me. Is anybody to home, as a manager?"

This one pretty girl, with a wide face framed by long black hair, looked at me and said, "Why you want 'em?"

"I'm lookin' for a guy I know. Thought he lived here."

"Who?"

"His name's Leonardo Díaz de Valdés." And I said it in my worst Texas.

Her pretty face turned into an ugly grimace and her friend spat on the ground. She had a longer chin and was heavier, with open rings in her earlobes and piercings in her nose and lips, and she snarled, "Maricón."

Meaning, queer. You grow up in Texas, you learn all the bad words in Spanish before you even know they're another language. I gritted my teeth to keep from snapping at her.

"We don't talk about him," said the Long-haired girl.

"What you mean?" I asked, putting on my best confused face.

"Padre says he sells himself," she continued, all wide-eyed and earnest. "It's sad. He is so guapo."

"I don't understand," I said, still playing the innocent. Sometimes you've got to dig through shit to find the diamond.

Piercings glared at me, nodding. "That puta pendejo is joined with the devil. He wants boys to sell their bodies."

The Long-haired Girl nodded. "Luis. Felicia's son. He was too close with Lemm."

"Lemm? Is that his nick-name?"

"Yeah. Luis — his parents can't afford nice things, but he borrows Lemm's clothes and he is happy to look good."

"Happy to look like that hijo de puta."

"Yeah. Now he is gone since two months."

"That should have told us. Lemm used nice things to make Luis like him. I think he sold him to some old fat culo."

"I thought he was nice."

"You listen to Gloria, too much," snarled Piercings.

"Gloria?" I asked.

"Lemm's brother is Tiago," said Long-haired Girl, "and she was close with him. Gloria was. She has a little girl by him. But he ran away. Gloria and Cara are still here."

"It's that maricón that should have run away," snapped Piercings, then she turned to me. "Tiago wasn't like that."

Long-haired Girl vaguely agreed.

"When did he leave?" I asked.

The Long-haired Girl cast her friend a worried glance.

"Why you askin'?" Piercings snarled. She'd be happy to smack me down, physically ... hell, smack anybody down. "You want that joto?"

Another rough word. Whooh. "He borrowed money from me, at work. I ... I ... man, I need it back."

"Too bad," she said, proudly. "When I learn what he is, I threw rocks at him. We all did. We ran him off, last week."

"You didn't know he was gay till last week?"

Long-haired Girl nodded. "Father Paul warned us."

I swallowed my anger. "He sounds like a good man. I'd like to speak with him. What church does he belong to?"

"San Sebastian." And she gave me directions. "But he'll be busy, today."

Piercings nodded. "It's the lunch meeting, until two."

"No, it's really a seminar," said Long-hair.

"Seminar?"

"To make a better life."

"Are you Catholic?" asked Piercings.

"Yes," I said.

"Join us, tomorrow." Long-haired Girl nodded. "Father Paul welcomes everyone. He's an angel sent by God. You'll see."

Looked like I was an okay guy, again.

They talked more about San Sebastian and how Father Paul was always making sure the kids had juice and cookies during Sunday School. Always helping the poor get food and health care and legal help. Always saying the right things about God and being hurt when people would not walk in his ways. They were crushing on him, big-time; I teased them about it.

"You can't do that," said Piercings, actually blushing. "He's a priest. Married to the church."

"But he is tall, with broad shoulders and a nice smile," said Long-haired Girl.

"His eyes are kind. Tender."

"The padre at St. Agnes is fat and puts his hands on you in

places you didn't like."

"Father Paul respects us."

The guy knows how to manage his groupies.

I thanked them then got back in the SUV and checked the addresses of the organizations Tone'd found for me. To zero surprise, San Sebastian was on it. It was on the way back to the fortress, so I swung by to look the place over.

— IV —

San Sebastian turned out to be an old, flat-roofed strip-center done in faux-Pueblo. A covered walkway ran its length, and a mom and pop food shop was at the far corner. The windows of the five storefronts between the chapel and the mom and pop were painted over and had the church's name lettered all the way across, nice and big and graphics-oriented. Conference rooms and church offices, sure, but also the office of PSALMS — AKA: *Palm Springs Accepts the Lord, My Savior.* Sub-heading — *To protect the pure and punish the sinner.* Made me laugh.

They were having a major seminar, all right, because the massive parking lot was packed, and people were starting to leave. I parked near the mom and pop, bought a Dr. Pepper and wandered down the covered walkway to watch.

The crowd was what you'd expect — mainly white, middle-aged, middle-class, dressed nice enough, only a hint of desperation to them, with just enough Latino and black couples to keep it from coming across as another meeting of the white sheet brigade. I saw Lionel Tinley come out, with his wife, followed by the guy I figured was George. No wife. Then I saw Ms. Ginty leave the building, wearing a casual outfit and in shoes that looked like ballet slippers. She headed straight for a huge SUV, not noticing me.

Colorful fliers were stacked near the side door and held in place by a stone, so I mingled in with the group to pick one up. It was for the luncheon with the theme — *You CAN capture God's blessing and build your bank book,* with the great and glorious Lamar Davis Lawton, CEO of C&B Trust, one of the three speakers. Tickets were a hundred bucks; one-seventy-five for a married couple; five hundred if you wanted to attend a prayer vigil with them, beforehand. It all but spelled Jesus with dollar signs. Made me chuckle.

That's when long, lean, clean Officer Roy came out of the building, wearing a suit instead of his uniform, with a small gold cross on his lapel. It took him two seconds to see me and stop, cold.

"What you doing here, Blaine?" he asked in a near growl.

I smiled. "I could ask you the same question, Roy. You off duty?"

"That's none of your business."

"Then what I'm doin' here is none of yours." I glanced at the people leaving. "Looks like church is out."

"It was a luncheon, not a service."

"For this?" I held up the flier.

"You make any trouble for Mr. Lawton, you won't get out of jail so easy, this time."

"What the fuck, Roy, you his bodyguard?"

"Get out of here, Blaine!"

"No!"

He pulled out a cell phone and headed over to a Cadillac, not taking his eyes off me. Looked like the cops would be here, in a moment. I pulled out my own phone and prepped it; I'd downloaded the ACLU's recording app for California so soon as they showed, it was getting fired up.

I shifted my attention back to the crowd just as a stocky, silver-haired man in a tailored suit exited, his face gleaming with self-assurance. The great and glorious Mr. Lawton, without a doubt, who would happily wave the flag with one hand as he picked your pocket with the other. He was followed by two young versions of himself ... and Grace Nieri, all in sharp suits. And she was almost smiling. Almost. Male and female fans of all ages swirled around them, and the lead guy worked them like a politician out to gain as many votes as possible.

A priest finally appeared — tall, broad-shouldered, salt-and-pepper hair, not bad-looking, if you like strong, Irish faces with eyes that were deliberately kind and lips that held a vague smile, out of habit. Father Paul and his dog collar. And like Cliff said, he did actually did resemble a former Marine in his Iran-Contra days, and he handled his adorers as neatly as Lawton, smiling here, nodding there, his eyes vaguely connecting with any and all. I wanted to hear their chit-chat, but the babble was too intense, so I moved closer.

Then a new black Camaro zoomed into the lot, big bad Chet behind the wheel. No suit, just casual clothes ... and a nice big bandage on his head. Guess that's why he wasn't part of Little Lord Lawton's entourage, today. Visible damage takes attention away from the great one. I made a mental note to ask Preston if they'd been suspended during the investigation, or if this was Palm Springs Police playing nice with a rich SOB.

The Caddy drove up and stopped beside Lawton's group. Roy hopped out, all but standing at attention, and one of Lawton's sleek clones held up her watch. The Great Man noticed, tapped the other acolyte's shoulder and they excused themselves, got in the Caddy with Grace and drove off. The crowd all but waved bye-bye in unison. Chet didn't move.

That's when I decided to have some fun and yelled, "Way to go, Father Paul! Rubbin' up against the rich and famous while you attack those who can't fight back. Very Christian."

Everybody looked around as he turned to glare at me. "Do I know you?" he asked in a voice that was oh-so-well-modulated.

"I'm Jacob Blaine, and I know what you did to Leonardo Díaz de Valdés."

His smile widened and he said, "I minister to many people, Mr. Blaine. Sometimes, despite having the best intentions, one is unable to change the dangerous path another has chosen."

"So you made it worse for him? Made him homeless?"

"He was an evil influence who was around children. That should never be allowed."

A middle-aged Latino man approached me. "I have my home there, me and my wife and kids. My neighbor's boy ran away because of that joto."

"How do you know that?" I asked.

"Luis was not like that, until he came," said an old man.

"If we had known what he was, we'd never let him live by us," added a stocky woman in black lace.

"Then why do you live in that complex?" I snapped back. "Your landlord's gay. You give him your money without a peep."

"You people should stay in LA!" snapped an old white lady.

"Friends, please," Father Paul said. "Mr. Blaine is built of confusion. Perhaps he doesn't believe the bible actually does say, in Leviticus — "

"Twenty-thirteen. *If a man also lie with mankind, as he lieth with a woman, both of them have committed an abomination: they shall surely be put to death; their blood shall be upon them.* I went to Catholic school. So you're sayin' I should be killed? Is that it?"

There were some people in the crowd whose looks said, *Yes.* He merely answered, "I don't call for anyone to be executed."

"You threatened Lemm with death."

"I merely invited him to join our clinic, to change from his evil path, and attempted to explain that if he does not do so, he will die and never see heaven."

"Do you call for people to give up bacon with their eggs? Are you tryin' to outlaw divorce? Make adultery punishable by death, too? Pretty picky as to what the bible tells you to do."

"Mr. Blaine, please do not think that just because you read the bible you know what it means."

"Maybe I do, maybe I don't. Maybe I don't care. But tell me somethin'."

"Do you really wish to continue this in public?"

"How'd you find out Lemm was gay?"

"It's perfectly obvious."

"No, it's not. None of these people knew till you told 'em. You didn't even know he was, 'cause you helped him and his brother get legal."

"His brother was not homosexual."

"Exactly, so you didn't think Lemm was, either. When did you learn? He lived in that apartment for years, but you didn't drive him out till last week. Why? Wouldn't he put out for you?"

BAM! His fake smile vanished. "I'll thank you to leave."

There were some in the crowd who wouldn't thank me to go anywhere ... except a lynching; the things they were muttering were not warm and fuzzy. And Chet was watching with a smirk. If they attacked, big bad cop wouldn't do anything to stop it. Hell, he might even hand them the rope. It was time to make a tactical retreat.

I strolled back to the SUV and drove away, pretending not to pay attention to them, but several men and women watched me the whole way. And it took everything I had in me to keep from laughing.

Man ... did I push some serious buttons, there.

— V —

I parked in the condo's garage, then Matt and Tone helped me move everything out of the SUV and back in place. Tone was cool enough not to ask me where I got it all ... that or Matt'd filled him in on the dealership. I didn't care. I didn't want them to know a thing about what I'd learned or what I thought happened. Sometimes ignorance is the only defense.

Once everything was in order, I asked Matt, "Could you find out if PSALMS runs an ex-gay clinic hear here?"

"Aren't those illegal in California?"

"Check Arizona."

"Do I want to know why you're asking this?"

I just smiled. He nodded and dropped over to his computer.

That's when I noticed Tone was fixated on the serigraph of me and Dion. I didn't want to, but I wandered over to him. "Did you ... uh ... did you ask Matt to get you what you needed?"

He nodded but didn't look at me. "This is beautiful."

I shrugged. "Now you know who I got my artistic ability from. See this hump on my right middle finger? It's just like Uncle Owen's. Comes from resting your pen or brush there, all the time. Nana called it our artist's hump."

He looked at my hand then looked at me then looked back at the serigraph. "You two posed like this after knowing each other for just a week?"

"Ten days. I came out on a Friday. Met Dion on Saturday. My uncle worked this up a couple days before I flew home."

"Where was his studio?"

"He didn't have one. He'd sling a cloth on the floor, pull out his materials and work that way."

"Then where're his art supplies? There's none here."

Shit, maybe they were at the dealership in one of those boxes. I'd better go back, to check.

I shrugged and said, "That'd be something to look into. It's not like he needed me and Dion here to pose. He did studies of us. Took a thousand digi-photos. They're probably in a file. On his laptop." His eyes were still sharp on the picture, so I kept on with, "Y'know, I had to talk Dion into this."

" ... Oh?" His voice was a thousand miles away.

I touched the frame of the picture. "That's why he wouldn't go completely nude. Why he's sittin'. He was self-conscious about his height. If he'd been standing, I'd only of reached his chin. Now he's totally the opposite."

I noticed Tone was looking at me. "Your smile when you speak of him ... so tender."

"Shit, Tone, we're talkin' about ten years ago. And this mornin' you told me to go home, so why're you actin' jealous?"

He hesitated, his eyes searching mine, then he looked back and the picture and said, "I'm not. I'm angry. Envious."

"About what?"

Another hesitation. He was working up to something. "He's open. Easy. Content. I'm not. But that's what you want."

I made myself chuckle. "Well, I ain't gettin' it from him; he's married."

"He wouldn't be for long, if you asked him. He still loves you. He'd love to make you happy." A snarl crept into his voice. "Which I can't do."

That made me nervous. "Don't go down that road ... "

"I've always hated people like that. People who know what they want. Comfortable in their lives when I never will be. Look at him. He hasn't changed. He's still this picture. He'll always be this picture. And that's how you'll always see him. Remember him. While I'm destroying your memories of us."

His eyes went ice cold. Mouth tight. Total focus on one the picture. Like a leopard getting ready to pounce. I'd seen it before, when he was about to attack a diver on his college's swim team. My hands grew cold and I whispered, "Tone, back off."

"I want to fuck him over, so bad," he continued, his voice growing colder with every word, "just to show him what life's really about and make him less perfect and beautiful because the world's not and he should see that in all its glorious brutality and hate and —"

I grabbed him and slung him around, onto the couch. Didn't even think about it, but my side sure made damn sure I knew what I'd done. I nearly doubled over from the sudden pain and had to steady myself by leaning against the wall.

He looked at me, stunned. I forced myself to stay still.

"You ever talk like that around me, again," I growled in a low, vicious voice, "so help me God I'll —"

"Jake ... ?" Matt got between us, concerned.

I swallowed the rest of my comment and forced my anger to step back as I croaked, "What?" But my eyes never left Tone ... and for the first time, he looked afraid of me.

I didn't blame him.

Matt's voice was uncertain as he said, "You ... you okay?"

I nodded. By then I had control enough to stumble into the kitchen, grab the bottle of wine, and down half of it in one gulp. But I was still shaky. I held the ice-cold bottle to my forehead. "What'd you find out about ... about PSALMS?"

" ... I'm not done yet ... "

"First, would you ... would you look at the laptop?"

I hadn't turned around, yet, so only heard Matt shuffle over to it. Then I heard Tone head up the stairs. Good. He could sulk in the bedroom all he wanted while I tried to figure out what the hell just happened.

That look on his face ... when I saw it focused on that diver, no question it made me angry, but I'd kept control. Pulled him back. Shown him he was being used. I could've done that, again.

But this time ... the knife in his voice when he threatened Dion ... I came close to hitting him. Hard. Like mom had said I would, eventually. And if he'd fought back, I'd have torn him to shreds. He would've had to kill me to make me stop. That scared me more than anything else that'd happened in the last few days.

Shit ... mom's poison was in me, too.

Matt cut through my darkening thoughts with, "Jake, you gotta see this. It's wiped clean. Like they were doing a fresh-install. All that's on here is the editing program, some Word docs, and video slugs."

Of course. His laptop was in his car.

"Why would you do something like that?" I asked.

"I wouldn't, unless the system was screwed up."

"Can ... can you reconstruct the files?"

"I can try. Info's never completely gone."

"Okay, my uncle vanished on August second; see if you can find anything that pops up before that date."

Matt pulled a disk from his briefcase, loaded it in and dove back into game mode, his fingers flying over the keyboard. I stopped him and added, "Before you get goin', the videos on here – will you burn the one that says *O-T* onto a DVD?"

He nodded and got back to work.

I took a deep breath and headed upstairs. Time to put an end to this.

Tone was sitting on the bed, staring at nothing. I stayed in the doorway.

"Go back to Texas," I said. "I've got Matt and Preston to back me. And Dion. We don't need you gettin' into more trouble for no reason. Leave now. Then once I'm done here, I'll fly straight back to Denmark. You can send me my stuff."

"So ... Dion means more to you than you're willing to admit." His voice still had that knife.

I snarled. "If I thought slappin' the shit out of you would get you to tell me what's goin' on in that fucked up brain of yours, I'd do it. But all that'll do is make my side hurt, more, and my hand. And it'll just prove to me that you don't really trust me. You've never really fuckin' trusted me. You always know better'n me what needs to be done, no matter how many times you fuck up. Well, I'm not gonna sit here and whimper and whine and hope you'll be back to normal, some day. I want you gone."

He nodded. "I ... I can't leave till Monday."

"Why not?"

He lay back on the bed but did not look at me. "I said that wrong. I'm not leaving until Monday. I'll sleep on the couch."

More of his goddamn stonewalling. "I don't want you in this house. I'll set you up in a hotel."

"I understand."

"Like fuckin' shit, you do! I don't get it, Tone. You get to have Collie as your perfect man. Your perfect memory. And you get to mope about him all over the fuckin' place and damn near get yourself killed on his behalf. But the second you find out I've got Dion as someone I still care about, you can't fuckin' handle it? What the hell? I told you years ago that you were my mate and how that works out is on you. And I've backed you up and done everything I can to show you that you're the only one for me, and you're tellin' me, so fuckin' what?!"

He sat up. He would not look at me, but I could tell I was landing some harsh body blows.

I was shaking. Had to fight to keep my voice down. "Okay, fine. Fine. You wanna lock your brain up from me, go ahead. But listen up, you psychotic little shit. Dion is a friend and he will always be a friend, and I want you to stay the fuck away from him. Am I bein' clear here?"

He gave me the slightest of nods.

"Now get your stuff. We'll find you a place to stay."

"I'll find my own place, thanks."

I rolled my eyes. "How you gonna pay for it?

"I have a credit card."

I sneered. "You mean, leave a paper trail for the Texas AG

to fuck you over with? Pretty fuckin' stupid."

That made him look at me. And suddenly all I could see is a scared kid with big, hurt eyes. They sliced into me. Made me even angrier. He didn't have the right to do that to me.

I spun and headed for the stairs. "You got ten minutes." Then I stopped and looked back at him. "And I mean it, Tone. You go near Dion or his family, I will cut your fuckin' throat."

I stormed downstairs and into the kitchen and downed more wine. Why the hell didn't we have some Tequila in the place? I was still shaking, I was so pissed. And scared shitless. Tone was being too easy about my blow-up. Accepting it ... like this was something he'd wanted. But why? Why can't I read him? Why can't I figure him out? Shit, why couldn't I just let it go and back away before things finally did go too far? It was freaking me the hell out.

I finally realized there was complete silence in the room, so I looked at Matt. He was watching me with wide eyes.

"How's it goin'?" I croaked.

"It's a disaster," he murmured. "It'll take longer than I thought."

"Then do me a favor?"

" ... Sure ... "

"Guess you heard everything." He nodded. I kept my voice soft. "I want you to stay with Tone, till he heads home. Keep him busy while I deal with everything else."

"What's going on?"

"I need to make sure he don't pull another dumb-ass stunt."

"Jake ... is this like what was gonna happen with that diver? What's his name? Grady?"

"Maybe you can find out; he's not sharin' with me."

"Damn, he was doin' so good, too."

"Was he?" I snapped. "What'd he have you find out for him?"

"The backgrounds of some people. Schedules. Statistics from the DA's office. A pile of news stories from the local papers."

"E-mail 'em to me, okay? What about PSALMS' clinics?"

"They're partnered with 18/20. Got them in Utah, North

Carolina, Texas, and El Salvador. I'm still researching those, so I can shove that off on him ... "

"Fine. Take my laptop. I got my phone so I don't need it. And, Matt — I don't want Tone out of your sight till he heads for home. And then I want you to call me the second he goes."

He smirked. "I could always tie him up, again."

I smiled. "Only if you leave his pants on, this time."

"Cut it out. I'll get my things."

"Thanks. Oh, and Matt, Tone's been makin' some calls, lately. Can you sneak a peek at his phone and find out to whom?"

"Okay. Oh, you might want to look at something I found hidden on Owen's computer. I left it open."

He headed upstairs as I sat in his chair and woke up the laptop. I almost stopped breathing.

It was a series of XL Spreadsheets with the budgets for shooting a bunch of videos, and for renting the dealership out to other video shoots. All beautifully detailed down to the penny, including several that had actual costs posted next to estimated costs. The dates on them went back over a year, and the date last input was two weeks ago.

It *was* a set-up. My uncle's laptop had been cleaned out to highlight these spreadsheets. His things had been moved over to the dealership to make it seem like he participated in their making. He didn't actually have anything to do with porn; it was theater to make the world think he had. Destroy his standing in the community and maybe even crush GALAIATH. As liberal as California could be, porn still brought out the moralistic puritan in too damn many people. And once the narrative's set in people's minds, it's hard as hell to change.

Thing is, while I was pretty damn sure about this, I had not one shred of evidence to prove it. Of course, at the moment I didn't necessarily feel the need for that. There are plenty of other ways to find justice, in this world. Some legal. Some not. Some poetic. Some perfect.

But considering what had happened ... what I was growing to believe happened ... there was only one type of justice I wanted to visit on the people responsible for my uncle's fate.

Annihilation.

And God help anybody who tried to stop me.

— VI —

Matt rode with Tone as I led them to a Best Western and checked them in. Tone moved like some machine programmed to drive the car and walk into the office and sign the register and nod to whatever I said and accept Matt as his roommate. He wouldn't look at me, wouldn't speak to me, just gazed straight ahead with a cool blank expression, like he didn't want me to know what he was thinking or feeling. But I knew him, too well; knew he was up to something and thought he was being clever about it, the little shit.

Once they were situated, I gave the Chrysler's keys to Matt, saying, "If he tries to take these from you, call me."

Tone shot me one of his little-boy-hurt glares, but I said nothing. Just left the room.

I drove over to the market where Lemm worked and talked to a few of the clerks and stockers. Everybody loved the kid, but only one girl saw a customer act threatening against him, about two weeks ago. I asked her if she could describe the guy.

"They were at the back of the store," she said. "I was at a register. But I could see he's taller than Lemm and bigger."

"Do you remember what he was wearin'?"

"Just normal clothes, like what you see in a gym or baseball game. Oh, he wore a cap on backwards."

"What made him leave?"

"I got on the call box for the manager. People heard it all over the store. The guy split, fast. Lemm was pretty shook up."

"How many times did it happen?"

"I only know about once. Is he okay? Lemm?"

I nodded. "I'm just out to keep that guy from makin' any more trouble for him."

"You like him, huh?"

"He's damn good-lookin'."

"Yeah," she sighed. "Why is it all the cute guys're gay?"

"'Cause we're arrogant assholes." And I winked at her.

She nodded at me and said, "Makes sense."

As I left, I called Preston's number to see if he had a minute to talk.

He laughed. "Aw, come on by the office; I'm here all day."

He gave me the address; it was the same as Dion's, so I drove over and headed up the stairs to the hallway. To the left was Dion's unit, in the back of the building; to the right past some offices containing an accountant, a dentist, and an import/export broker was Preston's.

He didn't put on much of a show — some padded chairs, an Ikea-style desk, with stacks of case-files piled on shelves and his desk and the floor, and copies of the Constitution and Bill of Rights on the wall behind him.

I rapped on the door; he looked up. "You didn't take long."

"I didn't realize you're Dion's neighbor," I said.

"Yeah, grabbed it the second I moved out here ... damn, five years ago. I told Don about his office when it come available."

"It's a good location?"

"It's cheap, but gonna move, soon."

"You doin' that well?"

"Lease is up and the new owner wants to tear it down and rebuild."

"Dion never mentioned he'd have to move."

"His lease is good for another year."

"Who's the new owner?"

He shrugged. "I only deal with the bank."

"Palm Valley West."

"How'd you know — aw, Dion. Right."

"What you workin' on?"

"I've got court on Monday. More bullshit cases."

"You know what's goin' on with Morrow and Harper?"

"The cops who busted you? IAD's investigating it and they're on desk duty or home with pay or something."

I nodded, smiling. Then I asked, "Preston ... does it seem to you like gay men are bein' targeted?"

I got a *You-gotta-be-kiddin'* look, in response. "When have they not been?"

"I don't mean the usual crap; I mean ... I dunno ... like a concerted effort to drive us away from Palm Springs."

"I have been busy, thanks to Owen putting the word out. Nuisance cases, mainly. Can't complain; pays my rent."

"So GALAIATH let people know they can fight back."

"Aw, c'mon, it's not like Owen was St. Joan of the gays. There's a dozen other organizations doing the same thing."

"But he had bigger plans, didn't he?"

"You mean, run me for DA?" I nodded. He shrugged. "Nice idea, but between you and me, not realistic. What's going on?"

"I dunno. Just tryin' to figure things out. Who'd you deal with at the bank?"

"Grace Nieri. Need her number?"

"No, I've got that."

"Aw, right, Dion'd be dealing with her, too."

"Tell me ... can I get a power of attorney or get declared guardian of my uncle's property?"

"He's run off, not dead."

"But if the bank declares his mortgage in default and taxes don't get paid, can't they still seize it?"

He gave me a long look, his eyes filling with hurt.

"If he doesn't answer a notice of default," he sighed, "the bank can foreclose on the property and sell it for whatever they want. Same for the county, on taxes. I'll try to get an emergency POA, but no promises."

"That's fine And is there any way to have the bank investigated? See if they deliberately set him up to default?"

"Jake." And his tone was so chiding, it embarrassed me. "The big banks and Wall Street screwed the country all over the place, not that long ago. And as for mortgage groups, they raped as many people as they could before they fell apart. And the feds did next to nothing; it was a few state AGs who went after them. Now you tell me how many of those assholes went to jail. And don't throw Bernie Madoff in my face; he screwed his rich buddies, so they made damn sure he got screwed right back."

"Figured as much," I said.

"It's always been that way, y'know. In law school, I read some books by Dickens ... he hated how screwed up justice could get ... and there's this one, *Little Dorrit*, that could've been set in today's New York City instead of London a hundred-sixty-odd years ago. A Bernie Madoff type's in it. So there's always wolves to feed on sheep ... and sheep to be fed on."

I stood up. "That, I learned in prison."

I took his card then bought a six-pack and drove back to the townhouse to sit in a dark, silent room. Let my brain go into calculation mode. Give my side a chance to calm down.

I started with the understanding that somebody, or some group, had a long-term goal in mind — not just to turn the straight community against the gay one, but make us the symbol of all that was wrong with society today ... according to their limited idea of what that was. But they weren't doing it just through speeches and demonstrations and loud noisy claims; they were doing it by infecting people with the poison of fear and distrust and hate. Like Fox News did to its viewers. Like the GOP did with its followers. Like my mom did with Tone.

And me. By proxy.

Uncle Owen had fought back in ways that made him a threat to their plans, so he'd been set up for neutralization. Question was, would they go as far as actually killing him? Even my paranoid brain said that's over the top. Murder is murder, no matter what your excuse.

Matt had sent me Tone's info, so I sorted through it on my phone. Tone sensed it, too. His statistics showed arrests for public indecency up by over ninety percent; lurid reports of every instance in the local papers; opinion pieces and political cartoons about how wonderful Palm Springs was before the gays took over, and how out of control things were getting to be, with the boys in nothing but bare-assed chaps and jocks and nipple rings during Splash and Pride and having sex in public and women who acted more like men; more anti-gay comments on the web, linking pedophiles and fags with every mention of a missing or abused child; the establishment of groups wanting to turn back the tide of gay lawlessness; local shops refusing to do business with queers; and on and on and on. Most of it had spread over the last few years ... with the trend shooting to the sky after the Supremes legalized gay marriage ... and once San Sebastian and PSALMS came to town.

On top of it, gay bashings were dismissed in the media as just robberies, and a lot was made about two gay men hanging themselves, over the last six months, adding to the slow-building idea that fags were broken people, to be feared and avoided, not lived with. Never mind we made up a fourth of the town's population and paid the same taxes as everyone else. Ideas have more validity than reality, way too often.

He also had info about *Future Dreams*, a multinational financial firm based in Dallas. Lamar Davis Lawton was on their board of directors, too. It handled banking, investing and insurance ... and healthcare. The 18/20 ex-gay clinics were a branch of one of those groups and had brought in nearly fifty-million in revenue, last year. Jeez, people were going nuts trying to un-gay their kids. Sounded like something my father would be part of ... hell, proud of ... not to mention my mother. Then I saw why Tone focused on it — Grace Nieri had been a spokesperson for the clinics ... on behalf of the *excellent work* they had done with her own son.

Jesus, no wonder I disliked the bitch.

Said son was not named in anything Tone could find, but he noted the guy was probably around thirty and married, now, based on when Grace had fronted for 18/20 and other details in the fliers and articles about it. I was glad he'd done the work on that, because there were dozens of those articles in all manner of right-wing, conservative, and *Christian* magazines. Just knowing about this was enough to bring back memories of my own brush with the ex-gay scum.

I'd been out of prison for a couple of months when a pair of priests showed up on Nana's doorstep in the middle of June, a couple months after I made parole. Seems my mother knew her mother would have slammed the door in their faces, so she waited till Nana was visiting Uncle Bert up in Dallas to send the twerps over. They both wore black short-sleeve shirts and pants, and that dog collar around their necks, their shoes polished to perfection. They'd have been twins if one hadn't been sixty and the other half his age.

I wasn't going to let them in the house, I was so pissed at mom for pulling that crap ... but the younger one gave me a glance up and down that put a tingle in my balls. I was in a ratty wife-beater and clingy nylon gym shorts, no briefs ... not because it was sexy but because it was cool ... and he was trying so hard not to look like he was wilting from the ninety-plus heat and hundred-plus humidity, he was close to fainting. Nana's window unit had the room cool enough to matter, so I opened the door, sat them on the couch, and provided tumblers of ice tea.

The old man was Father Boniface, from the Hollywood School of decent, loving priests; the younger one, Father Abel. He was short and trim, like an oversized jockey, with slicked back hair, dark eyes, a classic Roman profile and earnest expression. But here's the wild part; cute as he was, it was his hands that caught me. They were strong and masculine and I wanted to sketch them; told him so, as I pulled out my pad and got to work.

They sat on the couch and gave me their very meaningful line about Adam and Eve, not Adam and Steve, and that changing your orientation is all heart and mind over prurience, and that prayer solves everything if I really want to change and yap, yap, yap ... tho' when I say they I mean Father Boniface; Father Abel just nodded in agreement, like his hand puppet.

It was all white noise, I was so focused on Abel's hands. I nodded politely every now and then, as I sketched, and gave off single word responses to questions. I was positioned in Nana's ancient lounge chair, right by the ac unit so I wouldn't sweat. Nothing messes up Derwent pencils like perspiration.

Finally, the older guy's chatter began to irritate me and my jail training took over. I'd been bait for more than one butch-hound my owner wanted to put his collar on, so I set the pad aside and hooked both legs over the chair's arm, letting the shorts drift down to reveal a light tan line. Breathing in deep to emphasize my pecs. Clenching my ass every now and then to make everything move ever so slightly.

Abel's eyes darted down to what mattered, more than once, then jerked back up to mine. I kept my gaze sharp on him. Then let one leg drift down to straighten out, revealing my bulge. His eyes did not leave mine, after that point.

Father Ben finally caught on to what I was doing and bolted to his feet, furious. "You filthy animal," he almost screamed. "You dare to mock the men of God!"

"What you talkin' 'bout, Ben?" I said, all innocence and light. "I'm just sittin' here."

"My name is Father Boniface."

"I don't have a father," I whispered back, casually laying my hand by my erection. "Or mother. I was disowned. Kicked out with nothin'. So all I have is me. And part of that is that I love to suck cock. And fuck men. And I've been this way since I knew I had a dick and balls. That ain't somethin' you can change with thought or prayer. It's part of your DNA."

"Do you think this childish provocation proves anything more than you desperately need God's love and forgiveness?"

"I just think I'm horny, and I'm wonderin' which one of you wants to suck my dick?"

His face twisted into a nearly demonic vision of hate. "Your mother warned us you may have too much of the Muslim man in you to be treated as human, but we thought — "

I jumped up and cut him off with, "It's your guys who fucked little boys and girls, asshole, so cut this holier than thou crap. What's the matter? Am I too old for you? You like 'em half my age? A third? Still in diapers? Want me shaved?"

He almost hit me, but he forced himself to back to the door. His beefy hands shook from not being allowed to connect with my face. "You are beneath contempt," he muttered, his voice cracking. "And beyond salvation. Come, Father Abel."

"One moment, Father Boniface," he said in this fake empathetic way that always irritates me. "Jacob is a wounded creature, snapping even at those who would help him." Then he motioned to my ankle monitor. "Your mother told us why you were in prison. It's quite understandable you would have great anger and distrust. It can be very difficult for a young man in that sort of environment. Especially one who's known to be homosexual."

Oh, you wanna see difficult, motherfucker? I sat on the floor by his chair, laced my fingers over my knees and rested my head on them, letting the shorts ride back on my legs to almost reveal everything, and asked in an oh-so-innocent way, "Did she tell you why I was sent to prison?"

Again, his eyes stayed locked on mine. "You were arrested for drunk driving and attacked a police officer, actions which emphasize a cry for help — "

My inner wolf growled. "That's a lie. I got busted by a deputy sheriff who said I rammed his car and tried to take off. Then claimed he found drugs in my cup holder. Also a lie."

"Jacob," Abel choked, "to regain control of your life you must accept responsibility for your actions — "

"Like you? When all you're doin' is lyin' to yourself?"

"Of course — wait, excuse me?"

I stood up and stretched, my boner giving me some serious tent-pole action. His eyes still never left mine. "You use the church to hide from bein' gay. Is that why you were sent along with this prick? You ex-gay, yourself? You bein' tested, or testin' yourself? Provin' you're a nice well-trained puppy?"

"You have no idea what you're talking about," he said, then he got up. "You were right, Father Boniface, we ... we should have left when you said."

They headed out the door, Father Ben shooting me a look of pure condemnation as he said, "I believe only an exorcism could release the demon controlling your soul, Jacob. I'll discuss it with your mother."

"I'm twenty-four fuckin' years old, motherfucker," I shot back. "Mommy don't decide that for me."

He slammed the door closed. I chuckled and fell back into my chair. Let the cool air whisper over my body. Felt like I'd done my job as a gay man. So caressed my belly. Pinched my tits. Slipped my hand under my shorts and gripped my dick and ran my fingers up and down it and had a nice, long, lovely session of pretending Father Abel was sucking me off as his gorgeous hands gripped my ass.

And when I came, the world grew kind and gentle, again.

— VII —

I should've waited. Because just before midnight, as I was about to give up on a layout I was trying to pull together for Uncle Ari, a knock at the door proved me right about Abel. His eyes were starving, his breath deep and scared, tongue softly licking his lips ... and no dog collar.

"That story you told us," he asked. "Is it true?"

I just drew him inside and crushed my mouth against his and held his body close to mine and felt every nerve in me fire up at how hard and solid he was as he grabbed me around the waist and slipped his tongue across to mine and he tasted of Colgate and ... oh ... let's just say, within seconds my shirt became a rag as he ripped it open and bit my nips and groped my ass and cascaded his mouth down my belly to pull my shorts to my knees with his teeth and start a blow-job that made my knees weak.

I didn't let him finish. I pushed him back on the couch and proved I knew a thing or two about worshiping a dick. I also found out that when you're God's robot with too damn much abstinence stored up, it takes more than once or twice to be completely satisfied.

I wasn't into being fucked, back then; it was still too close to what had happened in prison. But he never asked, not even when I got really rough with him. All I can say is, he left at dawn with the most Zen of expressions on his face, swearing he'd come back if he could. I knew he wouldn't. Father Ben would notice and he'd be sent back to ex-gay camp. I got the feeling if that happened, this time, he'd either leave the priesthood or leave this world, completely. I made him promise if he reached that point, he'd call me, first. That kind of suicide is only a surrender to the control of others.

Then a month later, I found Nana asleep, forever, and between my grief and the lies I told so I could keep living in her place, I was too busy to worry about finding a guy. Helped that Uncle Owen talked mom and Uncle Bert into letting me stay there till my probation was up. A few months after that, Tone popped into my life, and a couple months later, my destiny was my own, again. All of it seeming like yesterday … and a century ago.

It was dark outside and I was beginning to zone, by this point, but there was too much more to go through for me to sleep, yet. Like about the right and honorable Lamar Davis Lawton. He'd been forced out of office due to the misuse of campaign funds, had built C&B into a major financial player, and had been in town six times over the last year — twice for seminars like the one at San Sebastian; twice to meet with the city councils of Palm Springs, Palm Desert, and Cathedral City about some sort of development; twice more for no known reason. All hush-hush, even though everybody was referencing it.

Dammit. If here was anything I did not want to do it was ask Tone why he dug this up. If he told me anything, it'd only be after an hour of arguing and snapping and growling at each other like a couple of pissed off mongrels. I figured I'd go over it, again, when I was clearer-headed.

Matt had the addresses of the vacant lots owned by OT & Associates. One was next door to the dealership; the other was behind it. A third one was off Dillon Road. They'd all been sold a couple years ago, according to the deed, but Matt snuck into the county tax records and found all taxes prior to last year's were paid by Palm Valley West Bank; all the loans were through them, too.

I checked who the previous owner of the dealership was, a company called Morengo Ford. Thanks to the purchase of those lots, they'd built up too much debt just as the economy crashed, so went under. The bank foreclosed and liquidated what they could. It was vacant till the porn biz moved in; that's when OT & Associates became the new owner, with the paperwork dated two years ago, long before Grace Nieri took over. Meaning, the paperwork was probably back-dated.

Okay ... so my first thought was that PSALMS Forever was working with Palm Valley West to hurt my uncle for fighting their anti-gay agenda. Paint him as a pornographer and child molester, drag Dion and Preston in by association, then PSALMS kills GALAIATH with a single story.

But that didn't explain the porn studio or the kinky projects that had been shot, both gay and straight. As rabidly moralistic as Christians can be about anybody but themselves, would they really go so far as to do BDSM porn? And would a supposedly reputable bank? That would also mean Cliff and Ned, two of Uncle Owen's friends, would be in on what the hate-crowd was planning. Which scrambled that idea up.

So I was back to the possibility my uncle did partner with someone to own the building, since he couldn't buy anything on his own, and did make porn, and the scum at PSALMS found out and planned to use that against him. Claim he'd used Tiago that way. And Lemm. And Harper had been the messenger for their blackmail.

Which also didn't really fit. Dammit, I needed to talk with Grace Nieri — but only as an equal; not when she could tell me to fuck off, again. I knew I could figure out from that bitch what her bank'd been pulling and why they were pulling it. Only that wasn't going to happen till I found my uncle's body.

Tone had also checked the coroner's offices of some other counties. He'd found three possible John Does — one in LA, one in San Diego, and one in Imperial, but the dates ranged over a few weeks. And there weren't enough details beyond height and estimated age to tell if they fit the bill. Plus one of the bodies was thought to be a victim of a Mexican drug cartel. I'd have to wait till Monday to check into these.

By this point, after three beers, relying on Advil instead of OxyContin, and not sleeping last night, I crashed and did not wake till the next morning. I hurt all over. That couch did not make a good bed, and yesterday's run was digging at my ribs.

It was after ten, so all I had time to do was grab a quick shower, yank on some wrinkled clothes, hit Price's for bags of chips and salsa and another six-pack, and head to Dion's.

If there was anything I did not want to do, it's be late for him.

I hit the front step at 10:59. Kent met me, in boardies and a t-shirt.

"Hurry in," he said, "It's too chilly for this outfit."

"We still doin' the pool thing?" I asked as he closed the door behind me.

"Back here."

He led me past the kitchen, and I had to say — Dion got himself a guy with a cute butt and great legs. Not much hair on 'em, but shaped like Da Vinci. Funny how slim he looked in regular clothes.

"Where's the rest of you?" he asked.

"Oh, uh, Antony had to head back to Texas. And Matt's not feelin' good."

"Sorry to hear it. You'll have to take him some food. We've got plenty."

"You cookin'?"

"Yeah."

"Won't be no leftovers."

He laughed and we exited to a bunch of kids running and screaming in and around the pool, all in swimming suits. There was a high cabana over the pool, Lucite sheets to the sides to cut down on the breeze and it was just warm enough, thanks to bowls of glass beads with soft fire whispering from them. They were positioned to give the best heat with barriers up to keep them out of the reach of the kids.

Straight and gay parents, all the same age as Dion, stood around with cool drinks, looking sedate in summer ensembles. The twins were gathered with some other girls at one corner of the pool while Joel and a couple of other boys tossed rings at each other. It was so suburbia, I felt totally out of place.

Dion was starting the grill with old-fashioned cedar chips,

and a table of bowls of food sat to one side of the door. He wore a pair of wildly-colored knee-length shorts, an athletic t-shirt, and flip-flops that made him male-model perfect.

He saw me and waved to the table. "Food goes there. Kent, put the beer in the fridge."

Kent took the sixer, introduced me around, then headed for an old refrigerator under a covered bar area. I put the chips and salsa on the table along with all the other chips and salsas that'd been brought.

"You alone?" Dion asked as he came over.

I just nodded and helped myself to a guacamole that was to die for. "Kent make this, too?"

"Oh, my God, honey, he's not the only cook in the house." Then he batted his eyes at me. I had more of the guac. "What's up with you and Anthony?"

"Antony," I said, softly. "Just stuff. Kent looks happy."

"It's Sunday. We're all getting in the pool, soon."

I dumped the shirt and flexed. "Got my beach bod on."

He laughed and said, "Wow. No kidding." Then he noticed the bruises, winced, and focused on my shoulder. "Oh, my God, I ... I love the tatt. C'mere." He led me into the house and down the hall to his bedroom. "I've got something for you, and a place for you to put your wallet, too."

"And passport and keys and ... "

He pointed me to a chest of drawers. "Top left."

I dropped my things in it and turned to find him holding some photo albums.

"Here."

"Family photo time?" I asked.

"These're Owen's. He left them here the night before the trial. I'd forgotten, till I went looking for this thing." He pulled down the shorts' elastic band to reveal a bit of the same electric blue Speedo he'd been wearing the day we met. His eyes twinkled as he said, "Remember?"

I caught my breath and said, "Let me see it."

"Don't be silly." But he was blushing.

I tugged at the shorts. "C'mon, Dion, don't tease. Let me see it on you. Don't it fit, no more? Is it all skanky lookin'?"

He swatted my hands away ... then hesitated ... then shrugged and pulled off his shirt. The shorts dropped, next, and I flashed back ten years to watching him remove those layers of costume, revealing himself section by section. Broad shoulders. Tight abs. Solid arms. Full chest. Sprinkled with golden hair gleaming in the sharp, hot sun that trailed down to that strip of nylon cozied across his glorious ass and crotch, pulled tight around his hips before letting his long, exquisite legs flow down to his lovely feet. His smile made him even more of a sun God, still every bit as beautiful as he was back then. No, more-so now that his belly was a bit softer and human.

"Still fits," he said, a bit bashful. "Hard to believe."

"Dion," I whispered, "if you wasn't married ... "

He grinned at me. "You're sweet. Kent likes it, too. I wear it, every now and then, when I want to spice things up." He cast me a wicked glance. "Like tonight, maybe. Once the kids're down. Pretend I'm the pool boy, Little Sir Innocent." He batted his eyes at me, again.

"I'd use you faster than on a porn shoot."

"You say that now," he chuckled. "Remember how nervous you were, our first night together?"

"I was scared everything was in proportion. Had no idea how I'd handle it."

"I think that was the tenderest I'd ever been," he sighed. "I'd always been into the slam-bam kind of hook-up, but with you, just holding you was close to heaven. God, I wanted you to come back. I even told Owen I did, but he said he wouldn't ask. I was so mad at him, for a while."

" ... He tell you why?"

"No, but Ian said later, when he saw that Owen'd given away our portrait, he asked him why, and Owen just said, *It proves that Jake stands on his own two feet, in control.* He never explained what it meant."

"When did he do it? Donate that portrait?"

"Last Christmas. It was part of an exhibit, and he let 'em keep it." He turned back to the photo albums. "He asked me to name all the guys I knew in here." I opened one and noticed a slip of paper in the front, with names by numbers. Inside, the photos were numbered, too. "I meant to bring them the night he showed us the video, but forgot. He said not to worry about it; he'd get them later. Then he ... he vanished."

They were nothing but photos of guys at a party or on a trip or dinner or a meeting of GALAIATH or just groups of friends having fun. Splash Party here and Pride Week there and around Uncle Owen's back yard, or Ian's or Meredith's.

"I don't know any of these people," I said.

"There's a few in there of you and me. Here."

Dion pointed to a photo of us on Uncle Owen's patio, at night, dancing close. There were other people around, but I couldn't see anything but Dion's arms around me, his hands resting on my butt, my arms holding him tight, his head resting on top of mine. I remembered exactly when this was taken; I was returning home, the next day. And I'd been hinting to Uncle Owen that I didn't want to go. Now I was thinking, if I hadn't ... if I'd stayed with Dion and grown to love the desert ...

"Why'd he bring this to you?" whispered from me.

"I got the feeling he was looking for someone particular. But he couldn't find him."

"Like who?"

"Some guy at a party. Couple of guys, maybe. He just asked me to name people. But I think ... what I'm thinking ... what I've been trying not to think ... it's got to be wrong ... that he ... he wanted these in safe hands and ... " His eyes grew tight.

"When was the last time you heard from him?"

"I ... I told you ... he called the night he vanished. He was crying, he was so upset. He kept saying, *I can't believe it. I can't believe it. Those motherfucking bastards. They couldn't do that to him.* But he wouldn't tell me what he was talking about. I told him to come over ... I mean, I couldn't leave; the kids were in bed and Kent was at work. He said he might ... after he did something. No, no, ended something, but he wouldn't tell me what. And I never heard from him, again. That ... that's really why I went to his place, a couple days later ... to see if he'd actually ... and everything was so neat and clean and all his plants were gone and he loved his plants and that's why I've been so afraid ... "

He was near tears. I pulled him into a hug and he rested his head against my chest. It felt so nice. So right.

"I don't know what that little fuck, Roy Harper, told him," he continued. "Oh, sorry. I just know it had to be vicious. Owen would never end it just because things got tough. He was the strongest of us all."

"Yeah," I said. I rested my cheek on top of his head and held him tighter. Shared the fear we both had about my uncle. Supported each other, in gentle ways. It reminded me of how great it'd been. My skin touching his skin. The hair on his chest tickling my belly. The hair on my chest mingling with his. The strength in his arms surrounding me ... I realized for the first time that Dion was more than just my perfect memory; he was my first real, honest, deeper than myself love. The fact that he cared about Owen as much as me. And feared for him in the same way I did. I didn't feel anything in the way of fight or conflict or secrecy with Dion. I felt whole and at peace, and God how nice it was, for a change.

"Dion," I whispered. "Did anything else happen with Uncle Owen around that time?"

He sighed but didn't move. "You know about Philby's crap. That bastard priest. The bank. None of it's easy to deal with, but that's all I know about. Oh, wait ... the bank charged him with someone else's property taxes, and Nieri wouldn't change it without something from the county saying it was a mistake. Only Owen could get that, and he was planning to ... "

"Why'd you even need a power of attorney?"

"Oh, it was stupid. I got caught shoplifting. Got 30 days. I was sixteen, jeez. The POA was part of the bank's crap. They wanted Owen to say, in a legal document, that it was okay for an ex-con to handle some of his finances."

"The bank bitch on that, too?"

"Of course. Have you found out something?"

"Nothin' concrete, yet."

"Shit, I wish I'd sold that hillside when I had the chance. Connie knew somebody who wanted to buy it. Then we'd just have this house to deal with."

"What d'you mean?"

"When I lose Playa Royale, I won't be able to keep my office. The bank's open to terminating the lease early, so I'm looking for a job. Best prospect's in Santa Monica. Kent's holding back, but ... if things get worse ... we've got kids to think of. Joel's problems at school ... "

"Yeah." I kissed the top of his head. Pulled him tighter.

He took a deep breath and patted my butt and said, "Enough of this maudlin crap. We got a party outside."

"They could wait," I whispered.

He tensed ... then slowly rose. His eyes locked on mine. A thousand emotions flashed through them as he looked at me. I realized I was holding my breath and my heart was screaming and the only reason I wasn't shaking was my arms were locked around his waist. And he caressed my cheek and whispered, oh-so-gently, "Jake ... you'll always be my Persian Boy."

I froze. Way to go, Jake. Shit, could you act more like a love-struck teenage girl? I could've kicked myself silly.

He gave my forehead a tender kiss and broke away, saying, "Lemme pull on a pair of trunks. My Neon Galaxy shorts are too expensive to swim in, and if I wear a Speedo to the pool, the twins will scream and Joel with laugh at me."

I growled and said, "Let 'em." Then I hooked a finger in the waistband and pulled him towards the door.

He reluctantly let me, protesting, "Jake, careful with those paws. I'm married to a protective man ... "

"I know," I said. "He better watch out."

He jerked away, laughing, back to the same old Dion. "No, I'm putting on trunks. Don't want to embarrass my kids."

I grabbed him around the waist, picked him up, fireman style, then staggered down the hall to the patio.

"Jake, cut it out! Stop it!"

Of course, if he'd really wanted to, he could've knocked me

on my ass. Instead, I stumbled straight into the pool with him, jolting the hell out of parents and kids. When Dion came up, still laughing, he pointed at me and cried, "I'm gonna get you for that!" Then he jumped me and pushed me under water and the twins piled in, laughing and squealing, and Joel sloshed water on us all as Kent jumped in to help Dion and the twins backed me up and we had a huge water-fight, making the other parents scramble aside to keep from getting wet. It was glorious, and my stupid move from moments earlier was completely forgotten.

Well ... forgotten by everybody but me.

— VIII —

I headed home about eight, exhausted but feeling more at ease than I had in months, finally accepting that Dion loved his man so much, he'd never dump him for me. I saw it when Kent was dozing in a lounger, holding a sleeping Samantha ... or Sarah, whichever. Joel sat at his feet, playing a portable PlayStation as Sarah, or the other one, watched him and yawned.

I was talking with Dion about nothing much when he noticed them ... and the loveliest, gentlest expression drifted over his face. He picked Sarah up and whispered, "Tired yet?"

She lay her head on his shoulder and said, "No." But didn't move.

His left hand drifted down to caress Kent's hair. The guy looked at him, smiled, nodded and got up still holding Samantha to follow Dion inside. Joel glanced up to watch them go, then turned back to his game. That's when the party broke up.

Okay ... so Tone was right about my feelings for Dion, but how the hell could he be so wrong about Dion's feelings for me? Did his jealousy throw his senses off? Who knew, anymore?

I called the hotel when I got home. Matt answered.

"Got some interesting stuff," he said. "And Antony's going after something I don't really understand, so he'd better tell you."

"Have you found out what he's up to?"

"No, all he'll discuss is stuff I asked him to research. It's all on your laptop."

"Fine, have him drop you off at the fortress, in the morning, then call me. And be sure to fix his ankle monitor to shift back to normal once he's home. I'm gonna talk to Philby. Soon as I get back, we'll go over everything."

Then I flipped through the photo albums. There was one whole section of Dion and me, including some of the photos he'd taken for the painting. The rest were friends, places he'd been, parties around various pools, all going back decades. Nothing jumped out at me. So much for that being any help.

The next morning, I called Philby's receptionist at 9am, sharp. I think the only reason she shoehorned me into his very busy schedule was, I said I knew why Owen Taylor vanished and I was leaving tonight, so he'd better talk to me now, now, now. With a nice little snarl in my voice. All she could get me was five minutes at ten past ten.

I grabbed breakfast at an overpriced diner that had *zero* idea how to cook hash-browns, then popped up at Philby's office twenty minutes early so I could check the place out. I got into the habit when I was under probation. The first couple of times I'd gone to my Parole Officer, I'd get pissed off that he was being such a dick, by the end of the meeting I was close to being sent back to prison for smacking him. Then I noticed that when the ex-con ahead of me came out without a slouch, things went better between me and the prick. So having a few minutes of watching people come and go and see what sort of emotional turmoil or joy they had going on helped me figure out what sort of attitude I could expect, and I could better prepare myself before I walked into his cubicle.

I didn't do it to be nice to the guy or make him happy or anything. Even on his best days, my PO treated me like scum, especially when it became obvious I'd be exonerated and met with him for our final face-to-face. He actually told me I didn't deserve to be let off on a technicality. But I did not want to go back inside, because even with the idiot restrictions and impossible demands and ridiculous attitude, it was better than being some fucker's personal slave.

I hadn't paid attention to Philby's reception area when I'd come through, the first time ... and God, was I glad. It was one of those cold, bland, nauseatingly serviceable spaces that fronts for a dozen offices hidden behind this big blank wall, with commercial chairs for seating. It could've been a doctor's waiting room or an airport terminal or the next step to hell, for all you could tell. The receptionist still had that *Do not fuck with me* vibe. Just the thought of coming back to that would've depressed the hell out of me.

The place was full of soon-to-be-criminals and their reps, but the only one that interested me was this guy whose hands were shaking, a little, as his lawyer oh-so-softly explained that the best deal he could get would ruin his life. The client was a little dumpy but dressed nice enough, not high-end but not Wal-Mart. Receding hairline. Closing in on middle age. A wedding band on his finger. He screamed closet.

His lawyer was hot. Sandy hair, sharp blue eyes and earnest features on a strong jaw, suit fitting perfectly, nails polished to perfection, no wedding band ... and zero pings on the gaydar.

Still, something about him seemed off. Like he was over-acting a part. His neck muscles were tense, and both of his hands gripped his briefcase so tight, his knuckles were white. He made angry jabs with his head to emphasize a point or word or something he really, really wanted the client to understand or accept or give into or something, and each one made the client even more upset. Unfortunately, the drone of other people in the room made it impossible to make out what they were saying.

Then the client snapped, "They can't do that to me!" That's when it hit me what was wrong about the lawyer. He wasn't angry or scared or tense; he was disgusted.

Without thinking, I popped off with, "Yes, they can."

They both looked at me, and the lawyer said, "Excuse me, but this is none of your business."

"They can do anything they want," I kept on with. "The DA has the power of the police and the state behind him. If he wants to screw you, he will."

"Hey!" the lawyer snapped. "Butt out!"

The other people in the room looked at us. The receptionist picked up her phone.

"You ... you're not helping, any," said the client.

"No, you're not helpin'," I shot back. "I don't know what you're accused of, but you picked the wrong lawyer to defend you. He's scared shitless you won't take the deal an' he'll have to publicly stand by your side, as if that'd be humiliating."

The lawyer bolted to his feet and snarled, "Shut up! C'mon, Gary, let's go over here." He started towards some chairs on the opposite side of the room.

Gary slowly got to his feet, his eyes hurling vicious pain at me. "You don't know what I'm up against."

"Don't I?" I said.

"I have a wife. Two kids! I can't go to jail."

"So you'll give into blackmail? All that means is more an' greater blackmail."

That's when Philby appeared by the door in the blank wall. He focused his ice-cold eyes straight on me.

"What's going on here?" he snapped.

Gary's lawyer all but jumped over to him and pointed at me. "Warren, this guy's messing with my client."

Warren? Oh, that was too damn perfect. I got to my feet, snarling as I said, "Jesus, why not just kiss his ring?"

Philby tried to growl me into submission with, "Blaine, what're you pulling, now?"

"Just givin' a bit of friendly advice," I shot back.

"Leave this office, or I'll have you arrested."

"On what charge?"

"Start with disturbing the peace, trespassing."

I laughed and turned to Gary. "Dude, you really do need a new lawyer. This one's gonna fuck you, dry."

"Shut up, faggot!" Gary's lawyer screamed.

Then he lunged at me. I stepped aside and he slammed into the wall, cracking it.

Philby snapped at the receptionist, "Call security. I want this man arrested for assault." He nodded to me.

I pulled out my phone and dialed a number as I said, "Fine. I'll have Gregory Mikkelsen put in an immediate request for the video, which will show I didn't touch him; he lunged at me." Then I looked straight at one of the ceiling cameras. "Should go well with everything else that's happened."

Philby gave a hint of hesitation then let this wolf's grin cross his lips. He stepped back, his voice warning but his eyes not. "Mr. Blaine ... why are you here?"

"To talk about my uncle."

"You have nothing of interest for his case, so I suggest you leave ... "

He'd backed down enough for me to shrug, say, "Have it your way," and head for the door. We could talk when we weren't in a pissing contest.

If ever.

I was halfway to the parking garage when someone yelled, "Hey," at me from behind. I got ready for it to be a cop, but it was Gary. He stopped a few feet away, winded, and I don't think it was from running. "Why do I need a new lawyer?"

"Didn't you see it?" He looked at me with complete and total confusion, so I added, "Gary! Your guy's Philby's boy. They work together. Shit. You want a lawyer the DA hates; not one he'll come out of his office to protect."

"That's not ... what happened." But he could see it, now.

"Did your guy even talk about fightin' the charges?"

"Yeah. He said it'd be next to impossible. And I'd have to register as a sex offender if I lost."

"What'd you get busted for?"

"Solicitation ... for prostitution ... "

"Shit, they got a fetish for that in this town."

"What do you mean?"

"They pulled the same thing on my uncle, about three-four months ago."

"What ... what happened? With his case?"

"He won."

"He did? Can I talk to him?"

"He ... he's not around, right now."

"Figures," he sighed, his voice breaking. "Who was his lawyer?"

"Tell me somethin'," I said, "did you do it?"

"Are you a cop?"

"Shit, Gary! What the fuck?"

"Okay," he said, then shrugged and added, "Yeah. Sort of."

"Sort of?"

"It was outside a bar. I had a couple of drinks in me. This guy talked me into showing him my ... my ... how big I am. He was the policeman that arrested me, and said I offered him money. Another officer saw me do it."

"What was the arresting officer's name?"

"Harper."

"Roy Harper."

"I ... I guess. I didn't pay attention to his first name. But he was so good-looking and I thought I'd got lucky and — "

"Is his witness named Morrow?"

"No. Stettlin."

"Hmph. Well, Harper's bein' investigated for perjury, for a similar case. And your lawyer didn't want to fight that?"

"Maybe he didn't know. He doesn't normally handle cases like this and ... and ... "

"An' that is bullshit."

Gary started pacing. "But my ... my wife was afraid ... Wanda was afraid ... if I was convicted of public indecency and had to register as a sex offender, I'd lose my kids."

"She'd take 'em away?"

"The state. She knows about me. Knows I need to be with a guy, every now and then. But our county DA is ... she's real ... so long as I play safe, and quiet, Wanda doesn't care."

"Wait, where you live?"

"Up the San Joachim Valley. On a ranch. I ... I guess from now on I'll have to go to West Hollywood or San Francisco."

I pulled out Preston's card and wrote his number on a slip of paper. "What's the name of that guy representin' you?"

"Scott Baskin."

"Shit, why am I not surprised?"

"I ... I was told he and his father have a well-respected practice here," said Gary. "I tried to go with his father but he doesn't handle cases like mine, anymore. And Scott's cute ... "

"That's only good if you want to fuck 'em." I handed him Preston's contact info. "Call this guy. He helped a friend of mine, and he hates Philby as much as he needs to."

"Will it make any difference?"

I looked at him, and he seemed so lost and scared and close to freaking out, I had to say, "Gary, what they're doin' to you in there is blackmail. It's got a pretty name an' it's all legal an' shit, but it's still mafia tactics. Give in or we'll fuck you up the rest of your life. That's tyranny, not justice. Now where're you parked?"

"Just over there." He pointed to the parking garage.

"Fine, follow me. I'll take you to Preston an' — no, no, wait, he's in court, today! Let's see if we can find him. And if he says the same shit as Scott did, you can call me an asshole."

"I already think you are," he muttered. "But you're even cuter than Scott."

"Thanks. I think. But I ... I'm with somebody."

"Figures."

We headed around to the Larson Justice Center and caught Preston sitting on a bench, inhaling a breakfast taco, a napkin tied around his front like a bib, drippings all over it.

"Got it from that truck, over there," he chomped. "Best ever, sloppy as hell, and cheap as shit. I'm packed the rest of the day, so I eat when I can."

"Want more business?" I asked.

"Will he pay his bill? Sit. And ignore the salsa."

So I introduced Gary to Preston, and in the space of two minutes, he saw how fighting back was anything *but* impossible. Get the cop's arrest record, focus on how he must've made a mistake and how the other witness couldn't have seen what he says he did, bring up the perjury investigation, object to everything the DA did ... and suggest during the trial that you'd appeal the verdict and make it too expensive for them to keep after you, and that should be that. By the time he got done, even I felt like I'd seen a wizard at work.

"At the very least," he said, "they'll wind up withdrawing the charges with jeopardy attached. Then I'll file a complaint against the arresting officer, just to be mean."

Gary smiled at that. "You really think that'd work?"

"He knows what he's doin'," I said.

Preston shoved the last of his taco in his mouth then mumbled, "This case'll give me one more excuse to rant and rave about injustice and the lack of follow-through on the part of the DA's office. It'll be fun."

Gary grinned, his face lost about ten years, and his hands weren't shaking. Now I could leave with a clear conscience.

I headed back to the parking garage, but halfway there Castillo called. I greeted him with, "Tell me you got a deal with the AG and I'll — "

"Jake, is Antony in California, with you?"

Oh ... shit. "Hasn't he been in contact with you?"

"Jesus, Christ," and I could hear years wheeze off his life. "I haven't spoken to him since last week. I just received a call from his parents. Their car has been impounded in Indio, and they are frantic. They think he may have been carjacked or something to that nature, because he knows perfectly well he's not allowed to leave the house without permission, let alone the goddamn state of Texas!"

"Oh, shit. Shit, shit, shit ... "

"What the hell was he doing!?"

"It's ... it's complicated."

"Fine, fine, fine, we can settle this, later. But as of now, I've received no phone call from him. Nor have his parents. Nor can any of us reach him. Perhaps you know where he is?"

Oh, I had this really bad idea I did. "I'll call you back."

"Do that. Fast." Then he disconnected.

I tried to call Matt but it went straight to voicemail, so I shifted direction and headed for the jail.

Man, Castillo being pissed was perfectly understandable. Tone's little stunt had just killed all the work he'd done with Texas' AG and given them the ball on our one-yard line. My only hope to kill the score was to sack the quarterback.

Oh, this was gonna be bad. So damned bad.

— IX —

Of course, the jail crew wouldn't tell me whether Tone was there, or at the facility in Yuba, or downtown Riverside, or anything. And were they obnoxious about it. As expected.

"You ain't married, and you ain't blood, so you got no right to know jack-shit," is how this one skinny, stringy-haired bitch put it. Laced in a twang nastier than Texas. What made it worse was, she was right. I wasn't.

I think they wanted me to start screaming and kicking things so they'd have an excuse to arrest me and beat me up. I considered it for a second because that would at least get me in to see him and make sure he's okay. Instead, I gave the bitch a tight smile and said, "Fine, I'll have my lawyer contact you." Then I walked out, very calmly.

A call to Preston got his voicemail; guess he was back in court tearing them a new one. I called Gregory; more voicemail. Must be on the golf course, making up for his missed session.

Then I remembered how I found out when Tone got busted the first time, back in Texas ... a guy I knew who worked in the jail's kitchen. If you ever need information fast, get a grunt who's low on the totem pole to pass the info along. I glanced at my watch. It was closing in on noon. Well ... there's more than one way to crack a detention firewall.

I returned to the food trucks and waited as people in uniforms and suits rolled out to make use of them. Just before twelve-thirty, the gods smiled and there came Dr. Sandoval, the medic who'd treated me last week. This time he was wearing a ratty t-shirt and holey jeans, but no mistaking the bopping walk or silver hair dancing in the hint of a breeze. I bolted towards him, waving and calling, "Yo, doc!"

He looked around, and it took him a moment to remember me. I let him take it; no sense spooking the rabbit.

"Oh, hey," he said, almost smiling. "How's your ribs?"

"Still ache," I said, smiling. "But Advil helps. Can I ask you a question?"

"What about?"

"A guy was brought in, this mornin'. A little shorter'n me. Slimmer. Brown hair. He's my cousin an' on the un-sharp side, an' my aunt's not gonna get here till tomorrow an' she's buggin' me to find out how he is, but that bitch at the front desk won't even confirm he's here. Have you seen him?"

He looked at me like I was crazy. "You know how many people we got in lock-up, from the weekend crap?"

"More'n should be."

He huffed. "No shit about that."

"C'mon, doc, all I wanna know is if he's in there an' he's okay. Okay?"

"Need a better description."

"You follow tennis?"

"Shit, no."

"Soccer?"

"Some."

"You seen pictures of that player the LA team brought in from Scotland?"

"No ... wait, yeah. Yeah. Mackey-something."

"Antony looks like him, only slimmer."

"Wait ... An-tony? Son-of-a-bitch."

Oh, shit. I made myself ask a casual, "Oh?"

"Little fuck damn near bit my head off when I called him Anthony."

"Yeah," I heard myself say, "he's a real dick about his name, like it matters." And I gave him a what-you-gonna-do kind of smile, but my brain was racing through *not again* territory.

Doc nodded and sighed, "He got a lawyer?"

"Yeah, but he's in court, right now."

"Better see if you can get him out."

Fuckin' shit. "C'mon, doc, what you talkin' 'bout?"

"I dunno what they did to that kid, but if they think it's gonna get swept under the rug, again ... "

"What happened!?"

"Oh, the idiots swear he slammed his own head against the table while they were talkin'. Like there ain't tape of it."

I grabbed his arm and snarled, "They BEAT him?"

Sandoval looked at me. "Cousin, huh?" I didn't move. He nodded. "Got a concussion. Gonna need stitches. He's at the ER."

"Which one?"

"Prob'ly the same one you went to but th' report ain't come through, yet."

"Thanks, Doc," I said. "I'm on top of it, now."

I stormed back to the jail's entrance, calling Connie's number. Voicemail, again, but her card had her office number on it, so I dialed that. A receptionist came on and told me she's in a meeting. I gently filled her in with my name and Tone's then said, "Antony St. Lazarre was arrested by Palm Springs police officers, taken to the jail in Indio and brutalized so badly, he's in the hospital with a concussion an' God knows what else. She better handle this, now, 'cause Palm Springs is facin' a huge lawsuit for police brutality. I'll wait for her call."

"This is not something a city councilperson has any control over, Mr. Blaine; you need to consult an attorney — "

I cut her off by snarling, "You tell Ms. Test everything I just told you, and remind her they did the same damned thing to me, last week. Without cause. That's two gay men come to your town only to get arrested by your city's police force, and both of us were beaten! That'll be great publicity for the city." Then I ended the call.

Connie called back within a couple minutes. "Jake, are you sure about this? Because our Chief of Police says — "

"If I don't know it, I don't say," I snapped. "An' they're layin' a claim Tone beat himself up."

"The reception clerk told you this?"

"It's lunchtime. Amazin' what a free meal gets you."

She chuckled. "God, Jake, you're a devious little bastard. That's why I like you. Come over to the side of the angels and join me for dinner. Just for tonight. I can keep secrets, and I have leftover chili."

I made myself chuckle. "Connie, if I could change, it'd be for you and you alone."

She just sighed. "Do you know why they arrested him?"

"Does it matter? It's all bullshit."

"What isn't, these days? We'll be there in twenty minutes."

I waited by the driveway to the jail's back lot. Nineteen minutes later, an unmarked sedan pulled up, a little blue light flashing, inside, Connie exited the passenger side as a guy jumped from behind the wheel and, man, you want to talk about a junkyard dog gone mean? He was old and white haired, with eyebrows that'd never been trimmed in his life, and a face only a basset hound could love. Plus, he made Consuelo look tall, and that's without taking into account her sensible heels. He wore a uniform that had never been pressed and walked like a Pitt Bull spoiling for a fight.

"My guys didn't do this, you little shit," he spat out.

"Did it to himself, right?" The ice in my voice killed his certainty. "Let's see what the tape says."

Connie stepped between us and said, "Uh, Jake, this is Chief Walinski, Palm Springs Police."

"I wanna see Antony," I snapped.

"You related to him?" the mutt snarled.

"Bill," Connie snapped, "don't make this worse than it already is."

He turned his snarl on her. "You want me to just shut up while fellow cops get maligned?"

"Without question," whispered Consuelo. "Let's find out where he's been taken."

I reached the door first so held it open for her. She glided into the warm sweat-socks smell of the building, nodding her thanks ... and giving me a quick pat on the ass. I gave the Pitt Bull a sneer and motioned for him to follow her. He did, trying to cut me with his glare. No butt-pat from him.

The second we walked in, the place snapped to attention in a way that reminded me of *The Three Stooges Do West Point*, pun not intended. Guess even sheriff's deputies pay attention to the chief of police.

Consuelo strode up to this paunchy new clerk and said, "What's the latest on Antony St. Lazarre?"

"St. Lazarre?" he gulped, now looking like a fish trying to breathe open air. "I ... I think he's been taken to the hospital."

"Which ONE?!" snapped out of me faster than I could even formulate the thought.

"Good question," Consuelo said to the clerk.

"I ... I'll find out, ma'am," he stammered.

"Good idea. Which interview room was he in?"

"T-t-two."

Consuelo led us through security into a cubicle that had nothing but a table and four chairs, and the typical two-way-mirror in the wall that fooled nobody, anymore.

And fresh blood on the floor.

BAM! Everything tightened into knots and I tasted metal on my breath. I spun on Walinski and rumbled, "I'm gonna feed your fuckin' balls to the fuckin' vultures, you fuckin' prick."

"Watch your language, you — !"

"Fuck you." I circled him, stooping lower, my glare locked on him as my hands clenched and unclenched. Even in my tunnel vision, I could see fear slip into his piggy little eyes and sense him backing away.

"Jake." Connie said, her voice authoritative but easy. "Back down. You have the high ground, now; don't lose it."

"High ground don't mean shit," I growled back. "Not when you got the whole fuckin' police force out to harass you. That's what his cops've been doin' since I got here. Any excuse to fuck with me. Like they fucked with my uncle, and they fucked with Dion, and with every other gay man and woman I've met in this piece of shit town! Well your guys went too far, asshole!"

"JAKE!" Consuelo yelled at me. "Control yourself or I'll put you in restraints, do you understand me?"

Yeah, like a leash on a dog, I thought, and I bet you'd love it, bitch. I forced myself to ease into a crouch in a corner, my eyes locked on Walinski, my breath rumbling with chuckles. That was as close to control as I could get, but it was enough. Especially since the cowardly little prick kept to the other side of the room, right by the door.

I didn't even look at Connie when she muttered, "Where's the camera?" Nothing mattered except me seeing Tone, right then.

We heard a knock, the door opened and the clerk popped his head in. He whispered something to the Chief, who beckoned Connie over. I rose and followed them from the room.

Still barely under control.

Turned out Tone was in the hospital I'd been taken to. I ran over; Connie and Walinski followed in his car. We found him in the same room I'd been in, curled up on the bed, facing a wall, barely covered by a sheet. I took a blanket and laid it over him ... and saw bloody bandages above his left eye and across his nose ... and his hands held tight to each other ... and his face slack and his breathing ragged and blood crusted his skin ... and I kicked myself a thousand times for not making damn sure he left, myself, as I kneeled by the bed.

His eyes fluttered open and he took a moment to focus on me and sort-of-smile. "Knew you'd come," he whispered.

"What? You gotta nearly get yourself killed, again, to make me talk to you?"

"Can't kill me. I'm too mean."

"Cut it," I said, softly. "How you doin'?"

He shrugged. "Been through worse."

"No shit. What'd they do to you?" I asked.

He fought a smirk, even as he said, "Dunno. We're talking. Then I'm on the floor. Can't see straight."

My hand shook as I touched the bandage on his nose. "You remember what they were sayin' 'fore that happened?"

"One said. I'm going back. To Texas. Had the ... the court order ready. Gonna leave. Soon as Rangers flew in. Leave in chains.

But being a fag. I'd like that. Like I'm into bondage. Guess won't. Happen. Now."

Holy shit, he *did* do it to himself. Just bided his time till one of the assholes was dumb enough to put a hand on his back or shoulder, then BAM! Head to the table-top. Stop the questioning. Stop the whole process. No way they could take him back to Texas, not till the doctor gave an okay. It's nuts, but that's my Tone ... batshit crazy.

"So how far'd you get before they caught you?" He looked at me, confused. "Down the Ten. Headed home?"

"Haven't gone yet. Got me at. Your uncle's. Matt not back."

My stomach flipped. "Matt's drivin' the Chrysler?" Tone gave me a hint of a yes. Oh shit, shit. "Where'd he go?"

"Breakfast. With Lemm."

"When?"

"Almost ten. Told him ... it's okay. Take his time. Wanted to talk to ... had to talk to you. Can't just ... can't just leave you like this."

"What you talkin' about?"

"Jake, don't yell. Hard to think."

I'd whispered. His hands were still clenched. I slipped mine around them, to pull them apart. "Y'know, I think the cop that said that, about the chains ... he's a closet case." I made myself smile. "Was he cute, at least?"

"Dunno. Couldn't get past. Ugly suit. That he's a she."

"Oh. Okay ... uh ... traitorous lesbian?"

"I'd laugh but ... too fuzzy."

"Fuzzy, huh?"

"All over. Stuff. For pain. Better'n the shit ... they gave you." His eyes dug into me. "Jake ... couldn't leave. Not before. Before ... " He stopped, again, then sighed and closed his eyes.

I caressed his ear. "Before what?"

He frowned and his eyes blinked open. "Huh?"

"What do you need to tell me?"

He looked at me, for a moment. His eyes grew sharp then unsure and soft. "Dunno," he finally said. "Uh ... it was ... was something 'bout a ... a body in the desert. On TV." He tried to look straight at me. "Dillon Road."

That third plot of land. I made myself look at Connie, nice and easy, and ask, "They arrested him 'cause they found a body in the desert? Really?"

Walinski rolled his eyes. "He broke probation. And illegals die crossing that desert all the time."

"This far north?" she asked, not so sweetly.

"Connie, it's got nothin' to do with — "

Her hard expression cut him off. He sighed, pulled out his cell phone, and left the room.

I turned back to Tone. He rolled partway onto his back, shifting his neck around. All of a sudden he looked like this scared little puppy who'd finally realized just how big the world was. He murmured, "Jake ... why I gotta lose you ... ?"

Right to the gut. I smirked and said, "Cut it; you know I'm yours forever, no matter how much of a dick you are."

"But I can't let you ... your mom ... no, can't ... "

Good ol' mom, again. "What did my mother say to you?"

"I don't want you hurt. You're better than us ... "

What the ... ? "Tone, what. Did. She say?"

He didn't seem to listen. "Can't believe. She'd rather you ... dead. Than with me."

I went cold. "What do you mean?"

His fingers encircled my arm. "Can't keep this up. Assholes who just ... just want to crush us. Me and you. Everywhere. Don't want you hurt. But look what they almost did. Almost. You hurt. I told her ... warned her ... had a deal."

My throat went dry, and I felt light-headed. His voice trailed off as he tried to regain control of it, but it was too late. He'd finally let slip what my mother really said to him. All the other crap he'd told me, that was just words. His way of hiding what he didn't want to reveal. That he roared out here to protect me because he ... he thought my own mother was behind the attacks on me. That she wanted me dead. But I couldn't see it. Not in my mother. She and I didn't like each other, but for her to go that far in her hate? I didn't believe it.

"Tone," I whispered, "did you tell Mira 'bout this?"

He got a bit tighter and held his breath for a second, and refused to give me an answer. In his world that meant, *Yes*.

So that's why Mira wanted to see me, in Paris. To get me to leave America for the relative safety of Denmark. Where I had family who cared. Meaning she thought it could be a real threat, too. Jesus, Christ, what do you think about something like that? What can you say?

"You came out here to mess everything up," I whispered.

"No ... no ... scared for you ... "

"I know, but you ... you called the cops on yourself, didn't you? That's why you sent Matt away. You worked it so you'd have to stay here. For years. In jail. Like that deal you worked out with my dad, once, where you were gonna go to prison so he'd let me back into his family. Never even seein' how he was usin' you for his own ends. Now you're workin' the same shit with my mother? So I'd have to go back or lose my job? Lose Mira and my brothers and sisters? Lose everything? I'd have to go home."

Again, he refused to answer me. I felt a ton of bricks lift off my soul. Oh dear God, I wanted to kiss him and smack the hell out of him, so damn much. "Why didn't you tell me this?"

Not a hint of wariness in his eyes, now. "She said ... if I broke up with you ... you'd be okay. She knows you. Knows you won't go with anybody else. Nobody after me. And that was good enough ... for her ... but if I told you ... she'd do it ... she'd know and ... don't let her know I ... "

His voice trailed off. I held his hand to my cheek. It was cold. I gently turned him to look at me and said, "But you're the one who needs protection, not me."

"Look what ... almost happened. Twice. I can live with anything, so long as you're in this world. But if you're not ... "

I drew his hand to my lips. "Listen up. We're goin' home, together. Home, you understand me? Not back to Texas. Neither one of us is."

"Jake ... I violated probation ... and your job ... "

"Tone. Trust me on this. Please, trust me."

" ... You sure ... that's what you want?"

"Nobody'll hurt you, again. Understand?"

His eyes opened up to me. No shadows. Only a couple of locked doors. "Always have," he murmured. "Love you. You're my rock. It's me that's shifting sand."

"No more of that."

He almost nodded. Almost smiled. "Better tell Castillo."

"We talked. He says, your folks're pissed about the car."

"Yeah. Told dad I'd bring it back today."

I chuckled. "Obviously, you lied, you little shit."

He sort of shrugged, sort of smiled, and closed his eyes. I stood up and touched my hands to his heart and he sighed.

That's when Walinski came back into the room. Tone looked peaceful, so Connie and I slipped out with the Pitt Bull.

In the hallway, he tried to scowl fear into me by snarling, "What d'you think you're gonna pull, Blaine?"

I figured the little bitch would listen in as Tone and I talked, but it didn't matter. I snarled right back, "What happens between me and Texas is none of your business."

"You were knowingly harboring a fugitive," he growled, like a dog that thinks the louder the bark, the more dangerous it is. "I could have you arrested, right now."

"Do it; see what it gets you."

Connie sighed and said, "Bill ... the body in the desert?"

"Don't know much, yet," he said, still trying to fuck me over with his eyes. "Somebody saw some vultures picking at a hand on the side of the road. Found the rest of him buried in the middle of nowhere, God knows how long ago. Looks like coyotes finally dug him up. Some parts're missing. It's been there long enough that we can't tell what age or race, yet. But cause of death's easy. Goddamn faggots ... "

"Watch it!" I growled right back at him.

Connie got still as ice. "Why will it be easy?" she asked.

"Feet tied; rope around the neck and his other hand. Torn underwear. Homosexual rape and murder, plain and simple."

Oh my God, there it was. The final link. Tiago. We'd found

Lemm's brother. The headline would write itself — *Local Man Raped and Murdered by Homosexuals*.

And thanks to that bit of video on Uncle Owen's laptop, they were going to blame him for it. Make him into another John Wayne Gacy or Freeway Killer or Dean Corll, and the anti-gay hysteria would be carved in stone. This was what everything had been leading up to.

I'd taken too long to figure it out, and now hell was going to have all kinds of fun.

— X —

I stormed outside and called Castillo to detail everything that had happened with Tone, not mentioning my mother, then I gave him Preston's contact information.

"He's in court, most of today," I said, "but he's damn good. He can put a nice long hold on everything."

"Jake, I need Antony back here, soon as possible — "

"No." The word shot out of my mouth. "Not gonna happen, and I don't care what you have to do to stop it."

"Are you out of your mind? We have no legal standing, now."

"For the money I'm payin' you!? Find some!" Then I ended the call.

Connie came out a moment later. "This is not good."

I forced a smile. "And I thought the English had the power of understatement."

"It's not funny, Jake."

"I know."

It was now as clear as a cloudless sky. The harassment, the crap in the papers, PSALMS and Father Paul. This would be the final nail in the gay community coffin. People on the right wing would be able to scream, *Fags rape and murder straight men; they're a danger to our sons,* and the media would fall in line without a hint of questioning it. Some would even claim all serial killers were queer, ignoring the likes of Ted Bundy and The Green River Killer and Jack the Ripper. I'd been run through that kind of hate after Tone revealed the crimes that sheriff's deputy and deputy district attorney had done. Right-wingers go nuts to defend animals who cause an innocent man's death as they blame everything from 9/11 to the economic crash to jock itch on gay men. Too many people never let facts or reality get in the way of a good bit of hate.

Now there would be a long, slow search for more bodies, whether there are any or not, and screams of how this was a ring of devil worshiping queers. Whack-jobs would demand laws to make the evil of homosexuality a crime, again. Attacks would increase and gay tourism would drop off. Some gay men might even get killed and the gay-panic defense would rear its ugly head, once more. It was all primed and ready, and the city would drown in the hate and intolerance. Then would come the cash-vultures to pick the bones of the living and the dead. This was not going to be fun to live through, and I figured what I'd need to do to stop it would be even nastier, but I was primed do it.

A news van drove by and turned down the street leading to the Larsen Center. Reporters were already beginning to haunt wherever they thought they might get a quote. My bet was, they were also lined up at City Hall and the DA's in Riverside and the Police Department. Wasting no time.

Connie noticed it, too, and looked at me in full politician mode ... meaning just try to figure out what she really thinks.

"If you have any idea where Owen is," she said, her voice soft, "tell him to come back, now. Now."

"I'll see what I can do," I said.

She frowned and was about to ask me something else, but Walinski came out. She just followed him to his car.

I drove back to the fortress. No sign of Matt. I didn't think there would be. Everything looked fine in the townhouse. His bag was by the door, his laptop right next to mine. I called his number, again; instant voice mail.

I knocked on Ned's door but got no answer. Then I heard

Geordi's yaps and noticed Meredith standing in her doorway. "He stepped out a little while ago, dear."

"Perfect," I sighed.

"Did you know Antony was taken away by the police?" I nodded. "Why did they do it?"

"Part of their evil plan," I said, trying to sound goofy.

"I wonder," she sighed.

"When did it happen?"

"About half-past ten. A man and a woman."

"Have you seen Matt, today?"

"No, but I've been tending my plants in the back for much of the morning. And talking with Ned. He can be ... tiring, at times."

I nodded. "Thanks."

Then she headed off to take Geordi for his walk.

Okay, time for the push-back to begin.

I left a note on Cliff's door for Lemm to call me, then I drove down to San Sebastian and went into their main office, which was plainer than plain. This little old lady receptionist greeted me with the sweetest, "May I help you?" I'd ever heard.

"I need to speak with Father Paul," I said. I figured he wasn't in; this was just to be as public as possible about everything, from now on.

She seemed genuinely concerned. "Oh, did you have an appointment?"

"No, sorry."

"He's out of the office, at the moment," she said, giving me a sugar rush. "Would you like to leave a message?"

"Sure," I said, keeping my voice just as sweet. She got ready to write. "My name is Jacob Blaine. I'm Owen Taylor's nephew. I believe my uncle is dead, and according to his will I will be executor of his estate. And I will do everything I can to shut PSALMS down and send Father Paul's ass back to Rome."

She blinked, but her voice stayed the same. "Is there a number where he can reach you?"

"No need to contact me. Thanks."

I was headed back to the SUV when Preston called.

"You're keeping me busy, buddy."

"That's my master plan," I said. "I'm backin' your campaign for District Attorney."

"I haven't said I was gonna run, yet."

"When's the election?"

"Aw, primary's still a couple years off."

"Now's the time to make up your mind, and I say go for it. You send me what you want to say and I'll work up some kick-ass fliers and mailers, web-ads, whatever you want. Start it now. What're the limits on contributions?"

"None for countywide office. Not in Riverside."

"Perfect," I said. "You talk to Castillo?"

"Yeah," he said. "I've already notified them we're filing a claim for police brutality. How does seven-hundred-and fifty thousand sound?"

"Ten million wouldn't be enough," I growled back.

"Seven-fifty, it is. They'll probably settle for two-fifty, and after my fee, he walks away with a hundred and fifty K. I'd ask for more, but he does have a record."

"So do I, apparently."

"And an exoneration. Makes a difference."

"Tell that to Philby. Whatever you get 'em to pay for what they pulled on me, after your fee, a third's to your campaign."

He breathed deep. "Aw, Mr. Blaine, you trying to bribe me?"

"Convince you. I'll soon be a property owner in this town, and I have its best interests at heart. I ask zero in return."

"Got you."

"You hear about the body?"

"Yeah ... oh, no, no, wait, you don't think it's Owen!?"

"No, I think they're still runnin' with the story that he split to Mexico. Did you get Philby's evidence on that?"

"He says Owen's car was checked through at the border, but he's quiet about whose passport was used."

"Meanin' it wasn't my uncle's. Keep hittin' him on it, because in a couple hours I think he's gonna tell the world my uncle's now wanted for questioning in a rape-murder."

" ... That body ... ?"

"Preston ... I think it's Lemm's brother."

He gulped in air. "Motherfuckin' son-of-a-bitch."

"Now you sound like a New York boy."

"Jake, you and Matt need to get the hell out of Dodge."

"I can't. Antony's in jail."

"Not good," said Preston, quietly. "Consider the reality. Few months back, some cops get caught committing perjury. The county responds by charging Owen with the molestation of a minor male. He vanishes and they make a huge deal about how he ran off to avoid rape charges ... only now they find a dead man who may've been raped and murdered. A man Owen knew? The city, county, the whole damn GOP in the state's gonna go after everybody who knows Owen, and the Democrats'll run like scared little rabbits. It'll get nasty. Very nasty. Very fast."

"No shit."

"So get thee to Arizona or Nevada, anyplace but here, right now. Because if they can lay any of it on you, they will."

"No."

"Jake!"

"I don't back down from fights, Preston. The motherfuckers want a war? They'll find out what scorched earth really means."

"Jeez ... one of these days you'll have to fill me in on what made you such a mean-assed bastard."

"Not a good idea, buddy," I said, smiling. "I like your curls black."

"Tell that to my wife. She says they make me look like I'm twelve — aw, wait ... did you just make a pass at me? And if you didn't, can I tell her you did? It'll impress her."

"Tell her I'm so hot for you, it hurts, but that I never diss married bliss."

"Yeah, right, she'll believe that." He took a moment then said, "I hope you got my number on speed dial."

"You and six others. And, Preston ... ?"

"Yeah?"

"Don't think you're immune to the hell that's gonna come."

"Jake, I'm from New York; we live for this kind of shit. Should I let 'em keep Antony in jail or fight for bail?"

Shit, there was that. "When's he up for arraignment?"

"Wednesday."

"Bail it is. By then, I should have somebody to keep an eye on him."

"Matt already split?"

"I can't find him. And he was drivin' Tone's car. And it's been impounded."

I heard him take in a deep breath then slowly let it out. "I'll see if I can find out anything."

"Thanks. Hope the next time I talk to you, it's good news."

"Me, too. Later."

I ended the call and headed back to the fortress.

Halfway there, Ned called. "Lemm's not home. He and Matt went out for an early lunch."

"Shit, they could be anywhere."

"I'd call Lemm, but he doesn't have a phone. Call Matt."

"Voicemail."

"Oh. Well ... check Panda Express, first. Over by that Home Depot, near the airport. Lemm has a thing for that place."

I thanked him, ended the call and Googled my way over to a neat little corner shop of painted brick and palm trees. They remembered seeing the guys, even remembered their orders — Beijing Beef for Matt, Sweet & Sour Chicken for Lemm. They sat at a corner table and ate for half an hour then left.

I noticed the restaurant had video surveillance of the dining room, so I talked the manager into letting me watch. Through the front window I saw Matt and Lemm wander out to the Chrysler, at 10:33. They got in and drove off.

That was barely an hour before Castillo called me about the car being impounded. Bureaucrats don't work that fast. But then I saw a new black Camaro follow them. I stopped the tape, my hands cold as ice. I couldn't see the driver but I didn't need to. It was Chet's car. I called Preston.

"I'm getting nothing out of impound, Jake," he said, "and I

gotta be back in court in a — "

I cut him off with, "They were bein' followed by fuckin' Officer Chet."

"They?"

"Matt and Lemm. From a Panda Express."

"What makes you think Morrow's following them?"

"Because Lemm's workin' with him and Harper and probably Philby. He set my uncle up for statutory rape, and — "

"No guessing games, Jake!"

"He told me he did it, and now the sneaky little fuck's helpin' them pull some kind of shit with Matt."

Preston let out a long, brutal sigh. "Listen, Philby coerced him into that confession." He spat the last word out.

"Maybe."

"I got the audio-tape! It goes on for three and a half hours before the kid breaks, and you can hear the other two assholes in the background, making their threats. And they were with the sheriff's department, not Palm Springs."

Wow, Preston. "How'd you get that?"

"I've been working here five years, asshole. I've got contacts. Owen knew I had it; that was our response to Philby's crap. That's why it didn't make sense for him to run off like that."

"He didn't."

Preston let out another long sigh. "Aw ... I know. But until there's a body, that's the official line."

"You get any information on my uncle or his stuff?"

"Philby says they're not done with Owen's computer. He said there was plenty of paperwork in the place for you to go through, so he's in no rush."

"Preston, there's no paperwork in that condo."

"None?" He didn't even begin to believe me.

"Nothing. Nada. Unless you count owner's manuals."

Another long silence, then his voice sounded shaky. "I'll go back to 'em with that. Oh, Jake, Philby's already been on the news, hinting-but-not-saying it was rape-murder and dragging Owen's name into it."

"Philby's an asshole," I snapped.

"You hear me arguing?"

I forced a chuckle, then headed back to the fortress.

I parked in the condo's garage and glanced at my watch. Two-fifty. I decided if I hadn't heard something from Matt by four-thirty, I was dragging the cops into it. I couldn't cover this area by myself. And I'd hit the media, too. Philby's not the only one who can give out interviews.

So I dug into the information Matt had gathered. First off, Tone had made a dozen phone calls to mom's new number with several from her to him over the last few months. None more than three minutes long. Man, I never got a hint of this when I was putting her back in her condo. But then, if she had really wanted me hurt or killed, she had plenty of opportunity to do that the weekend after I got back her townhouse. Obviously, this was just her way of driving me and Tone apart.

As for my uncle, Matt had found the names of a physician and a dentist. Neither one's receptionist would say he saw them, thanks to patient confidentiality, but when I laid out why I was calling and asked if a coroner could call to compare details, both agreed. That's as close as you can get to confirmation. So I called the coroner's offices in LA, San Bernardino and Imperial counties about the John Does and gave them that info.

A bit more discussion with Imperial County made me think the guy down there fit my uncle, too close. He'd been found by a border patrol agent on the side of a road rarely traveled, and had been there a couple of days, being picked at by vultures. Killed by a gunshot to the back of his head. The sheriff figured it was part of the gang warfare across the border, so they weren't all that invested in it. They said they'd get back to me if anything turned up.

A gunshot to the back of the head.

An execution. Of a man in the desert. His body left to the vultures and coyotes.

Dear God, what animals men can be.

— XI —

By this point, it was shifting towards darkness. I slipped into the back yard and wandered around the cacti and succulents to the back fence and called Matt's cell phone, again; still instant voice mail.

The back yard had a great view of the Ten in the distance, tiny cars and trucks humming along it. To the west, thousands of windmills whispered in the breeze, lights flashing on their crowns. The city's street lamps were just starting to glow with a surprising tenderness, and the far mountains were soft in the fading light. Small wonder Owen wanted to keep anyone from building anything that might block this view; it was like living on Olympus.

I was headed back inside to call the cops when I heard the entrance gate open, down below. I jumped back to the fence and caught a flash of a car on the winding driveway so bolted through the townhouse and opened the front door in time to see the Chrysler drive in! I was ecstatic ... until I saw who was behind the wheel. Officer Motherfucking Roy in casual cowboy, this time. He pulled around the circle and parked in front of Uncle Owen's, like he belonged there.

Oh, this was not at all right, but even though my first thought was to drag the prick out of the car and slap him around till he told me what he'd done with Matt, I only closed the door and crouched on the front step. Sure enough, the black Camaro rolled in with Officer Chet behind the wheel, non-cowboy casual, to park behind the Chrysler as Roy got out.

"How'd you get past the security gate?" I snapped at him.

He jolted to look at me. "We've got a by-pass code."

"So what's it gonna be, this time? Tasers at a hundred feet? A forty-five to the brain and throw-down pistol?"

"Are you recording this?" Roy asked.

I held my phone up to show it was silent. "No need to. We already got history. So I hope you ain't stupid-shit enough to pull anything 'cause from now on you need the backup, not me. Or maybe I should hope it."

"You got a big mouth for a stupid faggot," snarled Chet as

he got out of the sedan.

"Ain't me keeps fuckin' up, asshole," I shot back. Then I glanced at Meredith's window. Praise the Lord, she was watching.

Roy asked, "Don't you want to know how I got this car?"

I rose and wandered over to him, saying, "Why would I believe what some piece of shit like you tells me?"

Chet started over to me. "Watch your mouth!"

"Fuck you!" I shot back. "Perjury charges ain't goin' away just 'cause my uncle's not around to push 'em, any more. I'm doin' that, now, on top of what you pulled with me. An' I got two lawyers and the Danish Consulate backin' me up. If you can't see that means you're the one who's fucked, then you deserve what happens to you."

By that point, I was close to Roy, so I turned to Meredith and nodded at Roy. She nodded. He's who Uncle Owen argued with.

That's when Ned scurried out of his unit. "Everything okay, Jake?"

"We'll see," I called back. "Heard anything from Lemm?"

" ... No, have you?"

"I think I'm about to." And I looked straight at Roy when I said it.

Ned called to Officer Chet, "You know he's legal. Lemm's legal. He has legal residency."

"They know," I said. "They just don't give a shit." Officer Chet glared at me so I snarled at him, "And if either one of 'em is hurt, I'll cut your balls off and shove 'em up your ass." No sense letting anybody know I thought Lemm was part of their bullshit. Not yet.

Roy stepped between us. "They're fine, Jake. They're fine."

"It's Mister Blaine, and I know they ain't in jail, so where the fuck are they?"

"They're safe," Roy said. "We just ... we want you to listen, first. Just listen."

"And you think holdin' hostages'll make me make nice?! Iran tried that shit, once; didn't work out so well."

"No one's being held hostage," Roy snapped.

That's when Chet chuckled, "Sounds jealous. Were you

fuckin' that little Jew bastard, too?"

I looked at him, in awe. He wasn't even trying to hide his white sheet. Well ... now I knew what was going on. Lemm was keeping Matt busy for these two assholes while they pulled some other crap, and this little confrontation was to keep me off guard or something. So I pursed my lips at Officer Chat and said in my queeniest voice, "What's the matter, cunt? You want some?"

He acted like he was ready to attack, but he wouldn't, not with witnesses. The pussy.

Roy growled at Chet, "Wait in the car." Chet took a deep breath and returned to the Camaro, sulking. Then Roy turned to me and said, "When Chet arrested your uncle, it was due to miscommunication. He thought Taylor wanted to have sex with him, in public; he misread the signals. Unfortunately, when Chet makes a mistake ... well, he can't admit it."

"You backed him up," I said, forcing myself to keep even and cool.

"You have a copy of the trial transcript?" I nodded, even though I didn't. "Read it. You'll see, I never filed an official report or testified. And Chet said nothing that was strictly incorrect."

"So IAD's gonna whitewash it."

"There was no perjury, Mr. Blaine. The DA's office will not prosecute, and even if they do offer it to a grand jury, they will see to it no charges are recommended. Same for your accusations of police brutality against us. And do not think for one second your recording will help."

"What about the charges against my uncle?"

"Those are immaterial, since your uncle is now a suspect in a murder." Delivered as if that should be a surprise.

"So what shit did you hand him the night he ... uh, he jumped bail? Is that how you put it?"

"I don't know what you're talking about," Roy said.

"Cut it. Too many witnesses put you here."

"Not possible." And his voice was as calm as a placid lake. "I was in Riverside, that night, and can prove it."

"Ass totally covered, huh?" I snapped.

"Nothing needs to be, Mr. Blaine."

That's when it hit me ... he thought I had a copy of the trial transcript. Meaning, he maybe wasn't in on clearing out the paperwork from the condo.

Meaning, maybe I needed to rethink things.

I made myself ask loud and mean, "Where's Matt and Lemm?"

Roy frowned. "Are you backing off your legal threats?"

"No."

He looked at me, trying to read me, then shrugged. "Your choice." Then he handed me the Chrysler's keys ... and gave me the dealership's address.

The dealership? My brain shot straight to wariness.

I glanced at Ned. He was sneering at Morrow. Everything he'd said had been directed at him, not Roy-boy. Bricks began falling into place as it also hit me ... the condo's alarm was set, when I got here. Would the cops have given Tone a chance to do that?

Officer Harper turned to head for the Camaro. I stopped him by whispering, "Roy ... who told you how to find me, the other night? When you arrested me?"

He stopped but would not look at me.

"C'mon," I said, my voice still soft. "How'd you know where I was? Stettlin tell you? Janovich? Somebody else? And consider this — if you weren't here the night my uncle vanished, someone sure wants it to seem like you were. Who could that be?"

He looked at me then continued on to the Camaro. I watched Chet drive them away, the bricks continuing to line up. I turned to find Meredith was still watching. She motioned a question about what it was all about. I just shrugged.

Ned started over. "Jake, are you in some kind of trouble?"

"I'll talk to you, later," I shot back, then I got in the Chrysler and headed for the dealership.

Pissed as hell.

— XII —

Nothing had changed except the gate and door were unlocked. I snuck in, quiet, listening. Heard a bed creaking. I peeked around the corner to see shadows moving in the bedroom cubicle. A camera on a tripod was pointed at them.

I slipped into the private office. The monitors showed Matt lying on the bed, face to face with Lemm, who was having at it. Cameras recorded from two angles. One was a three-quarter-side view of both men, catching a great shot of Lemm's perfect legs and ass contrasted with Matt's trim, hairy ones; the other was a close shot from over Matt's right shoulder, showing Lemm's dick at work. It was so sharp an image, I could tell he was wearing a condom. He'd come prepared ... pun intended.

Well, boys'll be boys.

I checked the lower boxes for Uncle Owen's art supplies. Two of them were full of it. I quietly took them out to the car and put them in the trunk. When I went back in, they were still going ... this time with Matt needing the condom. We really had to get out of that dealership, but I just could not interrupt them.

They finished a couple minutes later and lay there for a couple more, holding each other, caressing, kissing, sipping from a screw-top bottle of wine. The look on Matt's face was beyond blissful, and Lemm's gaze was so focused on him, all I could see was two young men, deep in love.

Which washed this wave of sadness over me. Why couldn't love just be love, not something for politicians and preachers to use for fear and hate and control? Who cared who it was between, so long as it healed your soul and filled your heart and made you part of more than just yourself, even if only for a moment? Why do humans have to be so stupid and vile?

At least now it looked good for Tone and me, again. I could finally see what bullshit I had to fight to keep us both safe. Makes things easier.

Lemm finally got off the bed to head off-camera. I turned

just in time to see him come into the room. He yelped but didn't even try to cover himself. Man ... Matt scored.

Matt appeared behind him, a moment later, wrapped in the sheet. He grimaced and said, "Jake! How'd you find us?"

I just shrugged.

"Look, I ... I ... I'm sorry, but Antony said he needed to talk to you before he left and he was gonna call me, and I ... I figured if he didn't have the car then it'd be okay to leave him alone and if things didn't go right, I'd — "

I cut him off with, "Where's your phone?"

"In my jacket."

"It's powered down."

"Shouldn't be. Lemm, it was on when you put it back, right? Did Antony call? Aw, jeez, is he pissed? I was wondering why it was taking so long and — "

"Did you come here straight from lunch?"

"Jake, I'm really sorry. This was a good place to just talk and not be bothered and I really thought things were going good between you and Antony and — "

"They are, Matt. Everything's fine." I looked at Lemm, again. "How'd you get in?"

Lemm shifted to wary, his eyes locked on me. "Ned knows of this place. And the code. And a key. In a hole, in one of the window frames. He knows I wish to be alone with Matt. For a little while. For you to be alone with Antony."

Matt all but gleamed at him with happiness.

I nodded. "Then you guys haven't seen the news."

"We have other things to do," said Lemm. He put a gentle arm around Matt. Matt shared the sheet with him.

I sighed. This was not going like I thought it would. I focused on Lemm. "So you don't know about the body they found. Buried in the desert. Guy my age. My build. Black hair."

Lemm looked at me. His face went bloodless. He knew my meaning. That's when I slipped a knife into his heart and twisted it. "Way to go, Lemm. You may've just helped the guys who put your brother in his grave, and who're tryin' to set my uncle up for his murder."

He rocked. Matt steadied him. "Jake, what the hell?"

I shifted around so he could see the monitors.

"They're still runnin'," I said. "Your idea, Lemm?"

He paid me zero attention. Man, all the walls were down and he was close to being sick, and I could see the full impact of my words crashing against his soul.

Maybe I was wrong about him.

"No ... mine," Matt whispered. "I thought it'd be fun. Cut a copy. Prove I was with a guy like Lemm and ... and ... "

I nodded as I got up and went to them. "Can you shut down the system? Pull it apart?" He nodded. "Do it."

He looked at me, torn. "Why?"

"I don't want it here for the cops to find."

"Cops?"

He saw I meant it so let me take Lemm off him then bolted under the desk, taking that sheet with him. I guided Lemm from the office and back into the bedroom.

"Get dressed. We have to leave."

He wasn't listening. I shoved him on the bed. He bounced to his side, still lost.

"Listen to me, Lemm! I think Philby knows about this place. They may be gettin' a search warrant, right now. We have to be gone when they come lookin'. You guys're lucky they aren't already here. Get dressed."

His eyes grew dark and wet. He shook his head. "No. No. Is not my brother. Who ... could hurt ... Tiago? Is not my brother. Is not. Is NOT! IS NOT!"

I yanked him up. Slapped him and snarled, "Get dressed!"

Didn't help. He just curled up on the mattress and a soft moan whispered from deep within. No way could he function, so I slipped his feet into his pants then put on his shoes. No socks. I forced the pants up to his hips. He began to fight me so I slapped him, again, then I maneuvered an arm into a shirtsleeve and leaned forward to angle for the other one ... and froze.

There were whip marks on his back. They were so light, they

hadn't shown up on the video ... but no question what they were.

I made him look at me. "Lemm ... what's this? Who did this?"

I touched his back. He paid me no attention. I finished slipping his shirt on. Matt came in just as I was buttoning it.

"All done," he said as he grabbed his briefs. "That server was hooked up to a service. They'll still be able to find out what's on there. You gotta tell me what this is about."

"In the car," I said.

"But I'm in the Chrysler."

I held up the keys. "Harper had it."

Matt froze. "Harper!? How'd he get the keys?!"

"Lemm."

"What? No way! We were together — "

"Matt, when you guys got into the dealership, did Lemm forget somethin' in the car?"

Matt nodded. "The wine."

"After he borrowed your phone, right?" I made Lemm put on his jacket. "Harper followed you. Lemm gave him the keys and turned off your phone so I couldn't get hold of you, then they called Tone's folks to tell them the car was impounded."

"But ... why would they do that?"

"Keep Uncle Owen's condo empty. Give 'em time to plant something."

"But Antony was at the — "

"He's in jail." Matt gaped at me. I shrugged. "He got busted about ten-thirty. You got your clothes and his?" Matt nodded. "Let's get that video equipment out of here."

Matt was slipping on his shoes, so I pulled Lemm to the door, but he jerked away, muttering in Spanish, "*You're lying. You're lying. My brother is not ... he isn't ... you're lying.*" He rounded the cubicle like a wounded animal, primed for attack.

Matt gently made him look at him and whispered, "Shh, shh. C'mon, let's go. We have to go ... "

"He ... he lies. He lies. He wants to hurt me. He lies."

"Yes, he's lying. He is. C'mon."

Lemm let him guide him down the hall and out the door, still murmuring, "He lies. He lies. He lies." The two glances he shot at me were vicious in their anger.

Man, I felt like a shit. Those marks on Lemm's back — I didn't even know half his story, and figured half of what he *had* told me was bullshit. But now I wondered if he was cannon fodder, like his brother. If maybe he driven from his home to make it easier for him to vanish into a grave. His death would perfect to lay on my uncle. Who wouldn't lust after a beautiful kid like him? And the whole focus would be on the homosexual horror of his end ... add to the gay serial killer crap.

But if the official story was that my uncle's hiding in Mexico, wouldn't a fresh body on his land suggest he's still in the US? Or would Philby's claim his car crossed the border turn out to be fake. Or would they suggest he'd handed it over to someone else to take it to give a false trail, so he could continue to lurk and murder in the area? Giving the cops an excuse to search the home of everyone Uncle Owen had ever known or dealt with. Ian. Ned. Cliff. Dion. Kent. Billie. Beth. God knows who else. And so long as there was no proof of where he was or even if he was alive or dead, they could keep on doing it. Build on the harassment. Destroy anyone they wanted to.

And the way things stood, right now, I wasn't sure I'd be able to stop them.

— XIII —

Matt and I loaded the server, cameras and monitors into the Chrysler's trunk and front seat, then I wiped the place down as best I could. I think I got everything. Of course, their DNA was all over the room, but since neither one was in the databank and it was mingled in with God knows how many others, I decided not to worry about that. When I locked the door, I had Matt put the key back in the same place, using the tail of his shirt to hold it so he wouldn't leave any fingerprints. Matt got in the back, with Lemm, and we split.

When we were back on Palm Canyon, I called Preston.

"Jake, c'mon, I haven't had time to get anything more out of the DA's office, yet."

"I found Matt. And Lemm. And I've got the Chrysler. We're headed back to my uncle's. Listen, Preston, you better let Philby know you've heard my uncle owns some property. Emphasis on heard."

"He knows about the apartments and — "

"No, this is an abandoned dealership, he supposedly ... and I mean, supposedly also owns, along with two vacant lots next to it, and another one someplace, but I can't figure out where."

"He does? So what?"

"So it's better that you give him the information than if he gets to strut about how he discovered some secret crap about Uncle Owen. And seriously, emphasize that you never heard of it, before, and make damn sure he understands that it does not sound right, to you. In fact, send him an e-mail. Keep everything with the time noted on it."

" ... Okay. What's the background?"

"I ran across some papers that made no sense and looked into 'em and found references to it, and I told you."

"Jake ... what's so hot about the dealership?"

"Just tell the prick. He already knows about it, so, you'll be glad you did. Trust me."

"Why do I not, this time?"

"Preston ... does privilege apply if your client is ... oh ... committing a crime?"

"Aw, shit. What's the address?"

I gave it to him. "By the way, you know about the guys who committed suicide? Two gay men, this year?"

"Uh, no ... but what's that got to do with anything?"

"I'll make you a bet, Preston. Within the next forty-eight hours, those two guys'll be dragged into this as participants whose guilt became too great. Or maybe as victims, if it can be proven they had sex before they died. If I win, you run for DA and fire Philby's ass."

There was silence. "And if you lose?" he finally asked.

"What d'you want?"

"Aw ... double my fee?"

"Triple. Now get the coroner's reports on those two."

"I dunno if I can. I've never had to mess with them."

"C'mon, you're from New York. You'll figure it out."

"Okay, um, first I need to know the names and dates."

"I'll text 'em to you; info's on my phone."

" ... Okay, talk to you later."

He ended the call so I tossed my phone back to Matt. "Send Preston the info about the suicides." I finally noticed Lemm was now weeping. "Matt ... ?"

"I got this, Jake," he muttered back. "Don't worry."

"Did you see those marks on his back?"

Matt nodded. "Guy he used to be involved with. Got a little carried away."

"See if you can get him to understand — I think I know who killed his brother. If he wants to help rip 'em apart ... "

Matt just nodded. Then I heard the whoosh that said a text had been sent and he handed my phone back to me.

I parked in the driveway and we both guided Lemm from the back of the car. He was too lost in grief to pay attention. Matt wanted to take him upstairs, but I needed to know Lemm's part in this before I could change the narrative, so Lemm curled next to Matt on the couch, halfway between weeping and moaning. Matt kept caressing him.

I bolted over to Meredith's and rang the bell. Geordi did his yapping thing till she opened the door.

"Jake, did you find — ?"

"Do you have some alcohol? Like Tequila or Vodka or Bourbon or somethin'?"

"Brandy?"

"Anything stronger than white wine."

"Hasn't Owen anything?" she asked, heading back inside.

Wait — white wine in the fridge with mixers but no alcohol in the bar? "Was he tryin' to cut down on the booze?"

"Hardly," she called back. "But then, I never saw him with a drink before six, or ever get drunk."

"Did they drink a lot during GALAIATH meetings?"

She brought me a bottle, saying, "Ian always brings his own. Cliff barely drinks, but Connie and Ned love that beer. Dion has to drive, so he doesn't."

I took the brandy and said, "Thanks. Would you come with me? Bring Geordi. Please."

She didn't even blink, just closed the door and followed me back into Uncle Owen's, Geordi on her tail.

She stopped at seeing Lemm. "What's wrong, dear?"

He almost looked at her. Good sign.

"Have you been followin' the news?" I asked her as I headed for the kitchen.

"Yes, it's awful ... "

"Tiago ... " I whispered, but couldn't finish.

She caught it, instantly, and sat beside Lemm. "Oh, you poor baby," she murmured as she guided him into a hug. He let loose with sobs. Soaked her shoulder. She held him and stroked his back and kept whispering, "Poor baby."

I brought a glass of the brandy over and she took it. And she drank it. Then she said, "Another, please."

I poured it. She gently moved Lemm back, whispering, "Here, just a sip of this. Just a sip. Come along."

It took her a couple of tries, but he finally accepted the glass and sipped a little and choked on the sharpness of it and coughed. Then she patted the couch and said, "Geordi."

The little mutt jumped up and settled in Lemm's lap. Without thinking, Lemm began to pet him, bringing him back to earth's orbit. He handed the glass back to Meredith, and she downed what was left.

"Much better, dear," she smiled.

I squatted in front of them and whispered, "Lemm, did you and Harper have something goin' on?"

"Jake!" Matt snarled.

"I'm sorry," I said, "but I need to know this, now."

"What ... ?" Lemm murmured, still lost.

Matt hesitated then turned back to Lemm. "Buddy ... tell us about Harper," he whispered.

Lemm looked at Matt, his voice barely audible. "It is from him ... that Tiago knows ... I do not like the woman."

That jolted me. "Roy told him?"

Lemm shook his head. "Roy hurts me. Tiago saw ... my back is cut and ... makes me to tell him what I have done. Calls me puta."

Whore. Shit. "Did you meet at the dealership?" Lemm nodded. "He knew how to get in?"

Lemm barely nodded. "We go there very late. No one is to be seen."

"He did this more than once?"

Lemm nodded. "But I do not like this ... and Tiago is angry, so I stay away from him. He is angry with me for this."

"Roy is?"

Lemm nodded. His left thumb rubbed into the palm of his right hand as he kept on with, "For the rent ... Roy knows I need money. So he says, if I will let him use me. Be hard with me. One time. He will pay me. I think, I know him so it will be okay ... but I see what he plans to do and he ... he scares me and I ... I run away. When Father Paul tells everyone of how I am, Roy will give no more help to me. He does not want people to see us together. So I come to Ned and Cliff ... " His voice trailed off.

"You could've gone to Dion's."

He took in a deep breath and looked at me. His eyes were pools of sadness and pain. "If I live there, Father Paul will cry about the children."

Matt frowned. "Lemm, Harper dumped on you; why're you helping him?"

Lemm turned to him. "Ned says Roy came to him, and says the car is stolen. The police are to come for Antony."

"He knew before Tone was arrested?" I asked.

"Ned tells me," Lemm said, his eyes locked on Matt, "if you are with him. They take you. To the jail. I say I will get the car from you. He says this. He says Roy still likes me. So will help me in this."

Matt couldn't keep a tender smile from his face. "You were worried about me?"

Lemm nodded.

"So the guy calling you from the bank?" I asked. He looked at me, confused. "About the rent and Owen? That was just bullshit?"

He nodded, glimmers of fury and hate in his eyes. "Ned told me how the bank will work. He wants to be with me, but I have seen what he likes, and I am still afraid from Roy, and I say no. So he lies to me. Did he kill my brother?"

"Ned?" I whispered.

"Roy."

"I dunno. Maybe."

Lemm pulled back to sit up straight, his eyes locked on me. "Did he do to him what he ... he planned for me?"

"I don't know."

"When did he ... die ... ?"

"I ... I think it was back when he vanished."

Lemm nodded and absently scratched Geordi's ear. "So ... he did not run away from me. I think he did. Because I am ... I am a puta. He is angry with me. Yells at me. Gloria, she tells him he is wrong ... but then he is gone and people say he runs because he does not want Cara, and I say nothing. I ... I hurt from his words and I hate him but is not true he runs from me ... "

He lost it. Matt pulled him close, whispering, "Buddy ... buddy," as he all but threatened me with his eyes to let him take him upstairs. I nodded. Meredith started to take Geordi, but Lemm cradled the mutt so gently, as he rose, she left him.

As Matt guided them upstairs, I said, "Lemm, I'm sorry."

No reaction.

Man, I was a prick. A stupid fucking prick.

"I think someone should stay with him, tonight," said Meredith. "I'll get my pajamas. Matt and I can spell each other."

"You don't have to."

"Jacob, I spent half the day discussing plants with Ned in the back yard. Compared to that, this will be wonderful."

I nodded, grabbed the DVD Matt had burned of the porn

video and walked her back to her townhouse.

"This is a real mess," I muttered.

"Do you care to explain it?"

"Lemme talk to Ned, first."

"You don't really think he had something to do with this?"

"I dunno. I thought Lemm was in the middle of it all. Now?"

"He was very close to Tiago. Is it certain the body's his?"

"Not yet. Just a gut feeling. How long have Ned and Cliff known each other?"

"Ned moved in about three years ago. They've always been very quiet. Very pleasant. Very ... "

She wandered on to her home. I waited till she was inside before I headed up to Cliff's.

Now the fun was about to start.

— XIV —

Before I got to Ned's door, I could see him through the front window, watching the evening news. I knocked on it and he jolted. It took him a moment to get up and let me in.

"Have you heard?" he asked. I nodded. "Where's Lemm?"

"My place."

He took a deep breath and nodded. "Matt. They were sitting on the front step talking till like three in the morning. And his eyes've been happy and alive since they met ... and he's so beautiful when he's like that."

I just nodded.

He went to the bar and poured out a whiskey. "Want one?" I shook my head. He downed half the glass. "Cliff's working late, running tech on this story. He may not be home at all, tonight ... " He nodded to the screen.

It showed a telephoto shot of the coroner's wagons and cop cars in the middle of an open area of desert, tents behind them. A small window in the lower right corner had a news-chopper shot of a tent that was protecting the grave. The announcer yammered on and on about how there might be more bodies, according to unnamed sources, and how police and the district attorney's office were being tight-lipped, his tone breathless. Philby's narrative, to the max, and the news was backpacking for him. I had to work fast if I wanted to change the course.

"Does Cliff know a reporter I can talk to?" I asked.

"Why would you want to?"

"I got information for 'em."

Ned cast me a wary look but said, "Lemme see."

He called Cliff, who suggested a woman named Sousie Fornia, who was camped at city hall. He agreed to ask if she'd call me. I was happy for that much.

Ned ended the call and looked back at the TV. Nothing had changed. "It's sickening," he muttered.

I looked at him. Standing slouched, half-drunk, wearing lazy sweats, it was hard to picture him in those chaps and harness, having fun as Cliff fake-abused him. I finally sighed, "Why did you tell Roy Harper about Lemm and Matt?"

It took Ned a moment to understand what I asked. He finally looked at me and growled, "What makes you think I did?"

"'Cause somethin's goin' on between you and officer Roy?"

He glared at me, long and hard. I didn't move, so he sighed and said, "Okay ... Cliff's not really into my kind of games, but Roy loves to play. And we had lots of fun ... till he fixated on Lemm. I thought, if he knew the kid was interested in somebody else, we'd play some more. Didn't work out that way, did it?"

"So that story about him bustin' you ... ?"

"Honey, how do you think we met?" he sighed, then downed more of his whiskey. "After I was arraigned, he called me. And he fucked me every way from Sunday. That's how good I am." And his eyes all but tore my clothes off.

"You got it on with a guy who busted you without cause?"

"Oh, come on, you've seen him. Even had him ride your ass."

"Not exactly the same thing."

"Only because Chet was there," he purred, then he leered, "But if he hadn't been? And with you strapped down? Who knows?"

"Oh, shit. Just ... tell me about the dealership."

He grew more still. Did not look at me. "What's to tell?"

"I don't have time for this dance, Ned." I held up the DVD. "Start your player; I wanna show you somethin'."

He looked at me, saw the DVD and chuckled. "Okay, okay, now you know why I don't have to do the nine-to-five tango."

"You should see this 'fore you talk."

He frowned at me then took his remote and shifted to the player. I popped it in ... and there was Tiago's ass being mauled. Ned's jaw nearly dropped to the floor. He did not move as he watched the fingers tear at the cotton briefs and Tiago jolt and slur, "No — don' — " as the image froze and went to black.

Ned gasped for air, like a fish. "Was that Owen's hand? On Tiago's ass? How'd he get him? The guy's straight. I mean, I offered him money and he wouldn't even do a solo or pose for me, but he's letting Owen grope him? The son-of-a-bitch. Shit. Now it makes sense. Why he was so nice to 'em both. Beer and food and low rent for the bronze beauties — "

"Ned, that's not my uncle in that video." He cast me a sneer of disbelief, so I held up my right hand. "Look at this hump on my middle finger." It took him a moment to focus. "It's an artist's hump. Comes from resting your pen, pencil or paintbrush there as you use it, for years. My uncle had one just like it; the hand in that video does not."

Ned played the video, again, then froze the frame. He shook his head. "But ... but who else could it be? That's not Roy's hand."

"I know; he bites his nails. And it's not Cliff's or Ian's or anybody else's we know. So can you think of anyone who might know Roy's gay?"

"No ... nobody. He's one of those, quote, straight guys, end quote, who thinks so long as he's being sucked off and the one doing the fucking, he's not a fag. That's how deep in the closet he is. Hell, he was even married, once. And yes, Cliff knew. He was happy I was happy ... and played safe."

"How long's it been goin' on? This warehouse deal?"

It took him a moment to answer. "'Bout a year ago, we leased the building. Fixed up the inside. Roy even put money in on it. I used to do porn, in San Francisco, so I know people. They sent us production companies interested in renting the place for a couple days. New location. Decent rates. Gay or straight. Don't mind kink. Nice and private."

"Till the right wing nuts find out."

"Jake, shooting porn's not illegal in this state. In fact, it's the biggest business there is, short of the government."

"You really make that much?"

"Nearly two million, on rents and a percentage of sales."

"Bullshit."

"No shit. Companies come out here because LA requires they use condoms for fuck scenes and San Francisco's getting harder and harder to deal with."

"Barebackin'. Philby'll run crazy with that detail."

"He won't do a thing."

Whoa! "Is he a partner?"

Ned shook his head. "Try Samantha Fucking Ginty."

I laughed. "Are you fuckin' crazy?"

"It was her idea. When I got busted, she found out who I was. So I guess it got her little brain cooking. She connected me with the dealership, and if Philby ever did get interested, she'd redirect his focus. All for a percentage. Can't get better insurance."

"Who else knew about this?"

Ned took another swallow. "Just OT and Associates. They made the money look clean."

"But it went through Palm Valley West. Were they part of the deal?"

"Please. With that uptight bitch heading it?" He finally focused on me. "Why do you care?"

"C'mon, there's you, Cliff, Harper, and Ginty. So who else was involved? Is it Lawton? He helpin' you out?"

"He couldn't piss without detailed instructions."

"What about Grace Nieri? She runs the bank, so ... "

"Who fucking cares? You gone all moral on me?"

"Ned, open your stupid-assed eyes; this is a set-up. Who was your other partner?"

"You're crazy." He stormed to the door and opened it. "You should go!"

I grabbed the remote from him and played the DVD, again. "Look closer," I snarled. "Where do you think I found this? On the editing system in the dealership. Just this snippet."

"Our system? But that's not ... that wasn't what we ... um ..." He returned to the TV, his eyes locked on the image. "Oh, fuck, that *is* the bed in the cubicle ... "

I played it, again, and said, "Yeah. It looks like you tried to erase it but didn't get it all. When I first saw it, I thought Tiago was drunk. Now I think he was drugged. I think moments after it was shot, he was killed." Ned shot me a look of disbelief so I shifted into a growl to say, "Guess where his body is."

Ned jolted, grabbed the remote and slammed back to the news coverage, then he glanced between me and it, his face losing color by the second. Suddenly, he jumped for the kitchen. Barely made it to the sink before he hurled. I didn't move a muscle. Just let him do his thing until he was back in control. It took a while, and the stink was nasty, so I let him clean up, too. Finally, I heard him pour himself another drink, and could tell from the clinking glass his hand was shaking. He gulped it down; poured another. I ejected the DVD and returned it to its jewel case.

"No, that can't be, that can't be," he gasped. "Oh, sweet Jesus, we were just having fun in the place and ... and Jesus Christ. Snuff? Snuff films!? Did Harper go too far — ?"

"Too far in his S and M games? Has he, before?"

Ned ignored me. "No ... Roy bites his nails ... "

"You're supposed to think that's my uncle, since he's not around to prove otherwise. Who else were you partnered with?"

"No, we ... we're fine ... we ... we're okay ... Ginty will ... "

"Ned! There's a murder connected to that dealership now! Don't you understand that? There is no protection for you or anybody associated with that place."

"No, she said ... " His face went even whiter. It was finally cracking through his thick skull. "No ... Jake ... get out, please, just go! I ... I have to think ... have to — "

"Then DO it! Use your brain! Philby's probably already connected the dealership to my uncle!"

"Owen had nothing to do with the place!"

"You think that bastard gives a shit?!"

"Oh, God, you're right," he muttered, close to being drunk. "Oh, shit, it's all fucked up. I should've known it'd get fucked up. My whole life's been one fuck-up after another and now this. But the money was so good, and we didn't have to do anything but keep the place clean and equipped and ... and ... "

"Who else is involved, Ned? Tell me. Maybe I can deflect everyone's attention to them."

He looked at me with this sick, scary sneer on his face as he said, "Oh, you think you can, you arrogant prick? You gonna blame everything off on our silent partner?" He giggled. "All right, let's see what you can do. Because you know you'll be accusing? One of God's own chosen. The second fucking coming of Christ. The Lord of Angels. Also known as: Father fucking Paul, of San Sebastian."

And another brick fell into place.

PART FOUR

I burst out laughing, because it was perfect. According to Ned, Father Paul had heard rumors about how the dealership was being used, so calmly parked his sainted ass on Ned's couch and talked him into sharing the profits.

"*Think of it as a tithe*, is how he put it," said Ned. "And, since the money would come through OT and Associates, he'd have plenty of deniability. I handled the books, so Cliff ... he never knew how much we really made. I never mentioned Father Paul."

"Why'd you go along with it?" I asked.

"He said a couple of the girls who ... um ... participated were not of age, so he'd have us charged with kiddie porn."

"Were they?" Ned wouldn't look at me. "Do you have any proof that shows anybody else was involved in any of this?"

"It all went through OT and Associates," he murmured.

"Wanna bet their records don't reflect reality?"

"Oh, Jesus, oh shit, we're dead. Cliff. Oh, shit." He poured another drink. I'd stunned him out of being drunk and he wanted back in. "Cliff bought the cameras off the station when they upgraded. They'll be able to connect them — "

"I've got the cameras." Ned looked at me. "And the server and monitors and everything."

He bolted over to me. "We've got to get rid of them!"

"No fuckin' way! They'll figure out he had cameras, so we have be able to hand 'em over, when they ask. What we do is redirect 'em to what's really goin' on."

"Can you ... can you do that?"

"I dunno. But I can make it hell on earth for 'em if they keep pushin' this crap. So tell me everything from the minute you started using the dealership."

He nodded and unloaded. How many videos they'd made and when. Which companies. How much money he'd allotted to Ginty, Harper, and Father Paul. Showed me he had DVDs and files full of releases. All of it. He even tossed in how he'd been asked by Harper to keep Meredith busy in the back yard while they slipped into my uncle's townhouse. Now he could see how he'd been used, and he was a drunken wreck by the time we were done.

I dragged him upstairs into his bed. He was so out of it, I think he was snoring before his head hit the pillow. Then I hurried back to the townhouse. Meredith was heating up Connie's chili, thank God; I hadn't eaten since breakfast.

"Good thing you had some on hand," I said.

She smiled. "I hopped over to Connie's."

"Did you tell her about Tiago?"

"No," Meredith said, shaking her head. "I think it best to wait for verification. I honestly cannot handle more than one breakdown a night. This is the remains from Friday's pot. She always makes so much at one time."

"That's the trick to it. Cook it by the barrel, for days. It reheats good." I hesitated. "How ... how's Lemm?"

"Matthew's with him. And Geordi. It takes time to heal from a loss like this."

I nodded. "So, Connie's home?"

"No, she'll be at city hall, all night. I called her, and she said to take what I needed." I must've looked at her funny, because she added, "I have a key to her home. She, Owen, Cliff, and I swapped them, years ago. I water their plants when they're away. They take care of mine and Geordi, when I need to be gone. It was rather like a family."

"Do you still have yours for this place?"

"Yes. Do you want it back?"

"No. Just checkin'. Meredith, do you mind — can Matt and Lemm stay with you, for a couple days?"

She blinked. "They seem fine, where they are."

"Tomorrow the cops're gonna show up here with a search warrant, and they're gonna tear the place apart. I don't want Lemm to have to deal with that."

"Why would they?"

"Because Philby wants to blame that dead man on my uncle."

She hesitated then shrugged. "We'll take him over once he's had something to eat."

"You are perfection."

She smiled and said, "I know."

An hour later, after all but force-feeding Lemm some food, we moved everything of Matt's to Meredith's. Lemm let us guide him into her place and sit him at the counter, then she gave him a slice of turkey bologna and he absently fed a very happy Geordi. He almost smiled at the mutt's antics.

I was almost out the door when Lemm stopped me with, "Jake ... Matt says I may help you against my brother's killer."

I turned and looked straight at him. "Yes."

He nodded, vaguely. "Tell me how."

It looked like he was drifting back to life, so I said, "You willin' to look through some photo albums? Tell me who you recognize, in there?" Another vague nod. "Good. Lemme get 'em."

He found a picture of Harper in the first one, back to the camera and hair bleached half-blond. He was talking to a couple of men, one black, one white, both muscle queens. You couldn't see much of his face, but he wore a white wife-beater and it revealed part of a burn scar on his right shoulder; that was enough for Lemm.

"I have seen this skin," he said. "He tells me it happens when he is very young."

Meredith also looked at the photo and frowned. "This is five, maybe six years ago."

I removed it from its sleeve and looked on the back. No date or name. "How can you tell?"

"The hair styles."

"That cop's gay?" Matt asked. "But how could he keep that quiet, especially if he partied here? Someone'd recognize him."

"See if you can find a picture of his face," I said. "Can you find out what Grace Nieri's maiden name was? Or Married?"

Matt agreed. I headed back to the condo.

It was after ten when Sousie Fornia called. She was still haunting city hall for a statement, but the second she learned I was Owen's nephew ... and knew things Philby's office wouldn't share ... she all but teleported to the townhouse with an otter of a cameraman to get set up in time to be live on the 11pm news.

We used the living room. I explained who I was, then I said it looked like my uncle's body was at the coroner's office in Imperial

County, and had been since August 4th, as a John Doe. Murdered. No ID. Found by a border patrol agent on the side of a road not traveled much.

"Have you verified the body?" she asked.

I said, "I'm goin' down, tomorrow. Give 'em DNA."

"Assistant District Attorney Philby claims to have evidence Owen Taylor crossed into Mexico."

"As I said, the body was found without identification, so it may not be him. But Mr. Philby only has proof his car crossed into Mexico, so he may have been carjacked and killed. Problem is, Philby's so locked onto the idea of my uncle runnin' away to avoid some bogus charge about underage sex, I don't think he even checked. My uncle's attorney, Preston Niemczyk, asked for any and all additional evidence, but the prosecutor's office ignored him."

"Can they do that, with discovery?"

"There's always ways to delay and obscure things."

"I've also heard homosexual pornography ties into this situation, somehow."

So they'd already started leaking that. Okay. Time to feed her something verifiable to link the gossip to. "I've heard that, too, and I've been lookin' into it. I think my uncle was bein' set up."

"Set up?" The look on her face was simple — Bullshit.

"What I've heard is, the videos were shot in an abandoned buildin' somewhere in Palm Springs. I've even heard that my uncle owned this buildin' ... like a vacant warehouse or strip center, or somethin' ... but there's no record of it. In fact, at the time he supposedly bought the buildin', he wasn't even able to get a loan to purchase one of the townhouses that had gone up for sale, here; his debt to income ratio was too high. Looks like someone's spreadin' lies against him 'cause he pushed for gay rights. They figured the best way to stop him was to link him to pornography, by way of gossip. I think he found out who it was and confronted them, and they killed him. And left his body to feed the vultures on the side of a desert road." I added a hint of a quiver to my voice, to really sell it.

Sousie's bullshit look was gone. "Do you have any evidence of this?"

"Just that nobody has anything to connect my uncle to the

production of any videos. No contracts. No e-mails. No monetary transfers to him. Nothin' like that. Nothing. That and the fact that his total income could be accounted for through the rents he collected and investments he'd made makes me think somebody's cynically usin' this ... this horrifyin' situation to further their own political agenda."

"He could've had another bank account."

"Where? I can't find one, so if you know where it is, tell me. Please. I'm executor of his estate so I will need to know. And consider this, Warren Philby's office has a history with my uncle, and he was plannin' to help someone run for DA. Anything Philby could use to discredit my uncle could also be used to discredit whoever he had backed for DA."

"That ... sounds pretty conspiratorial."

I slipped into deep Texas to say, "Oh, honey, it's just politics, down and dirty. Nothin' new 'bout it. After all, Karl Rove got George Bush elected governor of Texas partly by spreadin' nasty rumors 'bout Ann Richards."

"That was over twenty years ago. Are you old enough to remember that?"

"Not the election, but I remember my grandmamma callin' Bush and Rove a couple of high school brats angry 'cause the cool girl wouldn't let 'em cop a feel."

Sousie laughed. "Your grandmother said that?"

"Oh, yeah. But a lot more graphically. Mom was horrified an' took me straight home, but I was already scarred for life."

I winked at her and she giggled. And we kept up a bit of flirtation through the rest of the interview, where I pointed out all the good things my uncle had done. Soon as Sousie's bit was over, Philby was fielding questions about it from reporters, and he was anything but pleased.

That's when Father Paul gave his own interview on how evil it was that good decent boys — and he emphasized *boys* as much as he could — might have been tortured and killed for someone's demonic pleasure, aiming his words at my uncle, suggesting he was still around. It was sickening.

The next morning, I heard from Imperial County's Coroner, way too fast for my liking, but Uncle Owen's dentist had sent over copies of his x-rays. That body had long been cremated, but they matched the John Doe's information ... every bit of it.

Every goddamn bit of it.

They were satisfied so, if I wanted, I could come down to pick up his ashes and a death certificate. I left the second I got off the phone, and took the Chrysler; I threw my satchel and jacket over the equipment in the front seat.

I zipped past a couple of news crews setting up at the entrance to the fortress. One guy tried to stop me but I just pointed to my watch and whooshed right by him. They'd be there when I came back, and I'd make damn sure they knew everything.

It's a nearly two-hour drive to El Centro, past the Salton Sea. A long, blank, straight, open road for miles and miles. Nothing but desert, with mountains hemming you in and so many warm shades of brown, red, and yellow, it's like the world had never heard of green and cool. Little billboards here and there. Occasional buildings that looked abandoned. But no buzzards in the sky. Nothing that could distract me from the fact that my uncle was dead for one reason and one reason only ... he was a fag who wouldn't play nice with the power-broker-bullies.

Nothing new about that, either. In prison I did a lot of reading ... mainly history ... and learned how the Railroad Barons were notorious for hiring thugs to run people off their land, or even kill them, if need be. Civilization hadn't made it better; look at Ford v. the unions and the GOP v. the world. Nor would anything ever change, because no matter how strong and right and honest you are, if the other side won't play by the rules, you play the game their way or lose.

The only good thing about this drive was the solitude of that isolated strip of asphalt. The endless sameness. It built and built in me till I began to howl in anger at the futility of it all. Empty my soul of some horror and sadness and pain. Over and over till I was hoarse. Even with my ribs snarling at me, it felt good.

This sheriff's office was actually nice to me. I handed over letters proving I was Owen Taylor's nephew, and they showed me the John Doe's blood type and his description in the doctor's charts matched. Then I saw proof positive in the x-rays they had taken. Nana once told me he'd fractured his right forearm, right in the middle. He'd had to have pins put in to hold it in place. They were still there.

Finally, I saw the body. Via a monitor. Video and still photos. Hideous images of his eyes pecked away and torso bloated beyond recognition. The thing they showed me looked nothing like my uncle, and I said so. That's when they took a swab of my mouth to run DNA … see if we were at least related. I knew it would come back positive, but I wanted … I needed that last little bit of proof, to make sure. Finally, they gave me a jar they called an urn, with details written on it in a Sharpie and a screw-on top. And the death certificate.

I couldn't move, for a moment.

Now I knew — the blood in the dealership was his, and the only reason everything was exploding was I had come here to find him. If I hadn't, he would have stayed vanished, and the people behind his death would have kept poisoning others against him and anyone associated with him for as long as they wanted.

I didn't cry while driving back. Not a single tear. No anger. Just a hollow space in my heart, like I'd felt the day Nana died. At least her death had been gentle and kind; she went to bed, alive, and just didn't wake up.

When I'd made the call to my mother, to let her know, all she said was, "I'll arrange the funeral. Nothing fancy."

Uncle Owen was one of the pallbearers. So was Uncle Bert. Neither his wife nor his children came. I couldn't go because that meant getting the okay from my PO … meaning I'd have to tell him my court-authorized supervision was gone, which would have been unacceptable to those who owned me. I'd have been sent to some facility to be watched and I couldn't have handled that. So I stayed home, my mind dark and hollow.

She was buried near the river, under a pecan tree. Then they had lunch at a Chili's and it was decided to let me stay in her house till I was released from probation. If my PO had to talk with Nana for some reason, Uncle Owen would handle it. He came to tell me; no one else was with him. All nice and calm and casual in the face of my desolation.

Some family I come from.

That was something else Tone gave me … the ability to go to her grave and say my goodbye. Finally. All they'd put up was a stone with her name and dates of birth and death. Not a thing more. It made me realize I had no idea what'd happened to either of her husbands. She'd never spoken of them, nor had my mother or uncles. I sometimes thought they'd been born from immaculate conception.

She never remarried. Nana felt two divorces was enough for one lifetime. So she focused on her career. She was a private nurse and the only other things that mattered were her children, and grandchildren. Especially me. First grandchild. I stayed with her so many times, when mom was off doing her thing, she was the one who raised me. Loved me without condition, even when I was a brat. And she gave me a home, again, twice. After I was kicked me out of my mother's condo ... and after prison. When she died is really when I knew I was an orphan, by reality.

I didn't head straight back to the fortress; I swung by the dealership and, sure enough, cop cars and forensics trucks were everywhere. People were milling about, watching, as more news crews tried to find something, anything, to put as the lede to their story. I thought about driving up to the address of the Dillon Road property, but that seemed a waste. However, I wasn't ready for the barrage of cops or news cretins, yet. Besides I did not want to arrive with all that video equipment in the Chrysler. So I whispered over to the Best Western, took a room for three days, and unloaded everything into it. My ribs were ready to kill me, before I was done, so I popped an Oxy and sat in a hot bath for an hour till they'd calmed down. Then I pulled my art pad from my satchel and did sketch after sketch after sketch of me seated on the bed and staring at the mirror, as if to prove to myself I really was there. The expression on every one of them was different but the same ... the blank, weary face of a man doing all he could to think of nothing.

Nothing.

Nothing.

— II —

Four news vans were parked at the base of the curving drive when I finally drove up. It was starting to get dark, and Stettlin and Janovich were standing guard, not letting anybody pass who didn't live there, so I stopped and told the news crews who I was.

Stettlin saw me and started over. "Hey, Blaine, we've been lookin' for you!"

"I was in El Centro," I shot back, every camera now on the both of us. "Identifyin' the body of my uncle, Owen Taylor. Somebody killed him and dumped him down there back at the beginnin' of August. I'm surprised you guys didn't check the morgues before claimin' he jumped bail ... or did you an' just keep it hidden?"

Well ... that got everybody's attention.

Stettin took in a deep breath and said, "I don't know anything about that, but there's detectives up there wantin' to talk to you. You should see 'em before you say anything more."

I smiled to the cameras. "If I come out in cuffs, remember — I didn't fly into town till last Wednesday. Okay?"

Then I got in the Chrysler and drove up to the fortress. Let Stettlin and Janovich handle the barrage of questions.

Police vehicles all but filled the cul-de-sac, with serious-looking men wandering between them and the townhouse.

Meredith saw me drive up and came over to the car.

"Jacob, I'm sorry," she said, "but they have a search warrant. I had to let them in or they were going to break the door down." Then she whispered, "One of them is the officer who arrested Antony."

"Have they ID'd the body they found, yet?"

"Not that I know of."

"Okay, Meredith, I want you to know, I ... I found Owen."

She grew very still. " ... And ... ?"

"Are you Jacob Blaine?" blasted over us.

I turned to see an older woman in an ugly suit striding over. She had been one of Ginty's guard dogs.

"Who wants to know?" I snapped.

Meredith touched my arm and said, "Jacob, this is deputy sheriff Pedrales, Riverside County. I told you of her."

I nodded.

"I understand you're Owen Taylor's nephew. We're looking for him. If you know where he is — "

I reached into the Chrysler and pulled out the urn with his ashes. I made certain she saw the location and day of death on it. She stopped cold.

Meredith sagged a little. "Is that date correct?"

I showed her the death certificate.

"All these months ... " whispered from her. She turned and walked back into her townhouse. My guess was, she was going to tell Lemm he had no one left in this world. But she would be wrong ... and I would make sure he knew it.

"When did you find this out?" Pedrales asked, her voice full of disbelief.

"Just now. Call a Dr. Descansos for verification. They're runnin' DNA, but it's ninety-nine percent sure."

"Stay here." Pedrales pulled out her cell phone and stormed back to the condo, huffing. Not only had I messed up her sneaky-assed arrest of Tone, I'd just ruined her theory as to who the killer was. Looked like I'd be busy for a while, so I called Preston and told him. He was ready for it, and said he'd get me declared executor, soon as he could.

Then I called Dion. He began sobbing and hung up on me. I slammed back to Preston, and he headed around to be with him.

I spent the rest of the day professing ignorance about everything that had happened since the beginning of time. I told them over and over they'd already confiscated his records and computer, and just to be nice, I let them search the Chrysler without an updated warrant. We had a lot of back and forth, but the more they dug into it, the more they saw they had nothing to link my uncle to the body buried in the desert except, according to Grace Nieri, he owned the property.

Bitch didn't waste any time.

They wouldn't tell me if they had paperwork to back that up, so I emphasized I didn't, either. None. They didn't believe me; it's like they honestly thought I'd taken all of my uncle's documents and hidden them or destroyed them. Which would fit in with my belief that it wasn't the cops who cleared out Uncle Owen's files.

Man, they dug through everything. Even tore up sections of the bedroom carpet to see what was hidden underneath. They also dug into the owners' manuals. Fortunately, I'd left the will in that hotel room with everything else. What they did find were some slim jewel cases holding DVDs that were probably of the dealership porn shoots. Of course. The thing made of Tiago was probably in with them, but there was nothing I could do about that, now.

Through it all, George came home and huffed around a lot. The circuit boys came and left, as did other people around the fortress, all fascinated by the non-stop police business. Ned watched it all from his front door, never-ending whisky in hand, while I figured Cliff was at work and Ian was populating his favorite watering hole.

I was able to catch some of the evening news, and the death of Owen Taylor was the lede. This was presented as a problem for the police because he'd been their number one suspect. Not so much stated as hinted at and wondered about and commented on. I figured the tide had at least been slowed if not stopped.

Sure enough, by the time the eleven o'clock news came around, Philby was hinting that some recent suicides might be revisited, to make certain they actually were what the coroner said. Anything to shift focus away from the growing idea my uncle was innocent of his charges. I just shook my head.

The cops finished about midnight. I asked Pedrales if she minded me staying in the townhouse, just to let her think I thought I needed her permission.

She shrugged and said, "We're done. For now." She cast that last line at me as if to shake me up. I just grinned.

The next morning, Preston and I got an emergency hearing before a probate judge, who declared me executor of my uncle's estate. What convinced him this was necessary now, now, now was me providing printouts of online records showing how Palm Valley West was screwing my uncle out of everything they could.

His comment? "Well, now they'll have to stop. It's up to you to decide how much they need to account for."

I nearly whooped for joy. Because my next visit would be to the bank. First, however, Preston and I had a quick chat.

"The only coroner's reports I got are the official ones, which are lacking in details." He handed them to me.

I glanced one over. Lots of medical jargon. Photos of the

corpse, and the guy was black; the other one was white. Nothing else stood out ... not that I had any idea of what I was looking for. "You hear what Philby said, last night?"

"Aw, he's gonna have to back that up. And those reports, once a coroner's made up his mind, you gotta have solid shit to make him change it."

"He will, even if he has to manufacture it." I folded them up and put them in my pocket. "Is Dion okay?"

"Aw, he was almost over it by the time I got to him. He'd been expecting it. Still a shock. Still a motherfucking shock." He eyed me. "Do you know who did it?"

"Maybe. But just gut, no proof."

"It is my fervent hope, Mr. Blaine, that you will find proof, and you will make that motherfucking son-of-a-bitching bastard pay for it."

There was real anger in his voice. So I nodded. "Totally my intention, Mr. Niemczyk. Got your campaign hat on?"

"Aw, I'm gonna kick that motherfucker's ass. Letting things get to this point. It's criminal."

I chuckled. "It'll be fun."

He blinked. "Wait, are you quotin' me, now?"

"Better get used to it."

"Shit. Hadn't thought about that." He leaned back. "Aw, now I've got to go back to speaking nice. Shit. You bastard!"

That made me laugh.

I got to Palm Valley West Bank twenty minutes later. In the parking lot was Lawton's Cadillac, Harper leaning against it. He hadn't seen me, yet, so I walked the long way around the Caddy to get a better view as I texted Matt, "Cross reference ex-gay clinics with Harper." Then I headed into the bank.

I bet you'll never guess what the receptionist told me. "Ms. Nieri is in a meeting."

I just said, "Get her out."

"Excuse me, but I can't even go in to talk to her. But if you'll come back in an hour, I'll be happy to try and — "

I pitched my voice at just below bellowing, so everyone in the building could hear me. "No, if I have to come back, it will be with the bank examiner, and I will have every goddamn one of your books audited to find out why your bank has stolen hundreds of thousands of dollars from my uncle's accounts! Now you get Ms. Nieri here and we clear this up right now! Or I'll have this goddamn bank shut down! Do I make myself clear?"

I noticed several people watching me, wary, as a security guard came over. I didn't budge.

The receptionist glared at me. "We are a reputable bank and have never — "

"I've got the proof, lady! Right here!" I held up a folder of printouts of my uncle's accounts.

The security guard stopped next to me, glaring into my ear. "You gotta go."

I kept my eyes on the receptionist. "Fine, from now on it's handled through my attorney. Make sure nobody destroys documents that the courts might want."

I started for the door, but she caved. Fast.

"Mr. Blaine, just a moment. Let me see what I can do."

I returned to her desk and sat as she scurried up an open staircase. The guard stood next to me, still glaring.

A few minutes later, Grace Nieri came down and strode over to me, and I noticed her perfect nails were lavender instead of French style, matching her sharp suit and careful hair, and she was in heels, trying to be even more imperious. Dion played the intimidation factor lots better.

Right behind her was Scott Baskin, looking just as intense as always and in an even slicker suit than what he'd had on, day before yesterday. Trailing them was the receptionist.

"Mr. Blaine," said Grace, "this is Scott Baskin, of — "

"Hi, Scott," I sneered in my queeny-ist voice. "Haven't seen you in a while. Where you been keepin' yourself?"

"Stop it, Blaine!" he snapped. "I know about your uncle, but you have no authority here and won't until — "

I cut him off by handing him the court order granting me control of my uncle's accounts. He read it and hesitated. Grace glared at him.

"Okay, he ... uh ... he does have authority. He can do what he wants with the accounts and — "

Grace sighed to the receptionist. "Get Roger."

The woman scurried back up the stairs.

"Grace, this is a court order," said Scott.

"Obviously, you are not your father's son," she said, her voice slicing into him.

"So what do you want to do? Go up against the court? Tell this judge to get dumped? They don't like that, much."

A man came down the stairs in such a smooth swoop, it's like he floated in — a long, lean block of serenity made from the finest marble, and just that cold, his suit tailored to a perfect fit and his silver hair blinding. If this was the senior Baskin, Grace was right — Scott took after his momma.

Without a word, he grabbed the court order from his son, scanned it and said in a voice that was perfectly modulated, "This is a legal and binding order. Ms. Nieri will be happy to make an appointment for you to come in and review — "

I snapped, "We do it now or we don't — "

"Mr. Blaine, the order gives you the right to handle your uncle's accounts, which will be frozen until such time as you and she agree on a course of action," he replied, unmoved. "It does not give you the right to determine Ms. Nieri's schedule. Lainey, when is she next available?"

"Friday, ten a-m," the receptionist said.

"Please reserve that time for Mr. Blaine." He looked at Grace. "I suggest you clear all appointments for that day; I'm sure this will be very time-consuming." Then he turned to me. "We'll see you at ten, Friday. I will also be in attendance. I strongly urge you to bring your own attorney. Everything will be done according to the law."

"That'll be a first," I snarled.

"Careful, Mr. Blaine. You're perilously close to having a libel suit filed against you."

That made me snort. He didn't even blink. I spun and started for the door, chuckling, then I caught Harper casting a hard glare my way ... but not at me.

I turned to watch Grace and Baskin stride up the stairs, quietly talking, pretending to ignore me, their movements too casual to be anything but a form of control. Her fingers held Baskin's arm, lavender nails bright against his dark suit, and in a vise-like grip. Scott trailed them like a lonesome puppy, ignored by both.

Then Grace cast a quick sharp glance back at Roy.

I turned to him. His glare was now focused on me.

Son-of-a-bitch ... he hadn't been allowed into her private world. He was tied to the car, like a dog that can't go into a cafe.

That's when the most important brick fell into place.

— III —

As I drove away from Palm Valley West Bank, I called Dion to let him know he'd be keeping control of the Fortress ... but he cut me off.

"I can't talk; Kent's been shot."

"What?! What happened?"

"It was at Joel's school and ... and ... oh, shit, oh, sorry." He put a hand over the phone to say, "No, please, just sit there. I'll be off the phone in a second ... daddy's fine ... he'll be fine. Just give me a minute, okay?"

"Dion, where are you?"

"St. Matthew's, on Gardena Road."

"I'll be right there."

Thanks to GPS ... and ignoring a few traffic laws ... I made it in ten minutes. It was a low-slung place with lots of black glass and desert landscaping, and as I drove onto the parking area I noticed that it had a recent name-change. I had to laugh. Only a Catholic would make a saint out of a tax-collector.

I found Dion pacing outside, talking on his phone. "No, Connie, he just needs stitches. Soon as he's done I'm bringing him home. ... Yeah, yeah. ... Listen, that offer you made? It still open? ... Good. I spoke with Lorinda. Drop by the office and we'll work it out." He saw me and tried to smile but what came out was a pained grimace. "Thanks. See you, tomorrow." Then he ended the call.

"Kent's okay?" I asked.

He nodded. "The bastard got him in the fleshy part of his

bicep. Forty-two stitches. It's a wonder somebody else didn't get hit by the bullet. It went through the wall and — "

"What happened?"

"He was called to the school by the principal. Joel was in detention. Some brats who popped out of a Minuteman's wife were calling him names because he has two daddies, so they got into a fight and he broke one kid's nose. Kent was talking with the principal about it when the kid's prick father arrived with a cop, to find out who the hell'd damaged his little angel. He was threatening assault charges and ... and they got into an argument and the son-of-a-bitch pulled a gun! The only reason Kent's not dead is the cop slammed the motherfucker against a wall."

"Shit."

"Joel saw it. Thinks it's his fault. The son-of-a-bitch did that with our child in the room!"

"Where's the kids?" I asked.

"Ian's letting them take each other's blood pressure and check reflexes and ... and ... oh, shit, Jake, I am so fucking close to going over to that jail and finding that fuck and slitting his fucking gut open — "

"Let me," I said. "That way you can stay with Kent."

He looked at me, and I could see him considering it, but then he shook his head. Reluctantly. "Wouldn't do any good. He's already bred into the gene pool." Then he led me inside.

"You called Connie," I noted.

He nodded. "I need to talk with you about that. She said if I ever got the okay from Owen, she had a buyer for the hillside. Since Owen's ... gone, Preston said you're executor. I'm hoping you'll ... you'll let me sell it. Same for Ian. He wants out of this place. It sounds so cold and awful, but ... "

"You're takin' the job in Santa Monica."

"I'm not giving Kent a choice. We've got kids. We can't have this happen around them."

"I'll buy you out."

He smiled at me. "Thanks."

We found Joel and the twins with Ian, sitting in a corner of the waiting room. He was reading them a goofy book so waved at us and Dion waved back then said, "I'm gonna check on Kent."

He started down a hall to the examination rooms, but a nurse stopped him. "Excuse me, sir, who're you here for?"

"Kent Mixta," he said. "I'm his husband."

The woman got as stiff as a statue and said, "Just a moment." She picked up a phone.

"What do you mean?" Dion snapped. "He was just brought in. I came in with him. I've already been in the — "

"I need to get authorization for anyone but a family member to see him."

"I'm his fucking husband, you fucking bitch!"

"Okay, you get out of here," she shot back at him.

Dion was about to explode when a doctor in scrubs and a white coat came out of an examination room, pulling her black hair into a pony-tail, and asked, "What's going on?"

"My husband is in a room down this hall being sewn up after being shot and this bitch won't let me see him," Dion snarled.

"Okay, this is a Catholic hospital," said the doctor. "We opted out of recognizing same-sex marriage and you are not — "

Dion went four shades of purple so I yanked him back by the shirt, hard enough to topple him into a chair, and I pulled out my cell phone as I said, "My friend's marriage is legal and binding, and that's not somethin' you can opt out of."

"I told you, this is a Catholic hospital and we are not morally obligated to recognize — "

"Texas might back you up on this, lady," I said as I hit speed dial for Preston's office, "but we're in California. Whether you like it or not don't matter."

Ian called to us, "Catholics Incorporated doesn't care about the law. Look how many times they helped their priests avoid being arrested for ... um, for the things they did. Some even got money to move along. Don't you just love religion?"

The doctor shot over her shoulder, "Janice, call the police and have these men arrested."

That's when Preston came on the line with, "Niemczyk."

"Hi, Preston, it's Jake. We got a problem at ... what was the name of this place, again?" I aimed that question at Ian.

"St. Matthew's."

"Who're you talking to?" the doctor asked.

"Our lawyer," I smiled. "We're at St. Matthew's Emergency Room. Kent was shot by a homophobe — "

"Shot?!?!?"

"The bullet cut some skin; he'll be fine. But the medical staff is refusing to let Dion see him. Seems they think since they're Catholic, they don't have to recognize his marriage."

"Let me talk to him."

"It's a her — Doctor ... ?" and I looked at the bitch with the sweetest expression I could muster.

"If you have a problem with how this hospital is run," she snapped, "you can call the chief-of-staff and — "

I cut her off with, "She doesn't want to talk to you."

"Okay, put me on speaker," said Preston, so I did. And she heard every word. "I will have a court order in your Chief-of-staff's hand in the next thirty minutes. If he fails to follow that order, I will have you all held in contempt of court. I am also filing a complaint with the AMA against you, and I will find out your name. I'll be asking to have your license revoked to practice in the state of California. I will also go after the hospital's charter to provide medical and attendant care and will demand a full and complete audit be undertaken by Medicare and MediCal to make certain all rules and obligations are being followed, to the letter, under the law, and I will also file a discrimination suit for half a million dollars — "

"Okay, fine, fine, fine!" she snarled. "This way." She started down the hall.

"You get that, Pres?" I asked as I yanked Dion out of the chair. Then I went off speaker. "The money got her attention."

"Of course, and I'm still doing everything I just said. Inform that doctor she'll be getting a call from her Chief of Staff, whether he agrees with her bullshit or not."

"I feel more like lettin' it be a surprise," I said.

He chuckled then said, "Suit yourself. Tell Dion I'll be over shortly. I want to deliver that order in person."

"You got it. Thanks."

"Aw, dude, thank YOU. I've gotten more solid business off

you in the last week than the last year. Buh-bye."

He hung up.

I watched the doctor huff down to a room down at the end of the hall, Dion right behind her. He cast me a quick glance of thanks then ducked into it.

Ian looked at me. "Do they pull this in Denmark?"

"They've had gay marriage for years. With no problems."

"I see why you moved."

"Totalitarian Christians." I joined him and the kids, who overheard every word. I put on a goofy expression and said, "So ... any questions?"

Ian just sighed and shook his head in disgust. "That doctor's name is Koskarov, and she was brought in about a month ago. She won't even talk to me, except to mention I'm going to hell. Bitch wants me to quit. Instead, I've become a model employee, like Meredith did, just to rub her nose in my gayness. I've only another six months to retirement; if she wants me gone before then, she'll have to get me fired and deal with the consequences. Now, you mind minding these little angels? My shift ended an hour ago and I'm desperate for a Manhattan."

"Glad to," I said then sat cross-legged on the floor and gathered some of the toys into a pile. "Okay, this is a campfire," I whispered, "so let's tell secrets. I'll start."

The girls happily plopped down with me but Joel stayed crouched in his chair, eyeing me with wariness.

"So ... did you know I was in jail? For nearly two years."

Joel's wariness became a frown. "Why?"

"A deputy sheriff got mad at me and had me arrested."

"Did you do something wrong?" asked Sarah ... I think.

"No, what I did was make a relative of his pay for damage she did to a car. It was owned by the city I worked for."

"That's not fair," said Joel.

"No, it's not," I said, looking straight at him. "There's lots of things that are not fair, in life. Lots of things happen that are wrong. But you know what else can happen? The people who do something wrong get punished. Like what that doctor said to your papa? That was wrong. And she's gonna regret it."

"How?"

"Your Uncle Preston's gonna take her and her boss to court. Because you live in a country where your two dads are legally married. She cannot ignore that. She cannot say it's not legal. She cannot refuse to follow the law."

"But she said she could," said Sarah. "She said she'd get us taken away from daddy and papa."

The fucking cunt. "Oh? When did she say that?"

"She said it as Uncle Ian was bringing us out here," said Joel. "She didn't like us being in that room with him."

"Did you have any problem being in that room with him?"

"No. He's Uncle Ian."

"Yeah," said Samantha. "He takes care of us, sometimes."

"Why would she say that?" asked Sarah.

"Because she's stupid and hateful," I said. "She can say whatever she wants, but you are protected by the law. You cannot be taken away from your dads, no matter what she says. No matter what anybody says. Kent is your father, and Donald is legally married to him. That is the law in America. And she cannot ignore that. And if she tries, she will really be punished. You remember that deputy sheriff? He got arrested, and I got paid lots of money for what he did to me. The fact is, a lot of other people got paid a lot of money, too, because some people in Texas acted like they can do whatever they want. And they can't.

"It's like that man that hurt your daddy. He's gonna be punished because you can't just shoot people." I shot a glance at Joel and added. "A punch in the nose is more manly. That's what I do when I'm about to get into a fight."

"You get in lots of fights?" asked Joel.

"I've been in a few. I don't start 'em; I finish 'em."

"I don't like to fight."

"Sometimes you have to. It's not fun, but sometimes if you don't fight back, it makes things worse."

Joel looked away. Oh, boy, I wondered if it was right of me to butt in. But then Dion came back and sat by Joel and pulled him into a hug and said, "Daddy's going to be fine. He's being bandaged up, right now. He told me what happened, and how proud he is of you,

Joel." The boy looked up at him, confused. "You stood up for yourself. You stood up for your family. And I am so proud of you, too. Sammi, Sarah, you have a great brother."

"We know that," said Samantha ... I think. Then she looked at me and asked, "Is it my turn to tell a secret?"

Joel was close to losing it so I nodded for Dion to get him away, which he did by saying they'd go get us all something to drink, then the girls and I shared the horrible things we'd done. Like how one's Barbie had to get surgery because she had breast cancer, like some friend's mom had. And how they'd often pretended to be each other just to confuse people (me included, I'm sure). And how I'd once stolen those cans of ravioli, and how I messed with people's minds. God, we were monsters. And through it all I could see Dion and Joel outside in an alcove, the boy bawling and Dion sitting cross-legged on the pavement, holding him and rubbing his back. A father comforting his son as best he could.

That's when fury slashed into me, deeper than anything I'd felt since I'd seen Tone being stabbed by that prick in that jail cell. A protectiveness so intense, I finally understood the true meaning of a scorched earth policy. It wasn't just some romantic notion or idea; it was self-preservation. Anyone who messes with me or mine? Destroy them so they can never be a threat. Period.

I didn't know exactly what I could do to change the tide of intolerance that had been building in Palm springs; neither did I care. All I knew was, when ten year-old boys are having to stand up for their families against hateful bullies while cowards run around thinking a gun means they've got a dick, it's time to stop being nice and whimpering, *Can't we all just get along?* Because you can't, not if the assholes don't want to. It takes both sides to make peace, but only one side is needed for war. So if that's what you want, you fucks, you got it. Full-scale all-out end-of-the-world devastation.

And I'm just the son-of-a-bitch to bring it to you.

— IV —

The Chief of Staff didn't show up before Kent was released, his left arm bandaged and in a sling. Dion was promising he'd do all the cooking for them forever as Joel and the twins clung to them both. Preston arrived just as we were leaving, got the okay to fire his load on the commie Christians, so he all but skipped into the hospital.

"Watch tonight's news," he called as he headed through the doors. "I've got a call in. They find it most interesting that retaliations are already happening against the gay community, because of the actions of one or two scumbags. Maybe it'll knock that other crap off, for a while."

Wait'll they see tomorrow's news, I thought.

I escorted Dion's family home then headed down to Indio. En route, I called Matt.

"How's Lemm?"

"Not so good. The coroner's office called and asked if he'd come see ... well ... "

"Shit. I've got the Chrysler."

"Meredith said she'd take us, about six."

"I'll meet you down there. Anything on Lawton and Harper?"

"Grace Nieri was married to a guy named Harper, but they divorced thirty years ago. What that means is, Roy Harper was at that ex-gay clinic. In El Salvador."

" ... Okay ... so ... "

"So they ... they tortured gay people to make them change. Suicides happened. They got shut down, it was so bad."

"Shit. Was he forced to go?"

"He was in his teens, so who knows? He joined the Marines when he got out, then he worked for Lawton and was married to one his daughters. That's how I found all this so quick — announcement for the wedding. They split up when he joined the Palm Springs Police ... that was three years ago."

"Must've been a pleasant divorce; he and Lawton still get along. Can you find out who Samantha Ginty's husband is? Her maiden name. How long she's been married. When they moved here."

"Now?"

"Fast as possible."

"Yes, sir. I'll do what I can, sir." His voice had an edge to it that hurt.

"Matt, I'm sorry I'm pushin' so much on you, now," I said. "But it'll be over, tonight. I promise."

"Yeah, I know, I know ... it's just ... Lemm's still ... I dunno. I don't want to take my focus away from him ... even though ... "

"Just keep him close to you, buddy. Hold him. Touch him. Let him know you're there for him. You're good for him."

"Nice fantasy."

"Matt ... Ned's jealous of you, over Lemm."

"Bullshit."

"Told me so, himself. And don't forget, Lemm helped Harper protect you. Now you're the one protectin' him."

" ... Yeah, I ... I guess I am ... "

He sounded better, so I ended the call and dialed up Castillo. He was not happy.

"You need to give me time to work out the impossible."

"You've had fifteen fuckin' months to handle this," I snapped as I pulled over. "Gimme the AG's number."

"Jake, it's almost six; they're gone for the day."

"Give me the fuckin' number!"

"Not if you're going to talk to me like that. You can get yourself another — !"

"You don't want me to haul your ass before the State Bar, you'll give me the AG's number."

He did. Three of them. I called the first two and got voice mail. *We're gone for the day so screw you,* kind of crap. I called the last one and it was the cell phone to one of his assistants, who was in the middle of fixing dinner.

After I told her who I was, she spit out, "You can call back, tomorrow. We'll talk then."

"Tomorrow's no good. It's now or not."

"I say not."

"Fine. You get the heat when everything crashes down

around you. And trust me, lady — it's gonna."

"Mr. Blaine ... is he even expecting your call?"

I just chuckled. "No, but he'll talk to me."

"Tell me what it's about and I'll see if I can — "

"No," I snarled right back. "You tell him call back, within the next ten minutes, because if he don't, my next call is to a lawyer, who will file a lawsuit against the state of Texas for a hundred-million dollars."

"Don't be ridiculous; you'll never get that mind of money."

"But I will get that kind of publicity, and watch what I do with it."

She sighed. "I have to offer some kind of explanation."

"Okay, fine — thanks to the state of Texas, I was arrested, beaten and held in a jail cell, overnight, because both the Palm Springs Police Department and the District Attorney's office for Riverside County say they were told I'd violated my parole, despite the fact that I have been exonerated and my record was supposed to have been expunged, years ago. You got that? Years ago! So he talks to me, now, or he talks to me in court."

"Mr. Blaine, I assure you, if that is happening — "

"Lady, the choice is yours. You don't want to call his precious little ass, don't. But I've already laid it out. It's now or never."

This time she heaved a royal sigh. "Ten minutes?"

"Not one second longer."

He called back nine minutes and forty-nine seconds later.

"Why'd you call, Blaine? You have an attorney — "

"The state of Texas was supposed to vacate my record more than two years ago. Why hasn't it been done?"

"I don't know that it hasn't."

"It takes fifteen seconds to pull up the site, fifteen more to find me. You're probably lookin' at it, right now."

"I'm not in the office."

"Shit, you really wanna play games?"

"Whether it's true or not, that was my predecessor's error."

"No, you're the AG. It's your lap. And I'm gonna be a motherfucker about it."

"No need to use that kind of language."

"Trust me, I'm holdin' back," I growled. "And if you keep pullin' this Little Sir Innocent crap, you'll find out just how much. The only reason I'm callin' is, I believe in offerin' everybody a choice, to make things easier for all concerned."

"And what do *you* consider a choice?"

"You can show me that you're a nice guy who is really doin' his best to correct the mess left behind by his predecessor, and I can focus my anger on the people of California who abused me. Or we can talk in open court under the glare of floodlights."

"And how might I do that?"

I sighed. "Really? After the roundabout we've been doin' for the last year, with your threats?"

"There's a new aspect to it. St. Lazarre's ankle monitor being reprogrammed."

"You go one step more down that road an' this call's over."

"... I see. How much do you expect from me?"

"I want Antony St. Lazarre free an' clear."

"That's a high price. I'll discuss it with my colleagues."

"Uh-uh. Its either a yes, right now, or that's a no."

"You expect me to make a decision of this importance without time to consider the ramifications?"

"Listen up! You spent nearly a year tryin' to make Antony responsible for everything that's ever gone wrong in the history of the world. The only reason you're fightin' me, now, is you think you finally got him. Well, you're right. He screwed up. He's all set for jail. All your cares are gone ... as regards him. And maybe ... maybe ... you can prove that piece of shit on his ankle didn't malfunction but was tampered with. But that does not mitigate the fact that I now have two broken ribs, a black eye, and a fresh arrest record, thanks to Texas. This calls for an investigation by the Department of Justice, to see if my civil rights were violated. Maybe there was collusion between you and the Riverside DA. You're both anti-fag and seem vindictive. Who knows? Maybe on top of a nice big jury award, I'll get the court to order your office to operate under a consent decree, like they did with the LAPD and Albuquerque. Them's your choices. Antony St. Lazarre walks free, or get ready to rumble."

"Well," he chuckled, "at least you're not insisting on a monetary settlement, because that really would be — "

"You're stallin' me? Seriously?"

"No! No, I ... um ... I was merely making a comment."

What bullshit. He probably had his bitch assistant checking into everything on another line, hoping he'd catch me out on some detail before he had to give up the store. Which pissed me off. "Y'know, if you'd just taken my offer, that would've been that. Now? You pay all my legal fees."

"WHAT?!" That yanked the plug out of his ass. "That could run into the hundreds of thousands of — !"

"So you wanna keep arguin'? Okay. I seem to recall Antony was damn near stabbed to death in a jail cell, an attempted murder set up by a Texas Ranger and a District Attorney — "

"Both of whom are en route to jail."

"For the manslaughter of a man named Collier Winston-Royce. Attempted murder's a whole new charge, and they'll be joined by some friends. Like a judge who was up to his eyeballs in it, and a state legislator and another Texas Ranger, all of whom also helped send me to prison, illegally, where I was abused and had years of my life ripped away — !"

"All right, all right, all right! It's a deal. It's a deal."

"Draw up the agreement. Castillo'll get it to us."

"You and St. Lazarre will need to come here to sign it."

"No. Fucking. Way. We are never returnin' to your fucked up state. My attorney'll FedEx it to me and I'll have my signature notarized. If that ain't good enough, you can kiss my ass."

"That," he sneered in a voice dripping with acid, "holds no interest for me."

"Thank you, Jesus," I snarled then ended the call.

I immediately called Castillo and told him about the deal. He damn near had a stroke.

"What the hell is wrong with you? Why didn't you let me handle it?"

"Because you didn't. Now earn some of your salary and make sure that prick doesn't pull some new shit."

"You can get another attorney to handle this — "

"I got one, but he ain't in Texas. You are. And you're billin' the AG's office for all your fees, includin' those I already paid. You'll give me every penny back, or I'll make damn sure you get stripped of your license. An' if you think I can't, then you go right ahead an' refuse the job."

"Dammit, Jake, there's no call for this! I was on your side."

"Bullshit. If you had been, we'd be done by now."

"What the hell happened to you?"

"You people on my side pushed me too fuckin' far."

I ended the call and cranked up the stereo. Time for some serious *Depeche Mode* to clear my head.

I managed to reach the jail just before five and waited, hoping I wasn't too late. After a few minutes, Doc Sandoval came out the back door and headed for a parking lot. I drove up beside him, saying, "Hey, Doc, remember me?"

He looked in the car and snorted. "Shit, I seen you more'n my wife, lately. What you want now?" He did not stop walking.

"Buy you a drink. Ask a favor."

"Depends on the drink. And the favor."

"You choose the joint. And you can decide on the favor after the first round."

He shrugged and got in, and we wound up at a nearby dive, where they have Coors, Coors and Coors. Yeah, total class.

We just chit-chatted until it was time for a second beer, then I hit him up with my request.

"Would you call the Riverside coroner's office and get some info?"

"On what?"

"A couple autopsies."

"What for?"

"Catch a killer."

He didn't even blink. "Whose autopsies?" he asked, pulling out his mobile phone.

I handed the official reports over to him. "Marco Samuels. Bruno Vrasky. Both died in the last few months. Suicide."

"These're official reports."

"Yeah, I read about the food and chemicals and stuff. I want to know what's not in them."

"Like what?"

"Like they could've been accidents. Or something?"

He nodded, punched in a number and said, "Both?"

I nodded.

He got hold of a buddy and fed the info into the phone then ended the call. "Gonna take him a bit to find the files."

"They're not in the system?"

His eyes dug into me. "Available to just anybody?"

O-kay, let's leave it at that. And what should come through at that particular moment? A freaked-out text from Matt with the info I'd asked for, on Ginty. My heart stopped for a second.

Doc noticed and said, "Should I end the call?"

"No," I said without even considering it. "No, I need that. It's just, I thought I was divin' into an Olympic sized pool. Turns out, I jumped into the middle of the fuckin' Atlantic."

Doc's phone grabbed his attention. "Yeah. Okay, hold on." He looked at me. "What you need to know?"

"A chemical screen was run on the bodies. They found Viagra and Ketamine, in large amounts. Does it say whether or not they actually had sex before they died?"

He asked, then shook his head. "Nothin' on that."

"Okay. The reports say death was by asphyxiation. Does that mean hangin'?" He nodded, his eyes locked on me. "Could it have been auto-erotic strangulation?"

He asked then said, "That's in the notes as a possible, but dismissed due to positionin' of the bodies when they was found."

"Positioning of the bodies?"

"They was hangin'. Feet off the ground, stool close by."

"Okay. It says there's marks and scars on their bodies, indicatin' they were into pain games. Were any fresh marks on their wrists? Ankles?"

"What kind of marks?"

"Like they'd been recently tied?"

"Son, what the hell's goin' on in your brain?"

"Just ... just ask. Please."

He did. He frowned when he got the info. "These boys was

into some kinky stuff, but 'round the wrists. Ankles, too."

There it was. The final brick. "Doc, do me a favor. Forget we had this conversation. If anybody asks you, tell 'em I ... I wanted to get info about Officer Harper from you."

The look he cast me would have sliced steel, it was so sharp. "Why would I know anything about him?"

O-kay ... "Keep it that way."

He looked at me, for a moment, then said into the phone, "Okay, son, put them folders back right where they come from and forget all about this. Okay? Thanks." He ended the call and looked straight at me, wary for the first time. "I wonder what I just got myself dragged into."

"You a religious man, doc?"

"I learned how to do without that a long time ago."

"Me, too. But there's people out there who haven't. And who'll do anything they think their religion wants or needs."

He snorted. "Tell me somethin' new. Look-it them *Muselems*."

"And Christians and Hindus and Buddhists, oh my." I shot back. He gave me a shrug of acceptance.

It was dark when we got out of the bar. I dropped him by his truck, then I parked and roared around to Philby's office.

I had it. Knew who'd killed my uncle and Tiago and even those two suicides. Now I just needed to prove it.

That was going to be the easy part ...

... And the scariest.

— V —

Samantha Ginty teleported down to see me the second she heard I was in the building. Preston had told them about the lots and the dealership, and they wanted to know how I knew what I claimed to know when I couldn't have known it. So we went into a blank interview room with a clerk and tape recorder, and sat at a blank table.

"Okay," she said. "Let's start with — "

"This," I snapped as I put my Iranian passport on the table. It had just expired, and it provided the world's best expression of confusion on her face.

"Let the record show Mr. Blaine has handed me an Iranian passport." She looked inside ... and her expression froze. "Why, I must ask, do you think this is of value to our investigation? It was my understanding you professed information regarding the property your uncle owned."

I smiled. "He's not the only owner."

"We know. It was purchased through a partnership, but it's a blind and he was the main — "

"I know who his partners were."

She looked from the passport to me. "And their names?"

I cast a hint of a glance at the clerk then looked straight into Ginty's eyes. "I also know there's somethin' more important to keep in mind." I pulled out the coroner's reports and handed them to her.

She glanced over them. "These are official coroner's reports for two homosexual males who committed suicide."

"Isn't your boss lookin' into the possibility they were murdered? They were."

"What makes you so certain?"

"Let me see better photos of 'em, I'll tell you why."

She blinked at that one. "Why?"

"Gotta see the pictures, first. Make sure."

"No, Mr. Blaine, what you have to do is tell me what you know before I have you arrested for withholding evidence."

"Got a better idea, counselor. First, let's compare the coroner's report on the body found in the desert to these two."

"I ... he ... he's probably still in the middle of — "

I shook my head. "He's done. We think the body is the brother of a friend of mine. He's been asked to identify it, and should be there right now."

Her look went wary. "I'll discuss this with Mr. Philby."

Shit. Stubborn. I wrote I hear someone's expecting on a sheet of paper and held it so the assistant couldn't see.

Ginty sighed in surrender and whispered, "You drive."

We slammed past the throng of shouting reporters as we

hurried to the Chrysler. A couple scrambled to try and follow us, but we were gone before they could even get out their keys. Then she directed me on the fastest way to the Coroner's office.

"I'll take you to a back entrance," she said. "There'll be fewer of those rodents there." It wasn't till we were on the freeway that she asked, "How did you know?"

"That you're Preston's wife? And work for my father?"

"Mr. Blaine ... or would you prefer Mr. Darya-Bendari?"

"I prefer Jake, if we're gonna be on the same side."

She looked at me, for a moment. "I'm Samantha. And I never worked for any company your father owned."

"You worked for a law firm that's on retainer to one."

"Hardly the same thing."

"Legally, but not really."

"What makes you think Mr. Niemczyk and I are married?"

"Wedding license in New York City, filed five years ago. Just before you and he moved here ... five years ago. I find it interesting you've both kept quiet about it. Now why would you do that? Except he works at representing gay men and you work for a man out to ruin as many gay men as he can. And Preston has a contact in the DA's office. And let slip his wife's pregnant."

"That's hardly proof of — "

"It will be in a few months. How'll you explain that away?"

She let out a long sigh. "I'm won't. Everyone in the DA's office thinks I'm divorced. I'm leaving before I have to explain anything."

"Is that okay with my father?"

"Faraz wasn't happy, but what can he do?"

"Faraz? First name contact? Seriously?"

"Spying has no place for a bureaucracy, Jake. Too much chance of something going wrong or someone wanting to curry favor with the powers that be, on either side."

"Did my uncle know?" Dead silence, probably meaning no. Okay ... "How'd you get a job here?"

"The man I replaced was ... well, he's now working as the American legal coordinator for a multi-national corporation in Paris, and doing a fine job, as I understand, despite speaking little French.

My credentials were ... oh, polished up and made more relevant to what Philby wanted. Didn't hurt that he likes how I look."

"Did you set up my uncle's arrest?"

"No, that's all on Officer Morrow. But I did know Owen had the security tape so viewed it and said nothing. Philby didn't even think about asking for it. When it came up at trial, Warren was not happy."

"Couldn't you stop him on the boy-rape charge?"

"And blow my cover of hate?" Her expression told all.

I laughed. "So you gave Preston a copy of Lemm's interrogation." She just looked away. "How'd you get close to Grace Nieri? She's a cold one."

"She's a founding member of PSALMS, from Texas, so I joined up. There's a lot of gossip at meetings ... when you're around like-minded people. Comments. Details about your plans. Faraz appreciated the information I was sending him."

"So that's what it was all about? Getting info? For what? Business dealings?"

"It wasn't just business."

"With my father?" I snorted. "Did he suggest usin' the dealership as a porn shoot site?"

She looked at me, for a moment, then said in very legal and careful tone, "That came from Grace. I learned Ned once worked in pornography and mentioned that at a meeting of PSALMS. Grace took me aside and suggested it might be useful in exposing the gay community for their venality and prurience. Her words, not mine."

"Grace came up with the idea? Really?"

"She said something about protecting the pure and punishing the evil. I put the idea to Ned, not mentioning her; he agreed we could make a lot of money. It began straightforwardly, but I noticed she manipulated the paperwork around it. To what end, I do not yet know."

"To hurt my uncle. That paperwork made it seem like he owned the building and was making money off immoral activity."

That made her think for a moment. "I've seen the evidence coming from the dealership. Apparently, it was much used, and now it's likely a murder was committed there, possibly recorded on video."

Shit, that meant they had a copy of Tiago's tape. "Is that where Philby's takin' this? Snuff films made in a warehouse connected to a gay man? And you'd let him do it? Even though you know the people involved? Know they couldn't be part of that?" She did not look at me. I let a snarl into my voice. "Daddy wants you to keep quiet. Let it play out, till he can decide whether it will help or hurt his plans."

"I don't know what your father's reasoning is."

"C'mon, Samantha. He doesn't give a shit about the anti-gay crowd or the damage they cause, so why's he got you here?"

She took a moment to answer, "The great and honorable Lamar Davis Lawton."

"Him? But he — " I cut myself off. "Palm Valley West Bank. It was declared insolvent. Daddy bid on it and wanted it, but it was handed over to C&B Trust."

"Our bid was the best offer."

"But Lawton had the connections. Had the bank repossessed property daddy wanted?" She said nothing. "Son-of-a-bitch, I'm helpin' my father on a fuckin' business deal? Shit!"

"How do you think you're helping him?"

"By bein' as big an asshole as him," I shot back.

She looked at me, half smiling. "On that, considering your language, you get no argument."

"Thanks a lot," I growled.

We arrived just as Lemm, Matt, and Meredith were leaving the building. Geordi pattered along, with them.

Meredith saw us, first. "Jake? What're you doing here with that woman?"

"Got somethin' to show her," I said, then added softly, "Is it definite?"

Meredith cast Ginty an evil eye but nodded, then she drew me aside, whispering, "They didn't actually show Lemm the body; it was too decomposed. He viewed images on a computer. Gave DNA samples. Answered questions." The same things I'd gone through when identifying my uncle. Jesus. "What made it certain is, Tiago was born with four toes on his right foot."

"Shit," shot out of me before I could censor it. "I was so

hopin' I was wrong."

"Exactly. Such a beautiful young man ... "

I looked at Lemm. He was seated in the back of Meredith's car, the door still open, Matt squatting beside him. All his tears had been shed.

"Can he and Matt stay with you a bit longer?" I asked.

Meredith smiled. "Don't be ridiculous."

"Thanks. I'll see you when I get back."

Ginty got me in to see the coroner, straight off. The estimate of time of death had been narrowed down to a few days, and it was right about the time Tiago vanished. Death probably caused by asphyxiation. Strangulation. Jesus.

I asked, "Were there drugs in his system?"

He frowned at me, but Ginty nodded to him, so he shrugged. "We found traces of Ketamine and Viagra."

I handed him the reports for the suicides. "Can you tell if they really did hang themselves?"

He glanced between me and Ginty. "I've already revisited these results. I'm still inclined to say suicide."

"The same drugs were found in them."

"I don't see what the relevance is. Many gay men take Ketamine."

"Tiago Díaz de Valdés was not gay. He was involved with a girl, and they were about to have a kid."

He hesitated, but still said, "That's immaterial ... "

"Can you tell if Tiago was really raped?"

"The body was too decomposed to be able to say."

"But his hands and feet were tied, just like these guys."

"I don't understand your meaning."

"Can you tell if someone's been strangled, not hanged?"

He looked hard at the suicide reports. Compared them to his notes on Tiago's body. "There ... are ways ... if it's truly suspected."

"It's suspected," Ginty said. "Call me personally when you have the answer, I don't care what it is, or when." Then she handed him a card. He gave a vague nod, and we left.

I drove her back to Indio, telling her everything. Well, except that I'd snuck the equipment out of the dealership. She didn't buy it.

"Conspiracy theories are for TV programs and action movies, Jake. Why do you think I have direct access to Faraz and your uncle was cut out of the loop? If five people work together to commit a crime, there'll be twenty-five ways for everything to go wrong or be exposed. And there hasn't been a hint of anything along those lines ... not till you popped up. PSALMS has not been quiet about what they want, and they're hardly the only anti-gay crowd. Father Paul's very vocal in his opposition to the gay community, but so are several Protestant ministers in the area. Are you suggesting they're all in this, together? Including extorting money from a pornography racket? Seriously? That's ridiculous. And there's been a lot of push-back, lately, not just from your uncle and gay organizations, but also on the city council, the courts, and the state, itself. People just don't buy the gays are evil and dangerous nonsense, anymore."

"So it's just about money? Maybe that's all it ever is."

She chuckled. "A time-old tradition, greed. It's believed the Salem Witch Trials were really about gaining control of some property, but the hysteria spun out of control and no one knew how to stop it before dozens of people were dead."

"Stupid's also been around since the dawn of time."

She nodded at that. "I'll send you photos we have of the two suicides. Will you then tell me who you think killed them?"

"If they're the same guys I think they are."

I dropped her off then picked up a few things we'd need for the next step and headed back to the fortress through a night that kept getting darker and darker. When Dion and I had been together, it seemed like Palm Springs was always well-lit and colorful. Not unusual when you're in love. But now? despite there being no clouds in the sky and the moon high and bright and stars gleaming, nothing cut through the shadows looming everywhere, deep and black. Matched my mood, perfectly.

Connie was at Meredith's door, talking with her when I arrived. She came straight over to me.

"Jake, things are getting awful," she said. "They may have found another body, and they're saying Owen was part of a rape-torture ring and was killed to keep him quiet."

I had to laugh. "Philby's trolls're workin' overtime to make it his fault."

"We need to figure out what to do and say in response."

"Already workin' on it," I said, smiling. "Let's talk."

I started for my door but Connie stopped me. "I have to eat, first. My last meal was a donut and cup of coffee for breakfast. How about I break out the leftover chili and we discuss this at my place?"

"I think Meredith brought that over," I said. "I could heat it up; we can talk here."

"That's even better," she gasped. "Let me freshen up. I'll bring beer and toppings."

"It's a date," I said. "But leave the handcuffs at home."

"Oh, you're no fun," she purred.

A few minutes later, Ginty's photos of the suicides came through, and I was right; they were the guys in Harper's photo.

I rushed over to Meredith's to find Lemm and Matt seated at the counter, nibbling at cucumber sandwiches. Lemm was numb. The photo albums were on her coffee table so I grabbed the top one, found the photo of Harper and showed it to him.

"This man did not kill your brother," I said. "But I know who did, and I think they killed Bruno Vrasky and Marco Samuels, the two men he's talking to."

Lemm looked from the photo to me. "But he — "

I cut him off with, "Do you still want to help avenge your brother's death?"

He almost smiled. "Tell me how."

I laid out my plan, right then and there, and saw life return to Lemm's eyes, bit by bit. Revenge can fire up emotion faster than any match, except greed. I had Matt assemble some of his information onto a thumb drive, just the stuff that would back up my thesis. I wrote out a quick brief outlining my suspicions, who I was fingering and why, and put that on the thumb drive, too. Once everything was lined up like I wanted it, I asked Matt to burn a dozen CDs to hand out to the news crews, including Sousie Fornia ... and Samantha. I wanted everything in readiness, just in case. Because this would change the direction of the whole story, and the easier it was for the media to follow, the more likely it was they'd follow it.

But I also did this because when you scorch your enemy's

earth; you can get just as burned, in the process. Only I was beyond caring what it took.

This was ending tonight.

— VI —

Half an hour later, Connie arrived dressed for success, and she meant business. Soft pullover blouse, loose skirt, sandals to mitigate the upscale attitude of her ensemble. She had a brown bag in one hand, a six of beer in the other, and a crooked smile on her face.

"Ready, willing, and able," she whispered, seductively.

"You left the handcuffs at your place, right?"

"Wanna frisk me?" she asked, fluttering her eyes.

I just took the bags and led her to the dining area by the patio door. She grabbed out a couple of bottles, first.

She caught an aroma. "Cornbread? You cook?"

"Got it from Meredith." I put the bag on the counter and the beer in the fridge. Negro Modelo. She must own stock in it.

"Jake ... not to get things off on the wrong foot, but I hear the first body found in the desert is Tiago's ... "

I nodded. "Lemm's wrecked, but Geordi's helping. And Matt."

" ... He's a good boy, your Matt." I smiled, in agreement. "He says he's from Florida. Is he going home after this?"

"Connie," I said, a chuckle in my voice. "Already set your sites on somebody else?"

"Don't worry, Jake, nobody comes before you."

"That could be read a whole bunch of ways." And I winked at her.

She swatted at me then twisted the caps off two bottles.

"I've been thinking," she said, "that interview you gave to Sousie Fornia changed the conversation."

"It wasn't that much."

"False modesty is as big a sin as an overactive ego. Don't fall into that trap. You come across well, on-camera. You're articulate.

You'd be a fine spokesperson for anyone, and a huge danger to anyone you opposed."

"Thanks. I try."

She handed me a beer then raised a toast. "To success."

"May our enemies be unconscious of our purpose."

"That's an odd thing to say."

"It's from an Alfred Hitchcock movie — *The Lady Vanishes*. Tone's into classic films, musicals. We watched *Cabaret* a dozen times before I asked him if he was hintin' at havin' a three-way with Liza Minnelli."

"I've been told I look like Liza." She batted her eyes.

I chuckled and winked at her as I brought the pot of chili over. I started to ladle it out, but she stopped me.

"I've got this," she smiled. "You unpack the goodies."

I dove into it. Tortilla chips. Bottle of Tabasco Sauce. Chili con queso. Grated cheese. Pico de gallo. Each in its Tupperware container. "Like Nana used to have," I whispered.

"Hmm?"

"Nothin'," I said as I set them on the table. "And no handcuffs. Hmph."

"Who needs 'em?" she chuckled. "So ... did you finish college?"

I pulled a hot tray of cornbread from the oven. "Nope."

"I'm surprised."

"That's life, full of left turns and right ones. Truth is, I didn't need it for my career."

"What do you do?"

"Graphic arts. For an advertising agency in Copenhagen."

I pulled out a chair for her, but she shook her finger at me. "I always sit near the kitchen. It's the host in me."

I used a chopping knife to cut some nice neat squares into the beautifully browned cornbread, put one on the plate by her bowl, then sat down and crumbled some into the chili, sprinkled on the extras, had a spoonful ... and it was just as good as the first time.

"Oh, Connie, if I wasn't a wiener dog, you'd be the girl I'd go for, you would. Believe me."

"My grandmother says, *The way to a man's heart is through*

his stomach. I've proven her right, more than once." She smiled as she sprinkled the extras on hers and slowly mixed them in.

I downed some beer. "You mind me askin' ... why don't you already have somebody? You're pretty. And, um, pretty ready, if you don't mind my sayin'."

She laughed and leaned back. "I have too much going on to handle a relationship, right now. Besides, I like to be the one on top, and not many men go for that."

"Oh, Connie," I chuckled, "you'd be surprised."

"Don't bet on it," she giggled back. "So, Jake ... are you thinking of moving here or returning to Denmark?"

I eyed her, then shrugged and sipped more beer. It tasted good and worked just right with the chili's spices. "I like Copenhagen. Like the people and the attitude. Like my job. But like everywhere, it's changin' ... not necessarily for the better. Now that Owen's gone, I'll have property here. So I've been thinkin' 'bout it. Makes too much sense not to."

"You could sell it. Market's good, again."

"True. But the fact is, there is a fight goin' on, and whether I like it or not, I got dragged into it ... and I don't run from fights. So maybe I will settle here. Find somebody to run for DA."

She blinked. "You're willing to back a candidate?"

"Somebody's gotta put a leash on Philby."

"Owen talked about Preston doing that."

I had to drink more beer, the chili was so spicy. I didn't remember it being like that, before. Not that I minded, but I like DP with something that burns so nice.

"Preston's not all that into the idea," I said, "and if he doesn't want to run but only does it 'cause he's talked into it, he'll lose. No, I want somebody who'll win."

"Become your own little power broker?" she purred.

"I've got some cash. I could get things goin'. If you had a law degree, I'd suggest you."

"I can check around. See who might be interested."

"Perfect. We may wind up in bed, together, after all."

"Now Jake," she leered, "don't tease ... "

I took another gulp of the beer. I could feel sweat under my goatee ...

Then my eyes darted about the room and everything shifted a little. "Whoa, that was weird."

"What?"

"My eyes just went squirrely and ... and ... "

The room whispered around me like a shape-shifting thing.

"What is it?" Her voice shrieked in its softness.

For some reason she was by the patio door and it was black and open beside her and the breeze was like icy fire on my skin.

I stood up. Tumbled back. "Connie, I ... sorry ... I don't feel so ... so good."

She was beside me. Supporting me. "Took you long enough."

Suddenly the stairs became an escalator as she whisked me up. I giggled. "Fourth floor, please," popped out of me. "Need shorts. Body wraps. Born to run."

"Sure, Jake. Whatever you say."

I fell face down on my bed, my head out around Mars.

"Shit, Connie ... what ... in that chili?"

"Just relax and go with it," she murmured as she straddled my ass.

It's weird, but while some part of me felt her hands grab me in places they shouldn't, and she had me locked in by her legs so I could barely squirm, none of it made sense. I'm a wiener-dog, not a pussy hound, and she knows it. That's when I floated off to God-knows-where for a second and came back to find I was face up and my hands were under me and my jeans were halfway down my hips and my shirt was torn away from my body. Wasn't it Dion who told me if I tried take her up on her moves she'd cut and run? Boy, was he wrong-wrong-wrong.

"God, Jake, boxer-briefs?" she was saying, her voice thick as daggers. "Circuit boys wear designer jocks."

Her hands grabbed my crotch. For some reason, what she was doing felt good, but I had the sense I wasn't really up for anything yet. I would be, soon, though. Not a good idea. Nope. Tone said not to be alone with her. So move your ass, Jake, before she does a strap-on with you, like *Myra Breckinridge*.

But I couldn't move. I started to drift to the ceiling and wanted to pull my hair to stop it but my hands refused to pay attention. I slammed my head back against the wall to jolt the flow and growled in a mutter, "So ... kill meeeee ... like you kill Tiago ... and Luis?"

She froze into stone and her eyes burned like fire and her face shifted into the wicked witch of the west and twice as cruel and fuck that revisionist musical and she drifted down to touch her nose to mine. Hands gripped my ears, like I was Dumbo.

"What did you say?" whispered from her like a lion's roar.

I giggled and sang, "I know what you're thinkiiiing. You wonder why I chose youuuuu. Out of all the suspects in Palm Spriiiiiings." She sat back, hair flaming around her face in furious hate. I kept giggling. "It's 'cause I know you did it. But how'd I know you did it? Ooohh, the biggest fuckin' cluuuue. Came the day that I met youuuuuuuuuu." More laughter.

"You're not making sense," she softly shrieked.

"First day. We met. You called ... cops on me."

"Of course. I thought someone broke into — "

"Why not think it's Owen? Ran off. Everybody thought. Gonna come back. No alarm. Couldn't be him. You knew. Already dead. So ... told Roy I come ... to find my uncle ... set him an' ... an' Chet on me ... "

The room whipped around. Her fingers floated to my chest. Claws ripped open my flesh. I burst into laughter.

"Tone ... right. You don't take no for ... answer, lady." I tried to roll over, but she was still straddling me. I felt my dick flop around. "Oh-oh, now you know ... I'm circumcised. Don't tell anybody. Will think I'm a slut." Then my voice dropped to a growl. "Like they think you're nice. When you really. Killin' us. My uncle. Tiago. Muscle bunnies. Boy name Luis. Now meeeee?"

Fire sparked each word. "You think I rape and murder men?"

"Oh, no. Tiago liked things like you. He's ... pussy-hound. You could'a had him. None of this shit. You're pretty. And pretty ready. Shit, you pretty ready. No, you didn't kill 'em. Prob'ly just helped. Like now."

That bounced her off the bed. She locked into stone, her face cold. Her hair straight and flowing like a river. Her voice echoing through canyons of forever. "I can't believe you're saying that to me. After all I've done for the gay community?"

"You done NOTHING! Just words! All words. I looked at ... at record." Her shadow grew big, behind her. Massive. Endless. "Speeches? Great. But action? To back 'em up-up-up? Zero. Zip! Nada! You bitch Nieri's Trojan Horse-lette? You're your plan? Help her drive the gay away without the pray?"

Connie jumped on the bed and flipped me onto my belly and straddled my back. Forced my jeans down my legs. My hands and feet kept frozen in place. I laughed, it hurt and tickled and tore at me so much. "Connie! CONNIE! Stop! I'm a wiener dog, not a pussy hound! Tone ... never forgive this ... "

She rolled me on my back, her face millimeters from mine and miles away. Her voice appeared in my brain. "How're you recording this?"

"Huh?" I said, in total eloquence. My shoulders screamed at me that this position was not at all right, and my ribs were too totally unhappy.

She showed me my cell phone. It was off. "You're not recording on this, so how're you doing it?"

"Oooooh! Oooh-nooo. No, thought I would ... but you jumped ahead on me of it. Like leapfrog." More giggles.

She slung the phone off to the moon. Her face was Medusa at her loveliest, her hair twisting and turning like snakes. She rose to sit on my legs, in slow-motion.

"How did you know?" echoed from her.

"Drug, bitch." I had to fight to focus. Fight to raise myself to my elbows to shut my shoulders up. Now my hands yelled at me and my ribs threatened to tear themselves out of my side. "Remains remain. All in coroner's report. Special-ilty K-K-K-K. That in one dead guy. No need for suspect-tion-ing. Two dead guys? Yeah, trend but ... coincidental-izing. So ... what? But four of 'em? Our own little *Dexter*."

Suddenly she was to my right, just standing there, cold and still. Her hands hidden. All dark shadows. Twice her size. And in front of me, at the same time. I didn't know which one to talk to, so I looked at the ceiling. Swirling like Van Gogh's *Starry Night*. My voice got tender and vicious. "Why Tiago? Pussy hounds like pretty-ready girls like you. No need for rape. Why do this to him ... to start? Was it ... kill him 'cause ... he might tell how ... Roy Harper's fuckin' his brother?"

"Roy Harper is not homosexual," rumbled from the shadows.

"Suuuuuuurrrrre. Suuurre ... "

Connie crawled up me, like a spider. "He's not. He came to me. And came in me. He was a wonderful lover. I can prove it."

"Bitch, pleeeeeeaase ... 'cause Roy was pretty ready for you? Ex-gay just ... go from a top to a bottom-m-m-m-m. Like you like-ike-ike ... "

Her legs spread around me. "What plan did you mean?"

"Kill Roy," I chuckled. "Hide with other deaths. Blame all on my uncle. Use to make people scared of gay-gays."

"You're being ridiculous ... "

"That's why argument ... that night. Meredith for witness. Says it's Roy. Him dead soon after. *Oh-my-God ... the faggot did it.* But Owen ... died that night. Uh-oh, can't blame him. Got to think. What if … the fag just … vanishes-es-es ... ?"

The shadows exploded into blinding light. Grasping noises echoed through my brain, like a devil's claw. Scratching. From a hollow room. Scratching. Shadows went gray and white and green and melted into walls of lavender and lace and blood and hands walked down my chest and over my belly and fingernails dug into my pubes. Made me feel it where it counted.

"If that's the plan," she screamed, soft and low, "why kill Tiago?"

"Told you." I giggled. "Momma found out Roy ... fucked Lemm. Momma don't like ... be lied do. Betrayed. Poster boy for 18/20 gonna prove 18/20's crap-pah? What's worstest? He's close to Mr. Money for God. Married asshole's daughter. But she thinks Tiago knows ... all a lie. Gotta keep Little Lord Flauntin'-Lawton safe from the ticky-tacky. Safe from gay guy tortured to pretend is straight. So can ... get the hell out of hell. Go back to bein' queer ... shadow queer ... an' look at Tiago. Looks like Roy. Hmm ... Owen … pain to Father Paul. Hurts PSALMS. What if ... serial killer? Kills guys like Tiago and Roy? All needed is proof. Like ... like video of his hand on ass of man about to be killed."

"Video? You've seen it?"

"Yeah. Kill couple more guys nobody cares about. Then kill Roy. Cop go missin'? People go crazy. Find his body. Raped and killed by faggot! *Ohmigod, queers is horrible! Drive them away!* Then it's buh-bye-birdie-bye-bye."

She didn't move. She was back to being solid stone.

"Ridiculous," growled from her. "Tiago was killed a year ago. If we were going to kill Roy, too, why wait until after Owen vanished?"

"Roy been with other men? Muscle bunnies. Wanna find out who they are. Kill 'em all. So no trail back to him when killed. There's Lemm. Been with Roy. But grab wrong kid. Look like him. Dress like him. Oopsie. Oh, well … kill him, too."

She all but chirped, "But Tiago and that boy were raped and murdered by some diseased faggot. No proof to the contrary."

"Drugs!"

"Party drugs used by queers everywhere? With Negra Modelo sold in stores all over California? That's your proof?"

"It's in beer? Good. Afraid was in chili. Super-secret stuff for kick-ass flavor. Would not be cooool … "

"So, that's the best you have? Really?" She pinched my tits hard enough to make the room stop moving, for a second. "No one can tie me to anything."

I growled and snapped. "Connieeeee, don't be stupid!" She pressed against me, gleaming like quartz. Cold. Unyielding. More giggles shot out of me, but I was not laughing. "Gettin' scary for 'em. Owen's found. Roy dies? Can't blame him. Even worse? Roy knew two dead muscle-bunnies. They were muscle bunnies together, once. Fuckin' like rabbits. Muscle bunny rabbits. Closet-a-go-go there. Suicides, no more, so … who has reason to kill? Roy? No … can't have that."

She leaned back. "The suicides have been reclassified?"

My hands and arms and neck threatened to walk away from me, they hurt so much. "Listen! Can't blame Owen. Can't blame Roy. Who next? Whooooooo? Connie. You're pretty ready. Liberal ID. Gay buddies. Man rape talk-k-k. Kill Roy, then suicide you. C'est complet. That's French. For all done."

A voice of ice and flame whispered over me. "Then how do you figure into this?"

"Dunno. 'Cause I figured-ed-ed it out? Maybe? Or maybe I got the look. I got the look. Like Prince says. Like Roy? Keep story goin' till Roy dead. All done. Over and out."

"What if this is all I want?" Her nails dug into my pubes.

It hurt and I gasped, "Connieee ... not pretty ready for you. Too wiener dog. Roy's dick is pretty readier than mine ... and when you strangle him ... it'll get to be big enough for you."

She slapped me and slapped me and slapped me and the world got clear, for a moment, as I tasted blood and snarled, then laughed and twisted around and the shadow-filled room fell on me, shrieking, and wrapped snakes around my throat and got above me on the bed and pulled tight and I couldn't breathe and heavy stones sat on my legs, holding me down, and I couldn't get the leverage to twist away because my arms froze behind me and my brain screamed from a thousand needles jabbing into it and I tried to howl or growl or yowl but couldn't get the sounds to come out ... and I couldn't breathe I couldn't breathe I couldn't breathe and the darkness was so heavy above me I couldn't twist away and I was hard from Connie riding me but that was crazy 'cause I'm a wiener dog and Tone'd go nuts if I fuck anyone else, no matter what my excuse, and that couldn't happen 'cause he's mine and I'm his and I can't die not now not so close to being back together with him and light flooded the room and Connie fell back and Tiago drifted down from on high like an angel but it wasn't him ... couldn't be him because he's dead ... so maybe I'm dead now ... but he's screaming filthy words in Spanish, words I haven't heard in years, and angels don't cuss and Matt's with him. Matt's with him? Matt? He's not dead and it's all wrong ... and then one of my feet jerked free from the stones holding it and I kicked and bucked up and pressed deeper into the bed and the snakes slithered away and Matt fought with Connie but she slammed him against the stone cold wall and turned on me and her hands gleamed like razors and she howled like a jackal so I twisted and kicked her back with my foot and she crashed against a dresser with a scream crueler than Satan's and Matt jumped up to cover her ...

... And the shadow vanished ...

... And Tiago flew back to heaven ...

... And I wanted to follow but my hands were on fire and the hell of screams and crashes and devil's shrieks filled my ears, going on forever and my head was pounding so hard and I could taste the chili coming back up and a noose hanging over a closet door reached for me ... laughed at me ... and I dissolved into more giggles.

And silence.

Blankets of silence.

All the craziness vanished. I saw Lemm float up beside the bed, his face pure in its horror. Blood dripped from his eyes.

Matt rolled me face down on the bed. I was barely able to gulp in air. My voice was raw and tore at me. I swallowed, over and over, trying to calm it ... and bit by bit the room stopped jolting and my hands were free and Matt was at my feet.

"Hogtied," he muttered. "They fuckin' hogtied you."

He made me stand. My legs were loose and wobbly, but he let me lean on him. "C'mon, just get your jeans back up."

Connie sobbed like a roaring beast deprived of dinner. I watched her slither around the bed to where blood painted the walls and Tiago was a ghost but not Tiago, but it was because it had to be ... but younger and I patted Matt's back and gurgled, "Matt. Lemm."

"It's okay, he's ... " He looked around and turned into ice. Lemm was white as a sheet and rocking back and forth. "Oh shit."

Matt sat me on the bed and I rolled over to watch him grab Lemm and hold him and force him to look away ... but then Matt's eyes focused on the floor and his voice shook like a 9.5. "Oh, Jesus, Jake. Jesus ... "

The fire in my hands grew soft. My legs could move, again. My fingers were red. Smoking. I forced them to flex. I looked at Matt, his big eyes hurt and scared and close to hysterics. I rolled off the bed onto the floor and realized my right foot had come out of my boot, and the boot was caught in a rope tangled around my other boot.

I forced myself to stand and grip Matt's arm and croak, "You see that?" I motioned to the bathroom door. Bright light flared from within. He forced his eyes away from the horror. Saw a noose hanging there. He gasped and nodded. "That was for. For me." He looked at me. Confusion and anger screamed in his eyes. I gasped out, "You get it all?"

"Yeah ... yeah, every word," said Matt.

Connie stopped slithering. She looked at me, her face torn up from the pain. No Medusa. Not stone. Just pathetic. Just sad.

"You did record this," she murmured.

"We bugged the rooms," Matt croaked. "I'm in the car. Outside. Close to pick up signal and ... and ... and heard Jake choking and ... and ... Jake, why didn't you tell us ... who ... ?"

"Cut it!" I growled.

I looked at Lemm, his eyes lost in a thousand-yard stare. One hand held the knife I'd cut the cornbread with, now covered in blood. He'd be gone, in a moment.

I made myself take the knife from him and grumble, "Matt, get him out of here."

"No, no, no," he whispered, "I can't leave you like this."

My wallet was on the dresser. I groped for it. Found the hotel key still in its envelope. Held it out for him. "I'm fine, Matt. I'm back. Get him out of here. Key to hotel room. Car key on table. Don't go to Meredith's. Clean up. Get rid of clothes. Do not let him near cops. Do not come back here."

"Jake!"

"GO!" I screamed. "He was never here. You were never here. Got me? Never. I'll call cops. Okay? You ... take care of him. Take care of him. Keep him away from here."

Matt glanced between me and Lemm, a couple times, then he accepted the key and guided the kid from the room. I waited till I heard the front door close then turned to stare at the scrunched up body on the floor. Black pullover and pants slashed and soaked to a dark red. Long lean hands curled in pain and fear, no artist's hump on the right middle finger.

Sure enough, it was the hand in the video of Tiago.

It was Grace Nieri.

I looked at Connie. "How ... she talk you into it? Kill a man. Strip him. Bury so long ... can't prove wasn't raped. She wouldn't tell you why ... she's really doin' it. To hide murder of her son ... 'cause he's a fag. She'd give you a story. You're not dumb, Connie. How'd she get you ... think this ... a good idea? Why think murder is okay?"

She just wept. Could not look at me.

"Okay, why ... why kill me, too? Except increase blame on you. For you. For everything?"

"No ... " she whispered. "No ... "

I dropped on the bed. My head wanted to fall off and the floor rocked back and forth. I know every inch of me hurt, but that was a concept beyond my thought process because the room shifted like a Rubik's Cube.

Maybe I wasn't as back as I thought.

"How'd she get you ... go along?" I whispered. "Why think this a good idea?"

"Grace ... " Connie said. I looked at her and she gazed back at me, haggard. Her voice grew strong. Deliberate. "She wasn't part of this. It ... it was Owen. Tiago ... I ... I slipped him some Viagra and the Ketamine. He was too focused on that girl, the one who got herself pregnant, so he wouldn't even ... and I just wanted to be with him. And I was ... but then he died. Just died. I called Owen, and he took the body away. I don't know what he did with it, after."

I shook my head. I think I was smiling. "You take blame for dead woman? And still blame Owen? Why? Is it PSALMS? Protect PSALMS?!" My voice grew to screaming. "It Father Prick's idea? Kill nobodies for God and blame fags 'cause no big deal if it turns back ... tide of queer rights?! That why you take blame?! For Father Fucking Paul!?"

"No." The word whispered from her, more like a breath than something spoken. Her head began to shake. "No ... you're wrong."

The room swirled. God, I'd have killed for some water. "Right. Right. Paul knew Lemm, so if Lemm was target, she wouldn't have killed wrong kid. I'm missin' something ... "

Connie sat up. Leaned against the dresser. "You're missing it all. You think people will believe a woman like Grace Nieri would commit murder?! Or a man like Father Paul would help?!" She laughed, near hysterics. "You're crazy! Everyone'll see that you're crazy! And I took you for smart."

I looked at her, feeling nauseous. God, she was horrifying in her nastiness. I had to make myself croak, "Never said I was, bitch.

Just enough of an asshole to fight as dirty as you."

I forced myself to stand so I could button my jeans ... but almost toppled over. My shirt was shredded and I could not figure out how to put on that boot, so I just steadied myself and headed down the stairs. The Rubik's Cube was back, twisting and turning, but I figured if I timed it right, I could walk over each and every colored square the second it paused. So that's what I did. And then I was by the front door, muttering, "Son-of-a-bitch, I made it."

Only the door was bolted from inside. How did Matt do that? Then my brain remembered the beer bottle I'd drunk from. Drugs in it. I wanted it, so danced back to the dining table grab it ... and saw I still held the bloody knife. My fingerprints on it. I chuckled. Let anybody even try to tie Lemm into this. He was in my pack, now, and if they tried to hurt him they'd find out what scorched earth means. I just hoped he'd be okay.

That's when I looked up and saw Cerberus guarding the patio door, letting no one in or out. Skin as black as ice. Eyes sparking flames of hate. Grace's head cold and cruel on one shoulder, Connie's laughing on the other. The middle one growling without a mouth, just a snout. All nothing but shadows. Smoke whispering from it. Body shining like polished leather. Someone I knew and didn't know ...

I think I smiled as I barked, "Ruff. Ruff."

Its paw raised a baseball bat and it swung at me and I ducked and pain exploded behind my eyes ... then I was on the floor, caught in thick smoke and coughing my brains out. Red and yellow light danced along the walls and over the carpet, and the shriek of wood popping and burning and floors collapsing tore at my ears. Drums slammed against all four corners of my skull, and the carpet under me was red and sticky and all I could think was, "Way to go, Jake. You didn't make it, after all."

Then my eyes closed.

— VII —

Burning embers hit my skin. Jolted me back to right now. Fire licked up the walls and stairs and into the kitchen, just visible through the thick smoke. Vague sirens called to me. I rolled over. Both bottles were busted on the floor. The knife gone.

Shit.

I rolled over, again.

Crawled onto the tile of the dining area.

Under the table.

Between the legs of the chairs.

Closer and closer to the patio door. The reflection of the flames followed me.

The door was closed. I couldn't get it to open. Couldn't make myself stand to grasp the latch. So I reached back. Grabbed one of the chairs. Swung it around to smack at the glass ... and nothing happened. Shit. Double-pane. I couldn't get momentum enough. My head swam in air as thick as honey. I was so close to not caring anymore. But what would happen to Tone if I wasn't there to kick some ass? And Matt and Lemm ... not in a good place. And someone to change the story ... lay blame ...

I hit the glass, again. Still nothing. Smoke was thicker. I hit the glass, again. Softer.

Nothing.

Then voices. Boots running up. Glass hit and hit and hit and shattering down around me. Fire exploding as hands grabbed at me. Flames licking my ass and legs. Suddenly I was weightless and then crashing back onto gravel and sand, coughing my lungs out. Choking.

God, the night air felt good and clean and pure. Ten billion stars in a sky of black velvet. A moon glowing in its tiny aura. Air kissing my skin like a lover. Washing away the sins of the world. No more shadows or darkness. Just Geordi's yapping. I wept from the beauty of it. I could have stayed there all night.

I was cradled up and gently carried through a fence to more people. Firefighters. Paramedics. Guided down to a gurney. Mask over my face. I could breathe. Rolled inside ... outside ... into chaos. Fire trucks and a host of people running about, some with hoses, some with axes, some with nothing as they watched the blaze, in horror.

I saw Ian spray the roof of Cliff's and Ned's with a garden hose to keep the fire away. It wasn't working. No Ned to be seen. Cliff probably still at work. I felt I should do my part, but the thought made my stomach flip and my head careen into space.

Another fire engine roared in and hooked up its hoses in a millisecond, followed by a cop car. Harper and Morrow in it. Talk about my own worst nightmare. But when they got out they didn't say a word; just watched the place burn as —

WHOMPH! The gas tank in the SUV exploded. Sent burning debris everywhere. Slammed Morrow to the ground. I smirked and thought, "That's what you get for being top-heavy, bitch." Only now the empty condo on the other side of Owen's was in flames, and someone yelled the scrub on the hillside was catching, so the firefighters focused on that as a third truck roared in and hooked up to the hydrant and fought to save Cliff's condo.

Meredith saw me and rushed over, shaken. "Jake!"

I couldn't find my voice to answer her; the mask felt too good to move, so I just gave her a vague wave.

One of the paramedics asked, "That his name?"

Meredith answered. "Jacob Blaine."

The other paramedic nodded to the fire and asked, "Jake, is that your place?"

I nodded.

The first paramedic pressed something icy to my head as the second examined abrasions on my wrists and marks around my neck. He nudged his partner. "Get those cops over here."

I don't remember much of what happened from that point. I do recall Chet asked me questions. And Harper stormed about, very intense. All I remember saying was, "Dunno. Connie. Came to talk. About body in desert. Ate chili. Beer. Next thing. I'm at back door. Hurt all over. Head killin' me."

I didn't mention Cerberus; it was too much like I had just fallen and slammed my crazed-up brain. I figured I'd deal with it when I was back from the fuzzy place.

The next thing I knew, I was in a hospital ER, intubated, being treated for a concussion, burns and smoke inhalation. A gash in my scalp took sixty-three stitches to close, and I spent the night in ICU ... and even though I don't remember it, I signed off on them doing a rape kit, thanks to abrasions where my boxer-briefs were torn off.

They tested my blood and it came back positive for Special K and Viagra.

The fire was huge news. It was seen for fifty miles in every direction, being on a hilltop, but it looked like a normal situation so it began to die down ... until a woman's body was discovered in the ruins. Then it shot back to top story, again.

Of course, Detective Pedrales came to question me the second I could talk. By this time investigators had determined the fire was arson. More big news. And Sousie Fornia had pointed out the condo was owned by a gay man who'd been killed and that I'd been gay-bashed, so speculation exploded about this being a hate crime. Helped that the DA's office turned stone cold silent about it.

That didn't stop Pedrales from suggesting I'd ingested all that crap on my own and killed the woman and set the fire, myself, to cover it up. I may have been fuzzy-brained, but I could tell she was bullshittin' me. She knew I was the one who got attacked. Made me very wary of her.

Of course, by this point it was public knowledge that Tiago was the dead man in the grave. So I, uh, let slip how Connie'd been fixated on him, and just happened to mention how she'd come on to me in front of Meredith. Talked of handcuffs and wanting to prove to me I really liked girls, and wouldn't take no for an answer. Then I played Little-Sir-Squirrel and let slip all sorts of information, like wondering if she'd killed Tiago when he wouldn't give in to her and planned to do the same to me. Pedrales didn't even try to hide her sneering contempt of the idea, but she called Ginty, who got a search warrant, then she went into Connie's condo and office to get something with her DNA. It matched what they found on me.

Now, Pedrales at Connie's office barely got a mention on the news, nor did anyone release the DNA info. But then a second woman's body was found in the ruins. And it turned out both of them died before the fire began. The media went nuts, hounding Philby and Pedrales and Walinski and anybody else they could find to get more details. Thank God I was isolated during the worst of that.

Except Philby appeared in my hospital room to question me about the two dead women. Ginty had warned Preston, so he just happened to be visiting when Philby arrived, and he and Philby had a lovely back and forth about what might have happened as I kept not remembering anything that ever happened in my entire life. Short story — the doctor confirmed I was struck from behind and firefighters confirmed nothing had collapsed on top of me, so it was too obvious another person was in the place.

Philby wasn't satisfied, but he had to storm off, empty-handed. After he was gone, Preston shook his head and said, "And he made it through law school? Wonder how many times he had to sit for the bar exam?"

I just smiled. Again, I said nothing about Cerberus.

I was finally released from the hospital on Sunday. My good healthy lungs and hard-assed head minimized the damage, leaving me with a non-stop migraine barely controlled by Darvocet. I had to be careful with my voice and exertion, but the consensus was I'd be back to normal in a few weeks. They kept my clothes, so Matt brought me a pair of Lemm's sweats and hoodie. They were tight, but the hood covered my bandaged head. We snuck out the back to avoid the reporters.

As he drove me to the fortress, Matt told me he and Lemm were still at the hotel, keeping a low profile.

"I ... I don't know what to do with the recording, yet," he said. "Listening to the stories on the news ... "

"Burn it to a CD-R," I croaked. "And clean it off your laptop. I don't want you or Lemm linked to this in any way."

Matt nodded. "He still thinks he should go to the cops."

"Don't let him. They're diggin' for blood, and they will tear him to shreds then blame him for everything."

"I ... I'm doing what I can."

"How's *he* doin' with what happened?"

Mat shrugged. "He won't talk about it. So we just watch movies. Futz with the camera equipment. Order in food. Sleep."

"That's it?"

He nodded, then shrugged. "Dunno if it means anything, but last night ... we were playing a game on my laptop and he laid his head on my shoulder. I mean, we were at a pause in the game and it was late but ... "

I patted him on the back. "It means something."

"But he's so beautiful and I ... I'm ... I've never felt like this for anybody, before. I hurt for him and I'm scared for him and I look at him and I'm so happy and ... "

"You'll be good together."

" ... You think?"

I nodded.

Of course, my uncle's condo was destroyed, along with all my things, and the ones to either side of it badly damaged. Ian let Cliff stay with him. Ned had vanished the night of the fire; I got the feeling Cliff didn't care. I got moved to Meredith's guest room, making Geordi happier than ever. Greedy mutt thought he'd get fed twice as much turkey bologna.

I waited till Matt headed back to the hotel to call Sousie Fornia to offer another exclusive, off-the-record, of course, about how Philby's office had a lead on who Tiago's killer was. They were keeping it hush-hush because it was somebody big in the community. I didn't know who, but it was serious. When she asked about the fire and me surviving it, I did a Philby and said I couldn't talk about it, but it had something to do with the murders. Best to let the scandal-hounds connect the dots. Then I called Matt and had him mail the CD-R to Ginty, with my uncle's condo as the return address.

It was only nine, but I felt so filthy and down, I sat in a scalding hot tub for an hour, just soaking and trying not to think. Didn't work. The Darvocet let too many thoughts scratch at my own locked doors, along with the cold reality of all those deaths: Owen, Tiago, Bruno, Marco, Luis, Connie and Grace. There was no emotion behind it. No pain. No sadness or fear. Just the calm acceptance that man is the devil's creation.

The last time I'd felt like this was the night I brought a new guy into Slaughter's fold. I'd belonged to that animal for twelve months, and I was back to wondering if I'd be better off in oblivion instead of three more years of that hell when a college brat was brought in because he'd baked hash brownies for his fraternity. Got twice as long as me. No question he'd be a braying animal in the space of eighteen days.

Except Slaughter took a liking to the guy. To me, he was just average — pale skin, leaner than me, not quite as tall, younger by a few years, lighter hair and less of it. A couple tatts on his arms felt wrong in contrast to his totally white-bread face. I also noticed how his hands had no calluses on them at all. But he had long smooth legs and a perky ass, just like a girl. So my owner staked his claim, straight off, and like I said, he was snarly enough for people to take a step back and see what was happening before making their own move.

Then that night, Slaughter told me, "Make him mine, he's yours, too."

I nearly wept. That meant I wouldn't be whored out for junk or favors; perky butt would. I could grow my hair back and be a man, again. All I'd have to do from that point on is watch the boss's back. And my reward would be getting to use the college brat when Slaughter wasn't busy with him.

Of course, now I think he did that because I was bulking up from exercising, which might cause a situation where I challenged him for alpha dog. Best to keep a potential enemy on your side, and truth is, I was so grateful, he got months of loyalty.

The guy ... his name was West; I don't remember if it was his first or last. I made friends with him. Got him to rely on me. Slaughter even helped me fight off a couple guys who cared more about getting their dicks serviced than whose territory they were poaching on. That made West my BFF, times ten.

Until one day, after he'd been in two, maybe three weeks, we were in the back of the library and I talked him into letting me blow him. He wasn't cut, which surprised me, but he loved me getting him off. That set him up for some reciprocation ... and I made sure it happened. It was really just a hand-job, with him making himself kiss the head of my dick, but it was enough to make me go nuts and fire all over his face. He nearly hurled.

But we kept it up, every few days, for two weeks, then I got him to fuck me. I made myself cum while he was in me, nearly making him scream when he let loose.

When he could speak, again, he whispered in my ear, "I could do that, again."

I nodded and said, "Let's see what happens."

That's when I gave the signal to Slaughter. He was ripe. He got West transferred to our cell. It was a two-fer but there was room for a fold-up cot and the guards loved that we were willing to not bitch about another guy sharing our space. Even if it's obvious why we weren't bitching.

I had West fuck me, that night, when Slaughter *dropped off asleep*. Which was part of the ritual; he was really jacking-off as West screwed me. He thought he was dead quiet as he used his hand but I knew his grunts when he was close to firing a load, and he made 'em, twice. The next night, after lights out but before West was asleep, Slaughter calmly talked the guy into letting him fuck him. Used the excuse that he'd been fucking me, so he must be into it and Slaughter'd protected him, so ...

They did it on the bunk under mine. West choked in pain through the whole thing. And when it was done, Slaughter had me clean him up.

He was bleeding, so I packed his ass with toilet paper and told him how lucky he was. If we hadn't been watching out for him, he'd have been torn apart by a dozen black guys or some of the Latino crowd; they loved making white boys hurt. Then I told him I'd show him how to make it easier on himself.

He thanked me as he drifted back onto his cot.

Then I crawled up onto my bunk. But I didn't sleep. Just stared at the ceiling, accepting how I'd become a devil, too. That's how it is, in prison — nothing but fire and flame. And the scum in high office want to make it more-so. Even as they make sick fucking jokes about it and sell off prisons to their corporate masters and find any excuse they can to send men, women and kids to their for-profit jails, and who want the country to think it's good and proper instead of grotesque and diseased.

Two nights later, I got the okay to fuck West. He let me, without a fight. Mainly because Slaughter was there to keep watch ... and to watch. I showed the guy ways to cut down on the pain and damage while not letting Slaughter know what I was doing. It was some trick. I also made sure he got off on it by massaging his prostate and dick. Slaughter wanted to see him cum; that made him officially ours.

When Slaughter dropped to sleep, I taught West how to fake a deep-throat blow-job and shared all my tips on how to keep safe and healthy in that hell-hole. He wasn't dumb; he figured out he was my replacement, and that eventually someone else would replace him in servicing Slaughter's needs.

Two months after that, I found out West's father had been running against a Tea Party Nut for Congress and they wanted him to back out. When he hadn't, West was targeted for conviction, and Slaughter'd been given the job to make his life hell. Then daddy was passed word that if he didn't end his candidacy, his son would be handed over to the African-American side to be fucked to death. It worked. When I heard that, I filled West in, and I didn't touch him, again. He and I just told Slaughter I did. Fortunately, he didn't need to see us doing it, anymore.

I also got him to bulking up, so that by the time I was released, he was able to take care of himself, and Sylvester had already given him the okay to share the next guy brought in. It was too late; West had let his father know the reality of what had happened, and now he wanted to get some of his own back. One of them would probably get killed ... but that was between them.

That's how much of an animal I'd become.

So now I was sitting in that tub, knowing I was slipping back to being a devil. Tone talks about his evil and psychosis and all that crap, but what he has is some quirk in his DNA or something. No family hating him. No molestations that I know of. No reason to be like he is. Me? Mira's right; I am my father's son. Push me too far, I'll rip you apart like a cornered wolf. Like I'd almost done to Tone, over Dion. Like I was about to do to the scum who'd helped kill my uncle. And I didn't care.

And hated that I didn't.

— VIII —

Monday morning, the AG's agreement showed up, so I called Preston and said, "Bail him out." A few hours later, Matt and I met Tone as he walked out of the jail. His eyes still purple but healing. Clothes rumpled and blood-stained. The second he saw the bandage on my head, he froze, unable to speak or move or anything until I said, "I'm still here." Then he let us lead him to the car. Even when we got to the fortress and he saw the taped-off ruins, he said nothing.

Lemm was there, waiting. He walked with more gravity and his eyes were sharper, now. No longer a boy. I took him aside to whisper, "Thank you."

He frowned, his voice just as soft. "For what — ?"

I cut him off with, "For savin' my life."

He looked at me, hard. "Do you say she kills Tiago?"

"You saw what she was doin' to me."

He took a step back, his eyes lost in confusion. "I ... I did not think it was a woman. That a woman would do such a thing." I let him take his time accepting it. "She did this to my brother? To those other men? To Luis? Luis!?"

"And you punished her."

"But I still should have the blame for — "

"You stopped her! She got what she deserved. Leave it."

He looked at me with confusion ... and he said nothing more, but he did not stray far from Matt's side. Tone noticed and shot silent questions at me. I just shrugged. But while he said nothing about it, I noticed he and Lemm weren't wary creatures with each other, anymore.

I sat Tone down at Meredith's dining table and showed him the agreement. He just looked at it, confused, so I pointed out the dozen places he had to sign. Of course, everything had to be notarized and witnessed and crap, but it turns out Lorinda was able to do that, so she swung by in her usual breathless manner, it got done, copied and on its way, by five.

Not, however, before she had taken me aside to tell me, "That Mexican boy, he's one of the illegals Owen used." Then she pointed to Lemm.

"Lorinda, he's from Chile, and he has a green card."

"He does?" And did she perk up.

"And he's gay."

"He is? Oh, like that is such a waste."

"Not to Matt."

She looked at Matt and frowned at me. "Him, too?" I nodded.

"Why is it like all the cute guys are gay?"

"Because we're arrogant assholes."

She nodded and said, "Well, like yeah – look at you." Then she was off to her next best prospect before I could react.

Matt took over as mother hen and set Lemm to making coffee for everyone. He bought clothes for Tone since his were ruined in the fire, too, and also brought in a bottle of whiskey then made sure every cup had some in it. I'm not crazy about my coffee that way, but it lowered the tension so much, I got a refill. Of course, Geordi helped by begging from everyone, and Meredith saw to it we each had something to give him. Then when Matt and Lemm finally headed back to that Best Western for the night, the kid looked at him in such a tender, loving way, I hoped they'd do some serious bonding.

Tone, I took up to Meredith's guest room, undressed, led him into the shower and washed him from top to toe. He watched me like he couldn't believe what I was doing. Stopped me as I was toweling him off and touched the bandage on my head, his eyes wide and wet.

"I mean it, Tone," I whispered. "I'm still here."

"Too mean to kill?" croaked out of him. The first words he'd said all night. I just smiled. He nodded. "Good."

Ian was home, by that point, so he dropped by to re-tape both of us, chirping happily about how he'd had more action in the last ten days than he had in the previous five years. His hands didn't wander, so I let him chirp.

Then I ordered in Mexican and made Tone eat ... as well as drink a beer. After some hesitation, he dug into the meal like he'd never eaten before, and his face started to shine, again. Finally, I guided him onto the bed and snuggled in behind him and laid my face in the nape of his neck and held him close till daybreak. For the first time in months, I felt nothing in the way of resistance from him. Even as he slept, he gripped my left hand tight to his chest.

Oh, God, the smell of him, lying there with me. Yeah, Meredith's salon products were all over him, but they added to the beauty of this gentle muskiness he had that felt so alive and welcoming and right. It was home, once more, just him and me. So even though I barely got a wink of sleep, I felt alive and fresh in the morning.

And that was all I needed, right then.

The next morning, Matt and Lemm brought in bags of groceries and we had a kick-ass brunch. Eggs, Rosemary potatoes, ham, fruit, bagels and butter and jam ... and a couple bottles of cheap champagne. Meredith and Geordi joined in, as did Ian and Cliff. By the time it was over, we were all a little drunk and queeny. Then while the others sat in the living room to chat and polish off the champagne, Tone and I cleaned up.

God, I felt so easy. My guy was smiling and laughing and touching me, every now and then, as if to make sure I was still there. And when he saw how Matt had an arm draped over Lemm's shoulders, he nudged me and gently whispered, "Them getting together, that would make me so happy."

So I popped off with an idea that had been building in the back of my brain. "What about me suggestin' Matt and Lemm stay in Palm Springs? I own property here, now. Dion's movin'; I need somebody to keep watch, keep the grounds up."

"You don't want to sell the fortress?"

I shrugged. That hadn't really entered the equation. "Insurance'll pay to rebuild Cliff's unit. Owen's ... I could use that insurance to take over Ian's mortgage."

Tone didn't even cast me a glance as he gave a little bop of his head and said, "I'll talk him into it."

I nearly shot to the moon from joy. He was granite.

By this point, both news and gossip had connected Connie to the deaths of several men and the molestation of God knew how many more. That two of the dead men were gay meant nothing, nor did that poor Latino boy who was, as so many subtly whispered, probably illegal; what mattered was Tiago and the fact that he'd been taken away from a beautiful young woman who loved him, and his adorable baby girl. Oh, the media loved it, especially the national weeklies.

Of course, Father Paul, joined by two gay-hating ministers, said Connie was corrupted by being close to the gay community. That didn't get much kick, and even brought a fair bit of push-back. The love thwarted by jealousy angle was way sexier. Didn't hurt that the DA's office was still with the *No comments* on the case. I found out later that Ginty had handed the audio of me and Connie over to Philby, and he had shut the leaks down.

The rental company was really pissed about the SUV, but I mollified them by saying I was checking to see if it was covered by the homeowner's policy; Matt got the insurance's info off the bank records. Still, they refused to let me have another car. Don't know why. So Matt got one for himself while Tone and I used the Chrysler.

I'd postponed my appointment with Grace Nieri to Wednesday morning; they still hadn't publicly ID'd the other body, and I felt no need to act like I knew she was gone, forever. So that day, Preston and I were there at 9:55, bright-eyed and bushy-tailed, as Nana'd say. Lainey was calmness, personified.

"Ms. Nieri is unavailable," she said. I just smiled. I hadn't even told Preston about Grace. Lainey continued with, "Would it be all right if Mr. Karadjian worked with you?"

"Wasn't Mr. Baskin going to be here, too?" I asked.

"I am here, Mr. Blaine," shot a commanding voice from behind me. I glanced back to see both father and son coming down the stairs with a slim, unassuming, rather nervous sort of man.

Preston greeted him with a smile. "Aw, this is great! So you're the sacrificial lamb?"

"Mr. Karadjian is familiar with Mr. Taylor's account," said Baskin. "He'll be more than happy to assist you, in any way."

"Let's get going."

It took ten minutes to see that they'd put everything back in perfect order. "I found a small error, on our part," said the very meek, very apologetic Mr. Karadjian, never telling me what it was. "I can't believe it was unnoticed until now, but once it was corrected, everything fell together. All past due penalties and fees have been refunded, and there is no reason to consider foreclosure proceedings. We have also sent a report of our error to the credit reporting agencies. They will update his record, accordingly. Again, I do apologize on our bank's behalf, Mr. Blaine. I assure you we have corrected the mishap in our system and everything will be above-board, from now on."

Yeah, right. It was obvious from Baskin Senior's casual demeanor he'd made them fix it so there'd be no way to track the mess back to anybody. I didn't know if that meant he knew what had happened or if he was just trying to minimize the fallout, nor did I care. I just made them add Dion as a co-signer for the trust account and delegated all responsibilities for the properties to him. He had to come in to provide his ID. I didn't bother mentioning he was moving, nor did he.

Baskin piped in with legal points a lot, quickly parried by Preston, but his mind seemed to be elsewhere ... until he got a call and settled into total calmness. Scott probably said twenty words during the entire meeting, and that included him taking orders for lunch and calling it in. He didn't meet my eyes once.

As we were headed back to our cars, Preston told me the city's attorneys offered to settle $1.2 million on me for the beating, arrest and harassment.

"I'd have told you, last week," he said, "but you were kind of preoccupied." Then he winked at me.

"What's your thought?" I asked.

"Take it. Insurance'll cough up a million; city kicks in two-hundred-K. With all this uproar, the council'll give it a quick pass. It's just a couple asshole cops who pissed on you. Now one's on permanent desk duty while the other's vanished."

"Harper?"

He nodded.

"Betcha he and Ned ran off together," I said.

Preston eyed me and shook his head. "Against you, I take no bets. As for Philby, he's county, and they'll fight you every dirty way they can. Better if I take care of the bastard when I'm DA."

"Go for it," I said.

"Glad you see reason, Mr. Blaine," he said with a smirk. Then sadness crept into his eyes. "I still can't believe Connie was raping guys."

"You never know about people."

He nodded. "Why is it shit like that never happens to me?"

"Be too much like pedophilia."

"Aw, cut it out. I'm older than you, and lots hairier."

"You're right, Preston; maybe you're too much man."

He snorted. "I'd call you an asshole, but you just put me into a whole new tax bracket." Then he got very still. "Plus my wife thinks Jacob is a good middle name, if we have a boy ... so I shall acquiesce to your better judgment."

"Can I ask you — how do you two work it?"

He smirked. "I think the best way to keep a marriage happy is by keeping separate apartments, meeting in hotel rooms and acting like a couple of sluts. And there must be millions of hotel rooms in Southern California. Every damn one of them a business expense."

Then he called the city's attorneys and gave them the news.

Ian was off work, so I had him meet me at his credit union to open an account. When the city's money came in, I could put it there; I had zero trust in any bank. Then I opened a separate account for Preston Niemczyk's campaign for District Attorney of Riverside County and started working up the graphics. Local politics was about to get very, very interesting.

We spent the rest of the day with Dion and Kent and the family, as did Matt and Lemm. Dion got taken on by a management firm in Santa Monica to handle his own set of buildings. Kent had just given notice and the kids were excited about living near the beach. I hated to see them run off, but no begrudging here; kids come first. Instead, I bought Dion's and Ian's shares of the hillside. That cut me tight till the city's money came in and Castillo refunded the legal fees I'd paid, but Uncle Ari sent me a couple of jobs, so I was okay.

Since Tone's ankle monitor was from Texas, soon as I knew the signed docs had been delivered, I borrowed gardening shears from Dion and sliced the damned thing off him to send back. COD. Let 'em try and charge me for it.

Then that night, after Matt and Lemm had slipped back to their hotel, and Meredith was sound asleep with Geordi, Tone and I were alone. Watching fucking *Cabaret*. Ian had a DVD. Bastard. It took me back to that night ... but I could live with it.

Fortunately, at the point where Liza and Michael started their affair and she sang about how she might get lucky, Tone kissed my neck. Which led to more kissing. And touching. And holding tight to each other. And turning the DVD off long before Joel sings to his gorilla. And let's just say, we made ourselves into one, all over again. And after we were done, I fell into the best sleep, ever.

And when I woke the next morning, I was ready to finish scorching the earth.

— IX —

That morning, the news got all excited, again. There was official word from the coroner's office that the suicides of Bruno Vrasky and Marco Samuels had been reclassified as murders. And the other body found on the land by Dillon Road had been identified. Now Luis could have a decent burial, at least. Naturally, that brought the worldwide media to town. As they say, *If it bleeds, it leads.*

Then the police released the news that the second body in the fire was Grace Nieri's, and they had found her car in airport parking. It had been there since the night of the fire. Their new theory? Connie and Grace tried to keep Ned from killing me, so they were killed and he ran off, thinking I was dead, too. In short — blame the killer faggot.

A nation-wide alert was sent out for Ned, so I snuck Sousie a note about the recording and told her Grace's voice could be heard on it. No way would I let either bitch look good, even in death. Sousie was very happy for the next 24 hour news cycle, and even found out on her own that Roy was Grace's son by Roger Baskin, and that Roy had been tortured in an 18/20 clinic. Now the firm of Baskin and Baskin was being hounded for details, and everyone was trying to find Officer Roy to talk to him, so the police had to admit he'd gone missing.

BOOM! More headlines.

The next afternoon, now that I knew the news was traveling in the right direction, I toodled over to San Sebastian's office and strolled on in. The same super-sweet-receptionist greeted me in the same super-sweet manner, and kept smiling when I said I wanted to speak with Father Paul.

"He's in a meeting," she chirped. "And you don't have an appointment."

"He'll see me," I said.

She buzzed him, told him I was here, and sure enough he said, "Come in."

She happily led me down a temporary hall to a temporary door, and I entered to find Father Paul behind a cheap desk in a cheap room. He put on even less of a front than Preston. The only difference was, Samantha Ginty was seated in a cheap chair, across from him, eyeing me. "Mr. Blaine," whispered from her.

"Ms. Ginty," I said back.

"It's good you know each other," said Father Paul in a voice that suggested he knew a hell of a lot more than he was letting on. "Have a seat."

"I prefer to stand," I said. "Easier for me to speak."

"How're you doing since the fire?" she asked.

"Better an' better. I may get back to runnin', next week."

"It's by God's grace you survived," said Father Paul as he sat behind his amazingly neat desk. "What can I do for you?"

"First, can I ask why I'm here when Ms. Ginty's here?"

"Allow me, Father Paul," she said. "Baskin and Baskin has had a bit of a shakeup and they've asked me to come aboard to handle some defense cases. For some odd reason they think they need to rehabilitate their image."

"Is Scott okay with that?" I asked.

"He is no longer with the firm. Since my husband and I are about to have a child, I'll be better able to manage my schedule than were I to remain with the District Attorney's office."

"Will you be counsel for San Sebastian, too?"

"No, that's what I came by to tell Father Paul. That will be handled by the elder Mr. Baskin. But I will, of course, offer any assistance I can." And the look she gave me said she was still working for my father. I barely kept from laughing. She continued with, "So ... why are you here?"

"You remember Gregory Mikkelsen?"

She blinked. "Yes. We did not get along well."

"Did you know he was once part of the diplomatic mission to the Vatican?"

She leaned back, watching me. "So?"

"So he knows some people there who are very high up."

"And your point is?" Father Paul asked.

I looked at him. He knew where I was headed.

"He was shocked to hear that Tiago Díaz de Valdés confessed to you that he caught his brother with another man. And named that man. And that you then told that man's mother about it.

Violating the sanctity of confession."

He sighed. "I would never do such a thing."

"You'll have a chance to defend yourself. I heard from Gregory, this morning. Seems certain members of the hierarchy are unhappy with your high-profile ranting, and you'll be recalled to Rome to determine whether or not the accusation is true." Then I whispered in a non-whisper, "Along with your bishop for allowing it."

Ginty popped in with, "They launched this investigation based on a story you told?"

"Along with certain info I provided."

"Did you provide this to the District Attorney's office?"

"Why should I? Nothing he did was actually illegal."

"It may have a bearing on some high-profile murders."

"Which Mr. Blaine will stress, I'm sure," Father Paul said.

I smiled at him. "Hard as I can."

He shook his head with a heavy sigh then said, "Ms. Ginty, would you excuse us? Mr. Blaine and I need to talk in private."

"Father Paul ... " she started.

He cut her off with a glare. "When a priest tells you a conversation needs to be in private, it will be in private."

She looked at me then rose. "Very well. I'm done, here. But I strongly advise against any private discussion with this man." Then she cast me a secret wink and left the office.

Father Paul looked at me, for a moment, and I saw an animal appear in his eyes. Vicious. Cold. Ready to attack. Not at all cornered. He smiled and said in a voice that was as calm and cool as if he was about to order dinner or a buy a suit, "You have it backwards, Blaine. Tiago did not know who his brother had been with. Nor did Grace ... until I told her."

"So much for honoring the sanctity of confession."

He leaned forward. His smile widened. "Did you not hear what I just said? This information was not ... *not* ... gained in confession. I would never violate so sacred an institution, especially since there are other, far better ways to gather information." Then he opened a video on his computer.

And I gulped in air, despite myself.

It was of the hallway at the dealership, pointed at the

windows around the back door, as Roy led an uncertain Lemm into the building. It cut to them leaving; Roy cocky, Lemm shirtless and walking slow. The whip marks on his back trailed blood.

"Where was the camera?" I was amazed I was able to keep my voice steady.

"The hallway has a false ceiling. A section of the tile was broken off. The camera was hidden above it and activated by motion sensors."

"Since when?"

"Since the moment I convinced Ned I should be a partner in his new enterprise."

"He helped you set this up?"

"He thought it just as good an idea as I did."

"Where'd it feed into?"

"A secure relay to a secret place."

"And not even Grace knew about it ... "

"If she had, would I have this?"

He brought up another video.

Of Connie ... guiding a drunk-looking Tiago into the dealership.

Then of her and Grace dragging a naked ... probably dead ... Tiago back out.

I looked at him. No more expression than before.

"Talk about withholding evidence ... "

"Merely protecting two good people."

"Two murderers. You ... you told Grace about her son. Did you tell her about Marco Samuels an' Bruno Vrasky, too?"

"It was very distressing. I merely let her know her son had returned to his evil ways and had seen those two men at this location. How could I know what she'd do with that knowledge?"

"She did what you wanted her to."

He stayed calm, on the outside, but his eyes smiled daggers at me. "That's a very strong accusation to make, without proof."

"The cops ... they must've found the camera."

"Ned removed it, after you and he spoke. He wasn't as drunk as you thought, and he was shocked to learn what happened to Tiago."

"He's seen all this?"

"Of course, and he wanted nothing which might lead the authorities back to him. Nothing like this."

He did a slide-show of video-capture images from the camera — Ned and Cliff, decked out in leather; Lemm and Matt entering happy; me and Matt talking equipment out the door ...

And Uncle Owen rushing in ... wearing the clothes that were soon to be covered in blood. In his, a car was visible through the windows, despite it being night and it being on the other side of the chain-link fence, that's how good the image was. I went cold to the tips of my fingers.

"He knew Owen Taylor was dead," whispered from me. "Ned helped Connie and Grace, knowing they'd killed my uncle."

"Yes. And this shows, without question, Owen Taylor was aware of the goings on at that dealership. In fact, I have video of every single solitary person who entered and exited." His eyes were locked on me when he said that. "Quite a catalogue."

"You devil. You knew my uncle had been murdered and who killed him, and you said nothing. You knew an innocent kid was killed in place of Lemm, and you said nothing. Then once you realized what she'd done, you drove Lemm from his home to make it easier for her to kill him, and you kept quiet while my uncle was blamed for it all, and you've got the nerve to say you weren't helping her?"

"Again, you make accusations without proof. I drove no one from their home — "

"You just scared Lemm's neighbors into doing it for you."

"Someone like that should not be around children."

"AND YOU SHOULD?!" I gripped the back of a chair. Refused to let myself sit down. "Well ... you fucked up."

"Watch your language — "

"You think Ned's under your control, but you fucked up. Now I see it. He was next door to my uncle's place. Had a key. Knew the alarm code. He worked with you and Connie and Grace. Till he realized Lemm and Roy were also targets. He knew what Connie was plannin', that night, for me. He let her go through with it, because he already had a plan. Connie and Grace kill me, then he kills them and burns the place down to hide it. Then he saw me and realized it'd fallen apart so hit me. And killed Connie. And set the fire. And ran.

And now I see why — to protect Lemm and Roy from you."

"You continue to make wild accusations — "

"Easy enough to prove, now that I know where to look. If I wanted to. But I've stopped you and killed PSALMS, so ... "

"By arranging my trip back to Rome? If you think it's going to make any difference, you'll be very sadly mistaken."

I fought the urge to punch him in his far too earnest face. Instead, I made myself say, "So you haven't heard."

"Heard what?"

"Your main backer is pullin' out. And you just showed me what made him do it. Self-preservation."

That made him blink. "What are you talking about?"

"It'll be announced tomorrow that a company by the name of Crédit d'Caisse d'Épargne is buyin' out all of C&B Trust's California holdings. Everything. And the great an' glorious Lamar Davis Lawton is steppin' down as CEO of the corporation."

Father Paul stiffened. "Nonsense. Lamar would've told me."

"Not if he can't use you, anymore," I snarled. "Grace Nieri killed five people, and you knew about it and you kept quiet about it and you worked with her through PSALMS. And with Connie. Ned knew about all of it and needed money, to vanish, so I bet he turned all this information over to someone who'd use it to force Lawton out. With him gone, well ... PSALMS can't operate without money, and the church won't back it, now that it's tainted, so it's dead. And so are you."

The daggers shooting from his eyes were as real as real could be. He fought to keep his voice level. "That makes the devil in you happy, doesn't it?"

"No," I growled back. "This devil's choice would've been for people to wonder where the hell you vanished to."

Then I stormed from the office.

I made it back to the Chrysler and got in and was able to start it up and drive down to another parking area, out of sight from anybody anywhere, before I started shaking, out of control.

I had thought my uncle's death wasn't part of the deal. I had thought it made a mess of Father Paul's plan to discredit him and, by proxy, the whole gay community and their supporters. But I was wrong; he'd always been targeted. He was disappeared to keep him from fighting the slander they spread about him.

Jesus Christ, the hate I felt for Father Paul and the diseased scum who'd put this plan into action. I wanted them all to burn, forever. To suffer, not die. But that son-of-a-bitch knew I'd never say a word about it. That I'd let all the blame be laid on Grace and Connie and Ned. That I'd never reveal who'd really killed my uncle.

How did he know this? Simple.

The car in Uncle Owen's photo was a silver ten year-old Lexus with blue and green racing stripes.

And duct tape on the driver's seat.

And now I knew.

I knew without question.

My mother had killed my uncle.

And she'd planned to kill me.

Jesus Christ ... she had wanted to kill me.

— X —

Three days later, Roy Harper came out during a telephone interview with Sousie Fornia and discussed that clinic in El Salvador. Sent pictures of burn scars left by their torture. More stories surfaced from victims of 18/20, as did lawsuits, so *Future Dreams* finally shut that subdivision down.

Of course, Lamar Davis Lawton disavowed any knowledge of anything and tried to claim that the gay community was out to persecute him and his fellow Christians. But the evidence was so overwhelming, he shut up and crawled back under his rock.

Father Paul broadcast my contact information during an interview about it, on Fox, so I got berated by online trolls and psycho-Christians calling and texting my cell phone. He even hinted I'd killed Grace when she confronted me about seducing her son, all said with the slyest innuendo possible. His parting shot as he left for *consultations with the Vatican.*

PSALMS disbanded within three months.

I didn't tell anyone about Ned. I understood why he'd done what he did — to protect Roy and Lemm as well as himself. I was just collateral damage. It's weird, but I felt respect for him over it, and was willing to let the cops do their search of the world for him.

Unless I saw him, again; then I'd rip him apart.

Crédit d'Caisse d'Épargne, a holding company owned by my father, bought Palm Valley West Bank for sixty percent of the price they initially offered. Dad couldn't have planned it better if he'd tried ... and I wouldn't be surprised if he had.

Tone and I stuck it out in Palm Springs till Riverside said they'd drop all charges if he agreed to a quiet settlement and no one had to admit guilt. He was happy with that, so I was, too. And Preston expedited the probate of Uncle Owen's will, so I was now the official owner of three condos, the remains of another, an apartment building and, because the paperwork surrounding OT & Associates was so wrecked it was useless, the dealership and three plots of land. I couldn't do anything about the crime scene properties till that was finished, but I did deliberately sell the two lots adjacent to the dealership to a gay-friendly investment group ... at a loss. Ha! I used that money to pay off the estate taxes and buy and repair the damaged condo next to my uncle's.

My plan was to set Matt up in it; he wasn't as put off by the desert as I was and liked being part of such a huge gay community. Plus, Lemm was learning how to write code as good as him, so they were working together, a lot. Lemm even brought in some Spanish-speaking clients.

So I sold the apartment building to a homeless advocacy group and bought Ian's townhouse for the boys to live in, then set Gloria, the mother of Tiago's daughter, up in the smaller one. That way, Lemm could see his niece, and babysit her, whenever he wanted. Didn't hurt that Gloria also made sure he knew Tiago would have grown to accept him being gay. And she loved being part of this new family, and they all loved baby Cara ... except for Geordi; she'd eat his turkey bologna instead of feeding it to him, which drove him nuts.

Once I was allowed to by the DA, I tore down the burned condo. Made it into a park with a sheltered wading pool, in my uncle's name, and buried his ashes there.

I gave Cliff his camera equipment back, nice and quiet. He said nothing. Barely even thanked me with a nod.

Lemm and Matt drove the Chrysler back to Texas and handled the move-out from the duplex ... which consisted of returning the furniture to Tone's parents, selling my car, and bringing a trailer of stuff back to PS. I know I should have done all that, myself, but I couldn't go back there. I just couldn't. In fact, it wasn't until the day before Tone and I were set to return to Copenhagen that I was able to make myself even think about calling my mother.

It was at that point in Palm Springs where the days are hot as hell as the nights are freezing. I was alone in the fortress; we'd seen Ian off just a couple days earlier, and Dion and Kent were set up in a nice little bungalow off Ocean Park, in Santa Monica. Tone went with Matt and Lemm to do some last minute shopping, and they were bringing home pizza and beer. Like college kids.

I used the solitude to work myself up to it. Then I punched the new number into my phone. And it rang. And rang. And when she finally answered, her voice was soft as snow.

"Jacob."

"Surprise, mom," I said. "What's goin' on?"

"My heart's failing," she wheezed. "I'm not strong enough to ... handle a transplant. Nothing else ... is working."

"I see. How long you got?"

I heard her breathe, for a moment, as if she was surprised at my casual attitude about her impending doom. "A couple of months," she murmured. "Maybe."

"Okay. Your church helpin' at all?"

A long intake of breath. "We ... are having prayer ... meetings here ... every day. I'm leaving them my home ... in my will."

"Deed's in my name, mom."

There was a long pause, then she wheezed, "That is between you ... and them."

"Sounds like fun. Tell me, your 401K, the money from your mortgage, did it all go to them?" Silence. I nodded. "So I helped subsidize that church. Hear from Father Paul?"

Another long pause. "Yes. He had a feeling ... you knew we knew each other." Then she coughed, lightly.

"Feelin', my ass. He knows you killed your brother an' thinks he blackmailed me into silence, with it." The words popped out before I could even think about them.

Another long pause. "But you said nothing. Interesting."

"Not really. I already knew he was up to his eyeballs in that mess. You gettin' mixed in complicated things, and I wanted that snake out of here."

"He's a good man," she almost snapped.

"He's a devil," I snapped back.

"You would say that. You're like ... your father. Only your needs matter."

"Could say the same about you, mom. Why'd you marry dad, anyway? I don't remember you two ever bein' happy together."

She took a while to answer. I could almost hear her thinking with each soft breath. "He wanted a son. I wanted his money. Almost like ... a business ... arrangement. No surprise ... you disappointed us ... both."

"Straight to the gut, every time." I tried to make it a laugh; instead, I just took in a deep breath. "So tell me how the hell that car of yours made it all the way out here. It's twelve hundred miles, each way. Your tires were damn near bald, for Christ's sake!"

"Jacob ... don't take the lord's name in vain."

"You can say that to me, after what you did?"

I could almost see her smiling. "Now we get down to it. Is that ... why you called? To berate me?"

"No. I want — I need an answer. You sent me those notes, with Uncle Owen's key." She said nothing; her gentle wheezing revealed it all. I nodded. "You sent me that text, usin' his phone." More silence, cut only by her breathing. My gut quaked. "You wanted me to come out here. To be killed. Why? You had a dozen other opportunities when I helped you ... "

"It would ... work better. Easy to make look like ... "

"Suicide? Or victim of my uncle? Who'd run off to avoid child rape charges, and was still rapin' and killin' guys who looked like me? Is that all it was? You toss me into the mix to add to the narrative that faggots are sex-starve maniacs out to rape and kill men to satisfy their needy dicks and — ?"

"Keep your vile thoughts to yourself!" snapped out of her. Then she was silent so long, I almost thought she'd drifted into permanent sleep. But she finally said, "Owen had a will."

"You couldn't just tear it up?"

"It was registered with the county."

"How did you know that?"

"I asked a lawyer." This time her sigh sounded sad. "If there had been none. I'd have been appointed executor. Of his estate. As his nearest relative. And could sign everything over. To PSALMS. Before I died. Instead, everything went to you."

"Unless I died." God, I felt so cold. "What if I'd left it all to Tone?" More silence. "That's why you messed with him. To drive us apart. Make sure I didn't do it. Okay ... that still don't tell me why."

"Doesn't it?"

"C'mon, mom, you want to play games now? Now!? Why now?"

With this breath, I could hear her shifting back to bitch mode. "I asked a priest ... to talk with you ... once. To save you."

"Right. Father Benedict Arnold and his sidekick, Abel."

"You behaved like an animal ... with them. Proved to me ... you were ... beyond redemption. Then I lost my job ... because of the cancer. Needed ... chemotherapy. Father Paul visited me. Comforted me. And told me of Owen. How he fought the city giving PSALMS a tax break ... on property. Father Paul had to ... establish a church there. To keep it. A lot of trouble. But he was doing good ... so good would come of it.

"Then Grace ... was in town ... with Mr. Lawton. She was sorry ... my home was gone. I knew her. Knew her from ... "

"From the bank."

"You have all the answers. You tell the story."

"She cry about her son still bein' gay?"

"We met with Father Paul. He understood our pain. Told us Owen was ... more trouble. And how sad it was. A man like that. Makes it seem all right. To be a devil. Influenced Grace's son. To return to that lifestyle. And converted you. As a boy. Made you like him. So you would spread the evil, too."

"Me!?"

"Father Abel ... left the church. The priesthood. Your doing."

"Good."

"Of course, you would say that. I knew ... something should be done. Both of you should be stopped. Before you spread more evil. More intolerance. So I ... had Grace meet with me."

I almost stopped breathing. "You ... you gave Grace the idea." Just her harsh breathing in response. "Kill me. Kill her son. Kill the guys her son'd been with. And blame your brother. It wasn't just the money; it was to show everybody they should be scared of people like me and your brother. Should hate us." More of that god-awful silence. "And you call me evil."

"It's not evil ... to protect the pure. Punish the sinner."

"Then what went wrong? Why'd you kill him early?"

"Owen ... attacked Father Paul. Threatened him. Blamed him for his arrest. I tried to talk ... with Owen. He ... refused to understand. Said vile things. Would not ... even see me ... after I drove out there."

"Why'd you have to? Grace'd already killed three men by that point. Why'd you have to come out here?"

"Thought I could ... reason with him. Make him stop attacking Father Paul. Keep things on ... on schedule."

On schedule? Jesus Christ.

"Sure you didn't just want to do it, yourself? Get satisfaction?"

More hideous silence. Finally, "Owen would not see me. So Grace told him ... a video. Being made. With a boy he knew. Tied down. Abused. For money. He came over. To watch ... I'm sure."

"No, no, he wanted to stop it, and you damned well know it."

"He ... he saw ... I was there. He was furious. Called me horrible names. Walked away. I ... carried a pistol for years ... in my purse ... and ... " Her voice trailed to silence.

"And you shot him." Again, that soft, horrible whisper of a breath. I dug my fingers into my arm to keep from screaming. "And you dumped him on the side of road in the desert for the buzzards to feast on. You hated him that much?" More silence. "Did my father know about this?"

She snorted a near laugh. "If he had ... do you think ... I'd be ... dying at home? Cared for by the ... only people who love me?"

"So me helpin' you don't mean a thing ... "

"You play the saint, now?" She tried to snarl, but her voice was too soft to make it happen. "Like your uncle? He and your father ... he backed him in that ... that development. Gave him money for ... vile political causes. Owen wanted ... you to move out there ... to live with him. After Faraz told me ... about you. And some blond man. Your father ... put an end to that. Your precious uncle ... he abandoned you ... for money. I suppose you will now continue ... down that path of evil."

"You're right. So you killed your brother for nothin'." My stomach was twisting and my hands were shaking and I was barely able to speak as I said, "Good-bye, mom."

"Jacob?" She sounded concerned. "What ... you going to do?"

"What do you care?"

"I told church ... they could have my home, Jacob. It's all I can ... give them. Now."

"Are you fuckin' kiddin' me?!"

"Don't swear. Prove to me you're not a devil, Jacob. Let me give this ... to them ... let me ... "

"I got a better idea. Tell your fuckin' church they can pay for your fuckin' funeral. 'Cause I don't know you, anymore."

I ended the call. Turned off the phone. Set it on the end table. A sharp fake-wood thing from Ikea. Matt and Lemm went crazy in that store, decorating the condo. At least the place looked right. Plants everywhere and photos back on the wall. The serigraph of me and Dion had been destroyed, but the museum made another one and it hung over the stair landing. Tone spent half an hour making sure it was just right. All so nice.

And so cold ... so fucking cold ...

It took me forever to stop shivering. No, what was hitting me were 9.5 earthquakes boiling up from the depths of my soul, screaming through my whole being. And I was sure that if I stood, I'd collapse and never be able to get up, again. I ached all over before they finished up. And, God, I needed a shower. Remove the filth and disease, if such a thing was possible. But I could not move until finally ... finally ... I had enough control to stop the shaking.

And could rise.

And wander to the stairs.

I found myself in the bedroom. Slipped off my shoes and socks. Stripped down to my wife-beater and briefs. My breath grew harsher and deeper and full of odd little sounds. I started to pull the rest off ... but weariness flooded over me, and I sank down to the bed and just sat there. Slumped over. My arms resting against my legs. Staring at nothing.

I couldn't think. I couldn't move. I needed space to even consider understanding it all. Needed silence and nothingness. Not grief. Not pain. Not anger. Just a still room filled with peace and quiet and solitude to give the screaming inside me a chance to regain at least a surface of calm.

So this is what it came down to. My mother hated me for being gay. And for being my father's son. And for being like my uncle. She'd rather I be dead. When Tone had admitted that's what she said to him, it'd hurt ... but I'd stupidly thought it was just words she used to manipulate him. When I had seen her ... helped her ... moved her back into her home, I'd caught none of that hate or disdain. But now that I'd heard the weak but still casual contempt in her voice for me ... even as she's lying on her deathbed ... that broke down every barrier I'd built to be able to cope with her condemnation.

What stunned me was how silently I accepted it. Some asshole says I'm going to hell, he gets a one-finger salute. My father treats me like a pawn in some game of cash-grab, I prove I'm as hard as he is, so he won't see how hurt I am. But my mother calls me evil. Blames me for her filth. And I ... I just roll over. Whimper *I don't know you anymore*. And crawl into a corner to lick my wounds. Why? Could I be, deep down, the self-destructive type? Is that why I accept her hate?

Is that why I stick with Tone? I'm hoping he'll help me destroy myself?

I had no answers to the unending questions. None of it made sense. Nothing mattered. Except that my mother and father ... the people whose genes I shared ... had shown me just how deep their disease went. In them.

And in me.

And now my mother was dead to me before she had died. And there was a crack in my soul, endless, terrifying, darker than any abyss could ever be, and it threatened to shred me, from within. And I knew ... I flat out knew that if I moved just one inch to the left or the right or even so much as raised my head, I'd explode into a billion bits of nothing. So I sat there.

And sat.

And wished to God I'd never come back to this country.

— XI —

I don't know how long I was on the side of the bed before I let my eyes focus on the floor and notice it was covered with darkness. And damn, I was cold. The doors to the balcony were open, showing the full beauty of the desert valley's lights for miles, but I could barely get the energy up to even look, let alone go close them. I maneuvered my coat onto my shoulders and kept sitting and the hell with the cold; I've been cold before.

But not like this.

Never like this.

I finally heard voices. Lemm, Tone, and Matt. Words about great pizza and how we were going to watch *Singin' In The Rain* because Lemm had never seen it.

Well ... they were. I couldn't handle its joyfulness.

They chattered and banged things around in the kitchen and glasses clinked. Every sound so innocent. So sweet and childlike in its joy, I wished I had tears to weep for them. I heard Matt say, "He's not answering his phone 'cause it's by the couch," followed by more shuffling about.

Then someone climbed the stairs and approached the room and the door opened and light from the hallway flooded across the floor.

It was Tone.

"Leave the lights," I croaked.

He jolted. "Jake?"

"Please, no lights."

He called over his shoulder, "Start without me," then closed the door, gave himself a moment to get used to the deep dark shadows, and carefully came over to sit by me. I didn't look at him. He didn't say anything. Just put his hand on mine. It felt so warm and alive and wonderful, words finally began to whisper from me.

"My mother killed my uncle. And wanted to kill me. Like you said. And my father knew, but said nothin' 'cause it'd interfere with his plans."

I heard him take in a deep breath. His hand moved up my arm to circle around my neck and softly, softly draw me close.

"I was born from snakes." His other hand squeezed mine, just a little. Just enough. "It was all about money. Usin' people's hate to make money. Wantin' more money for more hate. That's what I come from. What made me. I was born from snakes."

"Stop." Tone nuzzled my ear and muttered, "You're wrong. I won't let you beat yourself up, like this."

"But it fits. All I did when I was in prison, how easy it was."

"Shut up," he snapped. "It's different in there! You're out here, now, and ... and ... y'know, Preston told me about this guy named Gary. A guy who was set up on the same crap charges as your uncle. If you'd been inside and seen what was happening to him, what would you have done?"

" ... It'd be his deal, not mine."

"Exactly. But look what you did do, for a guy you didn't even know. You connected him with someone who could help him. You didn't have to do a thing, you were under no obligation, but you protected him. Like you protect me — "

"Tone, don't ... "

" — and Matt and Dion and ... and Lemm. You could have left him to be found in that dealership by the cops, but you didn't. You could have let him have the blame for killing that woman, but you didn't. You protected us. Would a snake do that? Would your father or mother? Your Uncle Owen did, for you. So did your Uncle Ari, and your grandmother. They are who you are."

"But you don't know the evil things I've done — "

"I know you!" He kneeled on the floor, before me, and pulled the coat tighter around me as he kept on with, "Okay, so there's a part of you, deep inside, that's dark and scary and hurt. Who doesn't have something like that? But what matters is what you do with it, and you use it to defend us. You got the good genes of your family, baby ... and maybe just enough of your parents shit to protect you. You've got a core of decency, not hate or greed, and I knew that the second I saw you walking down the street ... before we even met. Even then, I knew you were better than me."

I couldn't handle this, so I started to pull away from him, but he took my face in his hands and wouldn't let me.

"I know what I'm talking about," he snarled, "because I'm the one who goes batshit crazy and hurts people, no matter what. But you — remember when you saw me going that way? I was planning to make an example out of a guy who'd done nothing to deserve it. You stopped me. You pulled me back. If you'd really been nothing but your mother, you'd have stood by and let me destroy someone, just to prove a point. Or ... or like your father, found a way to shrug it off. But you didn't. Why can't you see what that means?"

His eyes locked on mine. I could finally see them. Bright. Completely open. No hidden doors or shadows for the first time in nearly two years.

"Hold onto that, Jake," he kept on. "Think about it. You even warned a man who'd hurt you. Threatened you. Hated you. You saw he was in danger and you did right by him. Don't you see that makes you so much better than all of us? Than me? I'm the one who's evil. I'm more your father's son than you are."

"Tone ... "

"You. Are not. Your parents. You're my proud, strong, beautiful wolf. Protector king of his pack. In total control and I believe in everything you do and I would give my life to protect you, which is silly because you're so much stronger than any of us and better and you're my Jake, and I will spend the rest of my life trying to get to where I deserve you, and I couldn't feel this way if you had no soul. I'd see a kindred spirit to have fun with, not someone I want to make proud of me. Not someone who's my mate and who I trust and who want in my life forever."

There was fire in Tone's eyes, warming me deep and gentle.

His hands gripped mine. I felt like I'd been returned to my body and was face to face with the truth of him and the darkness he'd hidden. I heard myself ask, "What're you sayin'?"

"I love you, Jake. You're my past, my present, my forever, and I want to make that real. Pure. Honest." He held my hands to his heart. Almost burned them with the heat. "I want to marry you. I want a home with you. A life with you. I want ... I want a dog with you."

Air, warm and secure, flooded into me. "You ... you want a dog with me?"

"Two dogs. One for you, one for me, both male. Geordi's cool; Georgina? Forget about it! Can't stand bitches. And considering what damn near happened to you, I'd think you'd feel the same way."

" ... What about Meredith?"

"She's not a bitch; she's a saint."

"Tone ... why you feel that way about women?"

He hesitated, sat back on his heels and sighed. "Fine. My first three years of school, I had the same teacher. Mrs. Kraus. She was beautiful and had the reddest nails ... and the sharpest. If you did something wrong, she dug them into your arm or neck. I got them two or three times a day. When I told my folks, they said, Behave. I tried. But she hated me and I still got dug once a day, no matter what. Even when I moved out of her class, if she saw me in the hall, she'd find an excuse to dig into me. I didn't understand why, then ... but she saw a kindred spirit, in me, and was having fun with it. And no one I told would stop her. It kept up till we bought a new house and I went to another school. And that's why I hate women. Haven't you noticed I still flinch when I see red nails?"

"That's it? That's all?"

"Told you — I'm psychotic."

I couldn't help but sort of chuckle. "A psycho who wants a dog with me."

"Actually, I want one more thing. A ceremony. There's just enough Presbyterian left in me to want something officiated. Did you know Cliff's an ordained minister? Off a website, but ... but we could put off the flight till next week and have something on the beach and Dion could be your best man and Meredith Saint of Honor and — "

I cut him off by standing and raising him up with me. Looked hard at his face ... his open, open eyes. There was trust in them, again, and they were begging me to accept it.

I slipped my arms around him. He did the same. The feeling of his cheek on my neck. The rise and fall of his breath. The warmth of him melting into me. My back grew straight. My shoulders strong. My world shifted from sand to rock. My mother, father, everything that had happened, that was all in my past. I had almost toppled into an abyss, and Tone had pulled me back. Emptiness drifted away and light filled my heart. I could howl at the moon and face anything the world was dumb enough to throw at me, now, and suddenly I realized ... I had misunderstood my uncle's pet phrase.

I remembered this one time when he came to visit me in prison. He brought more books and magazines; those were like gold, in that hell-hole. This wasn't long after I'd turned West into Slaughter's bitch, and I was feeling good about things. The second he saw me, he noticed the change.

"I don't know what it is," he said, "but you've never had such a swagger before."

"Been workin' out," I replied. Then I flexed my biceps.

"No, Jake, it's something in your eyes. You used to light up when you saw me. Like a puppy happy to find out its owner's come home and it hasn't been abandoned."

"Oh ... woof," I snarled.

He smiled. "I spoke with your attorney."

"So?"

" ... He thinks you have a good chance at an early parole."

I shrugged. "Okay."

He looked at me for a long time, then leaned forward and said, "Jake, this place is not your life."

I snapped back with, "It is this week."

"If you let it be. I thought you were stronger than that."

I snorted, derisive. "So what do you want me to do?"

He leaned back. "You know, I grew up in a state where it was illegal for me to love anyone, and I had to hide who I am in shadows. I'm still too caught in that habit. Harshly reinforced by my father; that's why mom kicked him out. I'm still trying to become truly unafraid, not merely pretend that I am. That's why I come here every other month to see you, and send you packages and letters — to not only support you but remind you that this is *not* who you are, no matter what others say. I let those *others* define me; do not let them define you. Stand on your own two feet."

"I've been in here fifteen months and I'm not even half done with my sentence and you're handin' me Hallmark crap?"

He looked at me for a moment. "Do you remember your father's brother? Ari?"

" ... Uh, yeah. Haven't seen him since he moved to Denmark. I think I was ten."

"He has a wife. Kids. Runs an advertising agency. I sent him some of the sketches you left at mom's."

" ... Why ... ?"

"With the internet, it's possible you could do some jobs for him. He's open to it. His letter's with the package I left at the desk."

"Jobs? From here?"

"This place is not forever. I'll bet you're out in a few months. When you are, he'll give you your first assignment. So long as you stop this descent into becoming an animal. Stand on your own two feet, Jake, not all fours. Don't let others decide who and what you are, no matter what the circumstances."

I didn't really understand what he meant, then, because I thought I *was* in control. But I'd let the lying system of justice decide I was an animal, and Slaughter was helping to confirm it ... and I was about to have that reality carved into my soul. Uncle Owen stopped it. I could see that, now.

It wasn't just about me standing on my own two feet; he was talking about me being my own man and deciding for myself who I was, and not letting anyone else determine what my reality should be, and he and my grandmother were backing me up until I was free to live my life on my terms, again.

That one little visit worked well enough to where I could stop growling and start listening. That's what let me find out why West was imprisoned. And why I helped him become more than just one of Slaughter's mongrels, so by the time I walked out of prison, he was ready to face down that beast.

I had also returned to working on my art; I'd stopped the day

I was arrested. So I got myself shifted to the library and clerical offices and in quiet moments did drawings. Portraits of inmates and doctors. And guards, who would bring me supplies and family photos to make more portraits. And who began to treat me decent. And sure enough, soon as I made parole, I worked up an ad for my Uncle Ari, and rocked it. Nana had to take it to a Kinko's to scan it to him, but little things like that helped me stumble along till Tone freed me.

Now here I am, two and a half years later, smelling my man's light muskiness, feeling him solid in my arms, and he loves me and wants to marry me and have a home with me and he trusts me and now I can trust him as much as I trust myself, because he's proven what I am to him, more than once, in his own dumb-assed way, and shown me he's my mate, forever, and he'll be granite under my feet, just like I will be, to him, and my heart is peaceful and calm, again, and ... and that is when I knew ... I finally, finally, finally knew ... I could answer Mira's question.

So why do I stick with Tone? It's not because I'm a stupid, loyal dog or needy or self-destructive or lost in worthlessness or stubborn or pitying or fooling myself into thinking this is more than a one-way street. None of that has any bearing on me and him. None of it. None of it. And now that I see how simple the reason is, I could kick myself for not realizing it, sooner.

It's because I love him.

And he fills the cracks in my soul.

And no one.

No one.

No one can ever tell me that's wrong.

The End

Kyle Michel Sullivan is a writer and self-involved artist out to change the world until it changes him ... as has already happened in far too many ways.

He has written books that range from sunshine and light (*David Martin*) to cold and dark (*How To Rape A Straight Guy*, which has been banned a couple of times) to flat out crazy (*The Lyons' Den*) to rom-com mainstream (*The Alice '65*). He has now ventured into SF-Horror-Suspense with *The Beast in the Nothing Room* and taken Capitalism to its logical extreme in *Hunter*.

The Vanishing of Owen Taylor is a follow-up to another of his dark books, *Rape in Holding Cell 6* (which has also been banned a couple of times; sample follows) ... but in this one, Jake is the protagonist instead of Antony.

He is now working to complete *A Place of Safety*, his Irish novel, using Tolstoy as his guide, and is also finishing up a character-study about a stained glass artist in *Dair's Window*. His goal is to build characters as vivid and real as possible, and has a lot of fun doing it — mixed with angst, anger, and amazement ... but that's the lot of a writer.

His e-books, paperbacks and hardcovers are available through Amazon, B&N and any independent book shop.

(Opening of *Rape in Holding Cell 6*)

— ONE —

I saw it on a local webcast — the Right and Honorable Nathaniel Carson Gilbert, III announced he was running for a suddenly-vacant seat in the United States Senate on the Republican ticket, intending to take it in place of the half-assed-but-decent-enough Democrat who was also running and *Return this country to decency and the rule of law*.

The two-faced-hypocritical-mother-fucking-son-of-a-bitch.

I guess it's needless to say he and I have a history — and not one that was fun, lemme tell ya — but if that pompous, fatuous, silver-haired piece of shit thought I'd stand by and let him get away with presenting himself as some Holy-Joe of the law even if it *was* to be from Texas, he was crazy as crazy can get.

Okay — so maybe I oughta backtrack and explain things a little, before you think I'm some half-cocked freak that hates all judges and cops and gives the salute to neo-Nazi scum and wants to bomb anything that I don't like and all that right-wing-nut batshit. Fact is, I'm the opposite of all that. To start with, I'm a card-carrying member of the ACLU — or used to be. Just like I used to be one of those guys who, if you left him alone to live his queer life, all would be rosy and cool. And yes, I DO mean queer. Not gay. Not homosexual. And sure as hell not a queen — just queer. Or faggot, if I'm feeling especially feisty.

No, that's not true; I used to be gay and proud of it, despite my family's reaction. I wasn't kicked out of my small-town home or anything (though we did live in a smallish town); my folks just sort of nodded and gave me a few words of advice and went about their business, very quietly. As did my brothers and sister. In fact, everybody in the family got quiet. And stopped inviting me to family events. And would be nice if I called but never bothered to call me. And while mom and dad paid for my college tuition and fees, they gave me neither car nor anything for living expenses outside my dorm and meal tickets (I guess they thought they could keep me from having too wild a party life, or something). And they never came to any of the events I was part of (I was on the tennis team and we were winning medals). Nor did my brothers or sister. Nor my aunts or uncles. Nor my cousins. Nobody. It was like I'd gone from being blood to being an acquaintance-in-law who wasn't quite right for the rest of us; someone to be polite to and not one damned thing more. I guess it made sense that they ignored my declaration of faggotry; after all, we *were* in a conservative Texas town of less than 100K population not far from a *big* conservative town where some things just were *not* discussed. Plus I've always had this streak of crazy-mean in me that could explode in a nano-second if I thought I or any friend had been slighted. But I think they really just feared for the sanctity of their sons' virgin assholes and seriously believed that if I made a pass at those boys, they'd be obligated to let me do as I wanted because we were related or something and —

Okay, now I'm getting off-track, so let's offer up some clarification. First off, I'm Antony Patric St. Lazarre, AKA: Antony (and if you do call me Tony, be prepared to get coldly corrected), from a nice upper middle-class family, and who was once told by an unimpeachable source I resembled John Payne — which I didn't get since I'd never heard of him, but then I finally saw a picture of him as a boxer seated in a corner, his magnificent legs splayed open, exuding this animal sexuality, and felt thoroughly pleased. I mean, the guy was a bit darker and prettier and rounder-faced than I saw myself to be, but then his eyes were more open to fun than mine and his smile almost sweet as opposed to mine being half-cocked. Plus my nose is more Roman in structure — and I'm getting lost in nonsense, again. It's not easy to concentrate, these days.

Anyway, I'm not quite as beefy as he was, either — just lean and solid. Not skinny. Not slim. I played tennis since I could hold a racquet and fit perfectly into that look, right down to my skin being tanned (despite a ton of SPF 45) and my choice of clothes being sports casual and borderline minimal. I mean, even in winter, which can get pretty brutal in Texas, I was usually in shorts and a tennis shirt, and the cold rarely got to me. Shit, if I'd had his legs, I'd be wearing a Speedo all the time.

You know, I think half the reason I was pleased to be considered his doppelganger was who it was that told me of the similarity — Collie. Collier. Problem is, Collie's the reason I loathe and despise that fucking judge — because he's one of the bastards who got him killed.

Collier Winston-Royce — talk about yin to my yang. So smart and kind and gentle and caring and full of affection, I wanted nothing more than to just walk beside him into eternity, my body molded into his. That he and I wound up lovers was a surprise, since he wasn't exactly my type — more sunshine and light than I look for — but it fit into every cliché you can imagine from the book on finding your soul-mate. And it was heaven.

I was two months into being twenty, and we met in the college refectory when he and I both grabbed for the last onion bagel. I was in a rush for media ethics class (talk about a misnomer) and hadn't noticed he'd opened the bin; he was busy dealing with a student who was being a pain. I grabbed the bagel (with paper), he groped my hand (with pinchers) and we both jumped ten feet.

"Sorry," he said. "Didn't even look."

"No, it — it's fine," I stammered out, feeling like a total idiot because I was looking into the bluest, most sparkling eyes I'd ever seen set into an chiseled face cut by a straight, manly nose and lips that looked ready to smile at even the hint of happiness in someone else. Laugh lines detailed his perfect proportions and thinning blond hair added to his aura of humanity. It didn't hurt that he had a body without a single angle to it — all round fleshy muscles covered by a layer of softness that made him achingly lovely instead of bulky, with hands that were picture-perfect and hair in all the right places (from what I could see) and then some — a buff, cheerful Golden Retriever in a button-down shirt and pair of Dockers that teased you with the brutal idea that they fitted around legs to die for. All I could think was, *Holy shit — he's gorgeous.* All I stammered out was, "Here." I offered the bagel to him.

"No, you take it," he said, and the hint of an accent in his voice would send a thrill down a nun let alone a sex-obsessed kid like me. "I need to drop a few pounds, anyway."

"Says who?" just popped out, without my thinking about it, because if I had I wouldn't have said it.

"Say my trousers, that're all thirty-three waist and warning me if I don't drop a few, I'll need a new wardrobe."

"Stupid trousers." And I wished I could take the comment back, it sounded so dumb. But he smiled and offered his hand.

"I'm Collier."

"Collie? Like Lassie?"

"Considering all the Lassies were actually male, yes."

His grin widened — and I realized what I'd said. Of course I blushed, and suddenly my light freckles looked like age spots.

"Antony — uh, Antony St. Lazarre."

That's when his student jumped in, eyes shooting bored darts at me. Orin Tedesco. I'd seen him around campus and dismissed him as an A&F kid who's so absolutely certain of his importance and attractiveness, he can't understand why he's not being paid attention to. No question he was hot — sun-blond hair, angular face, deep blue eyes under surprisingly bushy eyebrows, straight nose, curled lips and sharp cheekbones, all attached to a solid well-proportioned body by a neck that was just a bit too short. He wore training pants with a zipper up the leg that's only half-zipped and a hooded fleece jacket, and his calves were amazing. And amazingly hairy for a blond. But he looked like he belonged in high school (though he was a year older than me), and he spoke in a condescending *I'm being polite to you even though you're not worthy* voice.

"Excuse me," he snipped, "Professor, we're talking."

"No we're not, Orin," said Collie, still half-looking at me. "If your assignment's not on my desk by five, tomorrow, you'll be docked a grade, as I specifically stated at the beginning of the semester *and* noted in the syllabus."

"But it's not my fault!"

"We're a month into the semester and this is the third extension you've requested on an assignment. So, no. Period."

Orin stormed off. I shuddered, involuntarily. Something about him creeped me out, and I was glad he was gone. I don't know why I had that reaction, but sometimes I meet someone and I just take an immediate dislike to them. Just like I take an immediate like to others. And ninety-nine times out of a hundred, my gut's been right — as it turned out to be, about him. So I turned to my immediate-like guy and all but batted my eyes in mock-shock.

"You're a professor?"

"Creative writing. If these lads'd put as much effort into their course-work as they do their excuses, they'd all get A's."

"I gotta remember when I take your class — use my excuses as my papers."

"You plan to do that?

"Not till next year. I'm still programming."

"Computers. I'd never have guessed that."

"In a good or a bad way?" He smiled, in a beautiful way. I smiled back and continued, "No, it's really communications, but I want to be able to work my laptop even if it's freaking out in the middle of the Sahara."

"Excellent. You free tonight?"

Bam — right to the point, which made my breath quicken just enough to throw off my poor attempt at seeming cool. Fact is, I wasn't (I had a tennis student) but I said, "Yeah. Why?"

"Maybe we can get together. Have a bite to eat. I can talk you out of taking my class."

"Why would you want to do that?"

In answer, he took the bagel, split it in half and gave me a piece, then smiled and walked over to pay for it. And the way he walked — with those Dockers promising perfection underneath them — I got a boner and a half in point-two-nano seconds.

Needless to say, I rearranged my tennis session.

*****

We met at a Chili's. Seven sharp, though I was almost late; I spent two hours in my dorm room trying to figure out what to wear to say "Want me" but not look like I was saying "WANT ME!" I settled on a navy tennis shirt and board shorts with loafers — casual but still tight enough to show off, and I didn't care how chilly it was out.

I rode my bike over and walked in to find him wearing a simple cotton shirt, blue jeans, warm coat and — cowboy boots?! Obviously this was not gonna be a *take me home* date, not when he's wearing something that's nine kinds of hell to take off (I speak from experience, trust me). To say I was disappointed was to say the Empire State Building's tallish; in fact, I felt brutally let down. But then he saw me and smiled and my heart leapt into my crotch and I smiled back and decided to let the evening flow — and if I needed to, I'd do a quickie jack off in the men's room.

He ate the Tilapia as I chowed a burger and fries. And I found out he's from England but had lived in the States since he was five. He spoke perfect Italian because of his mother and perfect English because of his father. He had three brothers and two sisters and was the middle child. He'd been fat until he was in high school, where he'd begun to run every day and kept his weight under control by doing 5K every morning before classes. And he was just under twice my age. Woof.

I told him about my family's reaction to my coming out; my high school basically being supportive — except for some jocks who thought they could make my life miserable, until I used some Aikido on them (I'd started taking it the day after I accepted I liked boys instead of girls because I knew that would be a problem with some of the lesser-brained sorts); how I was paying my living expenses by teaching tennis and swimming because my folks wouldn't provide anything more than tuition and meals; and how I'd like to develop a Gay News Network to broadcast into homes all over the world — especially into those nations in the Middle East and Africa that liked to kill queers.

"I like tennis," he said. "We should play, sometime."

"I'll beat the pants off you," I replied.

"I figured that out already." His eyes twinkled.

"I'm going to take your class."

"Why?"

"It'll help me. I want to write as well as report the news, and anything I find that'll help me perfect my abilities, I go for." Again, I was saying something in a way to really mean, "I want to suck your dick."

He finished the last of his fish and leaned back. "You know what'll happen if you do?"

"What?"

"Nothing. I don't date my students."

I dropped a fry just before it hit my mouth and felt a quick scream down to my crotch. Seriously, if I'd been standing up, you'd have seen some tent-pole action, despite the liner in the board shorts.

"I — I don't date my professors," I replied.

"Then we understand each other?"

I looked at him — and those blue, blue eyes tore straight into me and that perfectly square chin emphasized the near-smile he was offering. And all I could think to croak out was, "Y'know — Chili's has the crappiest desserts."

He signaled for the waiter, paid the bill, chucked my bike in the back of his Land Rover and took me home.

Now, I know I sound like a horny little puppy here — and truth was, I was. I'd never had a relationship more serious than a couple of friends with benefits (which usually meant me sucking them off as they did me a hand-job and us never talking about it) and it'd been a month since I was with a guy (one of the University's quarterbacks, who was neither as big or as good-looking or as accomplished in fucking or sucking as he thought he was, but who was a good solid warm body, and with whom I *was* able to get off with, but whose *sessions* were built around his schedule rather than mine, and now baseball practice was underway, so...) so I was ready for some action.

But something about Collie told me he was the nesting type, and to be honest, I really wanted something like that. Needed it. I'd made no real friends on campus and was beginning to feel way too solitary in my life, so had already been scoping a couple of cute-if-lightweight classmates out as potential boyfriend material — especially a tall, sleek, golden number named Grady Lowenthaal, in Principles of Communication, who had gentle eyes and was openly gay and definitely worth going for. But Collie wiped all of that aside.

He lived in a condo near the university — one of those open, clean-looking places that felt surprisingly inviting. Gentle mixes of darks and lights. Hardwood floors. Big windows. Truly elegant.

He lead me in, let me pass him as he closed the door then stopped me with a caress on my left shoulder. His fingers trailed over to my spine and whispered down it and goose-bumps danced over my skin.

"Have you ever met someone and instantly thought, 'Yes, this is the one'?" he whispered.

I turned to him and nodded. "Right now."

"Are you sure?"

I spread my arms open. My first "come to papa" moment. He let his fingers drift up my sides to play with my tits and sent screaming lightning into my heart. I pulled him close to kiss him — and, sweet Jesus, what a kiss. Moist. Tantalizing. A hint of mint. A dream of perfection. Nirvana on this earth. I could have lived my life in that moment and never regretted a second of it.

I slipped my arms around him and felt how solid and comfortable he was — and how his body molded itself to mine. His hands caressed my ass — and I caressed his and loved how round and right it felt. I also felt his dick press hard against mine. Roll against it. So — he's a boxers kind of guy. I preferred the look and feel of briefs on a man's crotch, but in this case it whetted my appetite and I felt a great need to do some exploring, so I slid my right hand around his hip and slipped the back of my fingers over his crotch. Felt him move and react. Of course, all dicks feel big when they're touched this way but his — I knew I was underestimating.

He held me tighter and lifted me, still kissing, and carried me into his bedroom to toss me on the bed. I bounced back, laughing at the suddenness of it. The pure eroticism of it. My dick was pumped and ready for action and obviously so since I was straining at the liner of my board-shorts. He unbuttoned his shirt and I started to lift off mine — but he stopped my hands.

"Let me."

*****